The Player

Rockliffe Series Book 3

Stella Riley

Contents

PROLOGUE
Paris, August 1776

The dreams were back.

Dreams that remembered what his waking self only wanted to forget. Nightmares so bad that, once again, he dreaded sleeping. After the first, truly awful months, they'd gradually lessened in frequency and eventually stopped completely. Now they were back with a vengeance; vivid, vicious and debilitating enough to stop him spending his nights with his current mistress.

And all because of the letter.

Occasionally, he dreamed of the frigid disdain with which his parents had refused to accept his word and sometimes it was the man who had deliberately destroyed his life twice over in the space of a single day. But mostly he dreamed of Evie; heiress to a fortune, beautiful as an angel and addicted to risk. Evie ... who, from amongst an army of suitors, had inexplicably chosen him. Evie ... and the hour that had heralded his own living hell.

It was the night before his twenty-second birthday and three days before the wedding. At first, he wasn't sure what woke him. Then he realised that the door to his chamber stood open and, outlined against the darkness outside it, was a still figure in trailing white.

For an instant, with sleep still fogging his brain, he thought it was a ghost but, even as shock propelled him upright, he recognised Evie's husky, faintly unsteady laugh and saw her beckon him, then vanish like the apparition he'd briefly thought her.

The dream telescoped time and omitted his attempts to call her back as she led him through the unused and semi-derelict north wing with its smell of mould and mice and out into the clearer air of the roof. Then everything swung sharply back into focus.

She climbed on the low parapet, her body in its thin draperies haloed by the rising sun and the rippling rose-gold hair gleaming about her

1

shoulders. *Instinctively, he reached out to pull her to safety but she held him off saying, 'No. If you wanted to catch me, you should have run faster.'*

Her eyes were too bright and her voice too brittle. He'd seen her over-excited, highly-strung and wild before – but never like this. She frightened him as much in the dream as she'd often done in reality. He tried to speak but no words came out. And then, with a sudden dazzling smile, she said, 'I'm not going to marry you.'

The words hit him like a punch in the stomach.

'What?'

'I'm not going to marry you. Do you want to know why?'

He didn't. He wanted her to stop. He wanted her to laugh and say she was joking. He wanted the alarm bells ringing inside his head to fall silent. He said, 'I imagine you've brought me out here to tell me.'

'Yes.' The expression in the lovely cornflower eyes changed into something he didn't recognise and she took her time about replying. Then she said baldly, 'I'm pregnant.'

The sense of it was too far off to grasp.

'You can't be. We've never ...' He fought the hard knot that was forming in his chest. 'Evie, if this is some game ... you know that I love you. More – much more than is probably wise.'

'Of course. But it's no game.' She took a graceful dance-step along the broad, flat ledge and pivoted to face him. 'And it isn't about you. I'm telling you that I have a lover and that I'm pregnant by him.'

'I don't ...' He tried to focus and to accept that this was really happening. 'If that's so ... why wait till now? Why haven't you said anything before?'

'He's coming here today to fetch me.' She shrugged. 'I could have kept it to myself and married you anyway. Would you have preferred that?'

'I'd prefer there was nothing to tell.' His brain still wouldn't take it in and something was clawing at his insides. 'Who is it?'

'Guess.'

Guess? With half the men in London at her feet? How could he?

'I can't. Who is he?'

'Someone you know. Someone so very unlike you, he could be your opposite.' Her voice grew rhythmically hypnotic, as if she either had no idea of the torment she was inflicting or simply didn't care. 'One so dark, the other so fair. One with money, one without. One the heir to a high-ranking title, the other already possessed of a lesser one. Need I go on – or can you guess yet?'

He could but he didn't want to. Bile rose sickeningly in his throat and he said chokingly, 'Say his name.'

'I don't need to, do I? You know.'

'I shall know when I hear you say it.'

And so, with a smile and a shrug, she tossed him the name that ought to have been inconceivable but somehow wasn't.

Pain exploded in his head and drove the breath from his lungs. He couldn't speak, couldn't think and wanted, more than anything, to be sick.

Sometimes, when he was really lucky, this was where dream let go of him and he woke drenched in sweat, his breath coming in painful gasps.

Mostly, these days, it held him in its grip until the bitter end.

To the point where Evie, dissatisfied with his lack of response, had said, *'What's wrong with you? Haven't you anything to say? Don't you even mind?'*

He stood like a stone, not daring to speak or even to shake his head in case he shattered like glass.

She danced along the parapet again to within a few feet of him and, reached out as if intending to shake some reaction from him. And then it happened. He never knew if the heel of her slipper had become caught in the trailing hem of her chamber-robe or whether her foot had found some uneven crack ... but suddenly she stumbled, her balance faltering. For an instant, even as he launched himself across the intervening space, she seemed to right herself – only to somehow become entangled in yards of filmy white muslin. And then, crying his name, her eyes wide with terror, she toppled backwards.

Throwing himself against the parapet, he stretched out his hands to grab her ... but found himself grasping only a handful of insubstantial material which tore away as Evie continued to fall, screaming; down and down, to land with a sickening crack on the flagstones below.

The air hurt his skin and burned his lungs. He struggled to his feet and forced himself to look at the place where she lay like a twisted rag-doll in a slowly spreading pool of blood; and only yards away from a pair of startled gardeners who stared from the ruined body up to him, still leaning over the balustrade, clutching a handful of white muslin.

He wheeled away from the edge and was violently sick.

The dream, unfortunately, had the same effect.

Even though it had all happened a decade ago, he still woke up retching.

* * *

After a night spent staring up into the darkness with the letter clenched in his hand, he rose and began the process of closing off one life and opening up another. Some of what needed to be done was straightforward … other parts were unbelievably painful. All of it made him feel as if he was drowning.

He wasn't going back because he wanted to. He was going because his presence had suddenly become an unavoidable duty.

He doubted if anyone would welcome him.

ENGLAND

October, 1776

ONE

Considering the time of year, the crossing to Dover was unpleasant but blessedly uneventful. Despite having paid for a cabin, the man commonly known as Adrian St. Clare stayed on deck, staring out through the dark at the choppy waves.

Adrian St. Clare ... in one sense his own name and, in another, an alias. He had many such incarnations. So many that sometimes when, as now, he was quite alone and not required to be any of them, he was no longer sure who he really was; as if the man inside had somehow been scooped out, leaving behind nothing but a dry and empty husk.

Of his numerous personas, there were half a dozen he used on a regular basis, depending on the company and location. Among his favourites were the fussy, elderly Austrian, the nervous Frenchman and the clumsy, stupid Italian. He was also fond of the Scottish Major, the surly Russian and the outrageous Macaroni – though the last one had to be used with care. But all six were well-honed, ingrained ... and as easy to slip into as a well-worn boot. Old friends he must now leave behind. Then there were what he thought of as 'the others'. The roles he could create at will when the occasion demanded it and even, sometimes, when it didn't. And finally there was the one he had been born with; the one that, due to a sudden tragic turn of events, he would shortly be forced to resume ... if only he could remember who that had been.

He could have gone back three years ago but had chosen not to. He wasn't needed; he had a fair idea of the unpleasantness he'd be facing; and, more than either of those, he feared that return would lead him to exhume what exile had allowed him to leave buried.

Dawn came, tingeing the distant white cliffs with pink and heralding his imminent arrival on English shores. He wouldn't be sorry to leave the boat but couldn't think of anything else that was worth looking forward to.

Bertrand Didier, sandy-haired and deceptively slender, emerged at his side and, on an immense yawn, said, 'When's breakfast?'

'As soon as we're on dry land.'

'Oh God. Yesterday's bread and quantities of fried pig. Lovely.'

Despite the lead weight that had taken up residence in his chest, Adrian managed a wry grin. He'd come across Bertrand eight years ago in a Viennese back-street, running the Three Card Trick with men who were turning out to be very poor losers. Adrian had helped him out of a potentially lethal situation and somehow, without anything being said on either side, the two of them had remained together ever since. Of similar age, if not background, they'd pooled their resources and shared good times and bad, until St Clare's second and previously undiscovered talent had sent their fortunes soaring. Since then, Bertrand had slipped into the role of general factotum ... and he was still the only person who knew everything about Francis Adrian Sinclair Devereux, former Viscount Eastry and the current Earl of Sarre.

'Get used to it.'

Bertrand shot him a sideways glance and sighed.

'Are you really sure about this? They've managed well enough without you for years, after all – so there must be a way for them to go on doing it.'

'There isn't.' Adrian grabbed his cloak before the wind could blast it over his shoulder. He'd abandoned his hat hours ago and the majority of his hair had escaped its ribbon. 'Do you think I'd be doing this if there was a choice? My father's been dead for three years but my brother was there to take his place. Only now Benedict's in the ground himself, with no son to follow him and the only males left are myself and a couple of distant, octogenarian cousins.'

'But --'

'No, Bertrand. We've been through all this. My mother may not be pleased to see *me* but she'll be glad to have the vacant shoes filled – even if she can't bring herself to show it.'

Bertrand fell silent for a time, contemplating the rapidly approaching coastline.

'Mother the first port of call, is she?'

'Yes.' He shrugged. 'The road to London lies through Kent which makes it a matter of basic geography.'

'And you still want me to travel on ahead with the luggage?'

'Again – yes. See Henry Lessing, get the keys to the house he's leased for us and hire a cook and a maid if Henry hasn't already done so. Everything else can wait.'

'I suppose,' remarked Bertrand with a lack of expression that spoke volumes, 'you'll be wanting a proper valet now.'

'You mean you're not one?' retorted Adrian. Then, when the man who was more friend than servant didn't laugh, added, 'Don't be an idiot, Bertrand. Aside from the fact that I don't want anyone else knowing all my secrets, what would I do with a proper gentleman's gentleman?'

'Let yourself be turned out like a proper lord.' This time there was a glimmer of a smile. 'You know what a peacock you are.'

'That's just insulting. I'm not a peacock. My coats are the epitome of taste and restraint.'

'I'll give you that. But those pretty vests you wear under them?'

Adrian shrugged. 'There's nothing wrong with a touch of flamboyance. And everyone's entitled to one vanity.'

He wasn't ashamed to admit he liked dressing well. His boots and the lace at neck and wrist were of the best quality. His coats, plain to the point of austerity, had to mould his body; his breeches must fit without a wrinkle; and each of his long, embroidered vests had been chosen for their opulent originality. But clothes were his only extravagance. In every other aspect, he lived simply. The house he and Bertrand shared in Paris had not been in a fashionable quarter and was small enough to function with only one servant. He didn't own a carriage and when he needed a horse, he hired one. As for jewellery, the only item he possessed was a single, plain gold cravat pin. The heavy signet ring that had belonged to Viscount Eastry had been left behind on his wash-stand the day he said goodbye to England.

His hands clenched on the ship's rail until he dismissed that recollection.

It was a small thing but Bertrand saw it. He said, 'You'll be all right?'

Adrian heard the note of worry. It ought to have been amusing. Instead, it made something inside him feel a little warmer.

'On my own in the wilds of Kent for a couple of days? I think I can probably manage. And since I'm unlikely to be offered the fatted calf, I won't be far behind you.'

There was another long silence. Then, 'It doesn't sound like much of a homecoming to me.'

'No. But fortunately, I've never expected it to be.'

* * *

It wasn't a long ride. Dover, Deal and Sandwich were soon behind him and the main road with them. At a small village inn a handful of miles from his destination, he took a room and ordered food and a bath. Then, when his appearance satisfied him, he rode on through the network of narrow lanes until he arrived at the tree-lined driveway that led to his family seat.

From a distance, the house looked no more dilapidated than it had done a decade ago. It was a sprawling stone-and-brick mid-Elizabethan pile with all the usual additions, alterations and embellishments that rendered it either charming or ugly, depending on one's point of view. Closer inspection suggested that the north wing was probably still unusable ... but the main body of the house seemed in a decent state of repair. Adrian's London man-of-business – part of whose remit was to keep him informed of numerous matters – had notified him that, immediately following their father's death, Benedict had sold the London house. It appeared he'd done it in order to maintain at least a part of Sarre Park in a habitable condition.

Adrian was very careful not to let his eyes stray to the stone-flagged front terrace with its terracotta urns and box-hedge edging. He rode round to the stable-yard, dismounted and tossed the reins of his horse to a boy who looked no older than ten but was the only person he could see. Then he walked briskly back to the front door and pulled the bell.

The butler who answered his summons was a stranger. Adrian supposed he should have expected it. With a chilly hauteur he was far from feeling, he supplied his real name for the first time in a decade and watched the fellow's jaw drop. Then he asked where he might find the

Dowager Countess and, on learning that she was in the south parlour, nodded curtly and said that he would announce himself. The butler, finding himself in unexpected receipt of a cloak and hat, tried to look deeply disapproving but only succeeded in looking relieved.

Outside the parlour door, Adrian shut his eyes for a moment and tried to decide, not so much who he *was*, but who he was *supposed* to be. Then, opening them again, he straightened his back and turned the handle.

Startled, the woman on the sofa turned her head, her expression changing swiftly from annoyance to something approaching alarm as she took in the tall, beautifully-dressed gentleman standing just inside her parlour. She said sharply, 'Sir? What gives you the right to invade my privacy unannounced? And where is Seldon?'

'I imagine Seldon is regaling the rest of the household with news of the black sheep's return,' he replied with a hint of cool mockery. 'Perhaps I should have sent a written warning ... but I presumed that, as ever, your nerves would be equal to the shock.'

The book she'd been holding dropped from her fingers. One hand crept up to her throat and he watched the blood drain from her skin. Then, when she still seemed unable to speak, he said, 'Come, Madam. It's been a while, I grant you – but a woman ought to be able to recognise her own offspring.'

She drew an unsteady breath, swallowed hard and said faintly, '*Eastry?*'

'It's Sarre now, Mother. Or, if you find according me my title difficult, Adrian.' He paused, reflecting that he couldn't recall either of his parents ever addressing him by his given name. He'd never been other than Viscount Eastry to them since he came out of leading-strings. He put the thought aside and, a little more gently, added, 'I trust I find you well?'

'Under the circumstances, you find me as well as you might expect.'

'Of course.' He inclined his head gravely. 'I heard about Benedict. I'm very sorry.'

'Are you?'

His mouth twisted wryly.

'More than you can possibly imagine. But of course it's your choice whether or not to believe me.'

His mother rose to her feet, perhaps in an attempt to regain some composure. He had expected her to look different and she did ... but not so very much. The dark hair was threaded with silver and there were lines on her face that hadn't been there ten years ago. But she was still slender, still attractive, still beautifully-gowned; and still no more likely to throw her arms about him with exclamations of affection than she'd ever been.

'Is that why you're here?' she asked jerkily. 'Because of Benedict?'

'Yes. What else do you suppose would have brought me? I came because I assumed you'd be glad of any measure that prevented the earldom falling into abeyance.'

Her ladyship continued to look at him as if he'd dropped into her drawing-room from another planet. She said, 'If you wanted the title, why wait until now? It's been yours for three years, after all.'

'So it has. But perhaps I *didn't* want it. Then again, three years ago I was superfluous to requirements. As my late, lamented father pointed out when he told me to get across the channel and stay there, he had another son.'

The Dowager had the grace to look mildly uncomfortable, albeit briefly.

'He didn't mean it in that way. You make it sound as if he disliked you – when you know that was never the case.'

Actually, he didn't know any such thing but there seemed little point in saying so. He also wondered, if and when she decided to call him by name, which one she'd choose. Sighing inwardly, he recognised that he'd set the tenor of this meeting himself and that perhaps it might have been better done. The trouble was that he didn't know who the hell Francis Adrian Sinclair Devereux was, let alone the Earl of bloody Sarre, so he was crafting the role as he went along and hoping he was working along the right lines.

When his silence had lasted long enough to become awkward, her ladyship said brusquely, 'This is foolish. I have no wish to argue with

11

you when there are more important matters to discuss – so you had better sit down and I'll ring for tea.'

He didn't want to sit down and he hated tea. Given the choice, he'd have preferred to be elsewhere. But, since that wasn't an option, he took the chair she indicated, crossed one booted leg over the other and said, 'Tell me about Ben. I was told it was a riding accident. Is that true?'

She nodded, staring down on her fingers as they smoothed the impeccable folds of her black moiré gown. 'His mare stepped in a rabbit-hole or some such thing and Benedict was thrown. It would have been all right … it would have been *nothing* … except that he hit his head on a rock. He was dead before they brought him home.' She looked up, her gaze angry. 'He was to have been married next week. I would have had a daughter-in-law and, in time, grand-children. Instead of which I have a hatchment on the door and a new grave to visit. One would think that, under the circumstances, God might recognise that I already have enough to endure – but apparently not.'

Well done, Mother. Just another cross to bear, am I?

'I'd hoped my reappearance might be more of a blessing than a curse. If it isn't, you have only to say. No one of any consequence knows I'm in England so returning whence I came won't be very difficult.'

'Since your intonation sounds French, I needn't ask from whence you *have* come.'

French intonation? I'd better mend that.

'Quite.' He looked at her, his pale grey gaze unreadable. 'Is it completely beyond you to admit that my arrival is fortuitous? That you'd rather I stay than go?'

'It's necessary for me to state the obvious?'

'No. But it would be nice, just this once, to hear you admit that you need me.'

'The *earldom* needs you. As for myself … I don't know you.'

'True.' His smile was slow and not particularly pleasant. 'But whose fault is that?'

'Not mine, Eastry. It was --'

'I believe I asked you to call me either Sarre or Adrian. Perhaps you might strive to remember it.'

Her ladyship's expression grew positively arctic.

'Why Adrian? Your first given name is Francis.'

'Since you never used it, I'm surprised you remember.' *Only one person ever called me that and the last time she did so was when she was falling to her death.* 'I prefer Adrian. That or my correct title.'

'Adrian, then. To me, Sarre is still your father.'

'Doubtless his lordship would find that wholly appropriate,' he murmured sardonically.

His mother surged to her feet and then sat back down in a hurry as the butler arrived with a laden tea-tray. 'Thank you, Seldon. Set it down over there and then leave us.'

Seldon bowed and left the room as silently as he'd entered it. The second the door closed behind him, her ladyship said, 'You will speak of your father with respect.'

'I see little need to speak of him at all, Madam. But let us be clear on one thing. The current financial status of this family is attributable to my grandfather's love of the gaming table and my father's inability to recognise good investments from bad. It would be comforting to think that, during his brief tenure, Benedict managed rather better – but, since he had little to work with, I don't hold out much hope for it.'

'Now I see.' His mother finished pouring tea and held the cup out to him. 'You want money.'

Sarre accepted the cup and immediately set it to one side.

'A very banal assumption – and, as it happens, incorrect. Also, you appear to have forgotten that all the resources of the earldom, such as they are, are at my disposal.' He waited and, when she said nothing, continued smoothly, 'It may surprise you to learn that I have money. Not a fortune, perhaps – but a substantial sum, coupled with business interests which provide regular revenue. In addition to this – and entirely separate from it – every penny of the allowance I've received for the last decade, including the money Father shoved in my hand when he told me to get out of England, is sitting, untouched, in the account into which it was paid.'

13

Ask why. It's a natural enough question – or it ought to be. So unlock your jaws and ask me why I wouldn't touch it.

She didn't, of course. She continued to sit ramrod straight and look, not so much *at*, but *through* him. His mouth curled slightly and he said, 'I don't need the earldom, Madam. I don't even want it. I have a life in France to which I could return tomorrow and receive a warmer welcome than will ever be found in this house.' He paused and, with an elegant shrug, added, 'As I said ... I don't need the earldom. But if it is to survive, it most assuredly needs me.'

He watched her weighing his words and waited to hear what her initial response would be.

Predictably, she said, 'You've made money? How?'

Just for a moment, he allowed himself to imagine her face if he told her of nights spent at various gaming-houses, disguised as the Austrian or the Russian or the Scot ... or described the fight for seats at the Comédie Française on the days when the actor known to Paris as L'Inconnu was playing Molière.

Resisting the temptation, he said, 'Legally and by my own efforts. For the rest ... do you really want to know?'

'I suspect not,' she said dryly. 'Are you offering to put this house and the estate to rights?'

'When I have a clear picture of how matters stand, I'm prepared to consider it,' agreed Sarre evasively. Then, seeing how the rest of this conversation would go if he didn't take control of it, he said, 'Tell me ... why didn't Father have me declared dead? He could have done. And I'm sure he realised how much easier it would make things for Benedict.'

'He did. But there were always rumours. Never anything definite, of course ... just people who thought they'd seen you in this place or that. Enough to make any move on our part towards ...'

'Obliterating me?' he supplied helpfully. 'Yes. How disappointing for you.'

'Stop it!' Suddenly his mother was flushed with indignation and much less composed. 'You speak as if none of what happened was your fault. As if we cast you adrift without so much as a backward glance. But --'

'Didn't you?'

'No. We didn't. If you hadn't been set on marrying that dreadful girl --'

'That dreadful indecently *rich* girl. Let's not forget that. You may not have liked Evie but by *God* you wanted her money.'

'Her money,' snapped the Dowager, 'was the only thing that made her remotely acceptable. She was spoilt, atrociously behaved and wild to a fault. As to what came to light later, you'd never have been sure in *whose* bed your children were conceived.'

At last. Now we finally come to it.

'I told you what Evie said to me that morning. I very much doubt ...' He stopped, aware that saying the name would probably choke him. 'I doubt that her lover confirmed it. He was too busy announcing to you, the household staff – and later, to the world – that I'd pushed her off the roof because she was about to jilt me in his favour.'

Her ladyship made a gesture of impatience.

'It was enough, wasn't it? Enough to get you charged with murder.'

'But not – since there wasn't a shred of evidence to support it – to get me convicted.'

'You couldn't prove you didn't do it.'

'And no one could prove that I did.' Sarre paused, determined to stick to the point and trying to keep a grip on his patience. 'I'll say this for the last time. I did not kill Evie. She was flirting with danger as usual and she fell. I tried to catch her but I couldn't. It would be ... helpful ... if you'd accept my word. It would have been even *more* helpful if you had accepted it ten years ago.'

The Dowager made a small impatient gesture.

'We never said we didn't believe you.'

'And, equally, you never said that you did,' he returned, as lightly as he was able. 'But to resume ... no one witnessed what happened on the roof that day. So although there's no one to vouch for me, equally no one is in a position to make any kind of credible accusation.'

'That was never the point. Once you'd been hauled into court like a felon, the fact that you walked out a free man wouldn't have mattered in the slightest.'

He'd known it was true. He just couldn't believe she'd actually said it.

'Not to you, perhaps – but it would have mattered a great deal to me,' he retorted. 'You and Father, of course, were more concerned with the family name. You couldn't possibly allow your son and heir to face an enquiry which could result in him clearing his name. Perish the thought! *You* decided the family honour would be best served by what amounted to sweeping the mess under the carpet.' He leaned back and surveyed her over folded arms. 'Ten years on ... how well would you say that has worked out?'

'Well enough.'

'Really?' This time she didn't answer so he said, 'I believe we are agreed that it's necessary for me to assume the title. Unfortunately, this cloud of suspicion – that was none of my making – is still hanging over me. Ten years ago, if you and my father had listened to a word I said ... if you'd thought beyond the immediate moment and the family's thrice-blasted reputation in society ... if you'd stood behind me, the scandal would, by now, be a distant memory. As it is, as soon as I stick my head above the parapet, someone's likely to raise a question in the Lords. They won't charge me, of course. They're not about to attack one of their own and risk the Sarre earldom ending up in escheat. But the fact that the whole business has lingered on like a bad smell isn't going to make my resurrection any easier. And for that, I have you to thank.'

'Judging from what I've seen so far,' said his mother tartly, 'I'm sure you're more than capable of dealing with it. And since you're hardly going to be brazen enough to show your face in London, it's --'

It was the last straw. Sarre cut off her words with a harsh laugh.

'Not show myself in London? Is that what you think? That I'll skulk here in Kent like some gibbering relative, fit only to be hidden away? Oh no, Madam. That's not the plan at all. If I'm going to be the seventh Earl, I intend to fulfil all the requirements to the letter – including the dynastic ones. In short, I'm going to find a bride.'

16

'How? Every door that matters is going to be slammed in your face.'

'Perhaps.' He rose from his chair to loom over her. 'Fortunately, there are plenty of others to choose from and it doesn't matter who I marry so long as she's fertile. The daughter of any shopkeeper or lawyer or craftsman will do. After all, with my unfortunate reputation, I can't afford to be choosy, can I? And in the meantime, I suggest you make sure the dower house is habitable. Because however many doors may be slammed in *my* face, I guarantee that from the day I marry *this* one will be closed in yours.'

TWO

He spent the night at the inn where he'd bathed and changed for the meeting with his mother but got little rest.

He supposed it was inevitable he'd dream about the hour immediately following Evie's death. That small space of time before everything got inconceivably worse.

Half-blinded by tears, he'd run through the house like a madman. Stumbling down the endless stairs, tearing through the hall and out … out to the terrace where his love lay in a pool of blood, staring up at the sky out of wide, sightless eyes. Servants had appeared from somewhere but he hardly noticed them. He was on his knees, holding Evie's still-warm hand and being torn apart by violent, wrenching sobs.

The nightmare shifted.

They were carrying that broken body into the house; taking her away from him. He didn't want to let them … so he tried to follow. And was stopped by his father, demanding that he control himself and offer an explanation. Neither seemed important and both were beyond him. He raised his hands to his face and discovered they were wet with blood. His stomach rose into his throat and he threw up again on the floor of the hall.

'Eastry! For God's sake!' His father's voice was icy with disgust. *'Pull yourself together and tell me what happened. I assume the stupid girl managed to kill herself. What I need to know is how – and whether you were with her at the time. Well?'*

'Sh-she fell.' Shock and indescribable horror were making his teeth chatter so much he could barely get the words out. *'F-from the roof.'*

'Fell?' His mother now, cool and composed as ever. *'It was an accident?'*

'Yes.'

'And you were with her?' She sounded as if she was enquiring about a broken ornament she'd never particularly liked. But then of course she

18

hadn't liked Evie. Neither of them had. 'At that time in the morning? Why?'

So, in stumbling half-sentences, he repeated what Evie had told him; had been forced to explain that her baby wasn't – could never have been - his; and had endured the final cruelty of being made to name her lover. And, at the end of it, his father had looked at him as if he'd just crawled out from under a stone and said frigidly, 'One cannot be surprised. Only you could have made such a fool of yourself over a slut like that. Did you lose your temper and push her?'

'No! Of course I didn't. I would never have ... God! How can you even ask?'

'Because it is what everyone will think,' replied his mother. 'When the facts come out, how can they not?'

He'd woken up, drenched in sweat in the pitch-dark with those words still ringing in his head. *It is what everyone will think. How can they not?*

And this, God help him, was what he had come back to.

* * *

He arrived in London to find the narrow house in Cork Street warm, fully-furnished and ready to welcome him. Relieving him of his hat and cloak, Bertrand said, 'How was it?'

'Generally unpleasant. On both sides.'

'She wasn't pleased to see you? Or even grateful?'

'No.' He sat down and took the glass of wine Bertrand offered him, relieved to be speaking French again. 'She didn't smile or offer her hand or ask ... well, anything really.'

'Not even how you've been all this time?'

He shook his head and smiled wryly.

'She *did* ask if I intended to plough whatever resources I have into the estate.'

Bertrand swore softly.

'Is that when you left?'

'Oddly enough, no. I managed well enough until she said I should hide in the country rather than inflict myself on polite society. And that was when I said ...'

'What?'

'It doesn't matter. But I may have given her something to think about.' He looked around the pleasant parlour. 'This is better than I expected. Did you have any problems?'

'None. Monsieur Lessing had the keys to hand, the house aired and staff already in residence. A cook, two housemaids and a footman. The cook is adequate; one of the maids is pretty and the other would probably be grateful.'

Adrian grinned and felt himself start to relax.

'And the footman?'

'The usual sort. More brawn than brain,' shrugged Bertrand. 'He seems willing enough but I'm not sure we need him.'

'Keep him. This isn't Paris and our roles have to change. If I'm to be an Earl, that makes you the majordomo in charge of my household – and as such you shouldn't be demeaning yourself by answering the front door.'

'Answering it to who? Nobody knows you're here. And even if they did … how many of them are likely to come calling?'

'Not many.'

Bertrand raised one quizzical brow.

'All right,' sighed Adrian. 'As things stand, none … so I'm going to need help. Do you remember Nick?'

Bertrand laughed. 'That madman? Yes. Better than I'd like. What can he do for you?'

'His brother is a Duke – so I'm hoping he can prise open a few doors for me. I've no particular desire to be deluged with invitations – which is just as well, since I won't be – but society needs to at least be aware that Lord Sarre exists.'

'And what about the club?'

'I'll go and see Aristide tomorrow before he opens for business.' Setting his glass aside, he rose and stretched. 'Until I'm ready to announce my presence, I'll need some of the usual tricks if I'm to roam London unrecognised.'

'Everything's unpacked and waiting.' Bertrand sauntered towards the door. 'I'll find out if dinner's ready. I've warned Cook off producing any of those hideous suet puddings the English are so fond of ... but God knows what we'll get instead.'

* * *

On the following day, Lord Nicholas Wynstanton was enjoying a leisurely breakfast and congratulating himself on having quit the card tables last night while he was still ahead. He further congratulated himself on avoiding both the persistent attentions of Cecily Garfield and a third bottle of claret. All in all, his lordship decided as he reached for another chop, he was feeling particularly virtuous this morning.

His butler-cum-valet entered the room looking peevish.

'There's a – a *person* to see you, my lord.'

That explained the sulkiness. Brennon disapproved of anyone who called before noon and, in the case of Nicholas's friends, most who came after it.

'A person?' enquired Nicholas. 'What sort of person?'

'A man. French. One wouldn't like to designate him a gentleman.' Brennon's lips formed a tight little line. 'He presents an extremely oddly appearance. He is also most insistent on seeing your lordship despite being repeatedly told that your lordship does not receive at this hour.'

'Ah.' Nicholas had no idea who his mystery visitor might be but Brennon in a huff generally presaged something entertaining so he said, 'Best show him up, then.'

'But my lord – you are not yet dressed.'

His lordship rose and tightened the cord of his favourite brocade dressing-gown. It was patterned with gold and green swirls, slashed through with scarlet and had a tendency to make everyone but its owner feel faintly bilious.

'I'm decent. And, from what you say, I won't look any odder than this fellow downstairs. So send him up – and don't come back unless I ring.'

Brennon left the room with a barely-concealed shudder. Nicholas resumed both his seat and his breakfast. Then the door opened again and a pleasant, lightly-accented voice said, 'Is it just me – or does your man *always* look as if there's a bad smell under his nose?'

His lordship glanced up, a kidney half-way to his mouth, and stared.

His visitor was tall, broad-shouldered and swathed in an ankle-length cloak. That much of him looked pretty ordinary. But his dun-coloured hair supported a hat that hadn't been in fashion for decades – if ever – and his eyes were screened by the tinted lenses of a pair of spectacles.

'What's the matter?' asked this apparition with some amusement. 'Don't you know me?'

Very, very gently, Lord Nicholas laid down his fork.

'*Dev?*' he said incredulously.

Adrian Devereux, Lord Sarre grinned and strolled across to his friend, holding out his hand.

'Do you know … aside from yourself, no one's called me Dev in years.' *A good many other things – but not that.* 'It's good to see you, Nick.'

'And you.' Their hands gripped. 'But what the devil is that thing you've got on your head?'

Adrian removed it and twirled it on one finger, sliding easily into the light-hearted role he always played with equally light-hearted Lord Nicholas.

'It's called a hat.'

'*You* may call it that. No one else would. And why are you wearing that ridiculous wig – not to mention blue-tinted spectacles? No wonder Brennon didn't want to admit you. You look like a complete quiz.'

'I'm incognito.'

'That's one way of putting it.'

'And I don't look any worse than you do in that robe. It's making me go cross-eyed.'

'Everyone says that. I don't know why. Come and sit down. Have you breakfasted?'

'Hours ago.' Adrian tossed his maligned head-gear on to the chair, threw his cloak on top of it and removed his spectacles. 'I'll take some ale with you, though.'

Nicholas filled a fresh tankard and pushed it towards him. Then, reaching for the eye-glasses, he perched them on his own nose and said, 'What do you think?'

'You should keep them. They make you look positively intelligent.'

'Well they don't do anything else, do they? They're just … blue.'

'A stage-prop,' said Adrian. They weren't, of course but he didn't see any need to explain that he'd had them specially made.

'Am I allowed to ask *why* you're disguised as the kind of shady character who'd make me want to check my pockets?'

'I only arrived in London yesterday and don't want my presence known just yet.'

'Very wise. That coat's no better than the hat. Do you want an introduction to my tailor?'

'Not if he's responsible for that atrocity you're wearing.'

And that was when both of them gave way to laughter.

They had known each other since university and done part of the Grand Tour together. After that, and at more or less the same time Adrian's life had become unravelled, Lord Nicholas had spent a couple of years serving in the Hussars before deciding that military life didn't suit him and that racketing around Europe was more to his taste. He and Adrian had subsequently run into each other only a handful of times – most recently just over a year ago in Paris – but despite everything, their friendship continued to flourish.

Eventually, his night-dark eyes growing thoughtful, Nicholas said slowly, 'Benedict's death has made a difference, hasn't it? Are you going to assume your title and stay?'

'That's the general idea.'

'It's not going to be easy. Somebody's bound to rake up the business with Evie Mortimer.'

'I know.'

'And if anybody finds out about the club --'

'There's no reason why they should. You've managed to keep your own connection secret, after all.'

'I have – but it's taken effort. You know what Rock's like. He finds out everything sooner or later. Speaking of which, he mentioned thinking he recognised you on-stage in *The Hypochondriac* a few months ago.'

'Yes. I rather thought he had.' Adrian frowned a little, remembering the unpleasant moment when he'd looked straight into the Duke of

Rockliffe's omniscient gaze half way through a performance. 'Will he have said as much to anyone else?'

'Amberley, I should think – and maybe Jack Ingram. The three of them are still thick as thieves despite all having been caught in the parson's mousetrap. But much as he likes being three steps ahead of everybody else, Rock doesn't generally gossip for no reason ... and, as I said, I don't think he was completely certain.'

'Then I'll have to hope it stays that way or be prepared to brazen it out. I'll be *persona non grata* in enough places as it is without L'Inconnu coming to light.'

'That's the trouble with having such a colourful past,' said his lordship, pouring more ale. 'So what can I do to help?'

'Allow my name to crop up casually in conversation and see what the reaction is. Then, if there are a few people *not* making the sign against the evil eye, I was hoping you might use your connections to secure me one or two invitations.' He paused. 'Do you think I've any chance at all of gaining membership at White's?'

'We can try. I'll sponsor you myself and I can probably get Harry Caversham to join me. He's married my little sister, by the way – so being open-minded is something of a necessity. Of course, if we could enlist Rock the thing would be as good as done.'

'Considering that your brother is the one person with a fair idea of precisely how I've been spending part of my time recently, I don't somehow see him lending a hand in my social rehabilitation,' returned Adrian dryly. 'Do you?'

'He's done stranger things. As far as opening doors goes, he and Adeline are hosting a soirée tomorrow evening so I suppose ...' He stopped and shook his head. 'No. That won't do. You're going to run into Rock sooner or later but the first time needs to be on neutral ground. The night after, then. We'll put in an appearance at the Lintons' ball.'

'Since I have no idea who the Lintons are and don't have an invitation --'

'That doesn't matter. Lady Linton is the most disorganised hostess in Town and his lordship will most likely be three sheets to the wind so no one will care whether you've an invitation or not. You only need to show your face for an hour or so, so we'll time it for late in the evening. Tell you what … we'll dine at Sinclair's, play a few hands of piquet and fortify ourselves with a couple of bottles of decent claret before we go. Trust me. It's perfect. Just promise you can turn up looking more like an Earl than you do right now.'

'French tailoring, Nick,' came the smug reply. 'You'll be wholly cast in the shade.'

'Don't count on it. Where are you living, by the way?'

'I'm leasing a house in Cork Street.'

'Oh. Chuffy Hobart's place, I suppose. The word is that his wife gave him a choice. Stop catting around and tend the family acres or abandon hope of an heir.' His lordship shook his head despondently. 'That's what marriage does for you.'

'You're not contemplating it, then?'

'I'd sooner take up embroidery. And fortunately, being a younger son, I don't have to. Unlike yourself, of course.'

'Gloating is an extremely unattractive quality,' observed Adrian mildly, as he rose to replace his hat and cloak. 'I'm off to Sinclair's. Send me a note about the ball or anything else you think I need to know.'

Lord Nicholas also stood up. He said flatly, 'I'll say one thing right now. Tell Aristide to stop Marcus Sheringham's credit before it's too late. The fellow's so deep in debt, he's drowning in it.'

'I heard he was chasing an heiress.' Adrian strolled to the mirror, intent on placing his hat at precisely the right angle. 'Some cloth-merchant's daughter from Halifax?'

'Grand-daughter,' Nicholas corrected. 'Yes. He is. But he's in competition with every other fortune-hunter in Town. And the betting at White's is favouring Ludovic Sterne because the girl's being sponsored by Lily Brassington.'

'And that makes a difference because?'

'Like the rest of the family, Lady B is short of money so she takes on these girls for a fee – but she's good *ton* and is received everywhere. She's also Ludo's second cousin and, for years now, has been on the catch for an heiress whose family might not realise what a wastrel he is.

The cloth chit is the best bet so far – which means Sheringham's playing with a handicap.'

'I see. It seems I've a great deal of catching-up to do.'

'Dev, my dear fellow, you have no idea.'

* * *

The smart, exclusive gaming-club known as Sinclair's occupied a prime location in Ryder Street, just off St. James. Adrian surveyed the discreet exterior and devoted a moment's thought to the man he would meet inside. Although he knew that sooner or later he was going to have to settle into his role as the Earl of Sarre, there was no need to do it quite yet. Smiling to himself and eschewing the glossy front door, he slid around to the rear and let himself in with his own key.

It was a little after two in the afternoon and the quietest time of day. The main floor and all the private rooms would have been cleaned hours ago and preparations for the evening wouldn't start until around five o'clock. His lordship took the back-stairs, cut through one of several concealed passageways and emerged in the manager's office.

Apparently unruffled by this surprise visitor, Aristide Delacroix looked up from his ledgers and said in French, 'We were expecting you last week. I suppose it would have been too much trouble to send Bertrand round with a note?'

'I wanted to see if the plans you sent me of the geography of this place worked.'

'Plainly, they do. Equally plainly, if your memory had proved faulty, you might have ended up in my sister's bedroom.'

'In which case,' replied Adrian blandly, 'I'd have screamed.'

Fair-haired, blue-eyed and exquisitely-dressed, Monsieur Delacroix rose from the desk to shake hands with the man who, for the last two years, had been his business-partner. He said, 'I assume from your appearance that you've no wish to be identified.'

'Not yet – though you seem to have had little trouble doing so.' Once more removing the various parts of his disguise, he glanced around the office, noting an entire wall devoted to large drawers. 'Is there a gentleman in London you *don't* have a file on?'

'Very few.' Aristide gestured to a chair and turned away to pour two glasses of the very best French brandy. 'Do you want to see the books?'

'Not particularly. Your last report was sufficiently detailed. But if there's anything new, you can précis it for me. And then I'd quite like to visit your domain.'

Aristide nodded, swirling the contents of his glass as he warmed it in his hand. Like everything else, he took his drinking seriously.

'Membership has risen again in the last month and, on average, we're making seven to eight thousand a night. With all our improvements and refurbishments now complete, day-to-day running costs – wages, food, wine and so forth – are beginning to settle to a steady level and I should be able to put a fairly accurate figure on them in the next week or two.' He smiled suddenly. 'Your share of the profits for the last quarter is just short of twenty thousand and the return on the next quarter should be even higher. Personally, I'm delighted.'

'Personally,' remarked Adrian, 'I'm amazed. In the short time the club has been operating and with everything that needed to be done, you've made remarkable progress.'

'Getting the right staff was the key to that. There were a few mistakes in the early days – but lessons were learned. Mr Cameron, our floor-manager, has eyes in the back of his head and can spot a sharp at twenty paces. Naturally, that was one of the first tests I set him.'

A gleam of amusement lit his lordship's eyes. 'Caught you, did he?'

'Immediately,' replied the Frenchman with immense satisfaction.

Adrian sometimes found it hard to equate this new, business-like Aristide with the fellow he'd first encountered on the other side of a Parisian card-table. In the space of two lengthy sessions, they'd each discovered the other man's secret. Adrian had recognised that Aristide Delacroix was the best card-sharp he'd ever seen; and Aristide had eventually realised that the reason Adrian rarely lost and could detect dishonest play most men would never notice was because he had an uncanny ability to count cards.

Inevitably, the two of them together created a marriage made in heaven – and Sinclair's was its natural progeny.

'Lord Nicholas has been immensely helpful in bringing the place into fashion,' Aristide continued. 'He plays here himself occasionally – but never so often that anyone would remark on it. And his brother, the Duke, has been in a handful of times with the Marquis of Amberley and others.'

'That wouldn't have been Nick's idea,' murmured Adrian. 'Rockliffe has a certain reputation – of which his brother, like most people, is justly wary.'

'Well I can vouch for the fact that his Grace plays a fair hand of piquet,' came the faintly disgruntled reply. 'But to resume … Gaspard, our chef, is a true culinary genius; Jenkins runs the best security system in town; and Madeleine has charge of housekeeping and spends part of each evening in the more exclusive rooms upstairs – that being the only place she's safe from importunities.'

'In my experience, girls as beautiful as your sister aren't safe from importunities in even the most respectable of circles.'

'I daresay,' remarked Aristide grimly. 'But those girls aren't being guarded by a couple of ex-pugilists masquerading as footmen. She refuses to stay out of the club completely, so I set the rules. And our members know what's at stake. The last one who crossed the line was escorted from the premises forthwith and had his membership terminally revoked.' Aristide finally took a sip of his brandy. 'Speaking of which, I'm assuming you'll want membership yourself?'

'Naturally.'

'I'll see to it. But I'd appreciate it if you'd confine your activities to Hazard and Pharaoh. Anything, in fact, that doesn't allow scope for your particular skill. First off, we run a clean house here – and second, it wouldn't take Cameron long to become suspicious.'

'Duly noted. When do I get the tour?'

'In a moment. There's something I want to discuss first.'

'Ah.' *Of course. There would be.* 'I suppose it relates to that request I made of you some months ago.'

'Yes. I've done as you asked. But I'd like to know how much longer it's to continue.'

'I'm not sure. What is the current liability?'

28

'Ten thousand, give or take – and little or no chance of getting it back. The word is that he's mortgaged up to the hilt and the duns are swarming all over him.'

'And yet he still throws good money after bad at the tables?'

'Yes – in the establishments that will still let him. He's the worst kind of gamester – addicted and desperate.' Aristide eyed his partner thoughtfully. 'Are you trying to ruin him?'

'Not at all. He appears to be managing quite well without any help from me.' His lordship achieved an elegant shrug. 'On the other hand, I've no objection to allowing him to ruin himself.'

'That's what I thought. Am I allowed to ask why?'

'You can ask. But you must forgive me if I prefer not to answer.'

'Then I suppose there's no more to be said.' Monsieur Delacroix set down his glass and came to his feet. 'The grand tour, then. We'll start with the main floor. And when you've had a good look at the place, I suggest you sample the catering by dining with me in one of the private rooms. I may be biased ... but Sinclair's offers the best French food in this land of over-cooked beef and blood pudding.'

THREE

Two evenings later in a cramped rented house in Kensington, Caroline Maitland sat at her mirror trying to ignore her mother's unending stream of useless advice while her youngest half-sister finished putting up her hair in a style which didn't suit her in the least, needed hair which would retain a curl for more than half an hour and felt horribly insecure. As for the gown, it was an over-trimmed disaster in an unfortunate shade of yellow which had clearly been meant for a seventeen-year-old wisp of a brunette – all of which added up to sartorial catastrophe on top of another hellish evening.

She murmured, 'I think it's slipping, Sylvia. Perhaps a few more hairpins?'

'It's fine. Any more of 'em and you'll not be able to hold your head up.'

Caroline sighed and thought longingly of an early night with a book.

Mama's monologue was punctuated from time to time by her other sister reading snippets from some society magazine. Neither conversation had anything to do with the other and Caroline's head was already beginning to ache.

'I've said it before and I'll say it again. A plain Mister or an Honourable won't do, our Caro. No – nor even a knight or a baronet. They sound grand enough but, from what I can make out, they're not out of the top drawer. You can do much better'n that. And if we're to find well-to-do gentlemen for Lavvy and Syl, you need a husband with a *proper* title. A Peer of the Realm – so that means you've to land a Baron, at the very least.'

Not for the first time, Caroline wondered why – having endowed her three daughters with pretty names, Mama persisted in abbreviating them to something horrible.

'It says here that pale turquoise is the most fashionable colour of the season 'cos of Her Grace of R. wearing it to the Cavendish House ball,' said Lavinia. And, looking up, 'Who's the Duchess of R., Caro?'

'You must've met *some* peers,' grumbled Mama. 'If you haven't, I'd like to know what Lady Brassington is doing to earn her money. And I wish you'd pay more attention. I reckon we'd have had a few callers by now if you tried being a bit more pleasant.'

'It *says* pale turquoise but the book's two months old so that mightn't be true any more. Look about you tonight, Caro, and see if it is or not.'

'And after the education you've had and the fortune your Grandpa Maitland is settling on you, I don't see any reason why you shouldn't get a Viscount or even an Earl. You may not be much to look at but there must be some of them better sorts who need to marry money.'

Caroline winced. Whoever had first said 'Truth hurts' had known what they were talking about. The situation was simple enough. Her father had died when she was four and Mama had re-married. But Grandfather Maitland had maintained an interest in his only grandchild, paid for her education and promised a dowry of one hundred thousand pounds on the day she married. By contrast, Lavinia and Sylvia, issue of Mama's second marriage to Mr Haywood and also now fatherless, had nothing. Consequently, Mama had decided it was Caroline's duty to Save the Family by making a Good Match.

In essence, Caroline didn't mind this. Or not much, anyway. Owing to Grandpa Maitland's unshakeable conviction that girls shouldn't be married off straight out of the school-room, she was making her debut at the advanced age of twenty-two. This meant that she no longer had any silly, romantic illusions about being swept off her feet by a dashingly handsome fellow – noble or otherwise. She knew she was no great beauty and that the only reason any titled gentleman would marry a girl who came from a background of cotton mills and trade was the money she brought with her. Also, she was genuinely fond of her half-sisters who, having taken after Mama, were better-looking than she, good-natured and wholly devoid of jealousy. No. The problem wasn't doing what was expected of her. It was the manner of it … which closely resembled a cross between a slave market and a cattle auction.

Worse even than this were her clothes, which – however fashionable the dress-maker in Harrogate had thought them – were utterly and embarrassingly wrong in London. Lady Brassington had told her to throw everything out and start again but Caroline couldn't do that. It wasn't just that Grandpa had spent a ridiculous amount of money. It was the way he'd insisted she model every single gown for him and then, with tears in his eyes, announced that she looked 'champion'. He'd had no idea that the styles were too fussy and that the bright colours rendered her insipid. He'd just thought his little lass looked 'a reet picture'; so Caroline wasn't about to tell him that last night she'd actually heard a couple of ladies tittering behind her back. She looked into the mirror at the canary-yellow taffeta and sighed again. Tonight was a ball at the home of Viscount and Lady Linton, neither of whom she'd ever met. And tonight, just like the previous balls she'd attended, she'd spend most of the evening sitting with the chaperones because it seemed that the gentlemen who were interested in acquiring her dowry turned up for the first hour, then took themselves off to more conducive amusements .

Mama was still droning on about differing levels of the aristocracy when Lady Brassington's coach drew up at the door. Caroline pulled on her cloak, pasted a cheery smile on her face and went off to face the lions.

* * *

Marcus, Lord Sheringham arrived in Lady Linton's ballroom in time to see Ludovic Sterne leading Mistress Maitland through a gavotte. Suppressing a scowl of annoyance, he accepted a glass of her ladyship's extremely indifferent wine and glanced around the company in the hope of seeing any other viable candidates. Unsurprisingly, there weren't any. Although there were a number of well-dowered girls dotted about the room, not one was worth anything like the hundred thousand pounds the Halifax heiress would bring; and all of them had a father or brother who would summarily show him the door if he made even the most tentative approach. All of which meant that little Miss Halifax was his only possible option … and Ludo Sterne was a bloody inconvenience.

Basically, time was running out. Another week – two at the most – and his creditors would be blockading his door, leaving him with scant alternative other than flight. He'd had some luck at the tables recently but not enough to signify and the only reputable house still allowing him to play on credit was Sinclair's – though there was no saying how long that would last. The French fellow who owned the place had been giving him some very hard looks recently; and if the looks were followed by a request to settle his account, it would be the last, damnable straw.

He needed the heiress and needed her badly. So, unfortunately, did Ludo Sterne. Marcus knew he held three of the winning cards, compared to Sterne's one. He was younger, better looking and titled. It ought to have been enough. And if *would* have been if Sterne hadn't been holding an ace in the form of his cousin, Lily Brassington.

Marcus watched Caroline and her partner with an assessing eye. The girl didn't dance too badly and Sterne had said something that had made her laugh – which was more than Marcus himself had ever managed. But then, Sterne gave the impression of actually *liking* the chit. Marcus didn't, particularly. He found her bland and gauche. Her dress-sense was frankly appalling and physically, she wasn't at all the type of female he admired. Trying to engage her in conversation was like pulling teeth and, as for luring her into flirtation, he'd virtually given up hope. In short, if it hadn't been for the money, he wouldn't have looked at her twice. And the only way he could tolerate the idea of being stuck with her for life was by reminding himself that her dowry would enable him to redeem the mortgage on his least favourite and most distant estate and leave her there.

The dance drew to a close. Mr Sterne restored the girl to his cousin's side and lingered to exchange polite pleasantries. Marcus forced himself to wait and managed not to grind his teeth. Finally, Sterne made his bows and sauntered off in the direction of the card room. Marcus gave it another half-minute and closed in on his prey.

Caroline saw him approaching and felt the usual frisson of nerves. He wasn't at all like Mr Sterne who chatted easily about this person and that in a way she found both relaxing and informative. Lord Sheringham wasn't relaxing at all. He was extremely handsome, enormously sophisticated and a Baron – which meant he was the only gentleman currently showing an interest in her who would also meet Mama's requirements. She wanted to like him because she felt she should and because she knew she could probably do much worse. She'd been prepared to settle for any man who still had all his own teeth, so his lordship's good looks had to be considered a bonus. Consequently, if he made her an offer, she told herself she'd be a fool not to accept it. The trouble was that she didn't know quite what to make of him. He had a habit of fixing her with his startlingly blue eyes as if he was waiting for some specific reaction which eluded her. And when that happened, she always ended up feeling even more tongue-tied and stupid than usual.

'Lady Brassington. Your servant, ma'am. And Mistress Maitland.' He favoured her with a brilliant smile and bowed over her hand. 'You are looking particularly delightful this evening.'

Caroline knew she didn't look delightful at all but she gave him points for civility and tried not to dwell on the fact that it was the kind of thing an aspiring suitor was supposed to say.

'You're very kind, sir.'

'Not at all. Your gown is a refreshing change from the pink tones favoured by so many of the young ladies.' He smiled again. 'If you are not engaged and if her ladyship permits … perhaps you would honour me with the next dance?'

Caroline curtsied and cautiously returned his smile.

'I would be happy to do so, sir. Thank you.'

She took his hand and let him lead her on to the floor, gloomily wondering if she'd ever get beyond bland inanities or stop worrying that the ladylike accent she'd been taught four years ago at school might at any moment lapse into the broad Yorkshire of her Mama and sisters.

It was an old-fashioned, formal minuet … the kind that very few hostesses included these days. But it suited Marcus's purposes in that it allowed plenty of opportunity for gazing into her eyes in a way calculated to make her blush. She never did, of course. It was one of the things he was beginning to find most irritating about her. When subjected to his compelling stare, even the most experienced ladies were wont to become a trifle heated. Little Miss Halifax, on the other hand, merely looked perpetually baffled.

Deciding that, time being of the essence, some action was called for, he said, 'I feel that I have been remiss in not making the acquaintance of your mother, Mistress Maitland. If you are free, may I call tomorrow? And then, if she has no objection, perhaps I could take you driving in the park?'

Caroline's nerves went into spasm at the thought of his lordship in the dismal little house in Kensington and the likely nature of Mama's reception of him. She said abruptly, 'My mother is not – not well enough to receive visitors at present. I'm so sorry. Perhaps in week or two, if her health improves?'

Marcus suspected that he was being put off. Moreover, a week or two was longer than he could comfortably wait. He felt like shaking the girl but, instead, he summoned a sympathetic expression and said, 'Forgive me. I had no idea. Please accept my very best wishes for her swift recovery.'

'Yes. I mean – thank you, sir.'

Caroline groped for a change of subject but, as usual, her fund of social small talk proved inadequate and the conversation ground to a halt. Finally, his lordship said, 'Dare I hope to see you at the Overbury masquerade next week?'

'Perhaps. I'm not sure. Lady Brassington deals with all our invitations.'

'Of course. Have you ever attended a masked ball?'

'No.' *They don't tend to have them in Halifax.* 'Never.'

'Then you shouldn't miss this one. You will enjoy it immensely, I'm sure. And I,' he exerted just a hint of extra pressure on her fingers as the music ended, 'will not enjoy it at *all* if you aren't present.' Which, he reflected grimly as he returned her to Lily Brassington's side, had the merit of being absolutely true.

Lady Brassington watched his lordship saunter elegantly away, then looked searchingly at her charge. She murmured, 'Handsome is as handsome does, my dear. I'd remember that, if I were you.'

A little later, Caroline found herself marooned beside two young ladies she'd never met before, with no idea what to say to them. She smiled tentatively at Mistresses Delahaye and Garfield and wondered if she was correct in detecting a note of friction.

'Maitland? I've heard about you,' said the shrew-faced girl in pink. 'You're the new heiress.'

The other girl rolled her eyes and said, 'I wouldn't put it like that if I were you, Cecy. If she's the *new* heiress – what does that make you?'

Mistress Garfield shot her a venomous glance and returned her attention to Caroline.

'That's a perfectly awful dress. What on earth made you choose it?'

The blatant rudeness was sufficient to unlock Caroline's jaws and, without stopping to think, she said, 'Probably the same error of judgement that made you choose yours.'

Unexpectedly, Mistress Delahaye laughed.

'You asked for that, Cecy – and it's quite true. Pink doesn't suit you and all those ruffles and ribbons and roses are positively vulgar.' Then, smiling at Caroline, 'Don't mind Cecily. She's like that with everyone. I'm Cassie, by the way. And you?'

'Caroline.'

'Goodness. We're all C's. How odd.'

'Oh for heaven's sake,' snapped Cecily. She sent a searching glance around the room and added crossly, 'This is a waste of time. I've only danced three times all evening and there's nobody here now worth dancing *with*.'

'What she means,' confided Cassie, 'is that Nicholas Wynstanton isn't here.'

Cecily came sharply to her feet in a cascade of pink frills.

'That is completely untrue,' she snapped. And, turning on her heel, marched off in search of fresh prey.

'Thank goodness,' murmured Cassie. 'As you've seen, she's positively rag-mannered. If it wasn't for her money, I doubt she'd still be invited anywhere.'

Caroline stared down at her lap and said nothing.

'Oh – I'm so sorry!' Flushing with mortification, Cassie reached out and took her hand. 'I didn't mean that to sound as if … as if --'

'It's all right. I know you didn't. And I'm aware that I'm only here for the same reason as Mistress Garfield.'

'But with much, *much* better manners.'

'Not so very much after what I said to her.'

'She deserved that – and it was such a neat put-down that I very nearly applauded.' Cassie paused, and then added delicately, 'You haven't been in Town very long, have you?'

'A few weeks, only.' *It just feels a lot longer.* 'And you?'

'Oh – this is my second Season,' came the cheerful reply. 'Since most of the gentlemen I like treat me as if I were their sister and the rest don't meet Mama's standards, I'm likely to get a third one as well. Not that I mind, particularly. In fact, I rather like it.' She paused and then added delicately, 'I saw you dancing with Mr Sterne and Lord Sheringham, did I not?'

'Yes – and will be aware why they asked me.' Caroline also hesitated and then decided to grasp what might be her only opportunity. 'Would you tell me something? Truthfully?'

'If I can.'

'I know neither gentleman has any money. What I *don't* know is *why* they haven't – and all I hear from Lady Brassington are hints that don't really tell me anything except that she favours Mr Sterne.'

Cassie's brow wrinkled thoughtfully.

'Well, she would do, of course. She's his aunt or cousin or something. As for money … I'm not sure Mr Sterne ever had much. I don't think he inherited a great deal … and my Papa says he's a gamester.'

'I see. And his lordship?'

'Another of the same, I'm afraid – and equally deep in debt, if the rumours are true. The only difference is that rumour *also* says that, ten years ago, Lord Sheringham was a rich man.'

'You mean he's squandered a fortune at cards and dice?'

'Some of it, certainly.' Cassie cast around for something encouraging to say. 'I don't know either gentleman well, of course. But Mr Sterne is always pleasant and one can't deny that his lordship is very good-looking.'

'No.' *Handsome is as handsome does.* 'No. One can't.'

Though she'd hoped it might be otherwise, it came as no particular surprise to Caroline that both of her would-be suitors were addicted to gaming. More troubling was the knowledge that Lord Sheringham had already gone through one fortune and could just as easily go through another. She didn't think Grandpa Maitland would approve of his money being wasted over the card-table. She wasn't sure she approved of it herself. And when she took a moment to consider just how long Grandpa's hundred thousand pounds might be expected to last, she had the unpleasant feeling that it might not be very long at all.

Caroline had thought that she could do worse than Marcus Sheringham. Now she wasn't so sure. But persuading Mama that Lavinia and Sylvia could make perfectly satisfactory marriages without Caroline wedding a title was going to be virtually impossible.

* * *

At Sinclair's, meanwhile, Adrian and Lord Nicholas had enjoyed an extremely good dinner along with a couple of bottles of equally good claret. Then, despite Adrian's attempts to avoid it, they had settled down to play piquet and, within half an hour, the concentration it took *not* to count cards had made his head hurt.

At one point, Aristide had wandered in to watch the play for a few minutes – presumably in order to check that Adrian wasn't using his peculiar skill – and then, apparently satisfied, said, 'The main floor is busy tonight and there are any number of gentlemen down there who may know you. So if you're still intent on not being recognised, I suggest you leave by the back way.'

Glad of the interruption and feeling that even invading a stranger's house uninvited was preferable to another hour of mental torture, Adrian threw down his cards and said, 'Come on, Nick. For God's sake, let's go and get this over with.'

Nicholas glanced at the clock.

'It's only a little after eleven. Still early, really.'

'It's late enough.'

With a good-humoured shrug, Lord Nicholas surrendered what he hoped was another winning hand and said, 'All right. But since I'm only going to this damned party on your account, I'll demand we finish the game at some other time.'

'If we must.'

Aristide laughed and said, 'Dear me. Are you turning into a poor loser?'

'No. But I'm glad,' said Adrian between his teeth, 'that I'm providing you with some amusement.' Then, before Nicholas could ask what he meant, he snatched up his hat and cloak and headed for the door.

They were admitted to Viscount Linton's house in Clarges Street by a singularly incurious butler. Lord Nicholas led the way through the rooms, sometimes pausing to acknowledge various acquaintances and sometimes to introduce his companion. Adrian, who had braced himself both for playing the Earl and for having people turn their back on him, was cautiously surprised when no one did so. Undoubtedly, some of them would when they either recognised him or heard his name; and he was well aware he'd face more opposition from the ladies of society than from their husbands but he'd cross that bridge when he came to it. For now, it was enough that this first foray was going better than he had expected.

Mr Fox fanned himself languidly and said, 'Sarre? Well, well. How exciting. That *will* set the cat among the pigeons.'

Lord March said, 'A pleasure, sir. Care to join us in the card room?'

And Lord Philip Vernon, who was apparently the Lintons' son-in-law, smiled enviously and said, 'I don't suppose you'd give me the name of your tailor?'

Gradually, he let himself slide more deeply into his role. There was no room for error here. From this moment on, Society had to think of him as the Earl of Sarre ... and that wouldn't happen unless he thought of *himself* that way and projected the necessary presence. So he guarded his expression, kept his spine rigid and reminded himself to eschew French gestures and intonation – both of which tended to sneak in when he wasn't sufficiently careful.

Lady Linton, when Nicholas eventually ran her to earth, smiled vaguely and said, 'You're very, very late, Nicholas. Had you not brought Lord Sarre with you, I might have managed a scold. Or then again, not. Annoyance is so fatiguing. And you may atone by dancing with ... someone or other.'

Sarre watched her drift away.

'Is she always like that?'

'Yes.' Nicholas lifted two glasses from a passing footman and handed him one. 'Look over there. The two girls sitting on the sofa by that big leafy thing.'

'What of them?'

'One of them is the heiress from Halifax.'

His lordship's gaze sharpened almost imperceptibly.

'Which?'

'The one dressed like a dandelion.'

From what Sarre could see, it seemed an apt description. He said, 'Do you know her name?'

'Makepeace? Madeley? Machin? Something like that,' shrugged Nicholas. 'I've never actually been introduced to her.'

'What about the pretty brunette beside her?'

'Cassandra Delahaye?' Nicholas grinned. 'I know *her* well enough. Her father's one of Rock's friends and Cassie's a sweetheart.'

'Is she?' The Earl let a pause develop and then said, 'Introduce me, will you?'

'What on earth for? You can't be hunting for a leg-shackle already, surely?'

'I'm not. Call it a whim ... and humour me.'

'Oh God. All right, then. But on your own head be it.'

On the far side of the room, Cassie noted the newcomers and gave a gurgle of laughter.

'Poor Cecy. She bullied her brother into taking her home – and now here's Lord Nicholas, after all.' She leaned towards Caroline. 'He's the gentleman in blue – and he's the Duke of Rockliffe's brother. Cecily has been trying to catch his eye for weeks but he always manages to elude her.'

Caroline watched the meandering approach of two tall, beautifully-dressed gentlemen, only one of whom was smiling, and said, 'And his companion?'

'I don't know. But it looks as though we're about to find out.'

Arriving before the ladies, Nicholas grinned and said, 'Cassie, my love … you're looking especially delicious tonight.'

The disapproving tilt of her chin was somewhat spoiled by the twinkle in her eye.

'I am most certainly *not* your love. And delicious? What kind of compliment is that?'

'An honest one.' Then, 'Don't be cross, darling. I want you to meet an old friend of mine, newly returned from Paris.'

Although he made his bow and murmured all the right things, Sarre let the introductions and Nicholas's flirtatious banter flow over him. He filed the heiress's name away in his mind and surveyed her without appearing to do so.

It was difficult to look past the garishly yellow dress, adorned as it was with frills and rosettes and quantities of fluttering ribbons. And the dark blonde hair was arranged in such an elaborate mass of twists and puffs that it completely over-shadowed her face. But her skin was smooth, her waist looked trim and the little he could see of her bosom beneath that unflattering neckline suggested interesting proportions. As for her eyes … he was still waiting for her to raise them above the level of his sternum. She wasn't, by any stretch of the imagination, a beauty – but neither was she absolutely plain. For the rest, he couldn't decide whether her apparent inability to mouth more than the odd monosyllable denoted a lack of character, social ineptitude or mere shyness. Then, Nicholas said something particularly outrageous and she glanced up, half-way between shock and amusement, revealing warm, expressive dark brown eyes which went a long way towards transforming her otherwise ordinary face.

Sarre's brows rose slightly. Instantly, she caught him looking at her and froze, her expression changing to one he knew very well indeed. He'd seen it numerous times on the faces of actors when they weren't comfortable with the role in which they'd been cast or couldn't

41

remember the next line. Mistress Maitland was way out of her depth and frightened of either getting her words wrong or delivering them badly. He understood that and even felt a certain sympathy. His own position wasn't entirely dissimilar, after all … and *he* had a wealth of previous experience.

Very briefly, he considered taking pity on the girl and inviting her to dance but he knew that wouldn't do. At some point tomorrow, London society was going to learn that he was back in England and had assumed his title and, for a number of reasons, it wasn't a good idea for the gossips *also* to learn that he had been seen taking an interest in the Halifax heiress. Then again, Sarre didn't want to become acquainted with the girl just yet – or even at all. Until he had decided how he wanted the drama to unfold, he preferred to keep his options open.

Consequently, he let his gaze drift back to the other girl and, bathing her in a cool smile which didn't touch his eyes, said, 'Mistress Delahaye … will you take pity on a near-stranger and accept my hand for this gavotte?'

Cassie beamed and laid her fingers on his arm.

'Thank you, Lord Sarre. I would be delighted. And pity doesn't come into it at all.'

Lord Nicholas watched them take to the floor and realised that he was now stuck doing the pretty by the heiress. Drawing the line at asking her to dance, he handed her back to her seat and said, 'May I fetch you some refreshment, Mistress Maitland?'

Caroline had heard that particular excuse enough times to know exactly what it meant. She said colourlessly, 'Thank you, Lord Nicholas. By all means.'

And Nicholas, who was neither stupid nor unkind, immediately felt ashamed of himself.

'Or perhaps you'd prefer to dance? I don't generally, you know because I've a tendency to muddle the figures which most ladies find annoying. But if you care to risk it …?'

'Not if you'd rather not,' she replied with a faint smile. 'A glass of ratafia would be agreeable.'

'Of course.' He eyed her thoughtfully for a moment and then added bluntly, 'I know what you're thinking – and I daresay you have cause. But I promise I'm not abandoning you. A gentleman shouldn't, you see.' And, with a slight bow, he strolled away in the direction of the refreshment room.

Caroline stared at his retreating back, completely nonplussed. Of all the people she'd met, she would never have suspected that a Duke's brother ... moreover, a Duke's extremely *attractive* brother ... would not only understand but speak plainly of the slights she often endured. She wondered if his friend, the Earl would have been as honest. Somehow, without quite knowing why, she doubted it.

She looked across at him now, dancing with Cassie, his movements precise and his posture impeccable. He was tall, well-made and wearing a black coat adorned with a modicum of silver-lacing over an opulently embroidered vest. His hair, neatly fastened at his nape with a jewelled buckle, was powdered, leaving her with no idea of its colour. But his eyes, set beneath level dark brows, were a clear, pale grey; his cheekbones were clearly-defined, his jaw determined and his mouth, well-shaped but hard. It was an arresting face ... too shuttered and severe to be considered handsome but undeniably compelling.

A shiver ran down Caroline's back, as if a draught had suddenly found her or, as Grandpa might have said, someone had walked over her grave. Hurriedly, she withdrew her gaze from the Earl of Sarre and turned, with relief, to the comforting sight of Lord Nicholas walking back to her side.

Oddly, however, the chill still lingered.

FOUR

On the following evening, with the aim of making his presence in Town more widely-known, Sarre walked into Sinclair's through the front door for the first time. He had timed it well. The main gaming floor was alive with activity and a crowd was gathered around the Hazard table. His lordship strolled through the room looking perfectly relaxed and giving the impression that he had no particular goal in view. He was aware of the moments when the cheerful buzz of chatter around him became suddenly muted. He noted which gentlemen avoided eye-contact or turned their backs, which ones nodded a greeting and which offered him their hands. The snubs didn't trouble him. He'd taught himself not to feel anything a long time ago and now the habit was so ingrained that he didn't have to try. These days, when a show of feeling was a necessary requirement, he simply acted it.

He accepted a glass of canary from a footman, exchanged a few words with Monsieur Delacroix as if they were barely acquainted and continued on his lazy, seemingly idle progress through the heart of the club.

Aristide had given him the information he needed.

'The large card-room. There are two tables in play, he's at one of them.'

Sarre nodded, sipped his wine and strolled on. A lisping Macaroni he didn't recognise pointedly turned his shoulder and two fellows he might have put names to had he wanted to bother, froze in mid-conversation to stare as he walked by.

Giving the pair a haughty glare, Lord Philip Vernon strode to his side, hand outstretched, and said clearly, 'Good evening, my lord. A pleasure to see you again. You've discovered this place very quickly. I suppose Nick put you on to it?'

Sarre accepted his lordship's hand and the spirit in which it was offered.

'He was good enough to arrange membership for me. It's extremely stylish ... and new, of course, since my time. But popular, it would seem.'

'The play's deep and fair,' shrugged Philip. 'So how long has it been?'

'Since I was last in London? Ten years.'

'Good Lord. A lot of things must seem unfamiliar then.'

'Most of them, in fact.' Sarre eyed Philip thoughtfully and decided to find out how genuine were his intentions. 'Has no one told you about me?'

A hint of colour touched the lean cheek – more, it appeared, due to annoyance than from embarrassment. 'That lisping idiot, Ansford, started babbling about some ancient scandal – but I can't stand the fellow so I didn't listen. And if whatever happened took place a decade ago, it ought to be water way out to sea by now.'

The Earl smiled faintly.

'There are probably a good many people who remember what was said at the time; some who still believe it and one or two who will wish to resurrect it. You should hear what it is before offering any kind of support or possible friendship.'

'Perhaps. But I learned the dangers of basing my own opinion on that of someone else a while ago,' said Philip. 'It ended with me putting a bullet into the man who is now my sister's husband. So if *you* want to tell me what people will say, I'll listen. Otherwise, I'm not remotely interested.'

Sarre stared consideringly into his lordship's face for a moment. Then he said gently, 'I'm reputed to have pushed a girl to her death from a roof-top.'

The dark blue eyes widened then narrowed.

'Oh. And did you?'

'No.'

Against all expectation, Lord Philip suddenly grinned.

'Good enough. Come and join our party in the next room. No one's taking the cards very seriously but the company's good. Nick's not here tonight but I daresay you'll remember his brother ... and possibly also Lord Amberley and Harry Caversham?'

'Of course.' *Oh this is just perfect. I spent two months dodging Harry last spring and God knows how long hoping Amberley's French relatives didn't take it into their heads to bring him to the theatre the year before. As for Rockliffe ... there's no telling what he may say. And there they all are, just when I could do without that kind of audience. Hell.* 'It's extremely kind of you but I don't wish to intrude.'

'You won't be. I'll wager everyone will be delighted to see you.'

Not quite everyone.

'In that case, how can I refuse?' he murmured. And allowed Lord Philip to shepherd him through the doorway.

As Aristide had said, there were two tables both littered with bottles, glasses and cards. At one of them sat the Duke of Rockliffe's party. And, at the other, three men he didn't recognise, along with one he knew only too well.

Heads turned, conversation dwindled and there were several seconds of pure silence before Marcus Sheringham erupted from his chair so violently that he over-set it. He snapped, '*Eastry!* I heard you were back – and can only marvel at your effrontery.'

And there it was. The reaction he'd hoped ten years might have changed; rash, stupid and malicious.

You utter cretin, Marcus. Don't you see how very easy you're making this for me?

His tone cool and even a touch careless, he said, 'It's Sarre, actually. It may have slipped your mind, but I haven't been Viscount Eastry for three years. As to my effrontery ... I'm not sure what you mean. Did you expect me to remain abroad forever?'

'You damned well should have. Showing your face in polite society after what you've done? It's iniquitous!'

'And what, exactly, *have* I done?' *Say it to my face, you bastard. Just for once, look me in the eye instead of grubbing about behind my back.* 'Well?'

'Lord Sheringham.' It was Rockliffe who spoke, his voice as seemingly lazy as ever but sufficient to command silence. 'You are disrupting the evening.'

Just for a second, his lordship appeared taken aback. Then, 'My apologies, your Grace – but the interruption is not of my making.'

'Is it not? Whose, then?'

'That of *my Lord Sarre*.' The last three words were laden with sarcasm. 'I don't claim to speak for everyone in this room … but for myself, I refuse to sit down with a – a --' He stopped.

'Very wise,' murmured Rockliffe. 'You might wish to choose your next words rather carefully.'

'I will not,' said his lordship gratingly, 'sit down with a man who – whose hands are stained with innocent blood.'

This time the silence was hot and airless. Sheringham's three companions looked utterly blank and the Duke's expression remained enigmatic. But Philip was scowling, Harry Caversham and the fellow sitting next to him frowned and the Marquis of Amberley looked faintly contemptuous. Feeling that the entire situation was getting away from him, Sarre opened his mouth to take control – only to find himself forestalled once more.

'That is your choice, of course.' The Duke's fingers toyed absently with his wine-glass. 'But you are not required to … sit down … with Lord Sarre, are you? As far as I am aware, he has been invited to join our table – not yours.'

'Then I can only assume that your Grace doesn't know what he's done.'

Something that might have been laughter glinted in the night-dark gaze.

'It's certainly true that I don't know … indisputably and beyond any possible doubt … what his lordship *may* have done. But, unless I've mistaken the matter, neither do you.' He let a pause develop and then, when Sheringham said nothing, turned away in a clear indication of dismissal. 'Philip … if you're re-joining us, find chairs for yourself and Lord Sarre.'

Lord Sheringham remained, irresolute, beside his over-turned chair.

'If your Grace will excuse me for a moment,' murmured Sarre. He approached to within a couple of paces of the man who had once been his closest friend but who it seemed was still out to destroy him and

47

STELLA RILEY

said quietly, 'I offered to fight you ten years ago, Marcus. You refused and let my father stand between us. However, that offer still stands. Unless you're prepared to meet me, don't make me force the issue.'

And, without waiting for an answer, he turned his back and sat down between Philip and Harry Caversham.

'Well done,' said Harry, not bothering to lower his voice. 'If you need someone to act for you, I'll be happy to oblige.'

With a sound resembling a snarl, Lord Sheringham stalked from the room, leaving his erstwhile companions staring at his retreating back.

Ignoring them, Rockliffe sighed gently and reached for his snuff-box.

'If no one has any objection and the theatricals are over for the evening, do you suppose we might finish the game?'

'Why?' grinned the Marquis of Amberley. 'Because you expect to win?'

'I sense a certain probability,' agreed Rockliffe.

Sarre leaned back in his chair, avoided looking at the cards and attempted to understand what had just happened. The Duke had stepped in, seemingly on his own behalf and the others had followed his lead. In one way, this was easy to comprehend ... in another, it made no sense whatsoever. The best that Sarre had hoped for was polite acceptance but this had been much more than that and the reasons for it eluded him. Indeed, the only thing that might account for it was a possibility that had never previously occurred to him; the possibility that, in the last decade and in certain quarters, Marcus Sheringham had made himself somewhat unpopular.

While the others concluded their game, Lord Philip quietly introduced Sarre to Jack Ingram and explained that Lord Amberley was his own brother-in-law. The Earl's brows rose at this and he murmured softly, 'The one you shot?'

Philip flushed. 'Yes. And before you ask – no, he didn't miss me. He deloped.'

'Ah.' A hint of humour stirred. 'That can't have made it any better.'

'No. It damned well didn't.'

Rockliffe won the game by a generous margin. Harry Caversham called for another couple of bottles and, whilst gathering up the cards,

48

Lord Amberley said pleasantly, 'Welcome home, Sarre. It must be strange to be back.'

'It is. My apologies, by the way, for that unfortunate scene earlier.'

Amberley shrugged. 'Sheringham is still intent on raking over the coals, it would seem. But then, I've never had a particularly high regard for his intellect.'

'The fellow's an idiot,' remarked Harry. 'If he wasn't, he'd have stopped throwing good money after bad before he was completely rolled-up.'

'And is he?' asked Sarre, as if he didn't know.

'Yes. He's been trying to land an heiress for a couple of years, now.' With a glance in Amberley's direction, Harry turned to Philip. 'He made a push for Rosalind, didn't he?'

'Yes.'

'And then my Nell – and God knows how many others in between. Now he's got his claws into that shy little thing from Yorkshire; a girl with no decent connections to warn him off and nobody but Lily Brassington to put her wise.' He shook his head. 'Seems a shame, really. At the rate he's going, her dowry will melt away like butter on a hot day.'

'Is it at all possible,' drawled Rockliffe, 'that we could abandon the extremely tedious subject of Lord Sheringham's marital and financial prospects? Dominic ... will you take the bank or shall I?'

'It's yours.' Lord Amberley pushed the cards across the table and with a grin, said, 'Deal – and be prepared for the rest of us to take our revenge.'

Sarre watched the Duke deal him into the game and sank resignedly back into his chair. Before he'd sat down to a hand of piquet with Nicholas, he hadn't known the cost of shutting down his gift. For years in Paris, he'd frequented half a dozen different gaming establishments in a variety of different guises so that the consistency with which he won and the ability that made it possible went unremarked. Since his object had always been to earn a living, he'd never had any reason to try playing without using his skill. Now – because he'd promised Aristide and because he didn't want to profit from these men who'd shown him an uncommon degree of courtesy – he had to ignore what his own cards and the discards of the other players told him about the odds, probabilities and what was left in the stack. It didn't sound difficult. Most people would think it easy. In reality, it took a level of concentration that was going to leave him feeling as though his skull had been split.

The thought of having to endure many evenings like this was daunting. On the other hand, his sufferings wouldn't be without benefit. He'd thought his only ally in society would be Nicholas ... but if the men sitting around this table were prepared to accept him, his life would be a lot easier. Indeed, Rockliffe's support alone would be sufficient to smooth his way. Not that he was counting on that just yet. He suspected that, at the very least, the Duke was going to bring up L'Inconnu's career at the Comédie Française in order to have a little fun at his expense. Nicholas might think his brother wasn't sure what he'd seen. Sarre was under no such illusion.

As expected, by the time the game was over he had a monumental headache and had lost a reasonable amount of money. As the party broke up, Harry Caversham promised to send him a card for the party his wife was planning at the Pantheon and Philip Vernon offered to put him up for membership at White's. With a typically enigmatic smile, his Grace of Rockliffe bade him a perfectly civil goodnight and followed Amberley and Mr Ingram from the club.

Sarre took a moment to master the pain in his head and then went in search of Aristide. He said, 'With regard to the matter of Marcus Sheringham ...'

'Yes?'

'Give it one more week and then close him down.'

'And his debt?'

'Call it in.'

Aristide nodded. 'This is on account of tonight's unpleasantness?'

Sarre shut his eyes for a moment and then said, 'You heard about that?'

'His lordship made sure half the club heard about it.'

'Ah. So now you know some part of what this is all about.'

'Yes.' Then, '*Part* of it?'

'The only part I can do anything about. Don't you want to ask if it's true?'

'I hadn't thought of it,' shrugged Aristide. 'Should I?'

'No. Thank you.'

'*De rien*. And we shall let Lord Sheringham reap the rewards of his own folly.'

* * *

Back in Cork Street and having refused Bertrand's offer of brandy, he lay back with a cold compress over his aching temples and waited for it to effect some improvement.

Bertrand said, 'You look like hell.'

'Thank you.'

'Aside from the obvious, how did it go?'

'Better than I could possibly have hoped.' *Better than I deserved, perhaps.* 'It appears Sheringham isn't universally beloved – which is useful – and he made an exhibition of himself this evening.' He paused, then added, 'I've told Aristide to give him a week's grace before turning the screw.'

'Did you explain why?'

'Not precisely. He thinks it's because of what happened tonight – which is true enough in its way.'

'Is it?' Bertrand looked sceptical. 'You're saying you'd have left Sheringham alone if he'd let sleeping dogs lie?'

'No. But I'd probably have left him alone to dig his own pit.' Sarre tossed the compress aside and sat up, grimacing. 'As it is, I intend to ensure that when he falls into it, he stays there.'

* * *

Adrian slept for perhaps three hours and then woke with a pounding heart and a headache of epic proportions. He shoved the tangled sheets aside and sat up, pressing the heels of his hands to his eyes.

Marcus, this time. Of course. He ought to have expected it.

Marcus ... who had seduced Evie. Marcus ... but for whom Evie would never have been on the roof at all. Marcus ... who, arriving at Sarre Park to learn that his treachery had ended in tragedy, had immediately responded with vile accusations of jealousy and murder.

And all the while, Adrian's parents had stood by and said nothing.

'*You killed her!*' Marcus had yelled loudly enough for the whole house to hear. '*She told you she'd changed her mind – that she wanted me, not you – and you lured her up there and murdered her, you bastard!*'

Still numb with shock, Adrian had been unable to think lucidly. He'd been capable of nothing but a string of incoherent denials.

'*No! It's not true. I didn't … I wouldn't … I'd never hurt her, no matter what. Why are you saying this? It's not true!*' And helplessly to his parents, '*Why don't you tell him? You* know *me, for God's sake! So how can't you know it's not true?*'

But still they'd said nothing, but merely stood there as if frozen. And that was when, finally realising that he was on his own in this, Adrian had swung round to Marcus and said, '*Fight me, then. If you believe what you're saying, you'll fight. Now – outside. Swords or pistols. Your choice. Kill me, if that's what you want.*'

'*I don't soil my blade with murderers,*' spat Marcus insultingly. '*Nor do I need to when I can see you hang.*'

Adrian had lunged at him then, taking a wild swing which might have connected had Marcus not stepped back, leaving the Earl to block his son's fist and hold it fast.

Marcus laughed, albeit a little shakily, and turned towards the door.

'*Don't think I'll keep quiet about this, Eastry,*' he'd said. '*You'll pay for what you've done. And I'll see you at your trial.*'

Adrian sat up and dropped his hands to his lap. Of course, it had never come to that because that was when his father had ordered him to get out of England and stay there.

* * *

Mr Henry Lessing, Lawyer and Discreet Man of Business for the Discerning Well-to-do, occupied premises just off Chancery Lane. He had conducted the English affairs of Monsieur Adrian St. Clare of Paris for some time before learning that the gentleman in question was actually the seventh Earl of Sarre. Another man might have let this transformation worry him. Fortunately, Mr Lessing wasn't one of them.

He liked his work and particularly enjoyed his correspondence with the Earl. His only problem was that, when his lordship arrived at his office without prior arrangement, he failed to recognise him.

Ignoring the clerk who had been trying to herd him into the back office whilst establishing his credentials, Sarre walked into Mr Lessing's comfortable room, tossed his gloves on the desk and said simply, 'I'm Sarre. I assumed you'd be expecting me.'

Mr Lessing blinked and rapidly pulled himself together before he gave one of his favourite clients the idea that he was mentally-defective. 'Of course, my lord – though not necessarily today. However ... it is a great pleasure to make your acquaintance at last.'

'Is it?'

'Indeed. Not to put too fine a point on it, sir, a great deal of my work is both tedious and undemanding. Yours is neither.'

'I'm delighted to have provided you with entertainment. You had the note I sent just before I left Paris?'

'I did. If your lordship would care to be seated?' Mr Lessing opened a drawer in one of his many cabinets and withdrew a thick dossier. 'Do you wish to begin with that matter?'

'Later. Let's start with Marcus Sheringham.'

The lawyer nodded, placed a pair of spectacles on his nose, and opened the file.

'As instructed, I have a list of the gentleman's most pressing obligations and acquired, on your behalf, the mortgages on both his hunting lodge in Shropshire and his town house in Half-Moon Street. Ah ... did I explain that his lordship disposed of the house in Hanover Square some time ago?'

'You did. You also explained that, as far as you could ascertain, he didn't use any of the resulting proceeds to settle what you so elegantly term his obligations.'

'That is correct.' Mr Lessing rifled through a number of pages. 'My best reckoning suggests that his lordship is in debt to the tune of some twenty-five thousand pounds – excluding any debts of honour that he may have incurred, naturally.'

'Then you may add the ten owing to Sinclair's to your total.'

'Dear me ... dear me. I fear Lord Sheringham's prospects are somewhat bleak.'

'I rather think 'disastrous' is the word you're looking for.' Sarre crossed one long leg over the other and smiled coolly. 'The Maitland heiress could save him, of course ... but he's yet to catch her. And speaking of that – what have you found out?'

'Enough, I think. Her grandfather is Hubert Maitland, a cloth-manufacturer of Halifax. His only son, George, married Maria Turner, a weaver's daughter, in 1753 and their daughter, Caroline, was born a year later. Four years after that, George fell into the river whilst drunk and drowned.'

'Careless of him. And his widow?'

'Maria re-married almost immediately – one Roger Haywood, by whom she had two further daughters. Sadly, Mr Haywood is also deceased. He died ...' More rustling of pages. 'Ah yes. He died five years ago, since which time Mr Maitland has been making the family a small allowance. He has also paid for his grand-daughter's education and is meeting the costs of her debut in society. His only stipulation for all this appears to be that the girl spends a portion of each year with him at his home.'

Sarre nodded. 'Interesting. What do you know about Maitland himself?'

'He is a self-made man, my lord. Most of his earliest profits came from the export of cloth to Italy but, more recently, he has invested in extensive tracts of land in Yorkshire, Lincolnshire and Nottinghamshire. Virtually all of these are being farmed using the latest methods and produce very high yields. In addition to all this, Mr Maitland has lately begun buying government stock from which he receives a substantial return. His main residence is still a house in the centre of Halifax, with workshops and packing-sheds at the back of it.' Mr Lessing paused, as if for dramatic effect and looked up smiling. 'As for his net worth ... I estimate it to be in the region of seven hundred thousand pounds. Possibly more.'

The light grey eyes flew suddenly wide.

'Are you sure?'

'Perfectly. Mr Maitland is an extremely busy and astute fellow.' Mr Lessing allowed himself a small smile. 'And there is one more thing. He has fewer blood relatives than one might suppose. A half-brother, with whom he is apparently not on good terms; a nephew, currently living in York and a couple of cousins who I believe to be of a similar age to Mr Maitland himself.'

'All of which,' said Sarre slowly, 'suggests that the girl is his natural heir?'

'I believe that may arguably be the case. And even allowing for other bequests or charitable donations, it would still make the young lady quite fabulously wealthy.'

The Earl stared at him for a long moment.

'*Merde*,' he breathed.

FIVE

Caroline leaned back against the squabs of Lady Brassington's ancient, badly-sprung carriage and stared wearily out into the darkness. They had been to Viscountess Newlyn's ball at her house near Syon Park and now faced a return drive of an hour or more. Lady B appeared to feel the discomfort and inconvenience to be of small importance when compared to the prestige of the invitation. Caroline, who had spent a more than usually trying evening, wondered irritably how many more such treats her ladyship had in store.

The evening had begun well enough. Caroline had vetoed all of Sylvia's innovative ideas with regard to her hair and insisted on a smooth, simple style which suited her better and stood some chance of staying in place. In addition – on the advice of Cassie Delahaye – she and Lavinia had spent most of the day laboriously denuding one of her gowns of every extraneous ribbon, ruffle and bit of beading until it was as plain as it could possibly be. Nothing could be done about the colour, of course. It was still a virulent shade of green which bleached the life from Caroline's skin and made her look as though she'd been ill. But the whole *toilette* was a definite improvement on previous attempts and even drew a guarded compliment from Lady Brassington.

Unfortunately, after this promising start, the evening itself went steadily downhill. The Delahaye's were not present but Cecily Garfield and her brother were. Caroline hadn't met Lewis Garfield before and wouldn't be sorry not to encounter him again. Having been more or less dragooned into dancing with her by their hostess, he either stared over her head with an expression of long-suffering or interrogated her on the nature and profitability of Grandfather Maitland's business. By the time they parted company, Caroline wanted to tip a bowl of blancmange over his head.

Next and in rapid succession, Lady Brassington presented her to three young gentlemen who appeared barely old enough to shave. The first still had spots, the second kept tripping over his feet and the third was more than a little drunk. Gritting her teeth, Caroline stood up with all three of them and then, deciding enough was enough, took refuge in the ladies retiring-room where she enjoyed ten minutes of blissful tranquillity until Cecily Garfield came along to spoil it. Caroline let the first two patronising remarks float over her head. But when the wretched girl embarked on an impertinent and personal inquisition, her temper finally snapped and she said, 'Do you have any friends at all, Mistress Garfield?'

'What? Yes. Of course I do.'

'I'm surprised. But perhaps some people don't mind spiteful remarks and atrocious manners. Personally, I think it's a good thing you have money – because, as far as I can see, you've nothing else to recommend you at all.'

And she'd walked out while Cecily's mouth was still hanging open.

All in all, thought Caroline gloomily, the only positive thing to be said for the evening was the fact that Lord Sheringham had apparently not been invited – thus sparing her the necessity of evading any further attempts to meet her mother. But that was little comfort when this foray into London society was clearly doomed to failure. Worse still was the growing conviction that the only thing lying ahead of her was a humdrum existence of Duty and Making the Best of Things; years and years of being sensible and responsible and never, even briefly, knowing what romance felt like.

Lady Brassington appeared to have fallen asleep – though, with the bouncing and rocking of the carriage, it was a mystery how she had managed it. Caroline stripped off her gloves and tried to re-position a hairpin that was digging into her scalp. She realised, when a lock of hair dropped on to her neck, that she probably should have left well alone until she got home. She muttered something very rude beneath her breath and then, suddenly seized by a mood of pure rebellion, yanked out all the rest of the pins and tossed them in her lap. Her hair slithered over her shoulders in a long, untidy cascade and she pushed it back with hands that she discovered were shaking. She drew a deep, unsteady breath and then another. And that was when she realised how very close she was to crying.

Suddenly, a shot tore out of the darkness and the carriage gave a particularly violent lurch. The hairpins flew off Caroline's lap and Lady Brassington slid half-way from her seat, to awake with a strangled grunt.

'What on earth --?' she began.

And then the second shot rang out, followed by two voices shouting at once.

Highwaymen? thought Caroline, not sure whether she wanted to laugh or scream and conscious of a wish – rather stupidly, considering the circumstances – that she'd left her hair alone. *And there I was thinking this evening couldn't possibly get any worse.*

The coach lost speed and shuddered to a halt, causing her ladyship to whimper and clutch at her throat. Worried that she was either going to faint or have hysterics, Caroline said quickly, 'It's all right, my lady. They won't hurt us, I'm sure. Just try to stay calm and --'

The door opened abruptly on a gleaming silver-mounted pistol and a beautiful, charmingly-accented voice said, '*Bon soir, Mesdames* ... do not, I beg of you, be alarmed. If you will only remain tranquil, this small delay in your travelling will last but moments, *je vous assure.*'

Caroline peered out at this cheerful robber with his smooth assurances and discovered that he didn't look like a robber at all. His full-skirted coat was of good quality scarlet cloth, its deep cuffs lavishly ornamented with gold embroidery, and beneath it she glimpsed a black brocaded vest. Dark hair was tied back beneath a picot-edged tricorne and a narrow strip of black silk hid the upper part of his face, through which his eyes gleamed with laughter and *bonhomie.* He didn't *look* like a ruffian. He didn't even look dangerous. If he hadn't clearly been French, she'd have taken him for a bored young nobleman fulfilling a silly wager. Or she might have done, but for the small, deadly pistol that was making her heart beat unpleasantly fast.

Looking past him, she saw a second man on horseback pointing a blunderbuss at their coachman. Her pulse tripped and she called, 'Moulton? Are you and – and the groom all right?'

'Yes, Miss. No harm done. Yet.'

'Don't do anything rash, then.'

'No, Miss. Wasn't planning to.'

Lady Brassington shut her eyes and moaned.

Caroline squeezed her hand and, with more confidence than she felt, said, 'It will be all right. Just sit quietly and – and leave everything to me.'

She took a deep breath and looked back at the highwayman. She'd read novels and items in the newspaper so she had a fair idea of the correct etiquette. She said, 'Well?'

He tilted his head and his teeth gleamed white. 'Well what, mademoiselle?'

'Aren't you going to say "Your money or your life"?'

'But no!' It was difficult to tell if he was amused or affronted. 'Since we are not in a very bad play and I do not at all wish to kill you, why would I say such a thing?'

'I d-don't know. I thought it was tradition.'

This time he did laugh and the sound of it was curiously infectious.

'For some, perhaps. For myself – never!'

'Oh.' For a second, the whole scenario seemed so unreal that she had no idea what to say. Then common-sense re-asserted itself. 'Well, if you don't at all wish to kill us, perhaps you could put that pistol away? It's frightening her ladyship.'

The pistol didn't move.

'But not you, mademoiselle.'

'What?'

'This,' he gestured negligently with the gun, 'is not frightening to you.'

'It is – just not as much.' Caroline pushed her hair back and said baldly, 'We don't have any money.'

'No?'

'No. We've been to a party and one doesn't take a purse to a ball.'

'Ah. That is unfortunate.' He didn't sound particularly disappointed. 'One does, however, wear jewels.'

She laid her left hand over her right, hoping he hadn't noticed the only piece of jewellery she possessed and said nothing.

Lady Brassington, however, began fumbling with the clasp of her bracelet and said shakily, 'Take this – and the rings. It's all paste, of course. I had to sell the valuable pieces years ago.' She all but threw the bracelet at him and started tugging at her rings. 'Just ... please just leave me my pearls. They're not very good but they're --'

'Hush.' Forgetting about her own ring, Caroline laid both hands over her ladyship's trembling ones. 'Don't tell him anything.' She shot the highwayman a fierce look. 'I'm sure you can find richer pickings than us. We're not worth your time.'

His smile was slow and deliberately enticing. Lowering his voice to a simmering purr, he said, 'Not so, Mademoiselle. Not so at all.' And dropping her ladyship's trinkets in one pocket and the pistol in the other, he held out his hand. *'S'il vous plaît, mignonne* ... step down from the carriage.'

Caroline's nerve promptly deserted her.

'What? No. Why? I won't.'

'Ah. *Now* you are afraid, *n'est ce pas?* Afraid what the so-wicked robber may do?' Laughter danced in the masked face. 'Afraid to take just one tiny risk that will send the bad man on his way? *Quel dommage.'*

The idea that doing as he asked might get rid of him was tempting ... and the idea of taking "just one tiny risk", even more so. But, even as she wondered what had made him say that, Caroline's fund of sound Yorkshire sense took control.

'I'm not afraid. But I'm --'

'Prove it.' The beguiling voice gathered a note of mocking challenge. 'Step down with me and prove it.'

He was daring her. Worse still, he was offering her a moment or two of excitement and adventure; a moment or two that, only a very short time ago, she thought she'd never have. Telling herself that nothing very terrible could happen under the eyes of her ladyship, the coachman and the groom, Caroline straightened her spine and gave the highwayman her hand.

'Don't!' gasped Lady Brassington. But it was too late.

His fingers closed warm and firm around hers and he drew her from the carriage to the roadway beside him. Looking up at him, she realised how tall he was and knew a brief flicker of misgiving but he released her hand, smiled and said, 'You danced at your party?'

The question took her by surprise.

'I – yes.'

'With handsome, well-born gentlemen who flirted and praised the beauty of your eyes?'

'Not exactly.' It was so far from the truth that she couldn't suppress a puff of laughter. 'Not at all, in fact.'

'No? Then this should be remedied.' Without any warning, he stretched out a hand gave one swift tug at the strings of her cloak so that it slid from her shoulders before she could catch it. 'Come tread a measure with Claude Duvall.' His voice was a silky-soft invitation. 'Dance with me.'

'What?' She stared at him as if he was mad. 'Of course I can't dance with you!'

'But why not?'

'Because ... because we're in the middle of the road at night and it's dark and --'

'We have stars, *chérie* ... and a half-moon.' Again that magnetic smile, as he reclaimed her hand. 'You do not find it beautiful ... perhaps even a little romantic?'

'Well, yes. I suppose.' *It's beautiful and romantic and I shouldn't be doing it. I ought to say no.* Instead, she heard herself say weakly, 'There is no music.'

'There is always music,' he murmured, drawing her a little closer. 'One has only to listen.'

Somehow, he'd found her other hand and was using them both to turn her first this way and then that, in a sort of swaying motion. It *felt* like a dance, though not one she knew. Gentle, yet confident and supremely knowledgeable, his hands guided her to his left and a slow, pivoting turn to the right. He drew her in a lazy circle around him, then released one of her hands to perform the same movement himself. She felt his free hand trailing her waist and simultaneously became aware how very close he was. So close she could detect a faint scent of sandalwood and lemon and ... horse. The dreamlike sequence continued and Caroline stopped thinking; stopped doing anything at all except follow the silent commands of his body. It was almost as if the world had ceased turning; as if the two of them had strayed into a magic ring where no one else existed. The highwayman's nearness and the lightest touch of his hands filled her senses and sent them soaring.

After a while, his words a mere current of air against her ear, he said, 'You are not married, *petite*? Or affianced?'

'No.' He almost had his arms about her and she could feel him toying with a lock of her hair. A tiny, insignificant voice at the back of her mind told her she should move away but her feet ignored it. 'Why do you ask?'

Instead of answering, he whispered, 'Your hair is very soft ... like silk.' Inching back very slightly and holding her gaze with his own, he raised a strand to his nose. 'It smells of ... *lavande*.' A slight, elegant shrug. 'I do not know the English word.'

'Lavender.' His eyes seemed to be demanding something or perhaps promising it. She thought they might be blue but the mask and the shadowy light made it difficult to tell. Whatever their colour, something in them was making her pulse race and her blood run faster. She said, 'I should go.'

'Not yet.' His fingers stroked over her hair and somehow found their way to the nape of her neck. 'Not just yet. Our interlude is not quite done, I think.'

'It – it isn't?'

'No.' And, gathering her fully into his arms, he sought her mouth with his own.

Just for an instant because she'd never been kissed before, Caroline tensed against him in shock and confusion, alarmed because she didn't know what to do. But his mouth was soft and gentle ... it drifted lightly from her lips to her jaw, making her unconsciously tilt her face to meet it and to feel his breath, warm against her cheek. Her hands fluttered to his shoulders and stayed there. And by the time his mouth returned to hers, she was aware that she wanted more – even though she didn't know what that more was.

The highwayman knew. He deepened the kiss slowly and to just a tantalising degree and then, with a sigh of regret, he slowly released her.

Caroline remained absolutely still, staring at him.

Smiling faintly, he touched her cheek and then took her hand. She didn't know he'd slid her grandmother's ruby from her finger until he held it up in front of her. He said, 'Trust me with this ... and I promise to return it to you.'

She swallowed. Was he saying she'd see him again? Perhaps asking if she wanted to? Surely such a thing wasn't possible.

'How?'

'You will see.' He slipped her ring on to the little finger of his right hand. 'Do you remember my name?'

'No. Yes. Claude Duvall.'

He nodded and then asked curiously, 'You have not heard of me?'

'Should I have done?'

'Perhaps. Perhaps not.' He led her back to the carriage, picked up her cloak and dropped it lightly around her shoulders, saying softly, 'Your ring and my name. Our secret. And now I must do something you will not like.' He turned smoothly to Lady Brassington who was looking at him as though she couldn't believe what she'd just seen – which, in fact, she probably couldn't – and said, 'My lady, I regret the necessity ... but I must ask for your pearls.'

'No!' said Caroline before she could stop herself. 'You can't! They're the only real things she has left.'

'I know.'

'Then how can you be so cruel? How can you --?'

He shrugged again; elegant, easy, careless.

'How can I steal? I am a thief, Mademoiselle. Had you forgotten?'

'If I had,' she said, suddenly furious, 'you've certainly reminded me.'

'*Oui.*' And to Lady Brassington, 'The pearls, if you please Madame.'

Without a word, her ladyship unclasped the necklace and dropped them into his outstretched palm.

63

Claude Duvall offered Caroline his hand to step back into the carriage. She pushed it aside and climbed in unaided. He closed the door behind her, his smile every bit as charming and insouciant as ever. Then he removed his hat and made a low, flourishing bow.

'It has been of a pleasure quite remarkable, Mademoiselle,' he said. 'I think you will remember me.'

'Oh yes. You can be quite sure of that.' She hated the fact that her voice wasn't entirely steady and that her vision blurred slightly as she watched him stroll back to the horse which had been standing motionless beside the silent fellow with the blunderbuss all this time. 'They'll hang you, you know. One day they will.'

He swung up into the saddle and laughed.

'Probably, *mon ange*. Probably. But they'll have to catch me first.'

And he was gone.

For a full minute, while the coachman sent the groom to retrieve their own blunderbuss from the roadside, Caroline and Lady Brassington stared at each other. Then Caroline said, 'What now? I suppose we have to report this. But to whom?'

'Do you *want* to report it?' asked her ladyship unexpectedly.

'We must. Your pearls --'

'Are real, yes – but of very inferior quality compared to the ones I originally owned.' The merest glimmer of a smile dawned. 'And one might say he paid for them, in his way.'

'Did he? I don't see how.'

'He offered you a few minutes I doubt you'll forget in a hurry ... and he gave me the pleasure of watching a legend come to life, which is not a thing one sees every day.'

'A legend?'

'Yes. There was a highwayman many years ago who was famed for his gallantry towards the ladies. I daresay his name will come back to me when I think about it. Songs were written about him, I believe.' The smile grew. 'Perhaps our highwayman is following in his footsteps ... though, one would hope, not quite *all* of them.'

An odd sensation quivered in Caroline's chest.

'Why not?'

'Because the legendary one went to the scaffold, my dear. And, if the stories are true, a good many ladies shed a good many tears over him.'

SIX

Two mornings later, Adrian sat down to breakfast and looked, with some surprise, at the small stack of correspondence beside his plate. Aside from a note from Nicholas Wynstanton about a horse he thought Adrian might like to buy and another from Aristide Delacroix asking him to call at the club at his earliest convenience, all the rest were invitations. His lordship tossed Aristide's note across the table to Bertrand, then began flipping through the gilt-edged cards. Two, in particular, caught his attention. A belated invitation to the Overbury masked ball the following evening; and Harry Caversham's promised note regarding the party his wife was arranging at the Pantheon in four days' time. He kept these to hand for immediate acceptance. The others – two further balls and no less than four card parties – he laid aside for future consideration.

'What does Aristide want?' asked Bertrand, discarding the letter to reach for another slice of ham.

'Your guess is as good as mine.'

'From what I can see, there's a lot of guessing going on at the moment. I suppose you *do* know what you're doing?'

'Not entirely. Not yet, anyway.' Adrian picked up his coffee cup, discovered it had gone cold and pushed it away. 'I'm just … creating a few avenues.'

'Is that what you call it? Seems to me these 'avenues' of yours are as good a way as any of getting your fingers burned.'

'I know,' agreed Adrian with a half-smile. And then, 'But you can't begrudge me a little fun now and then. Or yourself either, come to that.'

* * *

A few streets away, Marcus Sheringham also sat at breakfast and found he'd lost his appetite. A small mountain of envelopes lay piled before him, all of them destined to remain unopened since he already knew what was in them. A couple might possibly be invitations. All the rest were renewed demands from his tailor, his bootmaker and the various tradesmen who supplied his now severely under-staffed house in Half-Moon Street. He couldn't pay any of them. Most had already refused further credit and, amongst the heap on the table, were probably others following suit. Worse still, he'd borrowed money from a very unpleasant fellow in Watermark Lane and was two months behind on the interest. If he didn't do something soon, physical violence was likely to be added to the general debacle of his life.

Marcus swept the envelopes to the floor and thrust his hands through his hair. He couldn't wait any longer for the thrice-blasted girl to give him permission to speak to her mother. He had no choice but to take the initiative and do it today.

Two hours later, exquisitely turned-out in dark blue velvet braided with pale grey, his lordship drove to Kensington and had to ask the way three times before he found the street he wanted. Mercifully, since his open town-carriage was the only equipage he'd been able to keep, the day was fine if a little chilly. Once he'd secured approval of the girl's Mama, he intended to take Mistress Maitland driving in order to pay his addresses somewhere other than the cramped-looking house he eventually drew up outside.

Although he was unaware of it, his arrival caused pandemonium inside the house. Seeing an elegant carriage stop at the door, Sylvia immediately shouted for her sisters to come and look.

'My goodness,' said Lavinia, impressed. 'He's vastly elegant – handsome, too. Who on earth is he?'

Caroline peered over her sister's shoulder and felt her stomach lurch.

'Oh God, oh God. I tried to stop him coming. I told him ...' She stopped, watching his lordship descend from the carriage and toss a coin to a nearby urchin, presumably along with an instruction to hold his horses. 'Mama's in the kitchen, helping Rosie with the baking. Sylvia – run and warn her. Tell her to let Rosie answer the door, then stay out of sight until he's in the front parlour. Lavinia and I will hold the fort while Mama changes her dress. Go! Hurry!'

Sylvia fled through to the back of the house. Lavinia, meanwhile, surveyed her elder sister and said, 'Mam's not the only one who ought to get changed. You can't want a town beau like him to see you in that old thing, surely?'

'He'll have to. There's no time.' Caroline groaned and squeezed her fingers together. 'I thought I'd managed to put him off. I told him Mama was indisposed – not well enough for visitors. Why didn't he *listen*?'

Light dawned on Lavinia at the precise moment the doorbell rang. She said, 'You think he wants to marry you?'

'Yes.'

'Well, that's good, isn't it?'

'Not necessarily.'

'Why not? God knows *I* wouldn't mind being courted by a pretty fellow like that and with a smart carriage of his own to boot. What --?'

'Shh! Rosie's at the door now. Be quiet or he'll hear you. Sit down with a book or something.' Caroline dropped into a chair and picked up the nearest thing to hand which happened to be Sylvia's knitting. 'And don't dare leave the room!'

There was a tap at the door and Rosie appeared looking flustered.

'Lord Sheringham, Miss. Do you want me to let him in?'

Aware that his lordship couldn't be more than three steps behind the maid, Caroline swallowed another groan and said brightly, 'Yes, of course, Rosie. Please tell Mama that we have company and then prepare a tea-tray.'

Rosie bobbed something resembling a curtsy.

'Right you are, then.' And stood aside.

Realising she was still clutching the knitting, Caroline flung it backwards over the sofa just in time to compose her features as her thoroughly unwelcome guest appeared in the doorway.

Smiling, Marcus strolled into the room and removed his hat to execute a perfect bow.

'Mistress Maitland,' he said with a nice blend of apology and charm, 'I hope you will forgive me for intruding unannounced. But I found myself unable to stay away any longer.'

Caroline swallowed hard. She'd thought him handsome before. But now, with his corn-gold hair unpowdered and gleaming even in the dismal light of their parlour, he was appallingly beautiful. Small wonder Lavinia was standing there with her eyes on stalks. No one, she thought helplessly, was going to understand why she was becoming increasingly doubtful about him.

Pulling herself together, she said pleasantly, 'There's no question of forgiveness, sir. It is most kind of you to call. But we weren't expecting visitors this morning and our mother is occupied elsewhere in the house – though I am sure she will join us as soon as she is able. In the meantime, may I present my half-sister, Mistress Haywood? Lavinia … you will recall me speaking of Lord Sheringham?'

Lavinia, of course, would recall no such thing since Caroline had taken pains never to mention the man.

Marcus stared at the dark-haired beauty and cursed inwardly. Why couldn't the heiress look like that? This was a girl a man wouldn't mind courting … and the way she was peeping at him through her lashes suggested that she'd be a damned sight more receptive and appreciative of his attentions than her dratted sister.

He bowed gracefully. 'Mistress Haywood … an unexpected pleasure.'

Lavinia dipped a curtsy and said cheerfully, 'Charmed, m'lord, I'm sure.'

Marcus barely repressed a shudder. At least the dratted sister spoke like a lady. The beauty sounded like the daughter of some northern farmer. Then the door opened on a younger and even prettier girl who, in the same unlovely accent said, 'Mam won't be long, Caro. She says to give the gentleman tea and the plum cake.'

Catching the look in his eye before he could banish it, Caroline gritted her teeth. She said, 'Thank you, Sylvia. Lord Sheringham … my other step-sister, Mistress Sylvia Haywood.'

Like Lavinia, Sylvia also grinned and curtsied. Marcus was grateful that she didn't speak. He just took the chair he was offered and wondered whether the heiress's family could be persuaded to remain silent at the wedding – after which, he sincerely hoped never to see any of them again.

In a rustle of purple taffeta and a cloud of ambergris, Mrs Haywood surged into the room on the heels of the maid and talking all the time.

'You've forgotten the plum cake, Rosie and I don't see no napkins either. Set that tray down and go and fetch 'em. And don't dawdle.' Then, beaming at Marcus who was once more on his feet, 'Well … to think we should be meeting one of Caro's friends at last. This is a right pleasure and no mistake.' She held out her hand. 'How do you do, sir?'

'Mrs Haywood.' Helplessly, Marcus took the proffered hand and found his own being enthusiastically shaken. 'I hope you have recovered from your recent indisposition?'

'My what?'

In an attempt to avert further catastrophe, Caroline used the brief, baffled pause to say swiftly, 'Mama … allow me to introduce Lord Sheringham.'

'Lord, is it? Oh my.' Mrs Haywood's smile grew even wider. She subsided on to the sofa and waited for his lordship to resume his seat. 'Well, your lordship … as I say, this is a rare treat. So how long have you and our Caro known one another?'

'A few weeks only, Madam.' He paused as the maid re-appeared with a plate of cake that looked as if it had been hacked apart with a blunt instrument. Then, when the door closed behind her, 'As I was saying, a short time … but long enough for me to be aware of a very earnest desire to know her better and to realise it would quite improper to strive for further acquaintance without first making myself known to her family.'

'And that's just as it should be, your lordship. I like a young man as knows his manners. Do you --?'

'Tea, sir? And you, Mama?' Caroline stemmed the flow by handing each of them a cup.

Mrs Haywood accepted hers with a nod of thanks but kept her attention on their visitor.

'Would your lordship be a London gentleman?'

'I reside in Town for the greater part of the year. But, of course, I also have an estate in the country.' He didn't bother to mention that, like everything else he owned, it was mortgaged. 'My mother currently resides there.'

'Whereabouts in the country would that be, then?'

'Sussex, ma'am.'

Caroline was fairly sure that Mama had no idea where Sussex was and hoped she didn't expose her ignorance by saying so.

She didn't. She did something far worse.

'If you don't mind my asking, sir ... exactly what kind of lord *are* you?'

He blinked. 'I beg your pardon?'

'What sort? I've not met many titled gentlemen but I know there's all kinds of different ones, so I'm wondering which of 'em you might be.'

Lavinia rolled her eyes; Sylvia put her hand over her mouth to stifle a giggle; and Caroline dived on the tray again.

'Cake, my lord?' she said, virtually shoving the plate in his hand.

Unused to being interrogated about his pedigree, Marcus was temporarily deprived of speech. Tea-cup in one hand, a hefty slab of cake in the other and nowhere to put either, he began to wonder how far he'd strayed from the edges of civilisation as he knew it.

As evenly as he could, he said, 'I am a Baron, Madam.'

He was rewarded with an approving, if not entirely thrilled, smile.

'That's nice. And what about your father?'

'My father has been deceased for some years now.'

'Oh.' The smiled wilted a little. 'So that means --'

'That he was also a Baron. Yes. The third in our line – thus making me the fourth. I trust that clears up any concerns you may have?'

Marcus decided that he'd had enough. He hadn't come here to answer impertinent and potentially awkward questions. He'd come to inform this common little woman that he intended to do her daughter the honour of paying his addresses – and therefore felt he had every right to expect a little respect. Rising, he deposited both tea and cake back on the tray and said, 'Perhaps, Madam, you might accord me the favour of a few minutes private conversation?'

'Well, of course, sir. Delighted to oblige, I'm sure. Girls – take the tray back to the kitchen but you can leave his lordship's cake in case he wants it a bit later. Go on – out with all of you. And no listening outside the door, mind!'

Slowly and with great reluctance, Caroline followed her sisters from the room. She half-considered trying to get a discreet word with Mama before it was too late but recognised that there probably wasn't any point. Lord Sheringham was going to say his piece and there was nothing she could do to stop him. As for Mama's reaction ... it was pretty much pre-ordained.

As soon as the door closed behind the girls and deciding that subtlety was a waste of time, Marcus came directly to the point. He said, 'Madam, I wished to inform you that I have formed an attachment to Mistress Maitland and intend to offer her my hand in marriage. I am presuming that such an offer would not be displeasing to you?'

'Well I never!' Mrs Haywood pressed both hands to her ample bosom and beamed up at him. 'I had no idea. Caro's not said a word about you, my lord. Not one word, the secretive little puss. And if she's told her sisters, it's more than I know to. So how it's all got this far without none of us having any idea, I just don't know! Or perhaps Caro *herself* don't know. I suppose that could be it. If --'

'I imagine the fact that I have been paying her marked attentions for some time now, coupled with my presence here today will probably have led her to guess,' he observed dryly. 'However, I am still waiting to hear if the match would have your approval.'

'Oh – no doubt about that, my lord. Not that – what with Caro's expectations and all – I wasn't hoping for a Viscount or even an Earl ... but there. If you've a fondness for my little lass and a house in Town so as she'll be able to launch her sisters into society, the rest don't matter one whit.' She sighed. 'Our Caro, a Baroness. I reckon her Grandpa'll be right pleased with that.'

Marcus didn't give a fig whether Grandpa was pleased or not and was positively furious that this vulgar female dared suggest that his rank fell below her expectations. Also, if she thought for a moment that he was going to foist her other, extremely *farouche* daughters on the *ton* – let her go on thinking it. He'd bleed to death before he wasted money that way or gave his friends the opportunity to snigger behind his back. He wanted the heiress and her fortune … and, once he had it, the rest of her family could go to the devil.

But he smiled, bowed and said smoothly, 'One would certainly hope so. But I have yet to pay my addresses to Mistress Maitland. Perhaps I might be permitted to do so now?'

'Of course. Of course, your lordship.' Mrs Haywood rose and reached out to clasp his unresponsive hands. 'You just wait here and I'll send her in to you directly. Not that there's any question but that she'll say yes. No girl in her right mind'd turn down such an handsome gentleman. And our Caro's no simpleton, I can tell you.'

Marcus said nothing in the hope that she'd stop talking, fetch the girl and allow him to get this business over with. Managing to prise his hands from hers, he raised one enquiring brow and waited.

'Just give me a minute, my lord. No more'n that, I promise. And try the plum cake while you're waiting. I made it myself only yesterday and, though I say it as shouldn't, I don't reckon you'll taste finer anywhere.'

Mrs Haywood left the parlour with a brisk step, shut the door behind her and tracked her daughters to the kitchen. Lavinia and Sylvia were agog with curiosity. Caroline looked as tense as a coiled spring.

'Well, Mam?' asked Lavinia eagerly. 'What did he say? Has he really come to ask our Caro to marry him?'

'Yes.' She shook her head at her eldest daughter and said rapidly, 'Later on, you can explain why there's been not a hint of this afore today and how come you've let it drop on us out of the blue like this. And for the Lord's sake, stop looking as though you've lost a shilling and found sixpence. He's younger and handsomer than I'd thought you'd find – you not exactly being a beauty. And he's got a title. Not the best sort, maybe – but a title for all that. What more do you want?'

'I – I don't know. I'm just not sure I like him very much.'

'God, Caro – you must be addled,' said Lavinia. 'He's *gorgeous*. I'd take him in a heartbeat.'

'It's not as simple as that.'

'Yes,' said her mother flatly, 'it is. It's you he's after and it's you'll he'll have – unless you've got another iron in the fire. Have you? Is there somebody *else* you haven't told us about? Somebody higher-ranking than this one or somebody you like better? If there is, you can tell the Baron you need time to think. If there isn't, you'll snap his hand off if you've any sense. Well?'

Caroline shook her head, feeling doom closing in all around her.

'There's only Mr Sterne. He's related to Lady Brassington.'

'That's all well and good but it's no answer. Your Grandpa's settled a fortune on you so as you can catch a title and you'll do more good for Lavvy and Syl as Lady Sheringham than you would as Mrs Sterne. There again, as Lavvy says, his lordship isn't exactly hard to swallow, is he? I'd have had my doubts if you was being sought by some old goat – but you're not. So it's time to cut your coat according to your cloth, our Caroline. Now pinch your cheeks and put a smile on your face. You've kept him waiting long enough.'

Marcus had spent the time scowling through the window, making sure that the urchin hadn't left his horses unattended. He decided that, once he was in possession of Mistress Caroline's hundred thousand pounds, one of the first things he would do – after settling with his tailor – was to buy a new carriage and bring his stables back to full strength. He supposed he'd also better pay off his gaming debt at Sinclair's so he wouldn't lose his membership and the loan in Watermark Lane before some hulking brute was sent to break his legs. As to the rest ... well, it would depend on which matters seemed most urgent.

He turned when Caroline came in and bathed her in the smile that had been known to melt even the coolest heart. He said, 'Your Mama has kindly allowed us a few minutes alone together and I don't wish to exceed what she would consider proper. But perhaps we might sit down?'

'Yes,' replied Caroline colourlessly. 'Of course.'

She perched on the edge of a chair, thus preventing his lordship from sitting as close to her as he'd hoped. Hiding the fact that the girl never failed to irritate him, he said gently, 'Don't be nervous, my dear. There really is no need, I assure you.'

'Yes. I mean – I know.'

Bloody hell. Is that the best she can do?

74

He'd considered going down on one knee. Now he concluded that, since she clearly had the social graces of a cabbage, it wasn't worth it. He drew a nearby chair up beside her, sat down with due deference to the full skirts of his coat and took one of her hands in both of his. Then, lowering his voice to a deliberately seductive level, he said, 'I have come to the realisation that you are the lady I had begun to think I might never find. In short, Mistress Maitland, I am hoping that you will make me the happiest of men by allowing me to keep this little hand.'

He waited. Then he waited some more. Finally, wondering if she really was so dense that she'd failed to understand him, he said patiently, 'I am asking if you will do me the honour of becoming my wife.'

'Yes. I – I know.'

Oh good. 'And?'

'And naturally I'm very flattered.'

You should be. And I shouldn't be sensing the word 'but'.

'It's just that I hadn't expected ... that is to say, we have only known each other for a few weeks, sir. It all seems ... forgive me, but it seems a little sudden.'

Caroline wished he would release her hand and move away. She also wished he'd stop pretending to be in love with her when it was perfectly clear that he wasn't. She felt crowded by him and weighed down by the expectations of her mother and sisters. She didn't want to say yes but was miserably aware that – since this might be her only chance of any marriage at all, let alone a remotely suitable one – she couldn't just say no. And all the time, hovering at the back of her mind and still refusing to be completely banished, was the memory of infectious laughter, a beautiful voice stealing its way through her senses and finally, a kiss in the moonlight.

It occurred to her then that Lord Sheringham hadn't tried to kiss her. Perhaps that meant he didn't want to ... or perhaps he was waiting until she said yes. She had the distinct feeling that the notion she might *not* say yes hadn't crossed his mind. She also had the uneasy suspicion that he might not take very kindly to a refusal.

Repressing a sigh and reminding herself about Duty and Making the Best of Things, she said hesitantly, 'Perhaps if you could allow me some time in which to consider ..?'

Marcus retained his clasp on her hands so he wasn't tempted to shake her. He said, 'If that is what you need, my dear ... and if you will at least offer me a little hope in return. Do you think you could do that?'

Caroline saw the trap but couldn't think of a way around it. Telling him he could hope was as good as accepting his proposal – just not quite as final. Or so she told herself as she prepared to bow to the inevitable.

'If you wish it, sir.'

'Thank you.' He rose, drawing her up with him. 'You won't keep me waiting too long?'

'No more than I can help.' She wished he would let her go. He was standing much too close and not knowing what he might do next was making her nervous. 'A few days. A week at the very most.'

A week? Oh no, my dear. You'll say yes before then. I guarantee it.

Instinct told him that kissing her wasn't going to advance his cause. She looked ready to bolt as it was. So he captured her other hand and raised each in turn to his lips, murmuring, 'A week can seem like eternity but I shall be patient ... and await my reward.'

Caroline stared out across the top of his head, her eyes wide and blank and her heart a lead weight in her chest.

SEVEN

While Lord Sheringham was doing his best to settle his financial future, Lord Sarre bought a sleek, grey gelding, promised to meet Lord Nicholas that evening at the Cocoa Tree and walked to Sinclair's to find out what Aristide wanted.

He arrived in the manager's office in time to hear Madeleine Delacroix saying crossly, 'I need another footman. A *real* footman – one who can serve at table – not one of those clumsy idiots of yours that I trip over every time I turn around. And the upstairs wine-store needs replenishing. Last night, Lord Shrewsbury asked for two bottles of Chambertin and I had to send downstairs for them.'

'I'll see to it,' said her brother.

'Today, if you wouldn't mind. Also, that other matter we spoke of. If you can't spare Cameron from the main floor for more than ten minutes at a time, you'll need to come up with another way of dealing with it.'

'I already have.' Aristide directed a wry grin past her to where Sarre was lounging in the doorway. 'You can come in. In fact I wish you would. She might turn her guns on you instead.'

Madeleine turned round and fixed his lordship with a long, cool stare.

'Ah,' she said. 'Adrian. Of course. I might have known.'

He smiled at her. 'Madeleine.'

She tilted her chin.

'I wasn't aware I'd given you permission to make free with my name, sir.'

'My apologies.' He managed to make his bow faintly ironic, despite experiencing the inevitable male reaction to her pale red hair, translucent green eyes and perfect body. 'Mademoiselle Delacroix ... as beautiful and razor-edged as ever, I see.'

'And Milord Sarre,' she retorted, 'with his arsenal of clever tricks.'

They'd been friends once – or, at least, he'd thought they had. It later turned out that Madeleine had imagined them on the verge of something more until, on the heels of a blazing row with her brother, she'd gone running to Adrian's lodgings looking for comfort only to discover him in bed with his current mistress. It had taken him some time to get over the fact that Madeleine had seen his bare arse. Presumably for other reasons entirely, Madeleine *still* hadn't got over it.

He'd missed her friendship. Unfortunately, she'd never let him explain that he didn't bed virgins and that, as Aristide's younger sister, he couldn't touch her – no matter how much he might want to. And now, years on, only two things had changed. She was older ... and, on the rare occasions when they met, she looked as though she'd happily stick a knife into him. From time to time, it had occurred to him that if he could have her naked in bed for an hour, that might be a risk worth taking ... if it didn't also risk his relationship with her brother.

Maintaining a bland smile, he said, 'If I've come at a busy time, I can wait.'

'No.' It was Aristide who spoke, his tone firm. 'I have a note of Madeleine's current complaints and --'

'They're not complaints,' she snapped. 'They are problems which need to be addressed.'

'And I've agreed that they will be. You shall have an additional footman, I'll see to the wine-store and, if you stop antagonising him, Adrian will hopefully clear up the other matter. So if there's nothing else ...?'

Madeleine narrowed her eyes and looked as though she could have thought of quite a few things, none of them pleasant, so Adrian said helpfully, 'I noticed a half-empty glass on one of the window-ledges downstairs. You could always go and persecute the maid who missed it.'

Recognising this for the provocation that it was, she didn't dignify it with an answer. She simply cast him another scathing glance and swirled from the room in a rustle of moss-coloured taffeta.

'Stop salivating,' said Aristide. 'Unless you can persuade her she'd like to become a Countess, she's not for you. And if you *did* so persuade her, the pair of you would cut each other to ribbons inside a month. So sit down and take a look at that.'

His lordship scanned the sheet of paper that Aristide pushed across the desk. It was a detailed list of Marcus Sheringham's gains and losses over the last quarter, most of them due to his predilection for basset. Marcus ought to find it horrifying reading. Adrian merely looked at the figure at the bottom of the page and skimmed it back towards Aristide.

'Pretty much as you said it would be. Are you going to acquaint him with this in person or by letter?'

'By letter – in which I'll also revoke his membership. He'll be in to see me, of course, as soon as he receives it. They always are. But I find it preferable to have these things in writing.'

Adrian nodded. 'And the other matter you wanted to discuss?'

'Ah. Yes. It's to do with something untoward in Madeleine's province upstairs.'

'The exclusive dining-parlour?'

'And the rooms adjoining it where men with abnormally deep pockets like the peace and quiet to indulge in abnormally deep play,' nodded Aristide. 'To be fair, it's not just gaming. Some of the most acute political minds congregate up there to pit their wits against each other. But mostly it's cards.'

'*Just* cards?'

'Yes. No dice and no house gaming-tables permitted.'

'And you think someone's cheating?'

'I think,' came the mildly irritable reply, 'that a fellow named Chatham – who certainly doesn't need the money – has an ability not dissimilar to your own. But neither Cameron nor I can be spared from the main floor for as long as it would take to be absolutely sure. So, in spite of everything I said to the contrary ...'

Adrian's mouth took on a sardonic twist.

'You thought it would be simpler to set a thief to catch a thief, as it were.'

'That's the general idea though I wouldn't personally have put it that way. Will you?'

'That depends on whether or not the existing players will welcome me.'

'I doubt that will be a problem. Rockliffe is one of them – in fact, it was he who first mentioned the matter.'

'Now why does that not surprise me?' murmured his lordship. And then, 'You realise that, however annoying it is for other players, counting cards isn't actually cheating? It's just playing with an added advantage. It's also – as I know only too well – a damned difficult advantage to shut down. So, assuming I confirm the Duke's suspicions … what do you intend to do about it?'

'I've no idea. At present, I'm just looking for an answer and hoping you can provide it. Needless to say, if you lose, the house will absorb your losses.'

'I won't lose.' Adrian leaned back in his chair, frowning a little. 'There is, however, a problem. If my peculiar skill becomes public knowledge I'll have more people looking at me sideways than I do already. In short, no one is going to believe I do my damnedest *not* to use it and I'll be black-balled at White's before I've even got through the door.'

'Only,' said Aristide, 'if you appear as yourself.'

Adrian groaned. 'Have you any idea what you're asking?'

'Yes. I've seen you do it a dozen times.'

'Not amongst men who know me, for God's sake! And not in the same room as bloody Rockliffe – who, even if he *didn't* know I'm an actor, is nobody's fool.'

'Are you saying it can't be done … or that you're not prepared to try?'

There was a long silence. Then, on a sigh of pure resignation, 'Neither. Damn you, Aristide. I'll do my best. But if it ends in disaster, it will be your job to pick up the pieces.'

* * *

'You're joking, aren't you?' asked Bertrand when told what was afoot. 'Haven't you got enough problems?'

Adrian shrugged. 'Aristide wouldn't have asked if it wasn't necessary.'

'It's not Aristide's reputation at stake, is it? But if you've already told him you'll do it, there's no point in arguing with you. So who's it going to be? Monsieur Montalban? Major Macpherson? Who?'

'Neither the Frenchman nor the Scot, I think. The Russian, perhaps ... or Signor Fiorelli. I'll decide later. For now, take a note to Lord Nicholas to let him know that I won't be joining him this evening.'

'What about that brother of his?' Bertrand knew all about Rockliffe.

'If his Grace comes to the club, Aristide is supposed to lure him elsewhere for a hand or two of piquet.'

'And if he can't?'

'If he can't, I'm just going to have to give the performance of my life.'

* * *

Monsieur Delacroix welcomed Count Julius von Rainmayr to Sinclair's and listened courteously to the gentleman's preferences, whilst drawing certain conclusions from his appearance. Although the diamonds flashing on his hands and in his cravat indicated that money was plainly no object, the elderly Count still held to the fashions of his younger days. The skirts of his plum-coloured coat were extremely full; his powdered shoulder-length wig was some thirty years out of date; and his once dashing military moustache had grown overly-bushy and exceedingly grey. Leaning heavily on his cane, he informed Aristide in flawless but heavily accented English, that he expected to be in London for only a brief time and that Sinclair's had been recommended to him as a place for deep play.

Aristide led him up the two flights of stairs leading to the most exclusive areas of the club. Owing to the Count's age and infirmity, progress was naturally slow and required frequent pauses. Eventually, however, they arrived at their destination and, when the Austrian gentleman had recovered his breath, taken stock of his surroundings and pronounced himself agreeably impressed, Aristide made the necessary introductions before melting discreetly away.

The men at the table were playing basset. There were six of them – amongst whom were the Earl of Sandwich, Charles Fox and Mr Chatham. Having bowed with Austrian punctiliousness to each of the six in turn, Count von Rainmayr accepted the chair he was offered and embarked on the lengthy process of settling down for the evening. He propped his cane against the table, then promptly knocked it over when he pulled a handkerchief from his pocket. Mr Fox picked the cane up.

The Count expressed his thanks, tried positioning it beside his chair ... and felled it again whilst searching for his spectacles. Once more, Mr Fox retrieved it. The Count polished his spectacles – wire-rimmed with oddly blue-tinted lenses – and, having positioned them on his nose, set about hunting for his purse. This time, instead of waiting for the inevitable, Mr Fox politely suggested that perhaps his lordship's cane might be put to one side until it was required. Since it appeared that Count Rainmayr's hearing was slightly defective, he had to say this twice before receiving a curt affirmative. And finally it seemed that the game might be resumed.

Over the ensuing half-dozen hands during which the Count lost consistently, he also managed to halt play completely no less than three times and slow it considerably with his fussy, beetle-browed deliberations. With the exception of Charles Fox, the other players at the table began to wear an air of mild exasperation. So when the Count announced that his preferred game was écarté and wondered if any of the gentlemen present would indulge him with a hand or two, Lord Sandwich immediately said, 'Of course. Écarté's your game, isn't it Chatham?' And was swiftly seconded by Viscount Derby.

Fortunately, Mr Chatham didn't seem to mind. Rising from his seat, he gave Count Rainmayr his arm as far as a smaller table in the corner and then waited patiently for the old gentleman to complete his lengthy preparations whilst a footman was sent for the required pack of thirty-two cards. Then, and only then, did they begin to play.

The Count lost all five tricks in the first two games and four of those in the third one. A substantial sum of money changed hands and Mr Chatham, expressing sympathy but appearing perfectly relaxed, ordered a bottle of burgundy. Count Rainmayr pronounced the wine excellent and gave it the credit for him losing only one trick in the next game and winning all five in the one after that. Mr Chatham started to look at his opponent a trifle oddly ... as though there was something he didn't understand and would very much like to. He still didn't appear at all worried.

Mademoiselle Delacroix appeared in the doorway and scanned the room, apparently checking that all was as it should be. Her gaze passed over the visiting Austrian, then returned to him and stayed there. Belatedly becoming aware of her presence, the elderly gentleman struggled to rise and, failing, bowed to her from his seat. For a second, Madeleine continued to regard him without expression. Then she dropped the merest suggestion of a curtsy and left.

The Count's luck apparently deserted him for a time and then surged back with a vengeance. By the time Mr Chatham had lost three consecutive games, Mr Fox had quit the basset table to come and watch and Lord March had wandered in from downstairs.

'Chatham's losing,' murmured Mr Fox to his friend.

And, raising his eyebrows, Lord March said, 'Is he now?'

At the conclusion of the next game, Mr Chatham leaned back in his chair and gave the Austrian gentleman a very level and yet somehow inviting stare.

For the first time and barely discernible behind the disfiguring lenses, a glimmer of humour appeared in the Count's previously austere gaze. Then he nodded and, as if answering a question, said, 'Just so.'

'Ah.' Against all expectation, Mr Chatham beamed at him. 'A rare pleasure.'

Not without difficulty, the Austrian heaved himself from his seat.

'For me, also. But now I fear I grow fatigued. Age is not a kind master.'

He looked round for his cane and nodded his gratitude when Mr Fox put it in his hand.

Mr Chatham also rose. He said, 'Should it be possible, I would greatly enjoy pitting my skills against yours on some future occasion, Count.'

'I would like this also. Sadly, my time here is all too brief.' He turned to go only to find his way blocked by another observer. He paused, infinitesimally and, with just a touch of irritability, said, 'Your pardon, sir. If you would excuse me?'

'Forgive me,' said the Duke of Rockliffe, stepping aside with a very slight bow. 'I was overcome with the odd notion that we had met before ... but believe I may have been mistaken.'

'Indeed, I believe that must be so – although my memory, like my eye-sight, is no longer what it was.' Another tiny pause as Aristide appeared in the doorway. 'Ah ... Monsieur Delacroix. This is fortuitous. I should be grateful for your support down your very many stairs, if you would be so kind?'

'Of course, Count. It would be my pleasure.'

Rockliffe watched the two men leave the room and then, offering his snuff-box to Charles Fox, said, 'A new member?'

'Only a visitor ... and blessed with a visitor's luck, it would seem. An Austrian Count, I believe.'

'Of which, as we know, there are a great number.'

'Indeed.' Mr Fox's attention had been captured by the Duke's snuff-box. 'That is a very unusual design, my dear ... but I am not convinced that I like it.'

'Do you know, Charles,' sighed his Grace, 'I fear I am inclined to agree.'

* * *

'Well?' asked Aristide quietly, as he descended the stairs with a hand on Count Rainmayr's elbow.

'We'll come to that,' said Adrian irritably. 'What the hell did you think you were doing letting Rockliffe up here?'

'I did my best to keep him away. But if you think one can stop his Grace doing whatever he sets his mind to, you can't know him very well.'

'I don't *want* to know him well. He knows too damned much about me as it is – and, if he recognised me just now and puts two and two together, he'll know a damned sight more.'

'Point taken,' sighed Aristide. 'And Chatham?'

'Isn't interested in winning. The first flicker of animation I saw was when I used my own ability to take a few tricks off him. He was surprised and then intrigued because he didn't know how I was doing it,' replied Adrian quietly. 'What do you know about him?'

'He's married, financially comfortable and has no known vices. He's also a Member of Parliament; a Minister in the Treasury, if memory serves.'

'That would fit.'

'Why?'

'I think he's a mathematician. He's not counting cards – or not in the way I do. So the only other solution is that he's using mathematical formulae to calculate probabilities. I doubt he even realises he's doing it. It's just the way his brain works. The poor devil probably even dreams about Pythagoras and quadratic equations.'

'So what do I do about him?'

'Tell him that other players have remarked on his inexplicable good fortune at the tables. Tell him that, though Count von Rainmayr has returned to Austria, you believe you may know another man with a similar ...talent. Then, if he appears both interested and discreet, send him to play cards with me. God knows, I'd be delighted to be able to indulge in a few hands of piquet without ending with mill-wheels grinding inside my head.'

EIGHT

By the time she was ready to leave the house, Caroline had come to
the conclusion that there was a lot to be said for a masquerade ball.
The tiny gold mask made her eyes appear very dark, while the bronze
silk domino not only covered her hideous mauve gown completely but
also seemed to turn her hair into antique gold. She tried putting up the
hood and looking sideways into the mirror. The effect was surprising.
She didn't look like herself at all. And if only Mama would stop talking
for a few minutes, she might not *feel* like herself either.

'When are you going to tell him you'll have him, Caro?'

'I don't know. It's only been two days, after all.'

'Two days is two days. You can't expect the man to wait forever.'

'I don't.'

'And you promised the girls and me you wouldn't turn him down.'

Caroline clenched her hands in the soft folds of the domino.

'I don't recall saying that exactly.'

'Words to the same effect,' shrugged Mrs Haywood. 'So, since you're
going to say yes, you might as well do it sooner as later. He'll be there
tonight, won't he?'

'I expect so. But everyone will be masked and one can never be
private at a ball, anyway.' She took a steadying breath and decided it
was time to make a stand. 'Please, Mama ... I know you mean well but
this is not helping. And if you won't let me think the matter through
properly, I'll just say no and have done with it.'

'You wouldn't be such a fool!'

'You may not realise it – but I'm trying very hard not to be *any* kind of
fool. And now I must go. Lady Brassington is here.'

Once in the carriage, her ladyship smiled and said, 'My goodness,
Caroline! That bronze is exactly the right shade for you. You look very
nice, my dear ... and hopefully tonight will prove a more pleasant
evening than some of the others. You deserve it.'

Their relationship had changed in some indefinable way since the encounter with the highwayman. Probably, thought Caroline, because they had a shared secret. Smiling back, she said, 'Thank you, my lady. That's kind of you.'

'Not particularly.' Lady Brassington folded her hands in her lap and said, 'In a moment, I've something bizarre and rather exciting to tell you. But first, I wanted to say this. Ludovic Sterne is my second cousin and I'm fond of him; but I've come to the conclusion that he's never going to change – so finding him a wealthy wife is pointless. What I'm basically saying is that, if and when he makes you an offer, you shouldn't even consider it. You can do much better than a well-mannered wastrel.'

Somewhat taken aback, Caroline said weakly, 'You think so?'

'I'm sure of it. And that brings me to Marcus Sheringham. Has he declared himself yet?'

She nodded, suddenly fascinated to see where this conversation would go.

'Ah. I'm presuming you didn't accept?'

'No. I said I needed time to consider.'

'Very wise. And what does your instinct tell you?'

'My instinct,' said Caroline wryly, 'can scarcely get a word in edgeways.'

'Your mother? Yes. She's seeing a good-looking fellow with a title, I daresay and not looking beyond it.' Her ladyship settled her grey silk domino more securely about her. 'Do you like him?'

'That's just the trouble. I can't decide. I feel as though I *should* ... but somehow I'm never quite comfortable with him. He's polite and attentive and he says all the right things --' She stopped. 'No, that's not true. He pretends he's fallen in love with me and thinks I'm stupid enough to believe it.'

There was a brief, thoughtful silence. Then Lady Brassington said, 'This isn't going to make me popular with your Mama ... but there's no reason for Sheringham to be so deep in debt other than his addiction to the tables and, as with Ludo, I don't see that changing. He'll fritter your money away the same as he has his own. And if, on top of that, you don't care for the man, marriage with him is unlikely to make you happy.' She leaned across and patted Caroline's hand. 'There. That's all I intend to say on the matter. You'll make your own decision when you're ready. Just remember that there are plenty of fish in the sea and you owe it to yourself to catch one you can live with.'

The turn of phrase made Caroline smile but she said, 'Thank you for your advice – and your honesty.'

'As to that, it was about time. Now ... to the other thing I've been impatient to tell you.' Her ladyship parted the folds of her domino. 'What do you think of this?'

It took Caroline a moment to recognise what she was supposed to be looking at. Then, on a sharp breath, she said, 'My goodness – your pearls!'

'Yes and no. These were found on the back doorstep this morning in a plain box, along with this.'

Caroline accepted the small pasteboard card and squinted to make out the writing in the poor light.

It has come to my attention that Yr. Ladyship was recently robbed of items of sentimental value. It is my fond hope that the enclosed will, in some small measure, compensate for this loss.

Yrs.

Sir Galahad

'Sir Galahad?' said Caroline. And then, rolling her eyes, 'As in the Knights of the Round Table and righting all wrongs and so forth?'

'It would seem so.'

'But who on earth *is* he? And who would even know what happened – let alone choose to do something like this?'

'I have no idea. Isn't it delicious? And there's more.' Lady Brassington paused for dramatic effect and then added, 'These aren't my pearls. As I told you, mine were inferior. *These* are the very best quality and are probably worth upwards of two hundred pounds.' She laughed. 'Do you know, Caroline ... our little adventure just gets better and better.'

* * *

Overbury House was ablaze with lights and the ballroom was already full of masked gentlemen in black dominos and ladies wearing ones of every colour imaginable. For a full minute, Caroline stared about her, utterly dazzled. Then she said, 'I had no idea it would be like this. How does anyone know who anyone else is?'

'Mostly, they don't – which is half the charm. The gentlemen have an easier time of it than the ladies, of course. But even so, one can rarely be *absolutely* sure with whom one is dancing. So accept anyone who asks, my dear and enjoy yourself. Just avoid dark corners and empty side-chambers. As the evening wears on, some of the gentlemen are apt to forget their manners.'

A young man whose dark eyes laughed through his mask swung to a halt before her and made a sweeping bow. 'Fair lady ... will you take my hand for the gavotte?'

'I – yes.' Caroline glanced at Lady Brassington and received an encouraging nod. 'Yes, sir. I'd be delighted.' And promptly found herself swept away into the dance.

Just for a moment, when she'd first accepted his hand, she had thought he might be Lord Nicholas Wynstanton. Then she recalled his lordship saying that he generally avoided dancing and realised that it couldn't be. So, after a little while, she said cautiously, 'Perhaps one isn't supposed to ask ... but have we met, sir?'

'Before this enchanted moment? No. Had we done so, I would have recalled looking into such dark pools of mystery.'

Her jaw dropped slightly and she stared at him, searching for mockery.

He looked back and shook his head, smiling.

'Your eyes, lovely lady. A fellow could drown in them.' And, after a brief pause, 'Also, no. One is *not* supposed to ask. One is supposed to guess and then wait for the great unmasking at midnight.'

'Oh. Yes. Of course.'

'This is your first masquerade ball, I take it?'

'Yes. It's very ... very ...' She stopped, unable to think of the right word.

'It is indeed,' he agreed solemnly. '*Very*.'

And, quite suddenly, Caroline found herself laughing.

By the time she had danced three consecutive dances with three perfect strangers, she realised that, for the first time, she was actually enjoying herself. She didn't know whether it was the anonymity provided by the mask or the relaxed formality of the occasion, but she suddenly stopped worrying about saying the wrong thing or laughing when she shouldn't – and it felt good. *Better* than good, in fact. It was totally intoxicating.

She quickly understood what Lady Brassington had meant about it being easier for the gentlemen to distinguish one lady from another. Only a handful of men had chosen to flout the fashion for powder. All the rest, with their narrow silk masks and black dominos, differed only in height, bearing and age. But the ladies, with their natural locks and dominos of every conceivable colour, were less well disguised … making it possible for a man to identify a lady he knew or to find again one he *wished* to know. When her first partner claimed her hand for a second time and flirted even more outrageously than he had before, Caroline felt more alive – more *herself* – than she had done since leaving Yorkshire.

Although she'd always known that she was no beauty, she'd never been a shrinking violet, afraid to speak up for herself. In the last weeks, however, she'd let Mama's expectations, Grandpa's money and the dismissive stares of fashionable strangers turn her into a ghost of her former self. Tonight, for the first time, she had regained her usual spirit … and, having done so, was determined to hold on to it. She was tired of being afraid to open her mouth in case she put her foot in it. From this point on, fashionable London could take her as she was or not at all. The days of Caroline the Mouse, she decided rebelliously, were over.

A little later whilst talking to Cassandra Delahaye, she glimpsed a gleaming, fair head and her heart dipped a little, thinking it was Lord Sheringham. Then the gentleman turned and she recognised her mistake. His face was finer-boned, his smile much warmer and his attention wholly focussed on the stunning brunette with whom he was dancing, one hand resting on her waist.

Noticing the direction of her gaze, Cassie said, 'That's Lord Amberley. Handsome, isn't he? And that's his wife with him. She's lovely, too. It's so sad that she's blind – though mostly one would never know. They are great friends with Rockliffe and his Duchess. You won't have met Adeline yet – which is a pity because she's the most elegant woman in Town. But she hasn't been much in society lately.' Lowering her voice, Cassie whispered, 'We think she may be in an interesting condition.'

'An interesting … oh. You mean she's having a baby?' said the new Caroline, unable to comprehend why this happy fact had to be whispered in code.

Cassie blushed, nodded and promptly changed the subject.

'I promised the next dance to Lord Harry – speaking of which, *his* wife is a particular friend of mine and she's planning a private party at the Pantheon the day after tomorrow. I'm invited and I've asked her to send you a card as well. I hope that's all right? Nell will arrange carriages for everyone and there'll be plenty of married ladies in the party so Lady Brassington needn't come.'

'That's kind of you,' said Caroline, surprised to have been thought of. 'But won't your friend mind? She doesn't know me, after all.'

'She won't mind a bit and I'll present you to her later. Meanwhile, here's her husband – so you can meet him right now.'

* * *

On the far side of the room, Lord Nicholas Wynstanton was trying to persuade Lord Sarre to join him in the card-room.

'Not tonight, Nick.'

'Why not? God knows, the rest of 'em are all here somewhere, doing the pretty by their wives. Rock, Amberley, Jack – even Harry and Philip. And not one among 'em I can tempt away.'

'You've tried, then?'

'Repeatedly,' sighed Nicholas. 'You're my last hope.'

'I'm flattered.'

'No you're not.'

'No,' agreed Sarre equably. 'I'm not. And for now, I believe I am inclined to dance. If you're so bored, you could do the same.'

'And break the habit of a life-time? I don't think so.' Nicholas scanned the room again and his eye brightened. 'Ah. I spy Charles Fox. He's usually pretty amenable.'

He walked away, leaving the Earl free to resume his thoughtful calculation of the risks involved with asking a certain lady to stand up with him. There were some, of course ... but hopefully none were insurmountable. He waited until the optimum moment and then strolled unhurriedly across the floor.

Caroline's skin was faintly flushed with exertion and her eyes sparkled. She smiled up at the tall gentleman offering her his hand, placed her fingers in his cool ones and felt a sudden, inexplicable quiver of awareness. She said, 'Forgive me, sir ... but I have the oddest feeling that I know you. Do I?'

'We have certainly met,' agreed Sarre. 'I will remind you, if you like. Or perhaps you would like to guess.'

Had the rich-toned voice not been as cool as his fingers and also slightly acerbic, the words might have hinted at flirtation. As it was, Caroline wasn't sure what to think.

'I'll try – provided you won't feel insulted if I guess wrongly.'

'I'm not easily offended, Mistress Maitland. On the other hand, if three guesses are insufficient, I may feel within my rights to demand a forfeit.'

Oh, thought Caroline. *That sounds rather daring. A bit* too *daring, perhaps?*

'What sort of forfeit?'

Drawing her into the dance, he shook his head and said, 'I haven't decided. Yet. So you see ... the risk would be all yours. It depends on whether you're brave enough to take it.'

Oh I'm brave enough. But I don't see why you should have it all your own way.

Tilting her chin, she eyed him consideringly and said, 'That doesn't seem very fair.'

'No. It doesn't, does it?' With easy grace, he completed the first figure and, when he was facing her again, said softly, 'Are you accepting the challenge?'

Caroline the Mouse would say no, murmured a taunting little voice in her head.

'Very well, sir,' said Caroline the Reckless. 'Why not?'

His expression remained completely enigmatic.

'Your first guess, then. Who am I?'

She looked at him, taking in the powdered hair and the strong, clean lines of cheek and jaw, and trying to determine the colour of his eyes behind the unusual silver-edged mask. Her sense of familiarity increased. There was something about that immaculate posture … not stiff exactly, but somehow unyielding … that tugged at her memory; and she'd definitely seen that firm, unsmiling mouth before. But when?

In desperation, she said, 'Lord Philip Vernon?'

'Alas – no.'

'Oh. Mr Ingilby, then?'

He shook his head, reprovingly.

'That was a poor shot. Mr Ingilby is much younger than I – and some three inches shorter.'

Damn. Who on earth was *he?*

'I think,' she said firmly, 'I'll save my third guess.'

'You have until the end of this dance.'

'Nothing was said about time limits.'

'It was implicit.'

She shook her head. 'You're making up the rules to suit yourself.'

'Not so. After the dance, you will be able to cheat, will you not?'

'Yes. I was counting on that.' She had hoped to look stern but something about the conversation was sending exhilaration fizzing through her veins, so she smiled and said daringly, 'A gentleman would allow it.'

His lordship looked into the warm, dark eyes and then at the inviting dimple beside her mouth. He said, 'I play to win, Mistress.'

Caroline swallowed hard, suddenly aware of a faint but discernible aura of something that was both alarming and exciting. It was more than the complete absence of expression in either face or voice; it wasn't even entirely caused by the slightly risqué style of his conversation. It was something she couldn't quite identify but which suggested that, though toying with fire was surprisingly enjoyable, losing the game might not be a very good idea.

The remainder of the dance passed in silence while Caroline racked her brains and Sarre watched her doing it. Finally, as the music approached its end and she sank into a final curtsy, she sighed and said, 'I don't know. I really don't.'

'No third guess?'

'No. I give up.'

'How disappointing.' He led her to the edge of the floor. 'If you abandon the game, then so must I.'

'No forfeit?'

'I waive my right to it. For now.' He paused. 'However, if you want to discover my identity, you will have to find me after the unmasking.' And with a small but very elegant bow, he strolled away.

Caroline watched him go, not sure whether she ought to be intrigued or amused.

If she had been able to read Lord Sarre's mind at that precise moment, she would have known that what she *really* ought to be was worried.

Marcus Sheringham arrived later than was his usual custom and then had to spend the best part of ten minutes trying to spot his future bride. In fact, his gaze passed over her three times before he recognised her and, when he did, he felt unreasonably annoyed. Normally, she stood out like a beacon in those garish gowns of hers. Tonight, she looked a damned sight better than he'd ever seen her look before – which was good; but she was also plainly enjoying herself more than a nearly-betrothed girl should in the absence of her fiancé – which wasn't. He stalked over to her side, sent the young buck who was just about to solicit her hand into retreat and said, 'Caroline, my dear. I feared I might never find you.'

Caroline rather wished he hadn't but she resolutely banished the Mouse and said brightly, 'Is that why you are so late? What a shame. But, of course, I had no idea you were looking.'

This wasn't the kind of reply Marcus either expected or found acceptable. Hiding his annoyance, he said, 'Would you care to dance?'

'Not really, if you don't mind. I seem to have danced every set so far and would be glad of a moment to catch my breath. Perhaps you'd be good enough to procure me a glass of wine? I'm quite parched and it's extremely warm in here.'

He stared at her, not at all happy at being virtually ordered to fetch her refreshments and even less pleased with her tone. But, since she had yet to accept his proposal, he swallowed his resentment and bowed stiffly.

'Certainly, if that is what you wish.'

'Thank you.' She smiled and made a vague gesture with her fan. 'I'll wait by the windows to the terrace where it is a little cooler.'

In the end, knowing that the refreshment salon was horribly crowded and that his lordship would likely take some time, Caroline wandered outside to the terrace itself. It was a wide, stone-balustraded strip running the width of the house and, presumably because of the sharp November chill, it was deserted. She drew a deep breath of clean air and gazed up at the stars while she enjoyed a small sense of triumph at the way she had handled Lord Sheringham. He would return wanting an answer, of course … but that didn't mean he had to be given one.

'*Bonsoir*, Mademoiselle,' said a light, charming voice from the shadows.

Caroline whirled round, searching for the voice's owner and finally finding him, half-hidden, by some leafy climbing plant. She said breathlessly, 'Monsieur Duvall?'

'*Bien sûr*. Who else?'

'But how – how did you get in? You shouldn't be here. It's dangerous. If someone sees you --'

Abandoning his place of concealment, the highwayman strolled towards her, loose-limbed and laughing.

'How is it dangerous? *Chérie*, that room is filled with men dressed exactly as I am dressed.' He came to a halt no more than two steps away and made a flamboyant, sweeping gesture with his black domino. 'No one will look at me. Why would they?'

Some of the light from the open windows fell across him, revealing dark brown hair and a bone-meltingly beautiful smile below the plain black silk of his mask. Caroline suddenly found it necessary to concentrate on breathing normally.

He was a highwayman and a thief and that night on the road she'd sent him away with impulsive angry words that were nevertheless true.

They'll hang you, you know. One day they will.

But knowing what he was and where it was likely to lead him hadn't stopped her thinking of him – even dreaming of him. She'd had to continually remind herself that, despite his words to the contrary, she was never going to see him again; that, even if she did, there was no point to it and never could be. Yet now here he was ... without any warning whatsoever and filling everything inside her with a pleasure that was almost frightening in its intensity.

She stared at him, unaware that everything she felt was in her eyes and said helplessly, 'Why are you here?'

'You need to ask, *mignonne*? I came to see you.'

'But you can't have known ...' She stopped, uncertainly.

'That you would be here? I knew.' He came a small step closer. 'I thought merely to look. I did not dare hope for a chance to address you – yet here you are.' Another step. 'And we have music.'

'There is always music. One has only to listen.'

His words from that night at the roadside echoed so clearly in her mind she was unaware of murmuring them aloud until he closed the final space between them to take her hands in his and raise them to his lips.

'You remembered. *Merci.*'

'I remember all of it,' said Caroline – and immediately wished that she'd bitten her tongue out. In an effort to banish the growing, dreamlike magnetism, she said, 'Lady Brassington's pearls have been returned. Except that she says they're better than the ones you took.'

'Vraiment?'

She realised that he was moving, causing her to sway and turn with him and re-creating his special magic with every easy movement.

'I don't suppose you know anything about that?'

'I? But no. How would I?' He spread his hands in expressive denial, taking hers with them. 'I am a thief.'

Suddenly, she didn't quite believe him.

'Are you?'

His smile, this time, was different. 'I'm many things.'

'That is no answer.' She tried to frown, tried not to think how warm and strong his fingers felt around hers. 'Tell me about the pearls.'

'Alas, I cannot. Perhaps her ladyship has a secret admirer.' He shrugged. 'It is a mystery.'

'It certainly is.' She knew she ought to pull her hands from his and move away but it seemed too difficult so she said, 'You must stop this. Someone might see us.'

'And what will they see?' he teased. 'A masked couple dancing innocently in the moonlight. That is all. Are you not enjoying it?'

Yes. God help me, I'm enjoying it far more than I should.

'That isn't the point. I sent a gentleman for wine and he'll be looking for me.'

'Ah. Then our time together is short and should not be wasted.' A subtle shift, an unexpected spin and they stood half-veiled by the creeper. 'Tell me you are pleased to see me.'

'Yes. But --'

'No buts, *petite*. Not tonight.' And, sliding an arm about her waist, he drew her into his arms and kissed her.

It was not like the last time. Caroline felt no shock or confusion; just a sweet, dizzying pleasure that made her melt against him in a way that, had she but known it, was both offer and invitation. Her fingers tangled in his domino, holding him as close as she could and wanting only to prolong the moment. But he, seemingly conscious that they might at any moment be seen, released her mouth with obvious reluctance and, looking directly into her eyes, said, 'I do not wish to leave you but I will not tarnish your reputation. And so ... *au revoir, ma chére* Caroline. Until we meet again.'

'Will we?' she asked unevenly. '*Will* we meet again?'

'Of course.' He stepped back, smiling and held up his hand so the light glinted off the ruby. 'Have you forgotten? I still have your ring.' And, with that, he slid back into the shadows whence he had come.

'Caroline?'

A faintly irritable voice pulled her back into the present and was just in time to stop her trying to see where her highwayman had gone. Spinning quickly to face Lord Sheringham who stood framed against the light spilling through the tall windows, she said, 'I'm here.'

He stepped out on to the terrace, a glass in each hand.

'What on earth are you doing outside?'

'I – I wanted some air.' Her heart was beating erratically at the knowledge of just how close she and Claude had come to discovery. 'Is that my wine? Thank you.'

He gave her the glass, considered ushering her back inside and then thought better of it.

'It's a very clear night ... though somewhat chilly, perhaps.'

'Just a little,' she agreed, taking a fortifying gulp of her wine. 'But a relief after the heat in the ballroom.'

'Indeed. You shouldn't really be here alone, however. A man finding you unaccompanied might be tempted to take advantage.'

'So Lady Brassington told me.' Another gulp. 'But you're here now – so I'm perfectly safe, am I not?'

Most women would have made that sound like a challenge or even an invitation. Caroline managed to make it sound as if she thought him the dullest, most stultifyingly staid fellow in creation. He wondered what had happened during the course of the evening in his absence. Whatever it was, he didn't find this sudden transformation an improvement. Still, it might be possible to turn it to his advantage.

His tone nicely threaded with amusement, he said, 'Not *perfectly* safe, perhaps ... but safe enough, considering I have offered you my hand.' He paused, allowing her a second to think about this. Then, 'Have you an answer for me yet, by the way?'

Caroline wished she'd had the sense to walk back inside the instant she'd seen him.

'Not quite yet, I'm afraid. But I have been giving it a lot of thought.'

'How very kind of you.'

'And *necessary*,' she said firmly. 'I appreciate the honour you've done me. But it's a decision that will affect the rest of our lives. So --'

'I am aware of that.' Marcus moderated his tone. 'Am I correct in assuming that your main concern is that we are not sufficiently well-acquainted?'

It wasn't – but it was simplest to let him think so.

'Yes.'

'Then there is an easy way to remedy it, don't you think?'

Belatedly seeing where this might be going, Caroline said cautiously, 'Time. Surely that is the only answer.'

'It's *one* answer. I wouldn't say it's the *only* one.'

He set his glass on the parapet of the terrace and reached out to take hers from her. Caroline tried to hold on to it but let it go when wine spilled over her hand.

'Lord Sheringham, I don't think --'

'Marcus,' he said, fastidiously drying the wine from her fingers with his handkerchief. 'My name is Marcus.'

'Yes. I know. But --' She stopped when he raised her hand to his lips and placed a lingering kiss in her palm. Then, trying again, she said, 'I should return to the ballroom. Lady Brassington will be wondering what has become of me.'

'Then she can wonder for a few minutes longer, can she not?' And he reached out to pull her into his arms.

Caroline rammed both hands against his chest. At the back of her mind was a bubble of faint hysteria caused by the thought that, having two men kiss her inside ten minutes, was a far cry from being the least desirable girl in the room. But she didn't *want* Lord Sheringham to kiss her. In fact, she actively wanted him *not* to. So she turned her face away, pushed harder and said, 'Please, sir – this is neither appropriate nor helpful.'

'How do you know? And why so prudish?' Marcus managed to grasp both of her wrists and hold them at her sides. Smiling, he said, 'Be still, my dear. I'm hardly about to ravish you. And if you give yourself the chance, you may even enjoy it.'

'I said *no!*' She wrenched her hands free with a strength that surprised him and simultaneously stamped hard on his foot, making him grunt. Then, stepping back, she said coldly, 'We are not betrothed *yet*, my lord. And this kind of behaviour is unlikely to persuade me.'

His lordship promptly forgot his company manners. He said, '*Persuade* you? Why should I need to do that? Who else is there, do you think, who will want you?'

His words produced a sudden silence broken only by the distant sounds from the ballroom. Then, from much closer, came the sound of a series of slow hand-claps.

'Bravo,' said a cool, sardonic voice. 'Bravo, indeed. With such a magnificent display of charm, I'm surprised the lady isn't swooning at your feet.'

Taken unawares, Marcus swore. Equally surprised, Caroline recognised the voice of her intriguing and unknown partner who now stood a few feet away, his mask hanging loosely from one careless hand and his body blocking the view of the crowded ballroom.

'Go to hell, Sarre!' snapped his lordship furiously. 'This is no business of yours.'

Sarre? Caroline stared. *He's the Earl of Sarre?* And finally recognising him, *Of course he is. The man at Lady Linton's who took one look and dismissed me out of hand. Then tonight... oh God. How long has he been watching? Did he see Claude?*

Her mouth went dry at the mere thought.

'None whatsoever.' The Earl advanced a little way towards them. 'But one can't help wondering if you've decided it might be quicker to simply compromise Mistress Maitland into marrying you. You know how that works, I'm sure. A supposedly secret embrace in a place where it's bound to be witnessed? If that's the case, I can understand why you find my arrival untimely.'

'Untimely, unwelcome and wholly unnecessary! I --'

'Did you?' asked Caroline sharply. '*Did* you try to kiss me because you hoped to compromise me?'

'What? No, of course I didn't. My feelings overcame me – for which I apologise. As usual, Lord Sarre is just trying to make mischief.'

'Not at all,' drawled the Earl. 'I was merely expressing a very natural concern for a lady's reputation.'

'*This* lady's reputation,' said Marcus, in a tone that could have cut bread, 'is perfectly safe with me – as is her person. A lot safer, shall we say, than it would be with you.'

'And there it is again,' sighed Sarre, boredom infecting every syllable. 'How very predictable you are. But I seem to recall having advised you to take care … and warned you of the consequences if you don't.'

'You don't frighten me, Sarre. Why should you?' Making a slight, contemptuous gesture in the direction of the other man, Marcus turned to Caroline and said, 'You should avoid his lordship if you value your health. It's said he pushes innocent girls from rooftops.'

Caroline's eyes widened but she said nothing, only too aware that whatever was brewing between these men needed no third party.

'Girls? Plural? That implies a habit, does it not? And said by whom?' came the mocking reply. 'Ah yes. Said by you, Marcus. Only by you.'

'One accuser is enough.'

'One slanderer is *more* than enough.' The Earl's brows rose but his gaze remained disconcertingly impenetrable. 'Shall I take you to law? I could, you know. And the difference between us now is that I can afford it, whereas you can't.'

'I doubt that,' scoffed his lordship. 'Your family's money was gone before you were born.'

'Unlike yours,' agreed Sarre. 'But then, unlike you, I've neither wasted the last decade nor spent it squandering every penny I could lay my hands on.'

For the first time, Lord Sheringham looked less than certain. He scowled and said nothing.

The Earl, by contrast, appeared perfectly at ease.

'If not a court-case – how about payment in kind? Shall I follow your example and tell this young lady that she should consider carefully before allying herself with a man who has no compunction in bedding unmarried, gently-bred girls … even those who are already promised elsewhere?' He paused, an unholy glint in his eyes. 'But there. I appear to have already done so, don't I? Poor Marcus. Unless you can repair the damage, you may have to look elsewhere for your fortune.'

'You bastard,' said Marcus, clenching his fists. 'You think I'll tolerate that?'

'You'll have to, won't you? I doubt, since you've no idea how I might retaliate, that you're about to hit me. And, having avoided my challenge ten years ago, it's hardly likely you'll rise to it now – though, as I said a few nights ago, it still stands.' Sarre waited, somehow making every second an insult. 'Well? Any time or place of your choosing. You have only to name your friends.'

Appearing to recall a degree or two of propriety, Marcus said, 'Caroline ... go back to the ballroom and find Lady Brassington.'

'It's a bit late for that, isn't it? If you were going to spare the lady's sensibilities, you ought to have sent her away ten minutes ago. On the other hand, if you'd rather she didn't hear you playing the coward again, I suppose now is as good a time as any.'

'Excuse me,' said Caroline, re-inflating her lungs and deciding it was time to take part in this duel of words. 'I don't need either one of you to tell me what I should do ... and having listened to all these taunts and insinuations, I've a piece of advice for the pair of you. If this quarrel is still unresolved after ten years, one or both of you must be mildly deranged. Eight year old *girls* can manage their squabbles better. Upon which note,' she said, gathering her domino about her, 'I'll leave you to insult each other in private.'

NINE

On the following evening, Adrian sat in his parlour staring moodily into a glass of claret. Last night's confrontation with Marcus Sheringham had been satisfying in some senses but a total waste of time in others. And Caroline Maitland, most surprisingly, had not only shown more spirit than he'd have expected but also managed to make him feel just a little ridiculous. The only consolation was that Marcus, due to his pressing need to marry the girl, probably felt worse.

The scene that Adrian had witnessed suggested that Lord Sheringham's chances of winning the heiress weren't high. Indeed, after the insulting way he'd spoken to her, he was lucky she hadn't hit him. Adrian wondered *why* she hadn't. He also wondered why Marcus was apparently blind to the warmth in those velvety dark eyes and oblivious of that beguiling dimple. Perhaps he couldn't see past the awful gowns ... or perhaps he was dazzled by the hundred thousand pounds. Either way, he couldn't ever have really looked at her.

Adrian frowned, plagued by an oddly uncomfortable sensation that he decided was best not investigated. Then, shrugging Caroline Maitland aside, he turned his thoughts to more practical matters.

He considered strolling round to Sinclair's and then decided against it. The morning's post would have acquainted Lord Sheringham with the news that his line of credit had been terminated and his current debt called in. This probably meant that his lordship had already called at the club, tried everything he knew to get both decisions reversed and been met with the brick wall that was Aristide at his most impervious. As far as Adrian was concerned, the details of what had occurred could wait until tomorrow. He drained his glass, re-filled it and reached for a pack of cards.

He dealt five hands face-down, then a sixth one face up and placed the remaining stack to one side, flipping over the top card. Then he let his mind move beyond what he could actually see, to the probabilities those things suggested to him. Usually, when he sat alone doing this, time passed without him even noticing it. Tonight for some reason, the sound of the hall clock chiming every quarter hour set his teeth on edge. Eventually, when he couldn't stand it any longer, he pushed the cards aside and stood up.

Unfortunately, he realised that he had no idea what else to do to pass the evening. He'd declined an invitation to a ball and another to a soirée. He didn't regret either one. As far as balls went, he'd accomplished everything he'd hoped to last night at the Overbury masquerade. And the mere idea of a soirée, with all those amateurs trotting out their party pieces, made him shudder. If he went to Sinclair's he'd have to restrict himself to the Hazard table because he couldn't play cards without giving himself a headache; and, though his membership of White's had apparently been approved, he'd yet to show his face there. He supposed the latter was his best option. He just didn't feel very enthusiastic about it.

In short, he felt both edgy and restless ... and didn't have to think very hard to work out why. Firstly, the two things guaranteed to relax him were not currently available. He couldn't play cards and he no longer had a mistress. He recognised that the second of these could be remedied – though perhaps not immediately. He didn't patronise whores; he hadn't been in London long enough to become acquainted with any pretty young widows; and the notion of a business arrangement with a courtesan wasn't particularly appealing. He wanted to spend time with a woman he actually liked ... not merely one who could provide physical release. He thought nostalgically about Angelique to whom he'd said goodbye in Paris. Then he banished the thought before it became pointlessly enjoyable.

Of course, he'd told his mother that he intended to marry and he realised this was a matter he ought to address. He'd also said it didn't matter who his bride was as long as she was fertile – but that wasn't entirely true. Birth was of no particular consequence. But the thought of being tied for life to a stupid woman or one lacking both kindness and humour was more than he could tolerate – which meant it wasn't going to be an easy decision, even supposing he managed to find a girl who didn't shy away from balconies in case he pushed her off.

In addition to everything else, he missed acting – which was ridiculous, considering that he'd been doing little else since he landed at Dover. One role with his mother, another with Nicholas, a third with Aristide and Mr Lessing ... and the impersonal, sophisticated aristocrat he showed to everyone else. Of his recent incarnations, Julius von Rainmayr had been particularly amusing. It was always fun watching well-bred men trying to hide their impatience or guessing which of them would pick up his cane and how many times he could get them do it. None of this, however, was any substitute for the chaos and camaraderie of theatre. It made the hollow space inside him emptier still and left him feeling as if half of his life was missing.

Adrian swore beneath his breath, first in French and then, even more irritably, in English. Then he swept out of the room and headed for the stairs. Bertrand, just emerging from the kitchen, said, 'Going somewhere?'

'Yes. White's, probably. I'll have to make my debut there sometime or other – so it might as well be tonight.'

'You'll need to change your clothes, then.'

'Oddly enough, I was on my way to do that very thing,' came the irritable reply. 'Is there anything else you think I might not manage to work out on my own?'

Bertrand shrugged. 'Yes. Do something about your mood before you walk into White's. Unless you want to pick a fight with somebody.'

And he sauntered back into the kitchen.

* * *

At around the time the Earl of Sarre was walking into London's most exclusive club, Lord Nicholas Wynstanton was abandoning Pharaoh for the Hazard table. He made a few casts, lost and decided he was bored. A hand of piquet with Lord March alleviated this sad state of affairs for a time but when March suggested joining the basset table upstairs, Nicholas – who enjoyed cards as much as the next man but was by no means a gamester – laughed and shook his head.

'No, no – from what I hear, the play up there is too deep for me.'

'Keep me company and watch for a time, then. Or we could take supper.'

Nicholas grinned. 'Supper sounds a good idea. Perhaps I'll finally get to meet Delacroix's sister – who I'll swear he's been keeping hidden from me.'

'Dear me. Just how much of a Lothario does Aristide think you are?'

'One of epic proportions.'

'Really?' drawled March. And then, 'You must have been boasting again.'

The two gentlemen enjoyed a leisurely and exquisitely-prepared meal but were denied any sign of Mademoiselle Delacroix. An idle enquiry produced the information that Mamzelle toured the rooms before service began and again later in the evening but generally occupied herself with other matters unless there was a problem or they were exceptionally busy. Lord March took the news philosophically and went off to lose some money at basset. Lord Nicholas elected to finish a bottle of particularly good Chambertin and promised to re-join his friend in due course.

It was just as he was leaving the dining-room and passing the stairs that led to the offices and private quarters above when he caught a drift of smoke. Nicholas stopped. *Smoke?* He sniffed the air. Yes, smoke. No question of it. And not pipe-smoke, either. As for the kitchens, they were two floors below. If something was on fire down there and he could smell it here, the whole house was going up – which, since there were no sounds of mayhem downstairs, it clearly wasn't. He set his foot on the stairs to Aristide's office, hesitated and then, hearing a crash and a muffled cry, went up them two at a time. By the time he reached the manager's door, smoke was curling beneath it.

Nicholas put his hand on the latch, took a moment to bellow 'Fire!' at the top of his lungs and then, opening the door as little as possible, slid inside and shut it behind him.

The room was swiftly filling with smoke through which Nicholas saw a situation that was bad but not catastrophic. Someone appeared to have tried to burn great quantities of paper, some of which had fallen from the grate and set the rug alight. Amidst this, a woman was tossing burning papers back on to the hearthstone whilst simultaneously trying to stamp out the flames around her feet. She was coughing, in imminent danger of setting her skirts alight and neither of her efforts was working.

The only useful skill Nicholas had retained from his flirtation with the military was that of quick thinking. Admittedly, he only normally needed it where bedrooms were involved – but the principle was the same. He ran across to the window and, with one savage tug, brought down the curtains. Then, wheeling back to the hearth, he caught the woman's arm and swung her out of the way while he used the curtain to smother the fire. He was just hopping about on top of it as he tried to extinguish any remaining sparks when two burly footmen stormed into the room and grabbed his arms.

'Mamzelle!' said one of them. 'What's this fancy-arsed bugger done to you? If 'e's laid a bleeding 'and on you, me and Dick'll cut 'is bleeding fingers off.'

'Now wait just a minute,' objected Nicholas, also coughing and trying to shake off hands the size of giant hams. 'If I hadn't got here when I did, Mamzelle would be burning like a damned beacon by now.'

'Shut it, you,' said the other bruiser, using his free hand to cuff his lordship about the head. 'If you was trying to burn the place down --'

'He wasn't,' said the woman between bouts of coughing, as she threw the window open. 'Let him go.'

'What?' This time both footmen spoke in unison.

'Let. Him. Go.' She spoke very clearly as if to extremely young children. 'Do. It. Now.'

The crippling grips relaxed, allowing Nicholas to brush down his coat and frown at the creases in his sleeves. With what, for him, was rare acidity, he muttered, 'My pleasure, Mademoiselle. Think nothing of it.'

She impaled him on a withering stare. 'What are you talking about?'

'I assumed you were going to thank me for my assistance and was saving you the trouble.'

'Oh – for God's sake.' She turned her attention back to the two muscle-bound idiots. 'Go and fetch my brother. I don't care where he is or what he's doing – I want him up here immediately. Have you got that?'

'Yes, Mamzelle.'

'So *move!*'

They moved.

Nicholas, meanwhile had recovered most of his usual good-humour. He had also become aware that the lady was uncommonly beautiful. Unfortunately, though he had naturally noticed the glowing hair and clear green eyes, he was primarily bewitched by the effect that trying to drag some clean air into her lungs had on her delightful bosom. By the time he managed to tear his eyes away from her *décolletage*, the lady's expression would have made hell freeze.

Colouring slightly, he said, 'Mademoiselle Delacroix, I presume?'

She nodded carelessly. Then, as if she didn't know perfectly well who he was and hadn't spent more time than she'd ever admit watching from the shadows of the gallery as he played Hazard or strolled with his friends on the floor below, 'And you are?'

'Nicholas Wynstanton.' He gestured to the mess on the hearth and added, 'In future, perhaps you should try burning your papers a few at a time. Or possibly in the kitchen?'

'I would if I had. But I didn't.'

'I'm sorry?'

'It wasn't I who tried to burn the papers,' she said patiently. 'My room is just through there. By the time I smelled the smoke, the damage was already under way.'

Nicholas frowned. 'You're saying that someone else was in here?'

'I would think so, wouldn't you? Either that or my brother's files had a sudden urge to incinerate themselves.'

Ignoring the sarcasm, he pulled back the curtain and crouched down on the hearth to begin picking through the debris. 'Is that what this is? Some of Aristide's files?'

'Yes. Isn't that what I just said?'

He glanced up and gave her an unexpectedly spectacular smile.

'I can understand you feeling shaky,' he remarked. 'Equally, having just saved your life, I think a crumb or two of civility wouldn't go amiss.'

That smile caused Madeleine a moment's hesitation. It was one of the things that, along with his easy laugh and light-hearted demeanour, made him dangerous to her peace of mind and the reason she'd spent weeks staying sensibly out of his way. She'd fallen stupidly in love once before and wasn't about to allow herself to develop pointless feelings for the brother of a Duke. So she folded her arms and said, 'I am not shaky – and you didn't save my life. I was managing perfectly well on my own.'

'And you'd still have managed perfectly well when your petticoats caught fire, would you?' He pointed to the singe-marks around her hem. 'You needn't be afraid to give me a little credit. I promise I won't expect you to fall on my neck in gratitude.'

'No?'

'No.' He stood up, holding some charred pieces of paper and added, 'I might *hope* for it, of course. But you can't blame a fellow for that.'

Madeleine opened her mouth on another acid retort and then closed it again as the door opened and Aristide burst in. Grasping her hands, he said in French, 'Are you all right?'

'Aside from ruining one of my favourite gowns? Perfectly. This gentleman,' she waved a careless hand in his lordship's direction, 'arrived in time to lend a hand.'

Releasing his sister, Aristide turned to his lordship and switched back to English.

'Nicholas? How --?' He stopped. 'No. That doesn't matter. I'm just grateful you were here. But what the hell happened, Madeleine?'

'I don't know. Clearly, someone was intent on destroying some files – this being the result.'

'Somebody got in here? *Here?* In my private *office?*'

'Yes.'

Aristide uttered a brief, pungent curse. Then, swinging round to the two beefy fellows hovering at his back, said, 'Get Jenkins up here now.'

'Mr Jenkins'll be on the door, sir,' objected one of them. 'Busy, like.'

'*Just get him!*' roared Aristide. They fled but it took the manager no less than three steadying breaths before he could say, 'Which files?'

Nicholas shrugged but Madeleine was already scrutinising the bank of drawers. She said, 'This one, perhaps? Unless you left it partly open?'

'Never.' Aristide pushed past her and yanked the drawer wide to reveal a large gap inside. 'S,' he said brusquely, rifling swiftly through the folders. 'Everything between Se and Sm. The bastard just grabbed a handful and tried to burn the lot. *Merde.*'

'Were they your only copies?' asked Nicholas.

'Yes. You can see how much there is – keeping duplicates of everything would take twice the space. And I pay a lot of money to keep the entire building secure so that this kind of thing can't happen.'

'Except that it has,' remarked his sister.

'Thank you for stating the obvious, Madeleine. It's such a help.' Aristide spun round as Alfred Jenkins skidded to a halt in the doorway. 'Jenkins. Excellent. Perhaps you'd like to explain to me how the *hell* an intruder managed to make his way through the entire club – apparently unnoticed – and set fire to my office?'

Mr Jenkins stared round at the damage and then back at his employer, the colour draining from his skin.

'I can't, sir. Not off-hand.'

'You can't. Wonderful. You realise, I hope, that my sister could have been killed and the entire bloody building might have burned down?'

'Yes, sir.'

'What exactly am I paying you for, Jenkins?'

'Security, sir. And all I can offer you right now are my apologies. But if you'll give me time to make some enquiries --'

'I'll give you twenty minutes to re-organise your schedules and have everyone previously on duty up here in front of me – and a further twenty to find anyone downstairs who saw anything. And I *mean* anyone – including the damned scullery-maid. Is that clear?'

'Clear, sir.' Mr Jenkins and ran back the way he had come.

'It may not be his fault,' suggested Nicholas mildly.

'It was,' came the grim reply. 'Ultimately, it was.'

'But if it was someone already legitimately inside the --'

'It wasn't.'

'You're saying,' remarked Madeleine, 'that you know who did this?'

'Almost certainly.'

'Then why didn't you tell Jenkins that? It would make his task easier.'

'I don't *want* to make his task easier, for God's sake. I want him to find the answer on his own – not merely confirm my suspicions because it saves a deal of trouble.'

'And what exactly are your suspicions?' asked a new voice from the doorway.

Aristide, Madeleine and Nicholas all turned like clockwork and simultaneously greeted the newcomer in three different ways and in a trio of differing tones.

'Adrian?' Relieved.

'My Lord Sarre.' Sarcastic.

'Dev?' Surprised.

Then, shaking his head, Nicholas said, 'I never knew a fellow who used so many names at once. It's damned confusing. However … where did you spring from?'

'White's. It was tedious.' The Earl saw no need to add that none of the men with whom he'd recently begun forging a friendship had been present and, of those gentlemen who *were* in attendance, most had chosen to ignore him. 'It's discreet mayhem downstairs – and now I see why. You were saying you think you know who's responsible?'

'Shut the door,' grunted Aristide. And when this had been done, 'Yes. My money is on Marcus Sheringham. This morning he received notification that his membership had been cancelled along, obviously, with his credit and that his debts to the club are due for payment before quarter day. An hour later he was in here trying to talk me out of it.'

'And failing,' said Sarre.

'And failing,' agreed Aristide. 'But he went through the whole gamut. Polite persuasion, empty promises, threats, entreaties … he tried them all. He even more or less said he'd landed the Maitland heiress.'

'Wishful thinking,' murmured Sarre dryly. 'He's yet to make it a fact.'

'That's what I assumed. By the time he finally left, he was hurling insults and virtually foaming at the mouth. But it never occurred to me that he'd try something like this.' He paused, running a hand through his already dishevelled hair. 'Not that there's any proof that he did.'

'Yet,' said Sarre.

'And if Jenkins finds some?' asked his sister. 'What then?'

'I'll have him arrested – after I've knocked his teeth down his throat.' Aristide looked at Sarre. 'I don't care whether the fire was started on purpose or through carelessness. If Madeleine and Nicholas hadn't got here when they did, people could have died and you and I would have lost everything. I'm not about to forgive that. And, aside from everything else, we've also lost the only detailed account of his debts to the club – which is likely to pose other problems entirely.'

'It would if it were true,' said the Earl calmly. 'As we both know, your memory for figures is exceptional. Also, Henry Lessing included an estimate of Sheringham's liability to Sinclair's in my personal accounting records so all you need do is update his information and have him furnish you with a copy. Then, assuming that you're right and it *is* Sheringham – it will be interesting to see what he does next.'

A little later, while Aristide was heaping burning coals on the heads of his entire security staff – none of whom had seen any sign of an intruder – Nicholas and Adrian strolled down St James Street, discussing the evening's events. Then, at the point where their paths diverged, Nicholas said just a little too carelessly, 'Tonight is the first time I ever met Aristide's sister. She's quite something, isn't she?'

'That,' responded Adrian, 'is certainly one way of putting it. Or were you speaking merely about her looks?'

'Oddly enough, no – extraordinary though they are.' He paused and then, still as if it were of no particular consequence, said, 'I suppose you know her quite well.'

'I used to ... until she took me in acute dislike.'

'Ah.' Nicholas nodded wisely. 'Like that, is it?'

'No. There was never any of 'that' between us and never will be. Also – just in case you were wondering – Madeleine may live above a gaming club and perform the duties of a housekeeper, but she isn't a demi-rep. And the man who makes the mistake of treating her like one had better be wearing armour.'

* * *

In his house in Half-Moon Street, Marcus huddled over the fire and waited for his hands to stop shaking. He couldn't believe he'd managed to get into Sinclair's and out again unchallenged. Wearing the darkest and plainest clothes he could find, he'd lurked near a side-door used for deliveries. Most of these were made during the day but he knew that the Gallic genius in the kitchen was always sending out for this or that, no matter what the hour. So he'd waited until a fellow came trudging back clutching a tray of something or other and taken it from him, saying, 'Thank God. He's been shouting for this for the last ten minutes. I'll take it – if you want to go and get warm.' And then he was inside.

Getting to Aristide's office had been easier than he'd expected. He knew where it was, he knew it would be unoccupied and he knew the areas Jenkins' fellows usually patrolled. He even, thanks to a bit of luck some weeks back, knew where one of the concealed passage-ways was – though not exactly where it went. But somehow, despite his terror, he'd managed to achieve his goal. Then it had been a matter of doing what he'd come to do as quickly as possible. He had no illusions about what his fate would be if he was caught. If Delacroix didn't beat him to a pulp, Jenkins most assuredly would. Worse still, they might hand him over to a magistrate. So he'd dragged a handful of files from the drawer so his own wouldn't be the only one missing and started feeding them to the fire. It seemed to take forever and the sound of a door opening somewhere had routed what was left of his nerves. He'd shoved the last few folders on top of the rest, stabbed at them with the poker and fled.

He didn't remember getting out of the club. He *did* remember running as though the hounds of hell were after him once he reached the street. And now, he sat by his fire, praying to every God there was that he'd done enough; that destroying the written evidence of his debt was going to be sufficient to cast doubt on the debt itself and, if luck was on his side, make it difficult – even impossible – for Delacroix to enforce it.

His hands were still shaking. They'd guess it was him. They'd guess … but they couldn't be certain. They couldn't prove it. It would be all right. And, to make sure it was, he'd stop Caroline Maitland dithering and drag her to the altar by force if necessary.

TEN

Caroline devoted only a modicum of thought to Lords Sheringham and Sarre and a great deal more to Monsieur Duvall. After much deliberation, she decided not to reveal his presence at the Overbury masquerade to Lady Brassington – not because she thought her ladyship's discretion wasn't to be trusted, but because she couldn't foresee where these Eulenspiegel-like appearances might lead. Also, she had never had a secret worth keeping before and she discovered that she rather liked it.

Mama continued badgering her to accept Lord Sheringham's proposal. Lavinia, wistfully but without rancour, said it was a pity that she and Caroline couldn't change places. And Sylvia said bluntly, 'If you don't like him, don't have him. A title's not everything.'

Privately, Caroline agreed with her. But, equally privately, she recognised that it didn't necessarily mean one could have the things one *did* like – even should they be offered.

On the evening following the Overbury masquerade, Mr Sterne declared himself and Caroline gently declined him on the grounds that she didn't think they would suit.

'I was afraid you'd say that,' said Ludovic wryly. 'I don't blame you, of course. But of all Cousin Lily's heiresses, you're the first one I actually wouldn't mind being married to.'

Caroline was surprised by the compliment and treasured it more than another lady might have done. She even felt a little sorry for Mr Sterne and tried to soften the blow as best she could but he merely smiled, shook his head and said, 'It's all right, you know. One gets used to it. But I hope you'll still dance with me.'

Having reduced her options by half, Caroline started to lose sleep about what she was going to say to Lord Sheringham. That she was going to have to say something very soon was becoming increasingly clear; but the problem was the same as it had always been. She didn't want to say yes but wasn't sure it would be sensible to say no. Then Lady Brassington told her something that brought the moment of decision inescapably close.

'I don't want to alarm you, my dear, but there's rumour going about that you and Lord Sheringham have an understanding.'

'We don't,' said Caroline, aghast. 'At least, *I* don't.'

'No. But it seems he's begun holding off his most pressing creditors by telling them that he's on the brink of contracting a very wealthy alliance. And word spreads, you know.'

'But he's no business saying any such thing! It isn't true!'

'It doesn't have to be true for the gossips to believe it and to pass it on,' replied her ladyship aridly. 'But it could place you in a rather awkward position. Of course, if you turn his lordship down, it will place him in a worse one – but that's his own fault. What *you* need to realise is that, the longer you don't answer him one way or the other, the worse the situation will become.'

'You mean,' said Caroline flatly, 'that if I dally long enough, I may end up having to say yes whether I want to or not?'

'It's a possibility. Yes.'

'Then I'll end it tonight. It's Lady Waldgrave's rout, isn't it?'

'Yes.'

'So Lord Sheringham is likely to be there?'

'Almost certainly, I'd say – particularly since he'll expect to see you and be hoping for the opportunity to press his suit.'

'And he shall have it.' *Though if he tries to kiss me again, I'll do a damned sight more than stamp on his foot*, she thought crossly. But was wise enough not to say it.

* * *

Caroline dressed carefully for the party that evening, maliciously electing to wear the only one of her gowns to have so far escaped de-ornamentation. The colour of bluebells, it might have been pretty had it not been made of extremely shiny and slippery satin and frosted in every conceivable place with over-lays of white lace. Lavinia shook her head over it and said, 'At least let me get rid of some of that stuff around the neckline.'

'No.'

'But it looks like a christening-robe.'

'Does it? I hadn't noticed.'

'It's awful and you know it,' said Sylvia. 'Why are you determined to look just about as odd as you possibly can?'

'I'll tell you later,' said Caroline, sounding more cheerful than she actually felt. 'Now ... where did we put the ostrich feathers?'

'You are not,' snapped Lavinia, 'putting those in your hair. I forbid it.'

'Forbid all you like. Sylvia ... be a love and fix these for me, will you?'

Downstairs, Mama – who had fought tooth and nail against what she saw as the wanton destruction of Caroline's wardrobe – nodded approvingly and remarked that it was a change to see her looking "something like".

Lady Brassington's reaction, when Caroline stepped into the carriage, was rather different.

'Lud!' she said faintly. 'Why didn't you powder your hair and have done with it?'

'Well, I *did* think of that – but it was too late to send out for some powder,' came the perfectly deadpan reply. 'It's a pity, really. Do you suppose pale blue might have looked pretty?'

Her ladyship shuddered and thanked God for small mercies. She said, 'Since you can't have achieved this result by accident, I suppose you have a reason?'

'Yes. I thought it might be instructive to test Lord Sheringham's ability to the limits.'

'What do you mean?'

'Well, if he can look me in the eye and tell me how lovely I look without wincing, he must be an extremely accomplished liar, don't you think?'

'My dear, if he can do *that*, he deserves a medal.'

His lordship thought so, too, when he caught sight of her from the other side of Lady Waldegrave's ballroom. Of all the hideous gowns he'd seen Mistress Maitland wearing, this one had to be the worst. The shine on that blue satin was almost blinding and every movement caused the layers of lace to flutter about like washing on a line. As for

117

those ridiculous ostrich feathers, they reminded him of his Aunt Agatha who was sixty if she was a day.

Marcus had spent a very nerve-racking day, lurking at home and fearing, at any moment, to hear fists pounding on the front door. He knew that, by now, Aristide Delacroix would have questioned every single employee in Sinclair's. He also knew that if any of them had so much as glimpsed him last night, he was going to be in a great deal of trouble. So he hid and he waited and would probably have gone on doing so but for the necessity of getting the Maitland chit to accept his proposal without further delay. And there she was on the far side of the room, dressed like a bloody maypole.

Feeling in need of suitable fortification, Marcus drained a glass of claret almost in one swallow before making his way across the floor. The only good thing to be said for the girl's appearance was that he was unlikely to have any competition for her attention.

Seeing him coming, Caroline stiffened her spine and snapped her fan shut. Behind her corset, her stomach was queasy with nerves but she drew a deep breath and smiled.

'Caroline, my dear.' He bowed with easy familiarity over her hand and met her smile with one of his own. 'That is a very ... original gown. Flanders lace, surely?'

'No. Every bit of it made in Yorkshire,' she replied cheerfully. 'It just goes to show that one doesn't have to buy foreign goods when quality can be had at home. Also, the Harrogate ladies who made this only charge eight shillings the yard as opposed to twelve for Brussels – and that's quite a saving, isn't it?'

'Yes. Indeed.' His lordship wondered why Lady B had failed to warn the cloth-merchant's heiress that discussing the cost of one's raiment wasn't much more socially acceptable than scratching or farting. In the hope of averting any other vulgarities, he said, 'Would you care to dance?'

'A little later, perhaps. I wondered if we might not just stroll the rooms for a while,' she suggested. 'I daresay you've a number of friends here tonight.'

In truth, he had far fewer friends than he'd had a year ago. Quite a lot had gradually distanced themselves as he slid deeper and deeper into debt – which told him how good those friends had been. As for those who remained, he had no intention of introducing them to his bride-to-be until he'd smoothed out what he was beginning to realise were quite a number of rough edges.

Smiling, he offered his arm and said, 'I doubt many of my intimates will be present this evening. There is a sporting event in Islington tonight which will likely draw a great crowd. And, truth to tell, I should much prefer to have you to myself for a time. Firstly, I must apologise once again for my behaviour the other evening. If I distressed you in any way, I am truly sorry for it. But I hope you will make allowances for the natural feelings of a man in love. A poor, foolish hopeful fellow whose soul is living in a turmoil of doubt.'

Oh dear, thought Caroline, suddenly thoroughly irritated. *We can't have that, can we? Time to put the poor, foolish hopeful fellow out of his misery.*

She murmured, 'Do you think that perhaps we ought to be having this conversation in a less public place?'

'If that would be acceptable to you – yes,' he said, looking a little surprised. And then, 'I'm sure Lord Waldegrave wouldn't mind us borrowing his library for a short time.'

A private room wasn't exactly what Caroline had in mind but she accepted that it was probably preferable to saying what had to be said where anyone might overhear so she nodded and let him lead her from the ballroom.

The library was beautiful and the array of books breath-taking but she couldn't allow herself to be distracted. It was important to keep her wits about her and to monitor her words very carefully if the next few minutes were not to get out of hand. And so, taking the initiative and trying to ignore the churning in her stomach, she said, 'I am aware that you have been extraordinarily patient in allowing me these few days to consider your proposal. I'm also, as I've said previously, aware of the honour that proposal represents. But I'm afraid that I can't accept it, my lord. I'm sorry.'

For a second, Marcus wasn't sure he'd heard her correctly and, when he realised that he had, it took him a moment to be certain he had his voice under control.

'May I ask why?'

'I – I don't think we would make each other happy.'

'You mean that you don't think I would make *you* happy.'

'I mean what I said. I'm not the wife for you. I'm not nearly sophisticated enough or socially adept or beautiful. And I don't think you will like becoming related to my family which would create difficulties as I've promised to help establish my half-sisters.'

Marcus didn't want to discuss that last part. In fact, he disliked her whole plain-spoken attitude. He purred, 'Darling ... how can you think yourself inadequate in any way? Surely the fact that I've told you that I love you should remove any such doubts.'

'It would if I believed you – but I don't.'

He stared at her, momentarily lost for words.

'What do you mean – you don't believe me? That's utterly ridiculous. Why would I say such a thing if it wasn't true?'

Because you want Grandpa Maitland's money.

'I think we both know the answer to that and can agree that it's better not discussed. You are not in love with me nor ever likely to be. And to be honest, I'd have respected you more if you hadn't tried to pretend.'

The blue eyes narrowed and a pulse throbbed in his jaw.

'Would you indeed?'

'Yes.' She spread her hands and pressed her attack. 'I'm not entirely sure that you even *like* me.'

He didn't ... and was liking her less and less by the minute. Unfortunately, if there was any chance at all of turning this around, he had no choice but to try.

'You distress me unutterably. Of course I like you. How can you possibly think I don't?'

'You gave me a clue when you said you didn't need to persuade me to marry you because nobody else would want me.'

Marcus opened his mouth and then closed it again. Finally, he said stiffly, 'I was angry – though not with you. Lord Sarre has an unfortunate --'

'Please stop. I realise that there has been bad blood between yourself and the Earl for a long time but that is nothing to do with me. And you made that unfortunate remark before you knew the Earl was there.'

Blast the girl. He could feel his temper beginning to rise in earnest. *Did she have to be so cursed literal?* He said sulkily, 'You also stamped on my foot.'

'In dance slippers, my lord,' she mocked. *Be grateful I was wearing too many petticoats to make my knee effective.* 'I don't like being mauled in public.'

'We weren't *in* public. No one was there.'

'Lord Sarre was.'

Marcus wanted to shake her until her teeth rattled. He said grittily, 'We seem to have strayed from the point. You are refusing my offer for reasons that exist only in your head – or so it seems to me. I have no right to ask, of course ... but is it possible that you have formed an attachment for some other man?'

It was unexpected and Caroline immediately felt her cheeks grow hot. She hoped his lordship would mistake that for embarrassment or annoyance ... or anything other than what it was. She said tartly, 'You're right. You *don't* have any right to ask. But since you have ... the answer is no. There isn't any other gentleman.' And that, she reflected, had the virtue of being true unless a Gentleman of the Road counted.

'You were not, then, considering an offer from Ludovic Sterne?'

She stared at him, suddenly as angry as she suspected he was.

'You go too far, my lord. And since this conversation appears to be at an end --'

'No. Wait. I beg your pardon.' With an enormous effort, he hid his fury behind a smile. He couldn't believe that this plain little nobody could actually dismiss him as if he was of no account. Who the *hell* did she think she was? He wished to God he didn't need her money; but, since she was his only way out of the quagmire that threatened to

121

engulf him, he said softly, 'You think I have no feelings for you? It should be clear by now that I have. Very strong ones, as it happens. So could we not turn back the clock and start again? Take time to get to know each other better? I've made mistakes. I recognise that. But doesn't everyone deserve a second chance? Can you not take a few more days to reconsider?'

He sounded so convincing that Caroline had to remind herself that he lied nearly all the time. She said, 'I don't believe that would serve any useful purpose.'

'I disagree. Do you really mean to be so cruel?'

'I'm not being cruel. I'm being truthful and practical. I won't marry you, my lord. And – and I would be obliged if you would put an end to the current rumours that we have an understanding – because we don't.'

She started to move past him on her way to the door only to freeze as his hand grasped her wrist.

'What rumours?' he snapped.

'The ones you started when you began dropping hints to your creditors,' retorted Caroline. 'Please let go of me. I wish to return to the ballroom. And I really don't think we have anything more to say to each other.'

Marcus let his fingers slide from her wrist and made a silent, sardonic bow as she left the room.

Don't you? Well … we'll see about that.

If he could deal with Sinclair's, he could deal with little Miss Halifax. He needed a plan and he needed it quickly. But first, he needed information … and he knew where he could get it. Purposefully but without obvious signs of haste, he left the library and strolled off to have a seemingly idle conversation with Lily Brassington.

ELEVEN

Lady Elinor Caversham's party arrived at the Pantheon in three separate carriages but at much the same time. Having cross-questioned Harry, Sarre knew who his fellow-guests would be. Philip and Isabel Vernon, Jack and Althea Ingram, Nicholas Wynstanton, Cassandra Delahaye ... and Caroline Maitland. The latter, said Harry, had been added at Cassie's request and because Nick's belated desire to join the fun had made the numbers uneven.

Sarre wasn't sure it was going to be fun. Philip, Jack and Harry had accepted him but their ladies, none of whom he had previously met, might feel differently. He prepared himself for cold looks and even colder shoulders ... and was relieved, less for his own sake than for those of the men who had befriended him, when he was met with neither.

Isabel Vernon was an attractive women whose manner was one of quiet confidence; Althea Ingram, a stunning blonde seemingly afflicted by shyness; and Lady Elinor's dark eyes sparkled with laughter as she immediately demanded to be told what the ladies of Paris were wearing this season.

If the wives were a surprise, the interior of the Pantheon was a greater one. Newly-built since he had last been in London, the Rotunda housing the supper-boxes and the dance-floor was of massive dimensions and set beneath an enormous dome with a glass cupola. Even in Paris, Sarre had never seen anything like it. A surreptitious glance at Mistress Maitland told him that she hadn't either.

She was wearing the tiny gold mask and bronze domino she'd worn to the Overbury ridotto. Beneath it, however, was a gown of bright turquoise taffeta which didn't suit her in the least and caused him to wonder if the girl had any colour-sense at all or was just cursed with execrable taste. His opinion, for what it was worth, was that she ought to stick to either end of the spectrum; pale gold, midnight blue ...

possibly even certain misty shades of green? He reined in his wandering thoughts. What the hell was the matter with him? The girl could wear a sack for all the difference it made to him.

Lady Elinor decreed that everyone should take to the floor before supper was served.

'Oh God, Nell!' groaned her brother. 'Have some pity, can't you?'

'I don't see why I should. You knew there would be dancing, Nick – yet you still more or less invited yourself and I'm not having one of the ladies being forced to sit tapping her toes just because *you* have two left feet.' She turned to the rest of her party, a diminutive General ordering her troops. 'And no husbands dancing with their wives! You can do that later. In fact, just this once, I think the ladies should choose their own partners. And I'm claiming Lord Sarre.'

With the merest hint of surprise, his lordship bowed.

'Willingly, my lady … so long Harry has no objection.'

'He hasn't,' she said firmly. And to Harry, 'Have you?'

'I wouldn't dare,' muttered Harry, gloomily. 'Down-trodden and truly under the cat's paw – that's me.'

Lady Elinor laughed, stood on tiptoe to kiss his cheek and then dragged Sarre away, saying, 'He'll dance with Thea – just see if he doesn't. And I expect Nick will foist himself on poor Cassie. That means Jack will lead out Isabel … leaving Mistress Maitland to Philip. Excellent!'

'Do you always organise your guests so efficiently, my lady?' asked Sarre.

'Usually. It's one of the privileges of being married.' She smiled up at him. 'And Harry's friends are permitted to call me Nell. Also, you didn't finish describing the latest styles. Harry has promised to take me to Paris in the spring and I refuse to be behind the mode.'

Once in the private box, everyone discarded their masks and sat down to supper. This was a cheerful affair with a good deal of teasing and laughter and, as often as not, several people talking at once. Sarre was reminded of post-performance gatherings at the Comédie Française where evenings like this were commonplace. Waging an internal war with nostalgia, he listened more than he talked … and was therefore aware that, beside him, Mistress Maitland said even less.

After a while, he looked thoughtfully at her and said, 'You are very quiet, Mistress.'

'Yes. I feel a bit of an intruder, you know. Oh – please don't misunderstand. It's not the fault of anyone here. They've all been very kind. It's just that I wouldn't normally be invited to private parties like this one and am only here now because of Cassie.'

His expression remained inscrutable as ever but the Earl bent his powdered head towards hers and murmured, 'I'm not generally invited to them myself.'

'No?' Caroline half-wondered if he was making fun of her, then decided that this man probably never made fun of anything. She also got the uncomfortable feeling that those unreadable eyes missed as little as they revealed – which made her wonder what was going on behind them. 'But you're an Earl.'

'Oddly enough, that's not a universal passport. There are certain … expectations. And, as I'm sure you know, appearances are everything.'

'Oh yes. I *do* know that.' She paused and then said tentatively, 'But someone – Lord Philip, I think – said you'd been abroad for a number of years?'

Long elegant fingers, bare of even the plainest signet ring, toyed idly with his glass and his gaze drifted past her in the direction of the opposite gallery. Caroline couldn't decide whether he was deep in thought or she had simply lost his attention. Then, still without looking at her, he said, 'Ten, to be exact.'

Suddenly the pieces dropped into place and her eyes widened. She thought of three things to say and wisely discarded all of them.

Lord Sarre's eyes returned to her face and his mouth curled in a sardonic half-smile.

'Putting two and two together, are you?'

Caroline flushed a little. 'I beg your pardon.'

'For what? You are guessing that my departure from England was somehow connected with my … what did you call it? Ah yes. My *squabble* with Lord Sheringham.'

This time she decided to be daring.

'And was it?'

'Yes.' He waited, as if giving her the chance to ask something else. Then, when she said nothing, 'My turn, I think. Rumour has it that you are to marry his lordship.'

She eyed him speculatively. 'Do you think I shouldn't?'

'Do you *care* what I think?'

'Not at all. But I imagine you raised the subject because you want to know whether or not the rumour is true.'

'And why would that be of any interest to me?'

'I don't know. Because of the ill-feeling between yourself and Lord Sheringham, perhaps?'

Sarre looked at her for a long moment, thinking that she was quicker-witted than he'd supposed. He said quietly, 'Congratulations. You've side-stepped my implied question very neatly.'

'As you have avoided my very direct one.'

His expression didn't vary by so much as a hair's breadth but his voice contained a distant note that might, just possibly, have been amusement.

'*Touché*. Very well. Since you ask, I would advise against marriage with Lord Sheringham ... but not for the reasons you may suppose.'

'Why, then?'

He shook his head. 'No, no. As I said before – it's my turn. So?'

Caroline sighed and then smiled.

'Rumour lies. I will not be marrying his lordship.'

The chilly gaze sharpened slightly. 'And presumably he knows that?'

'It would hardly be proper of me to tell you if he didn't,' she said primly.

'Of course.'

Sarre rose, shook out the folds of his black domino and then seemed to hesitate.

Caroline waited for a moment before prompting him.

'You were going to say something else?'

'No.' He half-turned away and then, with an irritated breath, looked back at her. 'Yes. Be careful.'

* * *

After supper came more dancing but this time Lady Elinor gave her guests *carte blanche* to please themselves. Caroline took to the floor with Lord Harry, then Mr Ingram; and finally with Nicholas – when it was proved, beyond any shadow of a doubt, that his lordship hadn't been making excuses when he'd said he couldn't dance. By the time the music stopped, Caroline was breathless with laughter and Nicholas, grinning back at her, said, 'You took that better than most girls do. Shall we try it again later?'

'You c-can't mean that,' said Caroline, still giggling.

'Can't I?' he replied. And managed a menacing leer.

Not far away and partnering Cassie Delahaye, Sarre found his eyes drawn to the source of that infectious laughter and noticed how animation improved the little heiress. It was also interesting how the candlelight seemed to be finding glints of amber and deep gold in that usually nondescript hair. She would never be a match for Nell Caversham or Althea Ingram, of course. But there was something rather attractive about her unaffected enjoyment. Something that made him want to continue watching it.

Meanwhile, Isabel Vernon had discovered that Dolly Cavendish was hosting a party only three booths along from their own. Since, with the exception of Caroline and Lord Sarre, everyone knew each other, the two groups began to merge and migrate between boxes.

Two of Dolly's guests turned out to be Mr Edward Chatham and his wife. Sarre accepted an introduction without the merest flicker of recognition, then watched Louisa Chatham's face freeze in open dislike before she turned away, drawing her husband with her. His expression becoming even more enigmatic than usual, Sarre gave a mental shrug and moved away to exchange greetings with Lord March.

Caroline, being ignored by two ladies from the Cavendish party who were chattering determinedly to Cassie, watched it happen. Earl or not, it seemed that – to some people – Lord Sarre was unacceptable company. Of course, he'd implied something of the sort but, if she hadn't seen it with her own eyes, she wouldn't have believed it. She wondered what exactly had happened ten years ago and why it hadn't been forgotten. What had Lord Sheringham said? *'He pushes innocent girls from rooftops.'* That was a particularly nasty allegation ... but then, Lord Sheringham often lied.

And he could well have lied about that. I wouldn't put it past him. But if other people also remember and believe it ... then, equally, it could be true.

Nicholas and Philip Vernon wanted Sarre to join them in a game of ombre. He begged them to hold him excused and slyly suggested they invite Mr Chatham instead. Then, when the three of them had settled around a table, he leaned against the wall, apparently content to watch either the game or the dancers on the floor below.

Caroline was hot and bored. Despite Cassie's attempts to include her in the conversation, the other ladies continually shut her out again by talking about people she didn't know. She endured it for another few minutes and then, rising from her seat, murmured an excuse and slipped from the box. The corridor stretched out in both directions and felt definitely cooler. Fairly certain that no one would miss her, she decided there could be no harm in walking the length of the gallery. She glanced into the Cavendish box as she strolled by. No one noticed her. Relieved to be alone for a little while, Caroline continued on her way.

His attention having been largely fixed elsewhere, it was a while before Lord Sarre noticed that Mistress Maitland was missing. He told himself this was no cause for concern. Althea Ingram wasn't there either and he'd seen the two of them conversing earlier in the evening. In all likelihood, they had transferred to Dolly Cavendish's box. Sarre glanced at the card-players. Despite a sheen of perspiration and a tightly-clenched jaw, Mr Chatham was already several guineas to the good. The Earl felt a distant sympathy. Aristide had plainly dropped a word in his ear and the poor fellow was trying. Watching him do it might have been enough to keep Sarre amused had it not been for the other thing. Without anyone appearing to be aware of it, he left Lady Elinor's box for the other. Althea Ingram was there, along with her husband and Isabel Vernon. Of Mistress Maitland, there was no sign.

Damn.

He'd told her to be careful – but plainly she hadn't listened. On the other hand, she didn't know what he knew. She didn't know that Marcus Sheringham had recently conducted a singularly rash raid on Sinclair's or that Aristide had that day sent him a politely-worded reminder of both his debt and the date payment was due. And she didn't know that, right now, his lordship was prowling the gallery on the far side of the Rotunda as though he was hunting for someone.

She ought to be safe enough, thought Sarre. He wasn't familiar with the building but, from what he'd seen, the gallery probably didn't run continuously – thus placing Marcus on one side and his quarry on the other. But if he was wrong, if there were passageways he couldn't see and more than two staircases … and if Caroline was roaming at will, the two of them could meet up at any time.

Hell.

Very briefly, Sarre wondered why he didn't want that to happen and recognised that it was not just about keeping Marcus trapped in the pit of his own making; it was also about feeling that the girl deserved something better than to drop like a ripe plum into the clutches of a fortune-hunter … and particularly *that* fortune-hunter.

All of which meant he'd have to do something. Quickly.

Bloody, bloody hell.

All the time he'd been thinking, he'd carried on walking in the direction that he guessed – and hoped – Caroline would have taken. His best chance was to catch up with her before Marcus did. He also realised that the Pantheon itself offered him two ways of managing this. One of them was safe and easy; the other … wasn't. He considered his options for a moment. Then, with a smile and a shrug, he made his choice.

Caroline, meanwhile, had arrived at the point where a staircase led down to the main floor and the gallery narrowed to circumnavigate the curve of the Rotunda. It looked to be no more than a maintenance corridor, presumably little frequented by guests; and her only other choices were either to return the way she had come or to take the stairs down. The latter was clearly not an option. She knew better than to appear on the main floor, alone and without her mask. But she didn't feel like returning to the rest of the party just yet so she chose the corridor.

She hadn't gone more than a few yards when she heard the sound of footsteps approaching from the other direction. She hoped it was one of the Pantheon's employees. Since her skirts were almost brushing either wall, she also hoped he wasn't carrying anything large because, if he was, they were going to have difficulty getting past each other. The idea of squeezing by anyone at all didn't sound like a good idea. Caroline turned round and retraced her steps to allow whoever it was a clear passage. She had just reached the landing when a hand was wrapped firmly around her elbow and a voice said, 'Dear me. This is fortuitous. I was still trying to work out how to prise you away from the Cavershams.'

Thoroughly startled and trying to pull her arm free, Caroline said coldly, 'I thought, my lord, that I had already told you I dislike being mauled.'

'In public,' said Marcus, pulling her towards the stairs. 'This isn't in public. But we can soon mend that.'

As best she could, she dug her heels into the carpet and tried to stand her ground.

'Let me go!'

He continued dragging her with him. 'No. I don't think I will.'

'But this is stupid! What on earth do you think to achieve? *I will not marry you*. How many times must I say it?'

'As often as you like. Though I imagine you'll stop quickly enough when a goodly number of people downstairs see you leaving with me through the main door.'

Alarm began to feather down Caroline's spine. Still struggling furiously, she said, 'They won't see it because it isn't going to happen! I'll scream my head off. If you don't let go of me, I'll start right now!'

By way of answer, Lord Sheringham twisted the arm he held behind her back and, spinning her round, clamped his other hand over her mouth.

'You won't, my dear. By the time I get you down those stairs, you'll be semi-conscious. And I have a carriage waiting – though it won't be taking you home.'

Caroline bit his fingers, rammed her free elbow into his gut and used her second of freedom to scream. At the same time and from just behind them, a furious, French-accented voice said, '*Merde alors!* What is this?'

Marcus dropped Caroline like a hot brick and whirled round to face a dark-haired fellow whose eyes, behind the black silk mask, threatened imminent violence. He opened his mouth but before he could get a word out, Caroline said breathlessly, 'Thank God!'

The Frenchman glanced her way and said curtly, 'He has hurt you?'

'No. Not really.'

'Not *really?*' The wild glare swung back to Marcus and its owner advanced slowly, step by step until the two men were barely a foot apart. 'You will answer for this, milord.'

'Answer for what? The lady is betrothed to me and --'

'No I'm damned well not!' shouted Caroline. And, to the highwayman, 'I'm not marrying him. I told him that – but now he seems to think he can force me.'

'Not,' said Claude Duvall, silkily, 'while I am here.'

'Look!' snapped Marcus. 'I don't know who the hell you are, but --'

'Clearly you do not. Otherwise you would not risk meeting me over a blade or a pistol. I am a master-swordsman and a deadly shot.'

Caroline knew a sudden insane desire to giggle.

Marcus also suspected a bluff but didn't feel inclined to call it. Drawing himself up ramrod straight, he said, 'I've no intention of meeting you at all, you interfering bastard.'

'Good,' said Claude cheerfully. 'Then we settle this now.' And, without any warning, he delivered a crashing blow to Lord Sheringham's jaw.

Marcus careened into the wall and narrowly avoided falling headlong down the stairs.

The highwayman flexed his knuckles, offered his arm to Caroline and bowed.

'Mademoiselle … allow me to restore you to your friends.' And, leaving Marcus clutching his jaw and staring after them with suddenly narrowed eyes, he led her back along the gallery.

She whispered, 'Thank you. I've no idea how you came to be there – but I was never so glad to see anyone in my life.'

'Are you quite sure he did not hurt you, *mignonne*?'

'Yes – though God alone knows what he had in mind.' Caroline suddenly realised that she was starting to shake rather badly. She said, 'Claude … I think I would like to sit down for a moment.'

'Of course. I saw an empty booth … yes. This one.' He drew her inside a box which, though littered with the debris of the evening and filled with the smell of recently extinguished candles, was blessedly deserted. Then, when she was seated, he said rapidly, 'I should not stay. Someone will surely be looking for you and if you are found with me, it will not go well for you.'

'I doubt,' she replied lightly, 'that anyone's even noticed I'm gone. But you're right. You shouldn't stay – but for your sake, not mine. In a minute or two, I'll be perfectly capable of making my way back alone.'

'I do not like this.' Dropping to one knee before her, he clasped both of her hands in his and placed a gentle kiss on each of them. Then, seeming to frown at her ruby ring which still adorned his little finger, 'I do not like leaving you, knowing that unpleasant fellow may try again to force you to wed him. I do not like the friends who take so little care of you. Where is your family? Have you no father or brother to protect you?'

'No. Just Mama and my sisters.'

'*Ce n'est pas bon.* Also, you have no affianced husband?'

She shook her head, wryly smiling. 'Nor likely to, I'm afraid.'

Claude relapsed into brooding thought.

'If this is so, I find it entirely inconceivable.'

'Do you? I can't imagine why.'

'And I cannot say. It would be to insult you.'

Caroline freed one of her hands to brush back the rich, brown hair with its hints of copper and bronze and wished she dared pull away the mask in order to see his whole face just one time.

'I'm used to being insulted, Claude. It happens nearly every day. So say it.'

He shook his head slightly and pressed his lips together. Then, on a ragged breath and as if the words exploded without permission, he said, '*I* would marry you.'

The chair on which she was sitting and the floor beneath it seemed to drop away and Caroline felt as if she was falling from a great height. She said feebly, 'What did you say?'

His head turned and he came hurriedly to his feet.

'There's no time. I hear voices. Tomorrow. The sunken garden in the Kensington Park at dusk. Can you do that?'

'Yes.'

'*Bon. À bientôt, chérie.*'

And kissing his hand to her as he made a brief bow, he was gone.

Caroline stayed where she was and waited for the world to stop spinning. From further along the gallery, she heard two voices. One belonged to Claude. The other, deeper, richer and with perfectly rounded aristocratic vowels was unmistakably that of the Earl of Sarre.

Oh God, oh God, oh God. Of all people, why did it have to be him?

Three booths further along was one whose only occupant was dead drunk and snoring. Adrian swiftly shed both domino and mask, dropped Caroline's ring into his pocket and freed the lace at his wrists which he'd tucked out of sight in case she recognised it. Finally, he reclaimed his powdered wig from its hiding place beneath a chair ... and, throughout all of it, he conducted a conversation with himself in two different voices.

Part of him was fizzing with sheer elation; the rest was still wondering what the hell had just happened and how come he'd lost control of the script. There was also the question of whether that immensely satisfying punch hadn't been a mistake. Up till then, he'd had Marcus fooled; after it, he wasn't so sure. But now wasn't the time to worry about what Marcus might suspect or what had come over Claude Duvall. *Now* was for completing the illusion.

Praying his wig was on straight and his whole appearance once more that of the ice-cool Earl of Sarre, he concluded his brief exchange with the highwayman and strode along to the box where he'd left Caroline.

Arriving in the curtained doorway and noticing that her expression was distinctly wary, he said abruptly, 'A French gentleman has just told me that you have been assaulted. Is it true?'

Not at all sure that she could rely on her voice, Caroline nodded.

'By whom? Sheringham?'

'Yes. You told me to be c-careful. I wasn't.'

'Are you hurt?'

His tone suggested he didn't care whether she was or not.

'No. He – he said he had a carriage outside. I think he meant to abduct me.' And quite suddenly the reality of what might have happened if Claude hadn't appeared struck her and she started to shiver. Hugging her domino around her, she said, 'Clau-- the French gentleman hit him.' She thought for a moment. 'Did you know he was here?'

Sarre pulled up a chair and sat down facing her. Caroline became aware that, at some point, he had discarded his domino and that, beneath the well-cut, dark-green coat, his vest was a riot of blue, green and silver. She stared at it, unable to reconcile its exuberance with the Earl's perpetual restraint.

'Sheringham? Yes. Perhaps I should have told you. But it didn't occur to me that he might attempt anything so drastic in a public place. That he did so, indicates desperation.'

'Do you think he may try again?'

'Possibly. Which means merely being careful may not be enough.'

Caroline's brain began to re-assemble itself. She said mordantly, 'What does that mean? That I should lock myself in my chamber for a week or two?'

'A somewhat extreme measure and not enormously practical,' he replied, as if it had been a serious suggestion. 'You can avoid empty ante-chambers, deserted corridors ... and private conversations such as the one we are currently having. You can put a notice in the *Morning Chronicle* stating that, contrary to popular rumour, there is no question of a marriage between yourself and Lord Sheringham – only, of course, you can't name either party openly.'

'I can't?'

Sarre shook his head. 'It's not done.'

'I don't suppose being forced to the altar is *done* either.'

'Not generally. No.' He leaned back in his chair, appearing to consider the matter. 'If it were anyone other than Sheringham, I'd suggest announcing your betrothal to someone else. But his lordship has been known not to let a mere betrothal stand in his way. And ... forgive my bluntness ... he needs your dowry very badly.'

'Yes. I've gathered that.' Caroline stood up and shook out her gaudy skirts. 'Thank you for your advice, my lord – and for giving me time to compose myself before facing the rest of our party. I appreciate it.'

Sarre also rose, a degree of calculation entering the normally expressionless face. He said, 'There is another option you might consider. Unfortunately, now is not the time to pursue it since we have both been absent quite long enough.' He held the curtain back for her to precede him. 'Do you ever walk in Hyde Park, Mistress Maitland?'

Her nerves jumped. 'Sometimes.'

He nodded. 'I ride there each morning before breakfast. If you wish to continue this conversation, I shall be on the Kensington side of the Longwater at eight o'clock and will wait for precisely ten minutes. Whether or not you come is entirely up to you. The only thing I must insist upon is that you do not come alone.'

The bubble of faint hysteria rising inside her at the thought of two secret assignations in one day almost caused her to say, *Why? Were you planning on abducting me?* But she stopped herself in time and said instead, 'I can't promise I'll be there. But I *do* thank you for offering to spare me some of your time.'

'Don't,' said the Earl. And under his breath, 'It's not exactly altruism.'

TWELVE

Caroline hardly slept. Though the encounter with Marcus Sheringham had left her shaken, it was thoughts of Claude Duvall that kept her awake. She spent some time wondering how it was he always seemed to know where he might find her and exactly when to make his presence known. But mostly she drifted on a little tide of joy that was caused simply by seeing him again and knowing that she would do so again tomorrow. Of the four unbelievable words he had spoken, she dared not think at all. It was too frightening.

She tried to imagine what Lord Sarre wanted to say to her but nothing sprang to mind. Surely he'd already laid out all the ways of keeping herself safe from Lord Sheringham, hadn't he? Meeting him privately hardly seemed necessary ... except that she was curious as to why the apparently cold-blooded Earl would offer his help.

The warmth of Claude's beautiful smile banished Sarre's tight-lipped control. Caroline sighed, knowing how foolish she was being. He was a highwayman; she'd only met him three times; and, for all she knew, he was as interested in her dowry as Lord Sheringham. Thinking that he might be as powerfully attracted to her as she was to him was downright nonsense and a sure road to letting herself be hurt. But if he were to turn those four amazing words into a question ... and if she truly thought he meant them ... she didn't know what she would do.

* * *

Adrian didn't sleep at all because he knew what was likely to happen if he did. Instead, he sat before the dying fire with a glass of brandy. When he'd first arrived home, he'd considered laying the tale of his evening before Bertrand but had decided against it. He *would* tell him everything, of course ... just not quite yet. Not until he'd had a chance to sift through it in his own mind and analyse, not only what he'd done, but why he'd done it.

He'd adopted the role of Claude Duvall because it offered both an easy disguise and the perfect way to find out what Caroline Maitland was really made of; to see what lay behind the social mask. Then again, what actor could resist the chance to play a romantic legend? The French highwayman who'd danced with the wives before robbing their husbands? Adrian hadn't even tried to resist it. Masquerading as Claude had been too great a temptation.

But now the highwayman had as good as asked Caroline to marry him. This had never been part of the plan. Adrian had no idea why he'd been foolish enough to let the words escape or where the notion had come from in the first place. And he *really* couldn't explain why the idea had suddenly seemed so perfect when, clearly, it wasn't.

Caroline had come to London bearing the carrot of a substantial dowry so she could marry well. Quite aside from having been dead for over a century, Duvall didn't qualify in the least – and any girl would have to be completely insane to throw herself away on a fellow she believed earned his living on the High Toby.

Ergo, Caroline couldn't possibly marry Claude Duvall.

Adrian frowned into his glass at the next and entirely logical progression.

Caroline couldn't marry Claude Duvall. She could, however, marry the Earl of Sarre.

The more he considered it, the more complete and poetically just it seemed. He intended to marry and didn't want to linger in London any longer than was necessary in order to accomplish it. Caroline had character, intelligence and, he suspected, a capacity for kindness and affection. A man could do a lot worse. And it would be a pleasure to get her out of those dreadful gowns and into something more flattering. Actually, remembering her response to a couple of rather enjoyable kisses, it would be no hardship to get her out of everything else as well. As for her money, that only mattered in one vital particular. He'd be damned before he let Marcus get his hands on it.

Adrian drained his glass and re-filled it. The passion he'd felt for Evie Mortimer had been all-consuming. Marcus – the man he'd thought was his closest friend – had known that. He'd known ... and yet had quite deliberately taken her from him. Not fairly, not openly and certainly not honourably. Then, within hours of Evie's death, he'd had been shouting the accusations of jealousy and murder that had forced Adrian into unwilling exile. Accusations that, even ten years on, had left mud clinging to his name. If there were any excuses for what Marcus had done, Adrian couldn't see them ... so it seemed appropriate that the favour should now be returned. And Caroline Maitland was the key to achieving it.

He wondered if she'd keep both of tomorrow's assignations. He was fairly confident she'd meet the highwayman but less sure she'd turn up for the Earl. Unfortunately, Sarre needed to make her an offer first and hope that she would accept it. Most people would think her answer a foregone conclusion. An Earl was an Earl, after all. Adrian, however, had a suspicion that Mistress Maitland was already half in love with Duvall ... whereas she didn't really like Sarre much at all. And if she did the unthinkable and accepted the highwayman, the immediate future was going to become distinctly complicated.

Only one thing was abundantly clear.

Bertrand was either going to laugh himself silly or ask if he'd completely lost his wits.

Adrian was beginning to wonder the same thing himself.

* * *

The early morning air was cold and crisp. Sarre allowed Argan one circuit of the park at a brisk trot – enough to keep him in a good humour but not enough to allow him to become over-heated – and then, on the stroke of eight, made his way to the Longwater.

He waited, reminding himself again why he was doing this but more than half-suspecting that Mistress Maitland was safely tucked up in her virginal bed. Then a cloaked and hooded figure detached itself from the nearby shrubbery and walked swiftly towards him. Sarre repressed an impulse to swear. Despite everything he'd said, the idiot girl had come alone.

Dropping from Argan's back and without giving her the chance to open her mouth, he said coldly, 'Why not simply trot off to Sheringham's house and have done with it?'

138

Caroline blinked. He actually sounded annoyed which, in a man whose emotions – assuming that he actually had some – were imprisoned in an icy tower, was tantamount to a full-blown tantrum. She said mildly, 'If I'd brought either the housemaid or one of my sisters, my Mama would have had chapter and verse within the hour. For obvious reasons, I wanted to avoid that.'

'Oh.' It hadn't occurred to him that she might not have a personal maid at all – let alone one whom she could trust. 'Then you'll accept my escort home.'

'You can accompany me to the end of the street and no further, my lord. But first – since I'm sure neither of us wants to be seen together at such an odd hour – you can tell me why I'm here.'

Sarre indicated a bench near the trees.

'Then let us sit and I'll be as brief as possible.'

He looped Argan's reins over a convenient branch and sat down beside her.

'Perhaps it would help if you understood Lord Sheringham's position more clearly. You will already be aware that, despite mortgaging most of his properties and selling a good many of his more valuable possessions, he is very deeply in debt. The reason for his sudden desperation now is a large debt of honour owing to a fashionable gaming-club which he has to pay within a month. If he fails to do this, he will find himself *persona non grata* throughout society and no gentleman's club in London will allow him through its doors. Marriage to you can spare him all that.'

'I see.' Caroline thought for a moment and then said, 'I thought such clubs were masters of discretion.'

'They are.'

'So how come you know of this debt?'

Sarre cast her a searching, sideways glance.

'How good are you at keeping secrets, Mistress Maitland?'

A sudden, extremely mischievous smile dawned, bringing the dimple with it.

'My lord, I'm beginning to think I'm quite excellent.'

'Good. Then I know of it because I'm part-owner of the establishment in question.'

Caroline turned her head and stared at him. 'Really?'

'Really. And please don't say *But you're an Earl!*'

'I wasn't going to. I was about to return to the point at issue. You're saying that Lord Sheringham is going to spend the next month trying to force my hand?'

'I think it quite likely.'

'And you don't wish him to succeed.' It was not a question.

'No. I don't.' His brows rose slightly and he added, 'Since it is your future which is at risk, I assume that you don't either.'

'No. But my reasons are clear enough. What are yours?'

'They are ... complex. Suffice it to say that the bad blood between Sheringham and myself is not of my making and neither is his financial predicament. But the first is hardly conducive to my wishing him well with the second.'

'No. I suppose not. Is there more?'

'There is ... but I'd rather not take up time with it now, if you don't mind. Like my horse, I imagine you're starting to feel the cold.' He stopped and added stiffly, 'Forgive me. That might have been better put.'

'Quite a lot b-better, I imagine,' replied Caroline, struggling not to laugh. 'So what *did* you want to say?'

Sarre cleared his throat and stared out at the Longwater.

'I told you that a betrothal announcement wasn't guaranteed to spare you Sheringham's attention. Marriage, on the other hand, would. If you wish it, I can make all the necessary arrangements by the end of today and we could be married tomorrow morning.'

An odd roaring seemed to be taking place in Caroline's ears. She said, 'I'm sorry. I think I must have misheard. Are you ... did you just ask me to marry you?'

'Yes.'

'But ... but that's ...' Words failed her.

'Insane? Not really. I need to marry – though not, I should point out, for money. I would, however, like to do it soon so that I can leave

London and set about caring for my estate and the people who live on it – that being the only reason I returned to England. Unfortunately, thanks to the stain on my reputation, my choice of a bride is likely to be limited as even the most open-minded of fathers will be reluctant to welcome an alleged murderer into the family.' Still without removing his gaze from the view in front of them, he added, 'I didn't do it, by the way – and will give you the full story if we are to marry, but otherwise not as I can't say I enjoy talking about it. As to the question of your suitability or mine … I'm financially solvent and I have a title. You have a great deal of character and are not at all stupid. I think we might deal agreeably together and I am willing to make whatever provisions for yourself and your family that you consider appropriate or desirable.' He stopped and at long last turned to look at her. 'I think that's everything.'

Still trying to grasp the magnitude of this torrent of words, Caroline simply stared at him. Finally she said weakly, 'You're proposing a marriage of convenience?'

'I suppose so. Yes. In the sense that it solves both of our problems.' Sarre seemed to suddenly appreciate what she was asking. 'But eventually I shall require an heir. Of course, I won't expect to share your bed until you feel ready for me to do so. But later … yes.'

'Oh. Well, I'm glad we've got that cleared up.'

The silvery gaze rested on her with a small degree of uncertainty.

'I'm sorry. I assumed you'd had as much romantic flummery from Sheringham as you'd ever wish to hear. I should have remembered that being hit with brutal honesty when one least expects it can be disconcerting.' He stood up and offered his hand. 'Naturally, you'll want time to consider. So now I suggest I escort you home before you freeze.'

She accepted his hand, then waited while he untethered his horse. For a time, they fell into step in silence until Caroline said abruptly, 'Will you tell me something, Lord Sarre?'

'If I can.'

'Have you ever been in love?'

Although he did not speak and his expression remained unchanged, she felt the air about them grow colder and colder still. She let the painful silence linger for as long as she could and then, just as she was about to withdraw the question and apologise, he said frigidly, 'Yes. Once. She died.'

* * *

Caroline slipped back into the house unseen by anyone but Rosie in the kitchen. Once inside her own room, she turned the key in the lock and sat down on the bed without even bothering to remove her cloak. She still couldn't believe what had just happened. Of all the unlikely occurrences in the world, the Earl of Sarre had asked her to be his Countess. It didn't seem possible. And her brain was still reeling from the enormity of it.

He'd offered her marriage with his characteristic lack of either warmth or emotion. And it was that, more than anything else, which told her he'd been honest. As far as it went, anyway. He didn't want her money. He just didn't want Lord Sheringham to have it either. As for the rest, he'd told her she might do whatever she wished to help Mama and the girls; he'd said she wasn't stupid and had character, and that he believed they might "deal agreeably together". He was offering a grander title than any she could have dared hope for and, it seemed, asking only for an heir in return. It was the kind of thing that happened in novels and Caroline told herself she should be dancing with joy. But she wasn't. Far from it, in fact.

She actually felt as though a lead weight had settled in her chest. She didn't dislike Sarre – though she suspected one could spend a lifetime trying to find a way through that chilly exterior only to find an equally chilly man within. She had never heard him laugh; indeed, she'd rarely seen him smile. But there was some kindness in him and that relentless honesty of his was a virtue of sorts. He was even rather good-looking, if one liked the stern, forbidding type. And of a certainty, he was no Lord Sheringham. In short, he was exactly the kind of husband Mama would have chosen and Grandpa had probably hoped for. And what *that* meant was that, unless she did the sensible thing and accepted him,

Mama must never, *ever* know he'd offered – or her life wouldn't be worth living.

She wanted to be sensible. She really did. And if Claude Duvall hadn't said those four words last night ... if he hadn't asked her to meet him in secret this evening ... she was quite certain that she'd have managed it. But he had. And, because she'd fallen in love with him one night at a moonlit roadside and wanted, more than she'd ever wanted anything, to know if he loved her in return, doing the right thing was monumentally difficult.

She suddenly had the oddest feeling that, no matter what she did, this would not end well for anyone. And that frightened her.

* * *

While he dressed for Claude Duvall's rendezvous in Kensington Gardens, Adrian reflected that the inflexible need to stay in character had its pitfalls. Caroline plainly thought Sarre was a cold fish and so Sarre's proposal had been about as tempting as an invitation to dive into the Thames. Equally, Duvall was a charming romantic of the type to sweep her, quite literally, off her feet. This, from Adrian's perspective, was decidedly awkward. Sarre could marry her in church in front of her family. Duvall couldn't. He'd have to run off with her. So it would obviously be best if the highwayman sacrificed his own happiness for the lady's good and retracted his impulsive near-proposal. That, thought Adrian, should do the trick – if only he didn't get carried away with his own performance.

Having donned the gold-braided red coat, shoved the black mask in his pocket and made sure he was wearing Caroline's ruby, Adrian avoided Bertrand's questions and set off for Kensington Gardens a little early in order to get there first.

The light was fading fast and the sunken garden was deserted. He put on the mask, replaced his hat and waited. Five minutes later, he saw a hooded and cloaked figure moving quickly across the grass towards him.

Curtain up.

She moved towards him, smiling and with outstretched hands. Duvall took them and raised each in turn to his lips. He said, 'You came. I feared you might not.'

She shook her head. 'I promised.'

He released her hands and stepped back, his expression troubled.

'Yes. But I was wrong to ask it of you.'

'I'm glad you did.' She wanted to ask him to remove his mask but realised he was wearing it out of a sensible regard for his own safety. 'Thank you for saving me last night. But for you, I might have been in a truly terrible situation by now.'

'He has not tried to come near you again?'

'No. And I'll take care that he doesn't have the chance.'

'Good. That will ... it will make me feel a little better knowing that.'

Caroline frowned slightly. He seemed different somehow; ill at ease and restless, as if something weighed heavily on his mind. She said, 'What's wrong?'

'Nothing.' Then, with an oddly helpless gesture, 'Everything.'

'I don't understand.'

'No. And that is for the best, I think.'

Nothing about this meeting was as she had expected it to be. The obvious conclusion was that he regretted what he'd said to her or perhaps had never meant to say it in the first place and was looking for a way out. If that was the case, she needed to make it easy for him. Anything else was likely to result in her humiliating herself.

Mentally straightening her spine, she said, 'Was there something in particular you wanted to say to me?'

'You know there was. Also, you must know that I cannot say it. I should never ... it was wrong of me to think it, even for a moment. I am a man of no honour.'

Caroline tried to decide if this was promising or not. Really, she supposed, it could be taken either way.

'I don't believe you have no honour. If I thought that, I wouldn't be here.'

He groaned. 'But you *shouldn't* be. This is what I am saying.'

'I understand that. But ... since I am?'

His face and voice became filled with regret and, for a moment, he seemed almost beyond speech. Then he said quietly, 'You are right. Since you have allowed me the very great privilege of this meeting, I must speak truthfully. But it is very hard for me, you understand. I do not at all want to say what I must.'

Caroline had noticed before that, at certain moments, his English noticeably deteriorated. That it should do so now didn't bode well. Folding her hands inside her cloak against a sudden feeling of chill, she said nothing and waited for the blow to fall.

Duvall drew a long breath and looked her squarely in the face.

'Of what is in my heart,' he said, 'I will not speak. It is too painful. But I cannot let you think I spoke idly or untruthfully last night. You should know that I would marry you if it were at all possible – but it is not. It is not and never can be and I was of an unbelievable wickedness to say what I did. I do not ask your forgiveness … but I am sorry.'

Her chill forgotten, a huge bubble of happiness welled up in Caroline's chest. He had meant it. He wanted her. He wanted *her* – Caroline Jane Maitland – and not because of money. She said softly, 'Why isn't it possible?'

He heard the note of wistfulness in her voice and wished he hadn't.

'I am not a gentleman. I am a thief. You know this.'

'I'm not really a lady,' came the candid reply. 'And … and perhaps you could stop being a thief?'

'I could, of course. But it does not change that I have been one. It does not change that I cannot give you the life you should have.' He sounded thoroughly miserable. 'That one little thing does not make everything right. Nothing can do that.'

'And if I said … if I told you that it didn't matter?'

Behind the mask of Claude Duvall, Adrian felt himself one step away from disaster and yet still couldn't help wondering if she was actually thinking of turning down an Earl in favour of probably the most wildly ineligible suitor in history. If she was, it meant two things; that she was almost certainly unique … and she was completely infatuated. And if the latter was true, there was no guarantee that – even if Duvall walked away in the next two minutes – she'd see sense and take Sarre instead.

Adrian considered his options, none of which were ideal. He could put an end to the entire situation by revealing his true identity; he could let her down lightly, as originally intended, and hope she'd recognise on which side her bread was buttered; or he could take the biggest gamble of all and play it to the end. If he told the truth now and she took it badly, the game was over – the same being true if he withheld a proposal and she didn't turn to Sarre. As for letting her think she was running off with the highwayman only to find herself marrying the Earl ... well, he imagined he could abandon any idea of cosy domesticity or getting her into bed for quite some time. If he'd tried something like that with Angelique, he'd have been fending her off with a chair.

And yet, even with the obvious drawbacks, every instinct was saying, *Roll the dice and see what comes of it. If you don't, you risk losing her completely.*

The mere fact that he was actually thinking this was too worrying to bear close scrutiny so he concentrated on the satisfying notion of giving Marcus Sheringham a taste of his own medicine and the fact that, once she got used to the idea, Caroline would probably like being a Countess. Then again, second-best though he undoubtedly was, Sarre was the closest she could get to what she *really* wanted. Though the Earl lacked the highwayman's easy charm, at least the two of them *looked* alike – something that, amazingly enough, she didn't appear to have noticed yet. And if it became absolutely necessary, he could always play Duvall in the bedroom.

His conscience, however, demanded that he make further efforts to render Claude less attractive. A slight smile curving his mouth, he said, 'It matters to me, *chérie*. And you should think for a moment. First, you know nothing about me. I have been many things – more than you can imagine. When you learn the truth about me, there is every likelihood you will be disappointed.'

'The same could be said of me,' argued Caroline. 'Isn't that a risk everyone takes?'

He shook his head. 'Not quite. For you, this risk is greater. I would be a very great villain if I did not make you understand this. For the rest, *if* I were to ask and *if* you accepted ... do you imagine your family would permit this? Will we wed in church after these English banns of yours have been called the three times? No. You deserve a beautiful wedding and this, with me, you cannot have. With me, it must be an elopement – which I think is not respectable. And afterwards? There would be no balls, no parties and, for who knows how long, no family for you.' He shook his head. 'You see what you would sacrifice? And truly, *mignonne*, I am not worth it.'

Caroline let his words sink in. The balls and parties and the beautiful wedding mattered not one whit. Even a temporary separation from her family was bearable because, though Mama would never forgive her, she rather thought Grandpa might feel differently – as long as he never found out about the highway robbery bit. But the elopement ... the mere thought of running away with her love in secret made her blood sing.

Her colour rose slightly and she said simply, 'You are worth it to me.'

'That is ... Caroline, I have no words.' In two strides his arms were round her, cradling her against his chest. 'You make me weak. What am I to do with you?'

'You could ask me the question you've been avoiding asking. Perhaps I'll say no.'

She felt his sudden quiver of laughter. 'Will you?'

'Will I what?'

'Will you say no?'

'You aren't playing fair,' she grumbled.

'True. This is something you should know about me.' He released her and stepped back. 'Well then, my Caroline. If you are sure ... if you are of a total and utter certainty ... will you do me the very great honour of becoming my wife?'

And lifting her face to him, incandescent with joy, she said, 'Yes, Claude. I will.'

He kissed her then. Claude did it because it was perfectly natural. Adrian did it because he thought it was the last chance he'd get for quite a while ... and because he wanted to know if her response was as sweet and intense as he remembered.

It was. Her arms slid around his neck and her fingers tangled in his hair as she melted into him. He found her combination of innocence and eagerness strangely seductive. But it also caused his conscience to smite him with the knowledge of his own deception. He knew that, in most respects, what he was doing was utterly wrong. He just hoped that, in time, those respects would be outweighed by the fact that his intentions were well-meaning and largely honourable. Having allowed the kiss to deepen a little further than was wise, he released her mouth and stepped back. Time to address the practicalities.

Brushing a strand of hair back from her face, he said, 'Listen now. There are many details to take care of and I will need a little time. All should be in readiness by the night after tomorrow, however. Do you have an engagement for that evening with the lady whose pearls I stole?'

'Yes. A rout, I think.'

'Then, some hours before, send a note saying you are unwell. I remember that her coach is plain with no crest upon the panels so I shall hire one similar and come for you in her place. Meanwhile, you should pack things you need and bring them here tomorrow at nine in the morning where a Frenchman named Bertrand Didier will be waiting to bring them to me. Is this possible?'

'Yes. I think so.'

'*Bon.* You will wish to leave a note for your family, of course. Tell them you are perfectly safe and will write again very soon.' He grinned suddenly. 'It might be best *not* to write that you are running away with the notorious Claude Duvall. It may give rise to anxiety.'

Caroline nodded. 'Will we have to travel to Scotland?'

'No. It is possible to obtain a licence permitting one to marry swiftly. This, I shall do.' The laughter faded and his eyes searched her face. 'Remember ... you do not have to do this, Caroline. If you change your mind – if you feel even a small doubt – hang something white from an upper window and I shall know not to trouble you further. Is this understood?'

'Understood – but unnecessary.' She would have liked to tell him that she loved him but held the words back. He hadn't yet said them to her; and, when he did, she wanted him to say them freely rather than because he felt obliged to do so. 'Is there anything else?'

'One thing.' Duvall removed her ruby from his own hand and slid in on to the third finger of her left one. 'I promised to return this and now seems the right time. Wear it as a token of my promise, *mignonne* … until I place another one beside it.'

THIRTEEN

'You belong in the mad-house,' said Bertrand flatly when he'd heard the entire story. 'It's the craziest and most asinine plan I ever heard. Why the hell didn't you just play the martyr and walk away?'

'I intended to – and I would have if she hadn't been completely besotted with Duvall.'

'What difference does that make? She'd have accepted the offer you made her as the Earl, wouldn't she? Christ, Adrian – what *else* was she going to do?'

'That's just the trouble. I don't know. Any female who'll take a highway robber in preference to a peer of the realm isn't exactly predictable. And Sheringham's desperate – which necessitates removing her from his orbit before he tries to abduct her again. Surely you can see that?'

'I can see a whole lot of *questions*. One of them is whether or not you actually *want* to marry the girl.'

Adrian shrugged and became suddenly intent on brushing fluff from his sleeve.

'I always intended to marry. We both know that. Caroline Maitland will suit me as well as any other – and better than most.'

Bertrand subjected him to a long, hard stare and thought, *Well now. That's interesting.*

He said abruptly, 'When she learns what you've done, she's going to hate you – and rightly so. You know that, don't you?'

'Of course I know it – but with roughly forty-eight hours in which to organise an elopement, I'm damned if I'm going to waste time worrying about that now. So are you going to help me or not?'

'It's enough that you're acting like a lunatic. You don't have to be an idiot, as well,' came the irritable reply. 'What do you want me to do?'

'Collect Caroline's baggage from her at nine tomorrow in Kensington Gardens and bring it here. By that time, I'll be back myself so you'll be able to take the horse. Then I want you to ride to Kent. I've a house on the coast near Sandwich. It's been empty for years save for a couple who act as caretakers. I need it setting in some sort of order as quickly as possible – not the whole house necessarily but the kitchen, main parlour and bedchambers. Hire as many hands as are required to get it done but don't keep them on afterwards – though we'll need a cook, of course, and possibly one maid. I'll leave that to you. Then, once everything is in train, come back. I'll need you here by seven o'clock on Monday evening at the latest.'

'The coast and back with a job in between? You don't want much, do you?'

'I know – and I'm sorry,' shrugged Adrian. 'But it can't be helped. And I've total faith in your capabilities.'

'Butter me up some more, why don't you? It's bound to make all the difference,' came the dry response. Then, 'And while I'm risking my neck flying *ventre à terre* about the countryside, what are *you* going to be doing?'

'I'll need to ride in the park early tomorrow so Caroline can refuse Sarre's offer. It's the only way she knows to reach him and I don't believe she'll leave without a word. Then --'

'Whoa!' Bertrand held up his hand. 'You've got to stop doing that.'

'Doing what?'

'Talking about the Earl as if he was a separate person. Sarre isn't *him* – he's *you*.'

'I know that.'

'It doesn't sound like it. It sounds as if you're not right in the head.'

'It's a convenience, for God's sake. With the current complications, if I used the first person all the time you'd never know who the hell I was talking about.'

Bertrand gave a snort that might have been laughter and said, 'All right. So you'll meet the girl – who is beginning to sound every bit as deranged as you are yourself – and then what?'

Adrian began ticking off tasks on his fingers.

'Procure a special licence, hire a coach – which, by the way, is why I need you back on Monday in order to drive it; write notes cancelling all

151

my engagements, call on Henry Lessing and see Aristide. And probably half a dozen other things I haven't thought of yet.' He leaned his head back against the chair and grinned. 'God alone knows what it's all going to cost. But there's immense comfort in the thought that, at the end of the day, it's going to cost Marcus Sheringham even more.'

* * *

On the following morning and precisely as Adrian had expected, Mistress Maitland waylaid the Earl of Sarre on his morning ride and politely declined his proposal of marriage. His lordship displayed all the appropriate signs of regret but was persuaded to take his defeat gracefully. Mistress Maitland then tripped off, presumably heaving a huge sigh of relief, to deliver her neatly-packed portmanteau to Monsieur Didier.

So far, so good, thought Adrian, riding home so Argan would be ready to carry Monsieur Didier to Kent. *Let's hope the rest of it goes as smoothly.*

He began by making application for a marriage licence and, when this was finally in his hand, turned his attention to hiring a plain, black travelling carriage and pair. This done, he visited Mr Lessing to ensure that all the requisite arrangements in the event of his forthcoming marriage were immediately set in hand. Mr Lessing primly congratulated him on his approaching nuptials ... and again, rather more warmly, when he learned the identity of the bride-to-be. Lord Sarre smiled, expressed his thanks and instructed the lawyer to wait for five days and then to put the appropriate notice in the newspaper.

Mr Lessing's brows rose.

'Five days, my lord? Why so long?'

'I'm merely erring on the side of caution,' returned the Earl pleasantly. 'In case there are any unforeseen delays.'

Once more back in Cork Street, Adrian settled down to write various notes which he had the footman deliver ... and another longer one, which he placed in his coat pocket for delivery later and in person. Then he sat down with a glass of wine and mentally examined his preparations. He had just two more calls left to pay, one of which couldn't be made until the next day. Tonight, however, he could

152

combine Aristide with a decent supper. He tossed back his remaining wine, made swift work of changing his clothes and set off for Sinclair's.

* * *

He revealed his intention to marry Caroline Maitland but withheld a few of the minor details – such as the fact that she thought he was a highwayman named Claude Duvall. Even so, in most particulars, Aristide's reaction mirrored Bertrand's.

'Doubtless you know your own business best – though tying yourself for life to a woman you've only met a handful of times sounds like a high price to pay to settle an old score.'

'An old score?' snapped Adrian. 'The man called me a murderer ten years ago and he's still doing it.'

'Not so old, then. And I suppose there's always the money.'

'It isn't about the money.'

'Of course it is,' came the impatient reply. 'You're marrying her so Sheringham can't. What else is it about, if not the money?'

'The girl herself. She doesn't deserve to be carried off and coerced into matrimony.'

The Frenchman's brows rose.

'Correct me if I'm wrong … but aren't you doing something pretty similar yourself?'

'No,' said Adrian uneasily. 'She's agreed to elope.' *Just not with me.* 'I suspect she thinks it's romantic.'

'God help her, then. And you, too.' He reached for the bottle and poured more wine. 'How long do you expect to be away?'

'It's difficult to say. A couple of weeks, perhaps.' A small square of pasteboard made its way across the table. 'If there's anything you think I should know or if you should need me urgently, that's where I'll be. I've told Henry to put a notice in the *Morning Chronicle* next Thursday, by which time I expect to married. Until then, you'd best be on your guard since there's a chance Sheringham may try something else against the club.'

'And after it?' asked Aristide.

'Oh … then he'll probably come after me instead.'

'Where's the point in that?'

'Probably so he can stick a knife in my back.'

* * *

With all his other arrangements securely in place, the next afternoon saw Lord Sarre dressing carefully for his final and trickiest meeting. He'd thought long and hard about the wisdom of this but had decided that, if all went as he hoped, the rewards outweighed the risks.

He was admitted without demur to the house in Albemarle Street by a butler who, in the absence of a footman, laid his lordship's hat, gloves and cloak aside before walking sedately to parlour and announcing him.

'The Earl of Sarre, my lady.'

Lily Brassington looked up from the letter she had been writing and stared across the room, plainly disconcerted. Then, rising, she said, 'Thank you, Soames. I will ring when I need you.'

'Very good, my lady.'

The butler bowed and withdrew. Sarre suspected he'd gone no further than the other side of the door. Meanwhile, her ladyship said coolly, 'My lord. I don't believe we have ever been introduced. Unless my memory is at fault?'

'It isn't. And your ladyship is quite right. It is atrociously ill-mannered of me to call without any prior acquaintance. But I'm hoping that, if you'll hear my reasons, you will understand why I came.'

She took a long, thoughtful look at him, noting the mask-like absence of expression, the hard lines of cheek and jaw and the exquisite tailoring. And, while she looked, she reviewed what she'd heard about him – none of which inclined her in his favour. Had she known that her steady regard was making the Earl want to fidget, she might have liked him a little better.

Finally she said, 'Very well, my lord. What is it you want?'

'I want your help – though not so much for myself, you understand.'

'Then for whom?'

'A young lady I believe you already hold in some affection. Mistress Maitland.'

Lily drew herself up very straight and her eyes shot daggers at him.

'And what, exactly, have *you* to do with Caroline?'

154

'Not what you may be thinking,' he said mildly. And with a slight, sweeping gesture of one hand, 'It's ... complicated.'

'Simplify it.'

Sarre began to admire Lady Brassington, not least because she hadn't bothered to offer him a seat or insisted on ringing for tea.

'I'll do my best. Two nights ago at the Pantheon, Marcus Sheringham attempted to abduct Mistress Maitland --'

'*He did what?*'

'He tried to abduct her in order to force her to the altar,' said Sarre composedly. 'Since you were in her company last evening, you will realise that he failed. Obviously she didn't mention any of this to you.'

Shock temporarily deprived her ladyship of speech. Then, 'Not a word. Are you *sure?*'

'Perfectly. Lord Sheringham's plan was foiled by a certain French highwayman, after which --'

'*A highwayman?* How --? No. Never mind. Just go on.'

'It was after the Frenchman spoiled his lordship's game that I entered the picture. I warned Mistress Maitland that Sheringham is now desperate enough to try again. I also offered her a way to make any further such attempt impossible.'

'How, exactly?'

'I asked her to marry me and assured her – truthfully, as it happens – that my reasons for doing so were not the same as Sheringham's.' His smile was faint and fleeting. 'She refused.'

By now her ladyship was staring at him with a sort of bemused fascination.

'Did ... did she say why?'

'She didn't. But then, she didn't have to. I already knew.' He paused. 'She refused me because she's in love with the highwayman.'

'*What?*'

'Quite. But for certain mitigating factors, my *amour propre* would have been quite destroyed – but that is of small importance in the overall scheme of things. Later today, you will receive a note from Caroline crying off from this evening's engagement. And at some point tonight, she and the fellow calling himself Claude Duvall will elope.'

Lady Brassington sat down very suddenly on the nearest chair.

'*Claude Duvall?* But he's dead. This is ridiculous. What on earth can she be thinking? And how do *you* know all this?'

'Well, that's where it becomes complicated.' Sarre withdrew something from his pocket and crossed the room to let it slide slowly into her lap. 'I daresay you'll recognise these.'

'My pearls.' She ran them through her fingers several times and then frowned up at him. 'I don't understand. How did you get them?'

Several seconds ticked by in silence. Then, with a rueful and very Gallic shrug, he said, 'I stole them. From you.'

She shook her head, frowning.

'No. That's not possible. You couldn't have --' And then she stopped, as the truth behind what he was saying finally hit her. 'You? *You* were the highwayman?'

He made a flamboyant bow. '*Claude Duvall, Madame. Et tout à votre service.*'

'Oh my God.' She continued to look at him as if she expected him to transform on the spot while the pieces slotted together inside her head. 'But that means ... that means Caroline's eloping with *you*. Except ... except that she isn't.'

'Yes. I did say it was complicated.'

'*Complicated?* It's a Chinese puzzle,' snapped her ladyship. 'What the devil did you think you were playing at? And for God's sake, sit down before I get a permanent crick in my neck.'

Sarre did so and said slowly, 'I could try to explain everything from the beginning. But perhaps you would rather know why I'm telling you all this.'

'I'm not naïve, sir. I *know* the answer to that. You want someone on your side when the world accuses you of ruining Caroline in order to force her into marriage for the sake of her dowry.'

'No. The world has been saying far worse of me for years. I'm used to it. What I want is to ensure that, when this is all done, Caroline's reputation doesn't suffer by it and I hoped you could help with that.'

'It's possible.' She eyed him narrowly. 'There are two things, however. Firstly, you can assure me that she'll return to society as the Countess of Sarre?'

'Yes.'

'And the unpleasant gossip one hears about you?'

'Is untrue. But denials mean little against such interestingly scandalous accusations.' He paused and added impassively, 'The truth would make an even juicier story. But the only person who could tell it is myself … and I won't.'

Lady Brassington continued to consider him for a moment. Then, nodding decisively and without troubling to pull the bell, she called, 'Soames?'

The butler appeared immediately.

Her ladyship said crisply, 'Soames – you will forget everything you have just heard.'

He bowed. 'Naturally, my lady. Does your ladyship require anything else?'

'Yes. Bring the best brandy. And *you*, my lord, can start again at the beginning and explain everything … including the story of my pearls.'

* * *

Bertrand arrived in Cork Street at a little after four o'clock, looking frayed at the edges.

Adrian said, 'Any problems?'

'Unless you count the fact that I'm tired, hungry and about to set off for bloody Kent again in the next few hours – no.'

'Well, at least you won't be riding this time.'

'Some comfort that is. It's damned cold out there.' He threw his hat and cloak on to a chair. 'I left Argan stabled at The Ship in Faversham, by the way, and rode the rest of the way on a hired nag. You'll be able to pick him up *en route*.'

'Good.' Adrian nodded. 'And the house?'

'Should be cosy enough by the time we get there. Your caretaking couple have kept it in reasonable shape. Mrs Clayton's prepared to cook for you and she's hired a maid.' He shot a sideways look. 'Not the easiest place to find, is it? Remote, too. Is that why you bought it?'

'I didn't buy it. I inherited it. The only thing I *did* inherit, actually – and that purely because, for some God knows what reason, it was entailed.' He handed Bertrand a glass of Burgundy and said, 'Drink that. Get warm, have something to eat and put your feet up for a couple of hours. I've packed a bag for myself and will see to the carriage and anything else that needs to be done. We collect the bride-to-be at eight.'

'Can't wait,' muttered Bertrand. And, with a sly grin, 'Bet she can't either.'

* * *

In fact, despite everything having gone surprisingly smoothly, Caroline's nerves were stretched as tight as violin strings. Lord Sarre had received her refusal with grace and a hint of mingled regret and concern. She'd delivered the one bag she'd permitted herself to the wiry, sandy-haired fellow who spoke truly awful English. She'd sent her apologies to Lady B and received a sympathetic note in return. And she'd written a letter to Mama and her sisters meticulously designed to reassure them. Following Claude's plan had kept her occupied. Once it was done, however, her insides shivered with excitement and nameless anxiety.

The trouble with making it appear that she was attending the usual sort of social event with Lady Brassington meant that she had to dress for that instead of being able to wear something suitable for travelling. Repressing a sigh, she chose the least dreadful of her evening gowns – a vivid pink shot silk from which nearly all of the silver-floss trimming had been removed – and laid out a gun-metal grey velvet cloak, lined with fine wool. Lavinia eyed the latter questioningly but made no remark. Sylvia, whose abilities as a coiffeuse had improved dramatically over the last few weeks, drew her hair smoothly back from her face and allowed only three long curls to fall to one shoulder. And suddenly it was time to go.

Caroline managed to leave Mama's letter in her room by dint of running back on the excuse of having forgotten her fan. Then a lump rose in her throat along with the realisation that, much as she wanted to hug her sisters and say goodbye, she couldn't do it. So she smiled and waved her hand just as she did every evening … and left her old life behind.

Claude's servant dropped down from the box to hand her into the carriage. Of Claude himself there was no sign – presumably a precaution in the event that anyone was looking through the window. Although she understood this, Caroline wished he was there beside her. Perhaps then she might not feel quite so sick.

Bertrand set the coach in motion. Behind it, sleek and swift as a cat, a dark figure moved back to the house and laid something white under a stone in the shallow portal. Then the same figure ran down the street in the direction the coach had taken, to the place where a brown mare stood waiting.

Bertrand pulled the coach to a halt and waited. Claude Duvall, no longer masked but with a peculiar hat pulled low over his eyes, opened the door and grasped Caroline's cold hands. She said shakily, 'You're here. I thought … for a moment I wasn't sure …'

'Foolish Caroline,' he reproved, his voice warm and caressing. 'Of course I am here. How could you doubt it? But there is no time to linger. We must be away.'

'Yes. I know. But aren't you going to travel inside the carriage with me?'

'Sadly, no. Bertrand drives, as you have seen. And I will need the horse – so of a necessity, I must ride him.' He gave her fingers a comforting squeeze and said, 'We are going to Kent – a journey of some hours, I fear – but will pause for a short time half-way. Until then, *ma belle*, you should try to sleep.'

And with that, the door slammed shut and he was gone.

Sleep? thought Caroline a shade wildly. *I'm running away to be married. How on earth does he expect me to sleep?*

Oddly enough, however, she did fall into a brief, uneasy doze so that the next thing she knew was when the coach drew to a halt in the stable-yard of an inn. Bertrand jumped down and set about arranging a change of horses. Several minutes later, Claude appeared in the doorway of the carriage with a mug of chocolate in one hand and a hot brick in the other. Handing her the first and busying himself placing the second beneath her frozen toes, he said, 'This is Faversham. It will be perhaps two hours more from here. If you wish to enter the inn and use the ... the facilities, I will find a maidservant.'

Caroline felt herself flush. He was asking if she needed to relieve herself. She said hurriedly, 'No. Thank you. I shall be fine.'

'*Bon*. Drink the *chocolat*. It will warm you. We will be off again in a short while.'

While she sipped the chocolate, she heard him conversing with Bertrand in rapid and presumably, since she couldn't understand any of it, idiomatic French.

Adrian said, 'Once Canterbury is well behind us, I'll ride on ahead. When you arrive, bring *mademoiselle* directly into the house. I'll see that the maid is waiting to take her upstairs so that she can refresh herself.'

'Make sure the girl understands that, for now, you're Monsieur Duvall not Monseigneur.'

'I am aware.'

'And where will *you* be while all this is happening?'

'Waiting.'

'Going to face the music tonight, are you?'

'Yes. Putting it off isn't likely to make it any better.'

'Suppose not.' Bertrand thought for a moment and then said helpfully, 'There's a lot of nasty sharp ornaments in that parlour – along with a good set of fire-irons. I'd put them out of harm's way, if I was you.'

'Thank you,' said Adrian dryly. 'I'll bear it in mind.'

Bertrand laughed.

Caroline handed her empty mug through the window to a passing stable-hand and watched Claude swing himself into the saddle of a grey horse that, even in the fitful light, looked vaguely familiar. She puzzled over this for a moment or two then forgot about it as the coach started moving again.

Aside from the occasional village, the road outside was black as pitch. After an hour or more, the coach rumbled through a large town which she guessed might be Canterbury and then passed into more darkness.

Time started to drag and Caroline's muscles began to protest at the hours of bumpy confinement. As best she could assess, the time had to be somewhere around midnight. Surely to God they must be nearly there?

They rattled through another small town after which the road disintegrated into a rutted track, causing Caroline to clutch at the strap in order to prevent being jolted to the floor. And then, just when she had given up expecting it, the coach drew to a halt. She peered out of the window and saw a house. It was quite large and clearly old, built of narrow bricks and furnished with tall chimneys. She wondered who owned it. Then, as Bertrand opened the door and let down the steps to help her out, she caught the unmistakable tang of the sea. She even thought that she could hear it which meant it must be very close.

Where on earth are *we? Can Claude be thinking of going to France?*

Bertrand, however, led her briskly up to the arched oak door and, without a word, handed her into the keeping of a maid who curtsied and said, 'I'm Sally, Miss. If you'll follow me, the master said you'd likely want a moment to refresh yourself after the journey.'

Caroline had expected to find Claude waiting to greet her. The fact that he wasn't made her uneasy. Reluctantly following the maid up the stairs, she said, 'Is Monsieur Duvall here?'

'Oh yes, Miss. Don't you fret about that.' The girl's voice quivered oddly. 'He'll be waiting in the best parlour when you're ready.' She opened the door of a pleasant, if shabbily-furnished bedchamber. 'Here we are. There's hot water in the jug and here's Mr Didier with your things.' She waited while Bertrand set the portmanteau at the foot of the bed. 'I'll unpack so you'll be able to change your gown – and I can tidy your hair, if you like'

Caroline didn't want to change her gown. She wanted to run and find Claude because something didn't feel right. But the pink silk was horribly crushed, her hair was escaping its pins and she felt distinctly grubby. Sighing, she gave herself over Sally's ministrations. And thirty seemingly endless minutes later, she was clean, tidy and had exchanged the ball-gown for an afternoon dress of poppy-red damask.

'I'll show you down to the parlour, shall I, Miss?' asked the girl. 'There'll be a bite of supper waiting, I reckon.'

'Thank you.'

Caroline managed a tense smile. She told herself to relax. Eloping was bound to be a little nerve-racking, after all and the moment she saw Claude everything would be all right again. She followed Sally back down the wide oak stairs and across the slate floor of the hall. The house was very quiet with no sign of other servants but the parts she had seen so far looked clean and well-tended. Then the maid tapped on the door, opened it so Caroline could step through and closed it quietly behind her.

He was standing in the shadows at the far side of the fireplace, so the first thing she noticed was the severe elegance of his clothes. A dark coat, beautifully-fitting but under-stated to the point of plainness. The second thing was the absence of a mask; and the third, his hair ... a thick, rich brown lit with shades of cinnamon and copper and bronze.

She said, 'Claude?' And hated how uncertain her voice sounded.

Turning, he moved unhurriedly out into the merciless light of two strategically-placed branches of candles. Slowly ... much more slowly than seemed reasonable ... she became aware of an exotic scarlet and gold vest; of the dramatic slash of cheekbones, previously always concealed by a mask; of the fact that he wasn't smiling and that his mouth appeared to be set in a rather grim line. And finally, she saw silver-grey eyes, fringed by long sable lashes.

Her stomach lurched and she grabbed blindly at a chair-back to steady herself. There must be some mistake. This couldn't be happening. She whispered, 'You aren't Claude.'

There was a long, very frightening silence during which he neither moved nor spoke.

Then, 'No,' replied the Earl of Sarre, a distant note of apology filtering through his impenetrable composure. 'I'm afraid I'm not.'

FOURTEEN

This time the silence was positively deafening. Sarre stood very still, watching Caroline closely and, when she swayed slightly, he was across the room in three strides ready to catch her if she fainted.

She didn't. She rammed the heels of both hands into his chest and, in a voice of mingled tears and rage, said, 'Where is he? What have you done to him?'

'Nothing.' *She hadn't understood yet. Of course she hadn't. How could she?* Stepping back, he said, 'Perhaps you should sit down.'

'No! Do you think I'm spending one more minute in this house? How *dare* you carry me off in this way?'

'It isn't quite as it seems. If you'll just listen for --'

'I'm not listening to *you*. You're no better than Lord Sheringham!'

Sarre winced inwardly. 'I --'

'*Where is Claude?*' The terrible seething in her chest was threatening to choke her. 'He – he was there when we stopped to change horses but I didn't see him after that. What have you done? Oh God. If you've hurt him ...' She stopped, trying to breathe. 'Tell me where he *is!*'

'I'm trying.' He let his voice sharpen into command. 'Sit down and listen.'

Caroline sank bonelessly into the chair. 'Well?'

'The man you know is not Claude Duvall.'

'Of course he is!'

'No. Claude Duvall went to the scaffold over a century ago. Your highwayman merely ... borrowed his name for a time.'

'Why should I believe that?' A small kernel of doubt started to grow amidst all her other emotions. 'What difference does it make, anyway?'

'Since Duvall doesn't actually exist, quite a lot.' Sarre paused and decided that the sooner this was over the better. 'I take it that you want to see him?'

'Of *course* I want to see him! What do you think I've been saying?'

'*Eh bien.*' With a smile, he slid smoothly into character. His posture, his accent, the timbre of his voice, his entire manner ... everything changed. 'Caroline, *chérie* ... I am so sorry. Never did I mean to cause this distress. I am, as you see, quite unharmed.' And, with the merest suggestion of a shrug, 'But – just as I tried to warn you – a disappointment, I think.'

Caroline stared at him, her eyes were huge and the blood drained slowly from her skin. She wanted to say that this wasn't possible ... but she couldn't. She couldn't say anything at all. She wanted to be sick.

In front of her, Claude Duvall vanished as easily as he had appeared, leaving only the Earl of Sarre who, with apparently unruffled composure, turned away to pour a glass of wine and set it on the table beside her.

He said, 'I can only apologise. It was never meant to go this far.'

Caroline wet her lips and tried, again, to find her voice. She said unevenly, 'It was you. All the time ... it was you.'

'Yes.'

'*Why?*' The word cracked in the middle.

'Not, as I said, to bring us both to this. For the rest, does it matter?'

Something inside her chest seemed to be breaking into pieces and her brain was sluggish with shock. 'Who *are* you?'

Good question. One I've frequently asked myself.

'Altogether?' he asked dryly. 'Well, then ... Francis Adrian Sinclair Devereux, seventh Earl of Sarre. Also, until recently, a player known to Paris as L'Inconnu. There have been other similarly defunct incarnations which need not concern you.' He waited and then said gently, 'Drink some wine. It will help.'

For a moment, she looked at the glass as if she didn't know what it was and when she finally reached out for it, she discovered that she was shaking so badly she needed both hands to steady it. Then she drained half the wine at one swallow and said tonelessly, 'I don't understand how ... how anyone could play such a cruel trick. Why anyone would want to. You are either evil or insane.'

'As it happens, I'm neither. Though I can see why you might think so.'

'How generous of you! But now you've lured me here under false pretences, what do you intend to do with me?'

'Nothing at all terrible, I assure you.'

Caroline pushed aside everything except the need to think.

'But I can't be assured of anything, can I? Everything you've ever done or said has been a lie. Everything – both as yourself and as C-Claude. So how am I supposed to believe a single word that comes out of your mouth?'

'Just at present, I understand that you can't. But in time, when --'

'Not,' she snapped, 'in a *lifetime*. I don't know who you are. And since you appear to be able to be anyone you want, I never will. So I'll ask you again. What are you planning to do with me?'

It was going no better than he had expected and, short of a miracle, he didn't know how to improve it. Sighing, he said, 'I am hoping that you will marry me.'

Her laughter was sudden and harsh, almost but not quite hiding the fact that she wanted to put her face in her hands and howl.

'Of course. The money *again*. Well, you can forget that, my lord. I wouldn't marry you if you were the last man on earth. God! Marcus Sheringham's a liar, too – but at least I knew he was doing it. I'd be as well off with him as with you, it seems.'

'No.' His voice was tight. 'You wouldn't.'

'Really? I suppose you're going to tell me that while you were acting the role of Claude Duvall you accidentally fell in love with me?'

'I'm going to tell you that the proposal of marriage I made to you on Friday morning was completely sincere and true in every particular. I don't need your dowry. I honestly believe we can be as happy as most other couples. I --'

'Yes. I remember what you said. I also remember telling you that I didn't want to marry you.'

'No,' he agreed blandly. '*You* wanted to marry a man who doesn't exist.'

'And whose fault is that?'

'Mine – though I neither intended nor expected it.'

'So why did you propose to me?'

165

'As myself? For the reasons I gave you at the time. As Duvall? Because you were so clearly infatuated with him that I couldn't be sure you'd recover your senses sufficiently to accept my own offer if he walked away. And unless you were happy to risk being abducted by Lord Sheringham --'

'To prevent which, you've abducted me yourself? Yes. Forgive me if I say I don't find that an improvement.' Hoping her knees didn't let her down, Caroline set the wine-glass aside and stood up, needing to get away before she started to cry. 'I don't see the point in continuing this conversation. Since it's the middle of the night and you've allotted me a bedchamber, I'm going to retire. But first thing tomorrow, I shall expect you to make arrangements to convey me back to London.'

Aware that he was unlikely to make any useful progress while she was still so angry and hurt, Sarre chose not to argue. He said carefully, 'I am truly sorry to have upset you and I'll do my best to make matters right. But, for now, try to get some rest.'

She looked at him as if he was a complete imbecile. Then, without a word, she walked out, letting the door slam behind her.

Adrian let out a long, exhausted breath. His stomach was in knots and every bone in his body ached. Some of this, he knew, was to do with the four-hour ride from Town ... but most of it wasn't. He wondered how much chance there was that tomorrow would be any better and came to the depressing conclusion that there was very little. Even if Caroline got over the worst of her shock, the news that her good-name wouldn't withstand returning to London unwed wasn't likely to be well-received. He'd thought he had known how bad the moment of confession would be. He realised now that he'd had no damned idea.

Bertrand walked into the room, took one look at him and said, 'It went well, then.'

'Brilliantly. In a nutshell, I'm a bigger liar than Sheringham, she wouldn't marry me if I was the last man on earth and she's going back to Town tomorrow.'

'Ah. She hates you. I told you she would.'

166

'She hasn't actually said that yet ... but I daresay she'll get round to it tomorrow.'

'When you tell her she's not going anywhere, you mean?'

'Probably. And a few more times after that.'

'Grovel,' advised Bertrand, reaching for the wine bottle and glasses. 'Women like that.'

'Earls don't,' retorted Adrian. 'They start as they mean to go on.'

'I'd have thought that, by now, you'd be sick of digging pits for yourself.'

'Christ. You have no idea.'

* * *

Caroline, meanwhile, locked her door, threw herself fully-dressed upon the bed and gave way to helpless, agonising sobs. She cried for Claude, who had never really existed; for herself – poor, stupid Caroline who'd thought a man like that could actually love her and given her own heart away without a second's hesitation; and she cried for the irretrievable mess she'd made of her life and the damage it was going to do to her sisters.

As for the Earl, she was still finding it almost impossible to believe what he'd done or that he'd managed to fool her so thoroughly. But of one thing she was perfectly certain. After deliberately practising such a wicked deception, she'd bleed to death rather than give him what he wanted. And if he tried to lay a hand on her, she'd very probably kill him.

She awoke, groggy and disorientated, to the sound of someone tapping on the door. Her gown was twisted around her legs, her hair was falling down her back and her eyelids felt as if they had been glued together.

'Go away,' she muttered, shoving her head under the pillow.

The tapping grew louder and a voice said, 'Miss? Miss! Are you all right?'

No. But why should you care?

'Go away!'

'I've brought the hot water, Miss. And some tea. If you'll just unlock the door?'

167

Caroline groaned and heaved herself upright. She supposed the day had to be faced sooner or later. Feeling as if she'd aged ten years overnight, she hauled herself off the bed and over to the door.

The maid took one look and narrowly avoided dropping her tray. 'Oh Miss! Whatever's happened?'

'Never mind.' She went to the window, pulled back the curtains and found herself gazing across a narrow sand and shingle beach to miles and miles of empty grey ocean. 'Sally ... where in God's name *are* we?'

'Sandwich, Miss – well, nearly. The town's a mile or so along the coast and inland a bit.'

Caroline shut her eyes and then opened them again. If one were searching for the bleakest most deserted spot one could find, this should surely qualify. Turning her back on it, she said, 'Where is he?'

Sally opened her mouth to answer and then thought better of it. 'Who?'

'Don't play games. We're done with that. Lord lying, cheating devious Sarre,' said Caroline between her teeth. 'Where is he?'

'I think ... w-waiting for you to join him at breakfast, Miss.'

'Is he? Good. Let him wait.' She paused, considering demanding a bath and then decided that putting a safe distance between herself and that clever, manipulating devil downstairs was more important. 'Help me out of this gown and then press it, please. I'll need to wear it again today. I can manage everything else by myself. And don't argue with me Sally.' This as the maid would have spoken. 'In case you haven't noticed, I'm not in the mood to be either tactful or polite.'

It was over an hour before Caroline entered the room where Sarre lounged at the breakfast table. Rising, he said, 'Good morning. I hope you didn't hurry on my account?'

'I wouldn't cross the street on your account.' She stopped and then, tilting her head, said with lethal sweetness, 'I'm sorry. I'm not sure how to address you. Who are you this morning?'

And Adrian, who had slept hardly at all and was in a mood every bit as precarious as her own, stepped completely out of character and drawled, 'Anyone you like, darling. If you want a manly shoulder to weep upon, I daresay I can summon up Claude for you.'

Before she'd even recognised the intention, Caroline slapped him so hard across the face that his head jerked back. She froze, half-aghast at herself and half-afraid of what he might do.

In fact, he did nothing though, for a long, unpleasant moment, something dark awoke in the silvery gaze. Then he said coolly, 'You were entitled to that, I suppose. But from this point on, it would be helpful if we could approach the situation in a more civilised manner.'

'*Civilised?* There's nothing remotely civilised about any of this!'

'Perhaps not. But I find that retaining at least the *veneer* of good manners usually helps.' And, gesturing to the table, 'Coffee?'

'Yes.' It came out as a croak. She cleared her throat and added a mumbled, 'Thank you.'

Sarre nodded and pulled out a chair. Then, when she was seated, he filled a cup for her and said, 'May I get you something to eat?'

Caroline shook her head. Swallowing the coffee was going to be difficult enough. A glance at the barely-touched plate on the other side of the table suggested he hadn't had much of an appetite either. She added milk to her cup and concentrated on stirring it round and round while she waited for him to speak.

He took his time ... partly because he couldn't decide where to start, partly because he had only the flimsiest grip on Sarre's habitual icy control and partly because it was painfully clear that she'd spent half the night crying. He tried telling himself that she probably felt better for it; then was forced to recognise that, if she did, it didn't show. She looked perfectly wretched. This time he told himself, very firmly, that she'd get over it. He considered apologising again but suspected it would be no more successful than it had been last night; and there was a limit to how many times one might say one was sorry without sounding witless. But somehow he had to salvage something from the wreckage, so perhaps conciliation was the key.

He said, 'I am only too aware that I am at fault in this. But we have to deal with it.'

'No. We don't. I'm not spending a single second more than I have to with you. Truthfully, I can scarcely bear to look at you. So summon the carriage and let me go home.'

'It isn't that simple.'

'I don't see why not. You created a myth and I was taken in by it. You did something unbelievably cruel and I – I was unbelievably stupid. So the best thing now is for us to go our separate ways.'

Sooner or later he was going to have to explain why that wasn't possible but he didn't feel ready to do it quite yet so he said, 'Would you mind if we digressed for a moment? I'd like to ask you something.'

She glanced up at him warily. 'What?'

'I wondered what you hoped for out of marriage. Not to me specifically – but in general.'

'Why on earth would you want to know that? I don't see the point.'

'Humour me. Please.'

She made a small sound of impatience and then thought about it for so long he began to think she wasn't going to answer. But finally she said prosaically, 'I never expected to marry for love. Women like me rarely do. But mutual respect and affection ought to be possible ... I would have wanted those.'

'Anything else?'

'My mother has very little income so I hoped to augment it from my dowry. And I'd like to do something for my half-sisters. They're good-hearted and much prettier than I ... so I think they could find suitable husbands if they were given the chance.' She stopped, coloured a little and added, 'And children. I'd like children to love.'

Adrian's throat tightened but he nodded and, without any particular emphasis, said, 'I offered you all those things myself. I *still* offer them.'

She went back to stirring her coffee. 'No.'

'Is marriage to me so impossible to contemplate?'

His tone was as level and impersonal as ever. Fleetingly, Caroline wondered what it would take to raise any sign of real feeling in this man. He was the most emotionless individual she'd ever met. He hadn't even been angry when she'd hit him.

'Now? After what you've done? Do you really need to ask?'

'I suppose not. But before that?'

'You mean before I learned that you've been deceiving me for weeks? I suppose I might have considered it then. You don't have an ounce of warmth in you but at least you seemed honest – which of course was just another lie. You're not honest at all. You made a complete fool of me with your play-acting – which means you could do it again at any time. And you're so very good at it, I'd never know, would I? In fact, for all I know to the contrary, you could be acting right now.'

'I could be,' he agreed mildly. 'But I'm not.'

'How am I supposed to know that?' she snapped. 'I can't trust you. I'll *never* be able to trust you.'

Aware of being neatly boxed in a corner, he thought carefully about what to say next.

'Can you at least accept that I didn't masquerade as Duvall out of any malicious intent?'

'I might – if I had the remotest idea why you *did* do it.'

Sarre leaned back in his chair and eyed her reflectively. He found it interesting that – even knowing that he'd been an actor and was part-owner of a gambling club – she was still seeing the Earl. That frigidly unemotional fellow who'd proposed marriage as if it was a business merger. He probably ought to make that last. If she got the idea that there was a whole other person lurking beneath, she really would think him a candidate for Bedlam. He suspected that there were days when, despite having known him for years, Bertrand thought the same thing.

'I'd be lying if I pretended it wasn't partly because I could and because I enjoyed it,' he said coolly. 'But I began it for what I thought was a very good reason.'

'Which was?'

'I knew Marcus Sheringham was planning to marry your money. In all fairness, I hadn't originally intended to interfere. But when he proved to be no less vicious and spiteful than he was ten years ago, I changed my mind – as much on your account as on my own. So I decided I needed to know who you were.'

Caroline's brows rose and she said dismissively, 'You could have discovered that in any ballroom.'

'No. I couldn't. Everyone puts a social mask on at such affairs and I'd already seen yours. What I *wanted* to see was the person behind it. And I did.' His mouth curled a little. 'If it's any consolation, had I not done so I would never have offered you marriage. It would be nice, therefore, if you could accept that my offer was an honest one.'

'I doubt very much if it matters to you whether I do or not,' she shrugged. 'I just want to go home and forget all this happened.'

And that, of course, brought them neatly back to where they'd started.

Sarre repressed a sigh and prepared to conjure up a storm.

'I'm afraid that isn't an option.'

Caroline finally abandoned her coffee and pushed the cup aside. Then, impaling his lordship on a fiercely stubborn gaze, she said, 'It's the *only* option. I can't stay here. And though I'd sooner not ask any favours of you, I need your help to get back to London.'

Since he couldn't avoid the issue forever, he grasped the nettle.

'Mistress Maitland … it appears that certain vital implications have escaped you. You left your home without female company. You eloped with a man and spent a night – to all intents and purposes, alone – in his house. Your family expects you to return married. If you go home unwed, your reputation will be tarnished beyond repair. In short, you'll be ruined.'

A flicker of doubt appeared in the expressive dark eyes and he thought, *Good. She's thinking about it. With luck, she'll see reason.*

Then she shook her head and said decisively, 'Not if I'm back by tonight. No one knows what I've done except for Mama and the girls. So long as I go home as quickly as possible and explain, everything will be all right.'

Sarre realised that this was undoubtedly his cue to tell her of the three things he had done which made her theory unworkable. All of them had been done to preserve her good name from any breath of scandal and enable her to re-enter the polite world as the Countess of Sarre with her head held high. Unfortunately, he hadn't bargained for the stone wall of her refusal. If he was forced to reveal what he'd done, she wouldn't see it as well-meaning measures designed to protect her. She'd see it as a deliberate move on his part to trap her.

Hell, he thought. *This is just getting worse and worse.*

'What did you put in your letter to your mother?'

'More or less exactly what Claude --' She stopped and clenched her hands until the knuckles glowed white. 'What *you* told me to. I said I'd met a gentleman with whom I – I'd fallen in love and that, for reasons too complex to explain in a letter, we were leaving Town to marry quietly elsewhere. I told her not to worry for my safety ... that I was very happy and would write again as soon as I had news.'

'I see. And if she or your sisters communicate this information to anyone?'

'Communicate it whom? The girl at the bakery? Old Mr Parker across the street?'

'I was thinking more of Lady Brassington – who might call to enquire after your health.'

'That's not very likely. And anyway, she wouldn't spread gossip about me.'

His brows rose, expressing mild disbelief.

'And Lord Sheringham ... who has probably still not given up and will soon wonder why he hasn't seen you lately? I take it he *does* know where you live?'

'Yes. But again, I don't think he'd call on Mama. Also – what possible reason would he have to blacken my name?'

'The fact that you'd rejected him in favour of someone else, perhaps? Not that his lordship needs a reason. Spite is usually sufficient.' Realising that the conversation was heading a direction he'd rather it didn't take just yet, he said flatly, 'Let us be absolutely clear about this. If you have your way, you run two risks. I've explained the first one. The other is Sheringham. I know him much better than you do. I've also told you how desperate he is and why. If you stray into his clutches, he'll find a way of forcing you. And if he does that, you can forget about helping your family. In fact, you can forget about pretty much everything except being shut away in the country while he enjoys squandering your money. Obviously, I have my own reasons for not wanting that to happen – quite aside from feeling that he doesn't deserve you. And one last thing. If word leaks out that you eloped but didn't marry, the resulting scandal can't be mended. If it leaks out that you eloped with *me*, I'll be in the public pillory with you. And since I'm doing my damnedest to persuade you to the altar, that seems a mite unfair.'

Caroline looked at him, hating the knowledge that most of what he said was true. She wondered whether, if her head and heart hadn't been full of Claude Duvall, she might have accepted Sarre's proposal. He had plainly taken it for granted that she'd do so now. In fact, he'd gone to great lengths to make it impossible for her to do anything else – which didn't make her like him any better.

Looking at it objectively, she supposed that, in every respect save one, he was a better bargain than she could have hoped for. Unless quite *everything* he said was a lie, he was financially solvent, would let her help Mama and the girls and make her a Countess. He was also alarmingly clever and quite good-looking in that severely-chiselled, slightly forbidding way of his. But none of that made up for what he'd done. She was utterly and mind-blowingly furious with him for making a fool of her; demons of misery were clawing constantly at her insides; and she would never, in a million years, be able to trust him.

She said, 'You make a good case. But I doubt the risks are as great as you say and I can't ... I just can't marry a man so capable of deceit. I want to go home.'

'Your last word, I take it?'

'Yes.'

Repressing the desire to swear, Sarre rose and walked to the door. He was about to do something else she'd better not find out about ... or he would be if Bertrand picked up his cue correctly. Taking a step into the hall and spotting the housemaid, he said, 'Ask Monsieur Didier to join me immediately, then go and pack for Mistress Maitland. She'll be leaving as soon as possible.'

And, returning to Caroline, 'There's obviously no point in trying to change your mind, so I'll have Bertrand harness the horses and drive you back to Town. I trust that will suit you?'

'Yes.' Something peculiar seemed to shift inside her but she put it down to the fact that she hadn't expected him to give way so suddenly. 'Thank you.'

'I won't say it's a pleasure because it isn't. I'd hoped --' He stopped when Bertrand materialised in the doorway and immediately switched to French. 'Mademoiselle insists on returning to London and I've failed to persuade her otherwise. She wishes to leave as soon as the carriage can be made made ready. I'm sure I can rely on you to deal with it.'

Without so much as a blink, Bertrand made a broad, helpless gesture and said, 'Milord – forgive me but it can't be done.'

Adrian scowled at him. 'What? Why not?'

'It's the horses, Milord. One of them has a badly strained hock and we were lucky to get here without him going lame on us. I've started applying poultices but he won't be fit to make a long journey for at least two days, if then.'

As previously, Caroline's school-girl French lagged woefully behind. She caught three or four key words but precious little else. So when Sarre turned back to her with a frown, she said, 'What is it?'

'I think you'd better hear it from Bertrand.' And switching back to French, 'Repeat what you just told me in English for Mademoiselle.'

Although he had a perfectly sound grasp of English, one of the small pleasures in Bertrand's life was mangling the language almost beyond recognition. He did so now, at such length and to such a degree that Caroline was hardly any wiser and Adrian, despite everything, was struggling not to laugh.

When he finally stopped speaking and fixed her with a woeful stare, Caroline said hesitantly, 'The horse's knee is on fire?'

'He has a strained hock,' supplied Sarre. 'He can't work today. Bertrand is sorry – and so am I – but there's nothing to be done. Sandwich doesn't boast an inn where horses can be hired and the horses that brought us here have to be returned to The Ship in Faversham so that I can reclaim my own cattle. I'm sure you see the problem.'

She stared at him, completely aghast.

'You're saying I'm stuck here until the horse is well?'

'Unfortunately.' He dismissed Bertrand with a wave of one hand. 'No! I *can't!*'

'I'm afraid there isn't any alternative.'

'There must be! What about *your* horse – the one you rode here? Can't he --'

'Argan isn't a carriage horse.'

'But I have to go home today!' she said urgently and then stopped, still half-unable to comprehend how badly everything was going wrong. 'If I don't ... if I don't ...'

'The heavens will fall?' he said acidly. 'Yes. I'm aware of it. But it's an ill wind, you know. At least you'll have the satisfaction of taking me down with you.'

FIFTEEN

Having been out to the stables and fixed a bran poultice to the perfectly healthy hock of one of the carriage-horses, Bertrand ambled back into the house and narrowly avoided colliding with Caroline, wrapped in a cloak and storming in the other direction.

He said, '*Mademoiselle?*' And very slowly, '*Où allez-vous?*'

'Since one hopes that, aside from being trapped here, I'm not actually a prisoner,' she snapped, not caring whether he understood or not, 'I'm going out.'

Bertrand stepped aside and let her go. Then he strolled into the parlour where Adrian was standing at the window, watching her pick her way over the shingle.

Without turning his head, he said, 'It's all right. She'll be back. If she walks far enough in that direction, she'll arrive at the mouth of the river and have no choice but to turn around. And if she burns off some of her temper, it can only be an advantage.'

'Mm. You've got what you wanted, anyway.'

'No. *You* got me what I wanted – although I nearly undid all your good work by laughing.'

'Pity you didn't,' muttered Bertrand.

Adrian turned away from the window. 'What?'

'Nothing. What now, then?'

'I'll have to *ad lib*. I suppose you've already put a dressing on that unfortunate horse?'

'Just in case she looks,' agreed Bertrand. Then, 'You're set on this, aren't you?'

'Marrying her? Yes.'

'Why?'

Adrian shrugged. 'She's got character. She's stubborn, not easily frightened and nobody's fool. She also knows something of the real world – and that will suit me better than one of those fluttering girls who've rarely stepped outside Mama's drawing-room.'

'I see. And that's all, is it?'

'You know it isn't.'

'Ah. Getting her down the aisle gives Sheringham his own again?'

'Exactly.'

For a moment Bertrand said nothing and, if Adrian had been looking closely, he might have detected a hint of worry. Then, bluntly, 'Are you going to tell her the truth about yourself? In particular, about what happened before you left England?'

'After she agrees to marry me and if she asks, yes.' He eyed Bertrand obliquely. 'What is it you're trying to say?'

'Nothing you don't know already.'

'Excellent.'

'But I'll say it anyway. You've deceived her in a way that's left her feeling humiliated. If she catches you out in any other lies, that stubborn streak you like so much is going to make your married life a bloody nightmare.'

'If you're talking about the horse, I shall claim ignorance and blame you,' shrugged Adrian. 'And in the meantime, I'm setting myself the task of worming my way into her good graces whilst simultaneously getting her out of those hideous gowns.'

Bertrand folded his arms.

'I know it's been a while – but surely you can wait till after the wedding?'

'Very funny. Find that pink monstrosity she was wearing last night and put it in a saddle-bag. If I can find a decent dressmaker in Canterbury, I'll need it.' On the point of leaving the room, he turned back to add, 'She hasn't eaten since God knows when. If she's not back reasonably soon, take some food and find her. At the moment, she'd probably rather it was you that chased after her than me. And it's not going to help matters if she passes out from hunger on the beach and ends up with inflammation of the lung.'

* * *

Since the strip of sand was wet, Caroline set off across the shingle and swiftly discovered that walking over small, slippery pebbles was both uncomfortable and tiring. In addition, the keen easterly wind froze her hands, found its way inside her cloak and made it impossible to keep her hood on her head. After roughly half an hour of determined tramping, her feet hurt and she was chilled to the bone. The only thing that stopped her retracing her steps to the warmth of the house was a very natural reluctance to give Sarre the satisfaction of seeing her defeated.

Not that she knew where she was going. As far as she could see, there was nowhere *to* go; just the choppy sea on her right, grassy dunes and fields full of green tussocks to her left and nothing else for miles apart from dozens of seagulls, all laughing hysterically at some joke only they understood.

She stamped to the nearest dune and sat down, huddling into her cloak and trying to tuck her feet beneath her. Then she stared out to sea and forced herself to think. Whichever way one looked at it, her current situation was a disaster. She had no means of getting home before tomorrow at the earliest – and that meant that everything Sarre had said about ruined reputations and scandal was going to be proved true. If, in addition to those ladies who already looked down their long noses at her, word leaked out that she was no better than she should be, she'd become a pariah. She would have to leave London and go back to Yorkshire. Mama would never let her hear the end of it, Grandpa would be disappointed in her and, for all she knew, running away might not solve the problem anyway. Halifax wasn't exactly the ends of the earth and people wrote letters, didn't they? If she became truly unmarriageable ... if no respectable man would have her ... it meant no dowry and no way of helping Mama and the girls.

And the weight of society's disapproval would fall on Sarre's head as well. She could try arguing that he deserved it and that this whole mess was entirely his fault ... but it somehow failed to convince her. He'd behaved atrociously, of course. But he'd known from the outset that he could and would put everything right, if only she'd let him. It made it difficult to paint him as a total villain. And then there was the other

179

thing; the thing she'd been doing her best to ignore. The small insistent voice inside her that kept whispering hopefully, *He was Claude. Perhaps some tiny part of him still is.*

She still couldn't make sense of any of it. She was filled with hurt and anger and, above all, confusion. It didn't seem possible that he could have taken her in so completely or that she'd never noticed that the Earl and the highwayman looked very much alike. Piece by painful piece, she went back over those meetings with Claude. That first night at the roadside; his sudden appearance on the terrace at the Overbury ridotto; and, more incredible than either of those, the evening at the Pantheon when he'd somehow managed to play both Claude and himself, switching roles so swiftly and easily. How had that been done? And why hadn't she had the slightest suspicion that something was wrong?

My God. Fooled by nothing more than a highwayman's mask and a French accent? Just how stupidly blind was I?

Then she went over the conversation with Claude in Kensington Gardens. What exactly had he said?

'You know nothing about me. I have been many things – more than you can imagine. When you learn the truth, there is every likelihood you will be disappointed.'

A harsh laugh shook her. Disappointment didn't even begin to cover it. Sarre had made her fall in love with an illusion. An illusion that had been everything its cold-hearted creator was not. And an illusion the loss of which she hadn't yet even begun to deal with.

The crunch of pebbles under booted feet made her turn her head. Monsieur Didier was trudging towards her clutching a basket and scowling dreadfully.

Bertrand absorbed the state of her in a single glance. She looked frozen, miserable and very, very lonely. Sitting down beside her, he pulled a stone bottle from the basket, poured something hot and steaming into a cup and handed it to her wordlessly but with a look that dared her to refuse.

She didn't. The smell of coffee was too tempting. With a whispered, '*Merci*', she wrapped her numb fingers round the cup and took a small sip. It was so good, she could have cried.

Bertrand fished in the basket again and came up with something wrapped in a napkin. He unfolded and re-wrapped it so that she could take it in her other hand. Warm pastry stuffed with apple and cinnamon. This time she had to blink away actual tears. She said, 'This is so kind. Thank you.'

He grunted. '*Ce n'est rien, Mademoiselle.* Madam Clayton makes good pastry, no? When you 'ave eaten and drunk, we will go back to the 'ouse, yes?'

Caroline narrowly avoided choking on a morsel of pastry.

'You can speak English. Properly, I mean.'

'Not so properly, perhaps – but of a sufficiency.' He sent her a fleeting, semi-apologetic grin. 'Before was my little joke. Not so funny for you, maybe. But 'e knows I do this and I 'oped 'e would laugh.'

She swallowed another bite of the tart and said bitterly, '*Does* he laugh? Ever?'

'Yes. Adrian is ... 'e is not so cold, you know.'

'Hadrian?' The other dropped aitches made it seem possible, if outlandish. 'Really?'

'No, no. In French, A-dree-enn. Or Ay-dree-ann, as you English say.'

'He told me his first name was Francis.'

'*Oui.* But 'e does not use it. In the many years we 'ave been together, 'e never 'as.'

Caroline decided to abandon this point in favour of another.

'And these many years were in Paris?'

'Some, yes. And before that, other places.' He reached for her cup, re-filled it and added simply. 'I am 'is friend. He does not 'ave so very many because ... what is it the English say? 'E plays 'is cards close to 'is chest.'

Caroline finished the last bite of pastry, licked flakes of it from her fingers and dried them on the napkin before taking back the cup. 'But not with you, it would seem.'

'No. Not with me.' He pushed the cork back into the stone bottle, shoved it in the basket and stood up. 'Finish your coffee, Mademoiselle and let us return to the 'ouse. This bit of England is very cold ... and if we are to talk, you and I, it will be better by a good fire, *n'est ce pas?*'

She looked up at him, her expression frankly disbelieving.

'*Are* we to talk, Monsieur? I don't somehow see you breaking his lordship's confidence.'

'You should call me Bertrand. And of course I shall not break confidences.'

'I also don't see us sitting down to discuss him when he's in the next room.'

'But 'e is not. 'E is not in the 'ouse at all.'

'Then where is he?'

'Out.' Bertrand took the empty cup, tossed it into the basket and held out his hand to her. 'Come, Mademoiselle. Time to go 'ome.'

They walked back along the beach to the sound of the receding tide and the crunch of their own footsteps. Caroline wondered what, if anything, the Earl's odd friend would tell her and whether any of it would make the slightest difference. She also wondered where Sarre had gone and what kind of devilment he might be up to now.

In the back parlour, Bertrand settled Caroline into a chair by the hearth and crouched down to turn the gently-burning fire into a blaze. Absorbed in this task, he said, 'Adrian says I know all 'is secrets and, of a certainty, I know most. Of these, I will not speak because they are the things 'e must tell you himself. But there are other things ... things 'e will never say because 'e does not see the importance. And me, I think some of this may 'elp you.'

'Help me in what way?'

'To understand 'im a little. And to decide what you will do.'

Caroline had her doubts but decided there was no harm in listening. 'Go on.'

Bertrand rose from the hearth and dropped into a chair.

'The day this story starts was the day of 'is twenty-second *anniversaire*. On that day, 'e was still the Vicomte d'Eastry, son of the Earl of Sarre. On the next one, 'e left England and became Adrian St. Clare.'

'Oh.' She frowned. 'That sounds rather ... drastic.'

'*Oui*. 'E 'ad no 'ome and little money. Until the day 'e saved me from evil men in Vienna and for a long time after, 'e lived on 'is wits.' He smiled suddenly. '*Heureusement*, Adrian 'as very good wits and also certain talents.'

'So I've seen,' agreed Caroline dryly. 'But surely his parents supported him in some way?'

'A little money was sent. Adrian would not touch it. Everything 'e 'as today, 'e 'as earned by 'is own efforts.'

"Ow? I mean – how?' The missing aitches were becoming contagious. 'By acting?'

'These last years, yes. But at first, by another means. Of this, aside from myself, only two other people are aware so I shall leave Adrian to decide whether you shall be the third. But the acting ...' He stopped and spread his hands in a wide, expressive gesture. "E is without equal.'

'He's certainly convincing.'

'Claude Duvall? Bah! That was nothing. The Comédie Française will not be the same without 'im.'

Caroline sat up, staring. 'He acted *there?*'

'But of course! For five years. He could have played the 'andsome young 'eroes but he would not. For Adrian, it was always the 'character' roles. And to see L'Inconnu perform Molière was an experience of the most unforgettable. Every seat would be taken and more persons fighting to get in.' Bertrand sighed and, seemingly lost in nostalgia, added, 'If only you could 'ave seen 'im play Argan. It was a joy.'

'Argan,' remarked Caroline, confused, 'is the name of his horse.'

'It is also the name of Molière's 'Ypochondriac. Clearly,' said Bertrand with some severity, 'you do not know Molière – which is a great pity but, one supposes, only to be expected since you 'ave the misfortune to be English. 'Owever. During this time, Adrian was 'appy. Not for the success, you understand – but because while 'e was on the stage the bad things could not touch 'im.'

'*What* bad things?' she asked. And then, when Bertrand merely smiled and shook his head, 'All right. But if that's so, why did he leave it all behind and come back?'

'For the family name.' And, scowling again, 'For the mother who does not deserve 'im. The father died three years since but there was a younger brother. Then, not so long ago, this brother fell from 'is 'orse and was killed. And so Adrian says 'e must return and be an Earl.' A pause and then, "'E is trying – but the role is not comfortable. 'E was 'appier playing Claude Duvall … but sadly that did not turn out so well, did it?'

'Not for me, certainly.'

'Not for either of you, Mademoiselle.'

'That's not how it looks to me. And neither does it excuse it.'

'Perhaps – perhaps not.' Bertrand came to his feet and stretched. 'You should remember what I 'ave said when 'e tells you 'ow it all began. If you think about it, you will also know that Adrian is more than 'e seems. 'E tells 'imself 'e does not feel 'urt, does not care. But if this was so, 'e would sleep better at night.' He nodded at her, his smile faintly grim. 'I will order food for you. Me, I do not think one pastry is sufficient. And if Adrian is late, dinner will be late also.'

* * *

It was raining in Canterbury. It was also more difficult than he'd expected to locate a *modiste* who not only knew her business but was also disposed to be helpful. By the time he'd located Madame Rambert at the far end of Castle Street, Adrian was damp, irritable and wondering why he was bothering. In her present mood, Caroline was unlikely to thank him for his efforts. She might also be unable to appreciate his taste. On the other hand, his self-imposed quest gave him something to do. And if he could go home with just *one* gown that didn't look as if it had been made for a fairground attraction, he'd consider the time well-spent.

Madame Rambert looked at the crumpled pink silk and winced.

'Mademoiselle's colouring?' she asked.

'Honey-blonde hair, brown eyes and a delicate complexion.'

'This, then, is completely wrong for her.'

Adrian relaxed. Madame was plainly a woman after his own heart.

'Completely wrong,' he agreed. 'As are all the others.'

'All?' asked Madame, in failing accents.

'Canary yellow, chartreuse, violet, peacock … and this.'

'Mademoiselle is bereft of any sense of colour?'

'I'm not sure. All I *do* know is that everything she wears makes my teeth ache.'

And Madame, who had been born in Dover, laughed and shedding her French accent, said comfortably, 'Well, we can't have that, now can we? So let's see what's to be done about it. I'm guessing you have some ideas of your own on what will suit?'

'A few. But I'm open to suggestions.'

Two hours later, he left the shop with a gown of misty forest-green figured silk which had apparently been made for a lady of changeable disposition and which Madame's seamstresses had worked like demons to take in here and let out there until it duplicated the size of the despised pink one he had brought with him. A further three gowns had also been argued over and ordered for delivery as soon as was possible; and Adrian rode back to Sandwich, lighter in the pocket, with rain dripping off his hat and a large dress-box banging inconveniently against his knee.

* * *

Caroline, meanwhile, sat by the fire drinking tea, nibbling lemon cakes and pondering everything Bertrand had told her. The majority of it didn't fit with the Earl of Sarre she knew. The idea of that cool, remote personage playing comedy roles in the most famous theatre in Paris was completely incongruous. There were other things, too. The implication that he'd left England with nothing yet returned, at the very least, comfortably-off. How had that been done? By means of that other, so far undisclosed, talent? The more she thought about it, the more Caroline began to realise that the questions far outweighed the answers.

In other respects, some of Bertrand's opinions were vaguely troubling because they suggested that Sarre was no more real than Claude had been.

He'd said Sarre was *"trying to be an Earl"* but the *"role was not comfortable"* and he had been *"happier playing Claude Duvall"*. Then, *"He is more than he seems"* ... which, in Caroline's opinion, was as good as saying *"He* isn't *what he seems"*; and finally, *"He tells himself he doesn't feel hurt ... but, if this was so, he'd sleep better at night."*

What, exactly, did that mean? Guilty conscience? Some emotional cataclysm? Nightmares? What?

She bit into yet another cake and thought, *Blast Bertrand. I don't want to be intrigued. I don't want to care how many masks Sarre is hiding behind. And I* particularly *don't want to end up feeling sorry for him. He doesn't deserve that I should and I've got enough problems already thanks to the impossible position he's put me in. As far as I can see, he's a lying, manipulating iceberg who I'd like to get as far away from as possible.'*

A chill rippled down her spine as practicality and sound, Yorkshire common-sense told her something she didn't want to hear.

Except ... except that, if I can't get home soon, I'm not going to have too many choices. It's either go back unmarried and wave goodbye to my reputation or give in and agree to marry the iceberg. Assuming, that is, he hasn't finally recognised defeat or decided I'm not worth the trouble. Damn.

SIXTEEN

Caroline sat down to dinner in the same poppy-red gown she'd been wearing all day. Sarre faced her across the table, immaculate in dark grey over Nile blue and silver. His unpowdered hair was fastened with long sable ribbons and, as always, his only concession to jewellery was a plain gold cravat pin. Bertrand, it appeared, had declined to join them. She wished he hadn't. Even if she was accustomed to dining *à deux* with a man other than her grandfather, conversation with the Earl was going to be littered with awkward moments.

Neither of them spoke until Sally had finished bringing dishes to the table and withdrawn. Then his lordship said politely, 'Did you enjoy your walk?'

'No.'

'A pity. Not the best weather for it, perhaps?'

'Absolutely not.'

'This part of the coast is a martyr to easterly winds.'

'So I noticed.' She relented a little and added, 'But for Bertrand's coffee, I think I might have turned into a block of ice.'

'One can always rely on Bertrand,' he remarked. 'No doubt his discourse proved equally beneficial.'

Ah. So he knew about that, did he?

'He didn't tell me anything he thought you wouldn't like.'

'I know what he told you. He's a well-meaning meddler.' He passed her a dish of carrots. 'It comes of knowing he is the only person alive who shares all my secrets.'

'You have a lot of them?'

'A few – some of which you already know.' He exchanged the carrots for roasted parsnips. 'You should be flattered. I am rarely indiscreet.'

She startled herself as much as him by giving a choke of sardonic laughter.

187

'Oh no. You're not *indiscreet*, my lord. That would be too simple. *You* just risk your neck by playing at highway robbery.'

Sarre's mouth twitched. He said mildly, 'I only did it once.'

'Once would have been enough if you'd been caught.' She took her time cutting up a piece of meat. 'As to your secrets … I assume you're referring to the gaming club?'

'That is one of them, certainly. I co-own it with a French gentleman who deals with the business on a day-to-day basis. It's been open for roughly two years now and it provides both Aristide and myself with a regular and quite substantial income. Needless to say, if the *beau monde* was aware of my involvement in such an establishment, I'd be even less popular in certain quarters than I am already.'

'You don't sound as if that thought concerns you overmuch.'

'It doesn't.' He shrugged and added, 'Few things do.'

That's not what Bertrand thinks. 'But?'

'But obviously I'd prefer that it remained private.'

Caroline nodded. 'And your theatrical career?'

'That, too.'

'Who else knows? Here in England, I mean. If you performed at the Comédie Française, presumably most of Paris does.'

'Paris knew an actor called L'Inconnu. Only six people know that actor is also the Earl of Sarre. Bertrand and yourself; Aristide and his sister, Madeleine; Nicholas Wynstanton … and, thanks to an unlucky accident, his brother, Rockliffe.' He paused and looked up from his plate. 'I assume you're not acquainted with his Grace?'

'Not at all.'

'He is … singular. I suspect he's both a very good friend and a very undesirable enemy.'

'But doubtless the Duke's knowledge doesn't bother you either.'

Sarre froze, then slowly laid down his fork. He said, 'You are very acute – but in this particular case, quite mistaken. One would be stupid to dismiss Rockliffe.'

This, thought Caroline, was interesting but she concentrated on her dinner for a while rather than attempting to pursue it. Eventually, however, she said lightly, 'According to Bertrand, the French stage is unlikely to recover from your … retirement.'

'Bertrand exaggerates.'

'Oh.' She allowed a note of disappointment. 'So you weren't *that* good, then?'

And there it was again. The suspicion of a smile, swiftly repressed.

'I was … popular. Particularly when playing certain roles. Like many of his countrymen, Bertrand has a great fondness for Molière.'

Caroline saw an opportunity and took it.

'As he does for yourself.'

He paused and then said curtly, 'It is mutual.'

If she hadn't been watching closely, she'd have missed it. Both eyes and voice remained completely unchanged … but the merest suggestion of colour touched those dramatic cheekbones.

Caroline looked on in fascination. *He's embarrassed by a reference to simple affection? A man who's performed before hundreds of people? Is that even possible?*

She decided to test the theory.

'He told me you saved his life.'

The colour in his face neither advanced nor retreated but this time she noticed that he took the precaution of letting his lashes veil his eyes.

'As I said … he exaggerates. He had the misfortune to upset some unsavoury gentleman and, since I happened to be passing at the time, I lent a hand. It wasn't nearly as heroic as it sounds.' He pushed a serving-dish towards her. 'Have some peas.'

'Thank you,' murmured Caroline. And thought, *He's different, somehow. Is this what Bertrand meant? Am I being allowed a tiny glimpse of the man behind Lord Sarre? If so, it's interesting. But though I'd like to push it further, I'd better stop before he realises what he's doing and crawls back into his igloo.* Purely at random, she said, 'You were out for a long time. Did you have a pleasant afternoon?'

'Not especially. It was raining.'

At some point on the ride home, it had occurred to Adrian that a gentleman didn't offer gifts of clothing to a lady who was neither a relation nor his wife. This meant that the green gown would have to remain hidden in his own room for the time being – and, quite possibly, forever if she didn't change her mind. More important, was the time frame he had set himself. Today was Tuesday and the notice of their marriage would appear in the *Morning Chronicle* on Thursday – which meant that he had two days in which to get her to church.

He looked at her now, apparently spearing peas one at a time and looking just a little smug. He'd answered her questions more fully than had been necessary and given her just a glimpse of himself in the process. He didn't know whether he'd done enough and had no idea whether – leaving the matter of Claude Duvall to one side – she liked him at all. He'd prefer that she didn't hold him in total aversion but would decide to marry him for the title and out of expediency. Despite the clinical evaluation he'd given Bertrand, he was starting to like Mistress Maitland rather more than he'd anticipated.

The door opened and Sally appeared bearing a blackberry and apple cobbler and a dish of cream. She said, 'Will there be anything else, my lord?'

'No. Thank you.' He waited until the door closed behind her and said, 'If you've grown bored with the peas, would you care for some of … whatever this is?'

Caroline shook her head ruefully.

'No. I ate a great many lemon cakes this afternoon. They are a weakness of mine.'

'Indeed?' Sarre re-filled both wine-glasses and decided it wouldn't do any harm to try testing the water. 'And is that the only one … or do you have others?'

Her nerves twitched but she kept her head.

'If I did, it wouldn't be in my best interests to admit them, now would it?'

'Why not? Do you think I might take advantage?'

'Given the right opportunity – or even none whatsoever – I think you might do all manner of things,' said Caroline, sensibly stepping back from flirtatious banter. 'The fact that we've managed a civilised conversation over dinner doesn't change anything.'

The ghost of something that might have been humour appeared in his eyes.

'You are an exceedingly stubborn woman, you know. Are you always this difficult?'

She tilted her head and thought about it.

'Probably not. But I never found myself in a situation like this before.'

'Odd as it may seem, neither have I.' He leaned back in his chair and toyed with his wine. 'I don't doubt that you're still angry. You have every right. And though I've answered some of your questions, I am sure you have others. I'm prepared to answer those as well in due course. However, as it stands, you already know enough about me to make my life very difficult should you choose – even without branding me the kind of man who ruins innocent girls. At this stage, I'm not sure what else I can do that will be helpful.'

You can stop hiding. You can stop refusing to smile even though you want to. You can stop weighing every single word before you utter it. You can stop behaving like an automaton.

But, deciding this was all a little too direct, Caroline chose another tack which was probably equally risky. 'Tell me what lies between you and Lord Sheringham.'

His face tightened.

'No.'

'Why not?'

Because it gives me nightmares.

'Because it isn't … pretty; because it reflects badly on someone who can't answer back; because, if we are not to be married, it isn't a tale you need to hear. Are those reasons sufficient?'

'You're saying you'd tell me if I agreed to be your wife?'

'Yes.' The mere idea of laying it all out before her filled his throat with bile. 'Yes.'

Caroline nodded. 'I suppose that's fair.'

'Thank you.' He took a swallow of wine. 'Is there anything else?'

'Just one thing for now, I think.'

Oh good.

'And that is?'

191

'I accept that your only interest in my dowry is your determination to prevent his lordship acquiring it. Aside from that being a very poor beginning, I don't relish the idea of being the instrument of anybody's revenge. But try as I will, I can't think of any other reason why you'd want to marry me.'

Sarre stared at her, his expression as usual defying interpretation. 'You can't?'

'No. Not one.' She waited for him to speak and when he said nothing, forced herself to continue. 'I'm twenty-two years old. I'm not well-born, I'm not comfortable in society and my looks are no more than passable – some might call me plain. The only thing I ever had to offer anyone was the money – and you don't need it.' She shrugged slightly. 'So it seems to me that, so long as I don't marry Lord Sheringham, you'll get what you want without having to marry me yourself.'

He felt something odd shift in his chest. Inevitably, he ignored it.

He said slowly, 'You don't have much of an opinion of yourself, do you?'

'I don't fool myself, if that's what you mean. And please,' she went on quickly as he would have spoken, 'don't misunderstand. I neither expect nor want any comforting platitudes designed to boost my faltering ego and I *especially* don't want to hear any declarations of spurious affection. I had enough of all that from Lord Sheringham.'

'He's an idiot.'

'I know that. But he's not blind. And neither are you.'

'Do you think we might forget Marcus completely and put your looks to one side for a moment?' He paused, seeming to consider for a moment. 'You want to know if I see you as more than a weapon? Yes. I do. You're strong and obstinate and shrewd. You don't faint when a highwayman points a pistol at you or when a different sort of villain tries to abduct you. You don't even have hysterics when you elope with one fellow, only to find yourself stuck with another. You are practical, quick-witted and impossible to predict. These things may not sound like compliments but, trust me, they are. If you want it in three supremely unromantic words ...' He stopped and then forced himself to go on. 'I like you. And I'd be glad of the chance to know you better.'

It was Caroline's turn to stare.

'Oh,' she said weakly.

'Oh,' he agreed. 'As to your looks ... it's true that you don't appear to advantage. But who told you that you are plain?'

'My mother mentions it from time to time.' *Two or three times a day, usually.* 'And, if you'd seen my sisters, you'd understand why. They're both exceptionally pretty – as was Mama in her day. I had the misfortune to inherit Papa's looks rather than hers so naturally I'm a disappointment.'

Sarre leaned back in his chair and said deliberately, 'Your mother isn't a man.'

Her jaw dropped. Then, 'Obviously not – though I don't see the relevance.'

'No. Of course you don't. However, let's return to safer ground and something I hope you *will* understand. To put it bluntly, you are the worst-dressed female I've ever seen. With the exception of that bronze domino, every single garment you possess seems to have been specifically designed to obliterate you. *You're* not wearing them – *they* are wearing you. And the effect is disastrous.' A sudden dazzling smile vanished as quickly as it had appeared. 'You wanted honesty. There it is.'

He stopped and waited for her to be offended.

For a moment, she continued to stare at him out of wide, faintly stunned brown eyes. He didn't know that, just for a second or two, his smile had knocked her sideways and, quite literally, taken her breath away. Then, incredibly, she started to laugh and said unsteadily, 'I know. My g-gowns are awful, aren't they? Every single one.'

'Yes.' He let her laugh, enjoying the sound of it. 'You didn't choose them?'

She shook her head. 'Grandfather wanted me to have a complete wardrobe before I got to London. The dressmaker in Harrogate said bright colours were fashionable and Grandpa liked them so ... so I let them have their way.' She paused, trying to quell her giggles. 'You wouldn't *believe* how many hours Lavinia and I spent removing most of the trimming, trying to improve them. It didn't work though, did it? They are beyond help.'

'They are. *You*, on the other hand are not. Correctly gowned, I believe you would surprise yourself.' For a moment, he contemplated giving her the green gown and then, with reluctance, decided against it. He rose, offering her his arm. 'Shall we remove to the parlour? If you feel disinclined for further conversation and would prefer to read there are books you might like.'

She didn't want books. She wanted more glimpses behind that invisible wall of his. Sitting down beside the fire, she looked at the playing cards he had left lying in seemingly odd patterns on the table.

'You were playing something earlier?'

'Merely passing the time.' He gathered up the cards and shuffled them out of habit. 'It was nothing of any consequence.'

Admiring the easy expertise of his hands, Caroline said, 'We could play piquet, if you like.'

'No.'

The word came out swiftly and with flat implacability, accompanied by an almost imperceptible shudder. Misreading the reason behind this, she said defensively, 'Grandfather taught me and I play reasonably well, I believe.'

'I daresay. But you don't want to play cards with me.'

'Why not?'

'Because I always win.'

'That sounds like an idle boast,' objected Caroline. 'No one *always* wins.'

'I do. Or, at least, I can.' He sat down facing her and swiftly set about discarding all the cards below seven to create a thirty-two card piquet deck. 'Do you want me to prove it?'

'Yes. But you can deal the first hand.'

'You think that will help you?'

'It gives me the advantage.'

Sarre shook his head. 'Normally, perhaps. But not with me.'

And he proceeded to demonstrate.

At the end of three hands in which Caroline had lost with disastrous consistency, he smiled a little and said, 'More?'

'No.' She sat back, baffled and frowning. 'How did you *do* that?'

'Another secret – which, if it got out, would see me black-balled at White's.' He waved his hand negligently at their discarded game. 'I count cards.'

Caroline looked blank. 'I don't understand.'

'I can tell what's in your hand with almost total accuracy. Of course, it's easier with piquet than most games. Any experienced player ought to be able to do the same thing up to a point. But I ... I have an extra ability that enables me to do it with any card-game.' He paused. 'Originally, I used it to earn my living and later, to finance my share of Sinclair's. *Now*, however, it's become something of a handicap because, although it's not exactly cheating, neither is it completely honourable. But trying *not* to do it gives me a headache – which makes sitting down to a sociable game of cards virtually impossible these days.'

'So you don't play?'

'Not if I can avoid it, no.'

'I couldn't tell what you were doing. Can other people?'

'They'd start to suspect something if they played against me often enough,' he shrugged. 'In the days when I relied on it, I had to take extensive precautions.'

'Such as what?'

'I played in numerous different establishments. And as numerous different gentlemen.'

Caroline stared at him in fascination.

'Will you show me one?'

To her amazement and for the first time ever, he actually laughed.

'Another time, perhaps.' He rose to offer his hand and draw her to her feet. 'I don't know if we've progressed at all from this morning. If we haven't ... if, tomorrow, you still find marriage with me an impossible prospect and want to go home, I'll arrange it as quickly as possible and do whatever I can to minimise the damage.'

She glanced up beneath her lashes, a look made all the more seductive for her being totally unaware of it, and said, 'You ... you may not be *entirely* impossible. For the rest, I don't know. The best I can say is that I will at least *think* about it.'

'Which is probably more than I deserve,' came the dry response. 'Thank you.'

SEVENTEEN

If you find marriage with me an impossible prospect ...

Caroline awoke with his words still echoing in her head. The truth, which she'd finally acknowledged to herself the night before, was that it wasn't. *He* wasn't. Somehow, in the space of a single evening, he'd become rather alarmingly possible and she didn't know quite how it had happened. She also had more sense than to accept it without question.

The man she'd sat down to dinner with last night had been the Earl of Sarre but the man she'd said goodnight to had been someone else; someone whose demeanour had spoken less of icy reserve than emptiness – or perhaps a long-held disbelief in happy endings. That man had been *human* and had awoken the first stirrings of liking. But then, she'd liked Claude Duvall, too. More than liked him. It wouldn't do to make that mistake again. And yet ...

There were complexities to him she couldn't begin to understand, though she suspected they had their root in whatever had happened ten years ago and which he was very reluctant to talk about. Plainly, this involved a girl falling to her death ... which, though quite bad enough, was far from being the whole story. She wondered why Sarre felt that, if she was to be his wife, he was duty-bound to reveal it. Then, putting the thought aside, she examined the other more pertinent things. Such as how – his deception aside – she actually felt about him now.

A tricky one, that. Self-possessed and generally a little intimidating, he wasn't an easy man to know. But just a tiny glimpse under the surface had shown her a fascinating puzzle that she'd rather like to unravel. He wasn't as hard and cold as he appeared. Indeed, she was beginning to suspect that the shell was there to protect a core of something he didn't want the world to see. As for the rest ... he was far from being typical of his class. He'd worked for his living and enjoyed it; he'd invested his earnings wisely, in a way Grandpa would undoubtedly applaud; and his peculiar facility with cards meant that he wouldn't be frittering away money at the gaming-table.

All these things were points in his favour. And there were two others which ought to have been of little consequence but weren't.

He'd smiled; just once and very briefly but it had stolen her breath.

And Claude Duvall's kisses had melted her bones ... except, of course, they hadn't been Claude's kisses at all. They had been Sarre's.

Never having kissed anyone else, Caroline wasn't sure what to make of this. But she rather thought that, unless he'd acted even *that* ... or unless all men kissed exactly the same – which she suspected wasn't the case – there was no reason to suppose that Lord Sarre's kisses would be any less bone-melting than Claude Duvall's.

At this point a rather shocking notion occurred, making her blush. Of course, she couldn't possibly *ask* Sarre to kiss her ... but neither did she have to actively discourage him from doing so. After all, it was a pertinent fact which might help her to decide.

She heard Sally tap at the door and climbed out of bed. It would be interesting to see who she'd be meeting over the breakfast table.

* * *

Sarre, by contrast, was reluctant to face his fate too soon and had therefore broken his fast early and taken Argan out across the fields. Then, returning to the stable, he spent a lot longer than was absolutely necessary grooming the horse and tidying the tack-room before slipping into the house through a side door so he could get to his bedchamber unseen and groom himself.

By the time he finally put in appearance downstairs, Caroline had eaten two slices of bread-and-butter and was finishing her third cup of coffee. The moment he walked through the door, the sense of disappointment she'd been telling herself she absolutely *did not feel*, melted away, causing her to say cheerfully, 'Good morning. You must have been up very early.'

'Moderately so.'

He busied himself pouring coffee. The truth was that, once again, he'd slept very little but had spent a large part of the night addressing the two possible permutations today would bring.

If she turned him down, he'd have to arrange to get her back to Town and steel himself to face the aftermath. This might be diluted a little by sending Bertrand post-haste to London with letters for Henry Lessing, Lady Brassington and, God help him, Caroline's mother. Then she'd be gone. Even after such a short time, he suspected he would miss her – but that was ridiculous, of course. What he would miss was the kind of female companionship he hadn't had in a while and which, once he was reputed to be an unprincipled libertine, he was unlikely to have again anytime soon.

The scenario if she changed her mind and accepted him was different but, in the immediate future, no less unpleasant. He couldn't let her walk down the aisle not knowing but he dreaded the prospect of putting it all into words. Since the day his parents had dragged the story out of him while he was still paralysed with shock, he'd told only one person. Sharing a lodging meant that Bertrand had seen the nightmares and knew what they did to him - so revealing their cause had become unavoidable.

Taking his coffee to the table, he sat down and said neutrally, 'It's a fine day. The wind has dropped somewhat. Perhaps later, if you wish it, we could walk to the town. It isn't far.'

Although he hid it well, Caroline sensed a shred of unease and realised that he probably expected her to demand that he take her home. She also realised that though this was what she *ought* to say, it was no longer what she actually wanted. So she drew a careful breath and said, 'Yes. I'd like that.'

A light flared briefly in his gaze and then was gone.

'I can't promise that there is a great deal there, but it's quite pretty and you might find the history of the place interesting. It's one of the Cinque Ports, you know.'

'Sink ports?' She shook her head. 'No. I don't know.'

He gave the merest hint of a smile and said, 'It's actually 'cinque' – the French for five because, originally, there were five ports – but no one pronounces it that way. You'll have to stop me if I become boring. Unfortunately, no schoolboy escapes that particular bit of history in this part of Kent.'

'*Is* it boring?' she teased.

'No. I don't think so – but then, I was brought up not far from here. I probably should have explained. This house is entailed to the eldest son and so has been mine since birth. Sarre Park is roughly ten miles away and is currently occupied by my mother.' He drained his cup and stood up. 'I have a couple of small tasks requiring my attention but I should be free in about an hour. Will that suit you?'

'Perfectly – though I'm happy to await your convenience.'

'A gentleman is never supposed to keep a lady waiting,' he replied with a trace of sardonic humour. 'Another inescapable and well-learned lesson.'

Caroline watched him go, her eyes thoughtful. Two things struck her. He was very carefully avoiding the question hanging over them both. And little splinters of ice had been evident in his tone when he referred to his mother. Both deserved some consideration.

* * *

Leaving the sea behind them, they walked to Sandwich along a rutted track that crossed the fields. For a time, neither of them spoke but finally Caroline said, 'Does this land belong to the house?'

'Most of it.' He glanced across the uneven terrain. 'It might do for sheep, I suppose, but very little else.'

'Do you know much about sheep?'

'Absolutely nothing.'

Caroline tutted reprovingly.

'They're not as easy as you might suppose.'

'No?' He sounded genuinely interested. 'I take it you *do* know about them?'

'I'm from Yorkshire,' she said dryly, 'where one could be forgiven for thinking there are more sheep than people.'

'Ah. Well, I suppose all that wool has to come from somewhere.'

She smiled. 'You see? You know more than you thought.'

'But not enough, it would seem.'

'Not quite. And if you're seriously interested in sheep, I'll educate you on the way back. But right now, I want your school-room history of the town.'

'Port,' he corrected. 'Or that's what it used to be before the river silted up and made it less viable for shipping. Do you *really* want the lesson?'

'Yes. I want to know how well you learned it.'

'By heart, if you must know. Very well, then. Sandwich was first mentioned as a Saxon stronghold in 664 AD and is listed in the Domesday Book.' He slanted an oblique smile at her. '1086, as I'm sure you knew.'

'I was just about to say that very thing.'

'You were?'

'No. Go on.'

Sarre shook his head and suppressed a tremor of laughter.

Caroline saw and wished he'd stop doing it.

'During the reign of Edward the Confessor, Sandwich and four other similar ports in the area were grouped together to become known as the Cinque Ports.'

'The other four being ...?'

'Dover, Hastings, Hythe and Romney. Who is conducting this lesson?'

'You, my lord. But you shouldn't miss things out.'

'I stand corrected. The Cinque Ports were required to supply the Crown with ships and men on an annual basis. In return, they received certain privileges – such as freedom from tolls and custom duties and the right to hold their own judicial courts. The first Charter outlining all this dates from 1155. The last one was given by Charles II in 1668.' Another sideways glance. 'I trust you're absorbing all this?'

'My memory is excellent, thank you. What else?'

'Not so very much, really. The last time Sandwich was called on for naval service was in 1588 which was the year of ...?'

'The Spanish Armada,' said Caroline triumphantly.

'Just so. In more recent times, what the town has lost in prosperity is more than made up for in character. It's changed very little since the plan of 1086 – that being the date of ...?'

Caroline rolled her eyes and began to realise that the Earl might actually have a sense of humour. 'The Domesday Book. Did you think I'd forgotten already?'

'Merely checking. The street lay-out remains largely medieval and there are a number of buildings dating between the thirteenth and sixteenth centuries. But if you want to know more about corbels and flying buttresses, you'll need another guide. My knowledge of architecture is limited to the basic difference between Norman and Perpendicular.'

After they reached the road and the first houses came into sight, Sarre guided her on to another pathway which he said was one of several which marked the edges of the town and which eventually led towards the river. Numerous boats were moored along the nearer bank and further upstream was a drawbridge giving access to the other side.

'The bridge is only about twenty years old,' remarked his lordship. 'I can remember it being built. Before that, one had to cross the river by ferry.' Then, pointing to an odd building comprising two conical parts connected by an arch spanning the road, 'The Barbican, on the other hand, pre-dates it by over two centuries. Tolls are payable there for every carriage, cart and cow wishing to use the bridge.'

They passed beneath it into the town and Caroline strolled along, admiring a row of black-and-white half-timbered houses over-hanging the street. She said, 'I've never been anywhere like this. It's charming.'

'I'm glad you think so. In the sixteenth century, these houses and others like them were probably occupied by Flemish Huguenots who came here to escape religious persecution.' He gave her a half-smile. 'Many of them, it may interest you to know, were weavers by trade.'

They continued a meandering progress through the town and were standing in front of the Guildhall when a voice said, 'M'lord?'

Sarre turned his head to find an elderly man with thinning grey hair and an extremely threadbare coat staring at him with an odd mixture of incredulity and joy.

'M'lord! It *is* you. I'd heard whispers that you was back but ...' He stopped, his eyes misting over. 'Oh m'lord ... it's that good to see you after all these years – and not a bit changed.'

'Mr Bailes?' said Sarre. Then, holding out his hand, 'Mr Bailes. Of course. It's a pleasure to see you.'

'Just Bailes, sir.' Shaking his head, the old man took the Earl's hand between both of his own and held tight to it. 'Fancy you remembering. But even when you was no more'n a lad, you always had nice manners. Never too lofty to pass the time of day, were you?'

'I certainly hope not.' Sarre retrieved his hand but said, 'I wouldn't have expected to find you here, Mr Bailes. Are you in retirement now?'

Bailes opened his mouth, then closed it again. Finally he said slowly, 'Of course. You wouldn't know. I heard as you never went back after that day.'

'I didn't. So what is it that I don't know?'

'His lordship, the late Earl ...' He stopped. 'I don't rightly know as how to tell it, m'lord. It don't seem right to burden you with it now. And t'weren't like you could have done nothing about it then even if you'd known.'

Sarre took in the thin coat hanging loosely on a too-thin frame and the swollen joints in the rheumatic hands. Then, turning to Caroline, he said, 'I'm being very rude. This gentleman is Mr Bailes. He was head-gardener at Sarre Park when I was young. Mr Bailes – this is Mistress Maitland. She is a friend of mine.'

'Honoured, Miss.' Bailes touched his shapeless hat and looked back at the Earl with a sigh. 'I'm glad to have seen you, m'lord – but I'll be on my way now. It's not right keeping the young lady standing about in the cold.'

His lordship detained him with a hand on his arm.

'It isn't – which is why we'll go over to the Old New Inn so that she can sit by the fire while you tell me everything.' And to Caroline, 'I'm sorry. I ought not to be taking you into a tavern but I need to hear what Mr Bailes has to say and --'

'It's all right. I don't mind. And I've been in a tavern before, you know.'

'You have?' He started shepherding both her and the old gardener across the street.

'My friend in Halifax owns one. I even helped out once when she was sick. Grandpa didn't know, of course, or he'd have had a fit.' She glanced up at him to add, 'And don't tell me *you* never did anything your parents didn't know about because I'll wager Mr Bailes could tell me differently.'

Sarre muttered something beneath his breath.

The old man cackled and said, 'I could that, Miss, and no mistake!'

'I'd rather you didn't, Mr Bailes,' said his lordship, ushering his guests into the inn. 'I'm barely managing to convince her I'm a gentleman as it is.'

Once they were all settled in a cosy corner, the Earl ordered ale for himself and Bailes and a small glass of local cider for Caroline. Then he asked for a large slice of meat pie with potatoes and gravy and while waiting for it to arrive, said, 'Now. What further crassness did my father commit after I left?'

'He – I'm sorry, m'lord – he turned off nearly all the staff. Inside and out. He got rid of everybody who knew and a fair few who didn't. And the worst of it was ...' He stopped again, plainly unwilling to go on.

'You needn't say it. I believe I can guess.'

Caroline watched as Sarre dropped his head back against the settle. She'd wanted him to stop guarding his expression but what she saw in his eyes now appalled her. He looked tired, defeated and as though the last bitter blow had finally slammed him into the ground. A lump formed in her throat and she knew a ridiculous urge to hold his hand.

Then, with an effort that could be felt, he summoned his usual control and said, 'So, Mr Bailes. There was yourself, obviously. Who else?'

'Old Matthew who worked with me, Mr Markham the butler, Thomas the footman, Lizzie and Sarah the maids ... and Betsy from the kitchen. Some others an' all. But them're the ones your lordship'd remember.'

'Betsy.' Sarre's tone was flat. 'I see. Do you know where she is – where any of them are? And how many found other work after being dismissed without a character?'

Oh, thought Caroline, shocked. *No wonder he looked so sick.*

'Old Matt died and I heard Mr Markham got a job in a tavern near Canterbury. Don't know about Thomas or Lizzie ... but Sarah scrapes by doing a bit of cleaning. And Betsy lives with her sister just outside town and makes a living with her baking.'

'And you?'

'Jobbing gardening when I can get it,' said Mr Bailes regretfully. 'Not the same as *proper* gardening but it's better'n nothing.'

The serving maid put down a laden plate and Sarre pushed it in front of Bailes who said protestingly, 'M'lord! There's no call for you to be doing this.'

'Yes. There is. And please don't argue with me. A slice of pie isn't going to make up for the last ten years, is it?'

'But it weren't your fault, m'lord. Not any of it. It was a terrible day – as bad as has ever been. And you was the one what suffered most.'

'Clearly, I wasn't.' Sarre shoved his ale aside. 'But we'll see what can be done about it. I'm at Devereux House at the moment – though for how long will depend on Mistress Maitland. However, I'll be keeping the place open. If you can speak to those in the same position as yourself, tell them there will be work for them with me if they want it. As for yourself, I'd like the walled garden restored to its former glory if you'd do me the favour of taking the job on.'

The expression on the old man's face made it necessary for Caroline to turn away, blinking back tears. He stammered, 'M'lord ... I don't know what to say. Truly, I don't.'

'Yes will do,' said his lordship, rising from his seat and tossing some coins on the table. 'Come to the bay when you're ready. I may not be there myself but I'll see that you and any others who come are expected and that arrangements are in place. No – don't get up. Stay and eat your meal.' He extended a hand and said, 'I'm in your debt, Mr Bailes. And I thank you.'

Once he and Caroline were outside, he drew a long almost shuddering breath and merely stood, frowning across the street.

She said slowly, 'You don't care about the walled garden, do you?'

'No.'

She waited and then, realising he was somewhere she could not follow, slipped her hand through his arm and said, 'While we walk back, I'm going to tell you all about sheep. There will be no need for you to talk – or even listen. In fact, I suggest that you don't because I'm going to be very, very boring.'

By the time they arrived back within sight of the sea, Caroline had run out of fascinating facts about sheep and moved on to the business of weaving and dyeing. Then Sarre, who so far hadn't contributed a single word, suddenly stopped walking and said stiffly, 'My apologies. I've been very rude. And you've been extremely patient. Thank you.'

'Thanks aren't necessary. You needed time to think.' She looked up into eyes that were still as bleak as a December sky. 'That was an extraordinarily kind thing you did.'

'But not enough. Nothing I can do now will ever be enough.'

'Perhaps not. But you couldn't have known.'

'Couldn't I?' he asked bitterly. 'I might have guessed my father wouldn't stop at just being rid of me. But to turn servants off without a character and for no fault of their own ... how could anyone do that?'

'I don't know.'

Drawing a long breath and seeming to reach a decision, Sarre said, 'I'll take you home tomorrow. I ought to have done it today.'

Something she tried not to recognise settled in her chest. She said carefully, 'If you'd done that, you wouldn't have met Mr Bailes. And you couldn't anyway because the horse --'

'There's nothing wrong with the damned horse,' he snapped. And then, more moderately but with great weariness, 'Bertrand knew I wanted some time, so he offered it and – and I let him. I'm sorry. It was stupid of me to think I could change your mind. Stupid and naïve. So we'll --'

'You weren't,' Caroline blurted out. 'You weren't either stupid or naïve. And if I'd wanted to go home, I'd have told you so this morning.'

He turned the full intensity of his gaze upon her.

'What are you saying?'

She swallowed hard, knowing that her next words would herald either the best or the worst choice she would ever make.

'I'm saying I'll marry you.'

He looked completely stunned.

'You will?'

'Yes.'

'Even ... even knowing I lied about the horse?'

'Yes.' *Haven't you punished yourself enough for one day?* 'Even knowing that.'

'That's ... generous of you.'

'Well, you'd know all about generosity, wouldn't you?'

'Oh. I see.' He smiled crookedly. 'You'll marry me because I bought Mr Bailes a meal.'

'No. Not because of that. Nor because you gave him both dignity and hope – nor even because you're still calling him *Mr* Bailes when he's no longer here to hear you.'

'Then why?'

'I'm marrying you because you're a good, kind man who – despite one rather large error of judgement – is intent on doing the right thing. And if you lavish half as much care on your wife as you're giving to Mr Bailes, the woman who marries you will have nothing to complain about.' She harnessed all her courage. 'And there's something else.'

'Yes?'

Smiling, she stood on tiptoe to place a kiss at the corner of his mouth. 'This.'

EIGHTEEN

By Tuesday evening, the absence of both the Earl of Sarre and Mistress Maitland had become noticed in certain quarters.

Not having run into his friend in any of the usual places, Lord Nicholas Wynstanton had called in Cork Street and come away baffled on being told that the Earl had gone out of town.

And Lord Sheringham, having failed to clap eyes on Caroline since his attempt to abduct her from the Pantheon the previous Thursday, was finally forced into making enquiry of Lady Brassington.

She looked him over with overt distaste.

'Mistress Maitland is visiting friends in the country,' she said coldly. 'And, even if she were not, I don't imagine she would wish to see you, my lord.'

He flushed slightly and tried to brazen it out.

'I don't know why your ladyship should think so.'

'In that case, you must be singularly obtuse. I know what you tried to do. And you may count yourself extremely fortunate that I haven't made the information public. But if you accost Caroline again, you may count on that situation changing. I trust that makes the matter perfectly plain?'

And she walked away without giving him the chance to answer.

Marcus scowled at her retreating back. He'd realised that, if Caroline told anyone what had happened at the Pantheon, it would be Lily Brassington and he'd known that the consequences of that were potentially dire. He had, however, counted on being allowed to make it all sound like a misunderstanding. Of *course*, he hadn't intended to abduct the girl; he'd merely found her alone and unchaperoned at a public ridotto and wanted to offer his protection. Not realising her peril, Caroline had resisted and they'd quarrelled. It was all very unfortunate and he had been hoping for an opportunity to put matters right.

Lady Brassington had not only blocked that avenue but also issued a threat which he couldn't afford to completely ignore. On the other hand, Caroline was still his only hope of avoiding ruin so he needed to find her and quickly. Then he'd better come up with another and more fool-proof abduction plan.

Since he had no other option, the following morning found him once again being admitted to the dingy house in Kensington – hoping against hope that he'd find the girl there and that she hadn't given her mother chapter and verse on what had happened at the Pantheon. If she had, he had no idea what the hell he was going to do.

As it turned out, he had timed his visit better than he knew for Mrs Haywood was not at home. The sisters, however, seemed perfectly happy to see him which removed his worst fear. But when he enquired after Caroline, the elder one shook her head and said brightly, 'Oh – Caro's not here, m'lord. Hasn't been for a couple of days, now.'

'Indeed? Then perhaps you can tell me where I might find her?'

'No,' said the other girl. 'We can't.'

'You can't?' he asked pleasantly. 'Or you won't?'

'Can't – because we don't exactly know.' Sylvia's smile became lightly edged with acid. 'And it'd not do you much good if we did, m'lord.'

'I'm not sure I understand you.'

'No. But I expect you'll find out soon enough.'

'Syl,' hissed Lavinia. 'There's no harm in telling him, is there? And being as he was hoping to marry Caro himself, he's maybe got a right to know.'

Marcus didn't like the sound of that. He said, 'Know what?'

Ignoring him, Sylvia shrugged at her sister.

'So tell him, if you want. It's hardly going to change anything now.'

The bad feeling in Lord Sheringham's gut intensified.

'If there is some significant circumstance of which I am as yet unaware,' he said grittily, 'I would appreciate being apprised of it.'

'Oh my!' grinned Sylvia. 'What a lot of long words.'

'Syl – don't be mean.' Lavinia smiled at his lordship. 'It's like this. Our Caro has fallen in love with another gentleman and run off to be married. I daresay she's wed by now.'

'She's *eloped?*'

'Yes.'

It's not possible. Who else would want her? And where could she have met him without me knowing?

'With whom?'

'Well, that's the romantic bit. Caro left a note saying how happy she was but she never told us the name of her intended. We couldn't understand why she didn't, could we, Syl? And Mam were right mad in case it was a Nobody.' Lavinia gave a tiny laugh. 'Only then the next morning, we found another note outside the door. And it was from *him.*'

'Him?'

'The gentleman Caro's marrying,' said Sylvia in the kind of pitying tone usually reserved for imbeciles. 'Who else do you think?'

Marcus cast her a filthy look and restored his attention to the less annoying of the two.

'And presumably this fellow signed his name?'

'He did,' nodded Lavinia. 'And you could have knocked us down with a feather 'cos she'd never said a word about him before. Mind you, she never said a word about you neither. Proper secretive our Caro's become lately.'

'Do you think,' asked Marcus through his teeth, 'that you might come to the point and tell me who this *gentleman* is?'

'Well, yes, if you like. I suppose you'll probably know him.' Hugely enjoying herself, Lavinia paused, purely for effect. 'It's the Earl of Sarre.'

Just for a moment, Marcus thought he must have misheard. Then, somewhere beyond the strange roaring in his ears, came the thought, *Sarre. Of course it would be him. The bastard's having his revenge.* And then, struggling to apply a few grains of logic, *But whatever he's said and whatever these two idiots think, he won't marry her. Oh – he'll bed*

210

her. But he won't marry her. He'll send her back to me and wait for me to pick up his leavings.

With enormous difficulty, he dragged some air into his lungs and said, 'I'm sorry to say it but I fear that your sister has been most wickedly deceived.'

'How do you work that out?' asked Sylvia, plainly disbelieving.

'I know Lord Sarre. There will be no wedding – nor did he ever intend that there should be. He has a long-standing grudge against me and, knowing I had hoped to win Mistress Maitland's hand myself, is using her to hurt me.'

'I can't say as that sounds very likely,' said Sylvia sceptically. 'Sounds more like something out of a novel to me.'

Marcus managed a grim smile.

'Then you can't have considered the matter. Sarre is an Earl. If his intentions were honest, why would he persuade your sister into an elopement when he had no need to do so?'

''Cos it's romantic,' sighed Lavinia.

'No. It is merely dishonourable. A thing no true gentleman would do because it has compromised your sister's reputation beyond repair. Worse still, he has had time now in which to debauch her person.' He, too, knew about dramatic pauses. 'Your sister, ladies, is by now almost certainly ruined.'

The two girls exchanged doubtful glances.

Sylvia said, 'If you're right and this Earl doesn't intend marriage – why did he bother to leave Mam a letter telling her not to worry and that Caro'd come back to Town a Countess? I reckon you're just jealous and out to make mischief. Our sister isn't stupid. If she's fallen in love with him, it's because he's worth it. Unlike yourself, my lord.'

'I see that I'm wasting my breath,' said Marcus, wishing he could shake the damned girl until her teeth rattled. 'You say Mistress Maitland isn't stupid. Allow me to add one final bit of information. Lord Sarre has been abroad for ten years due to a very nasty scandal. For all any of us know to the contrary, he may have left a wife behind him.' He gave a perfunctory bow and said, 'Upon which note, I'll bid you good afternoon.'

When the door had slammed behind him, Lavinia said, 'What if he's right?'

'I doubt if he is. He may be pretty to look at but, if you ask me, there's something nasty inside.'

'That's as maybe. But the question is – what do we tell Mam?'

'Nothing. If he is right, the damage is done by now. And if he's not … what's the point in worrying her when there's nowt to be done about it? Let's just wait and see.'

* * *

Back in Half-Moon Street, Marcus nursed his grievances, contemplated his remaining choices and cursed Sarre at great length over a bottle of brandy. His luck, throughout, had been bloody awful; his only alternative to bankruptcy was Caroline Maitland; and he couldn't think of Sarre without wanting to commit murder. Unfortunately, none of these things was constructive.

At some point as he started to become inebriated, he found himself thinking back to how it had all started. At school, Eastry – as he'd been then – had been his best friend. They'd done everything together, even during the holidays. But at Oxford, things had begun to change. Marcus had noticed that, where he himself was merely tolerated, Eastry had been popular; so popular that Marcus had often found himself competing for his friend's company. Then had come the Grand Tour. Eastry had made his accompanied by the brother of a Duke; Marcus's had been done in the company of his old tutor. Worst of all, had been their first season on the Town when the young ladies had clustered about Eastry like flies round a jam pot. And Marcus hadn't been able to understand why. While Eastry was heir to an impoverished Earldom, with a country house going to rack and ruin, he himself was already in possession of both his title and a tidy fortune. He dressed better than Eastry, was better-looking than Eastry … yet the girls still sighed over the Viscount's smile. None of it made any sense. And somehow, amongst it all, envy had turned to something darker and more dangerous.

Evangeline Mortimer had been the catch of the Season. Her exquisite looks and her fortune ensured that she could have had any man she wanted. But, watching from the side-lines, Marcus had concluded that she'd really only chosen Eastry because, although the match-making mamas dismissed him, their daughters all vied for his attention and Evie enjoyed watching her rivals turn green with envy.

She hadn't been like the other girls. There had been a streak of wildness in her; a spark of something that was easily fanned into a flame. Give her a whiff of danger, challenge her a little and she could be lured into almost any escapade. And so, in order to prove something to himself as well as showing Eastry a thing or two, he'd drawn Evie first into a flirtation and then into bed. For a time, it had been fun, laughing behind Eastry's back whilst tumbling his affianced wife. Only then she'd got pregnant and, instead of simply going ahead with her wedding, she'd insisted on telling Eastry the truth. On the whole, Marcus wouldn't have minded watching his bastard being reared as the next heir to the earldom but Evie would have none of it so he'd reconciled himself to marriage and impending fatherhood. It hadn't been very difficult. Having already discovered the pleasures of deep basset, he could see that Evie's money might come in very useful indeed.

Only he'd never had it because the silly bitch had gone cavorting about on a roof-top and got herself killed. Knowing Evie, it was all too easy to imagine how that had happened. And he knew Eastry better than to suppose for a moment that he'd had any hand in the tragedy. But when Marcus had learned she was dead, something angrily powerful had filled every bone, vein and muscle; and, almost before he realised it, he was shouting accusations of murder.

Of course, they weren't the kind of accusations one could take back ... so he hadn't. And now Eastry – Sarre – was back in England and intent on vengeance. Vengeance Marcus was determined he would never have.

If Sarre and the girl had eloped, they'd gone in one of two directions. Lord Hardwicke's Marriage Act had put an end to Fleet weddings ... so it was either Scotland for marriage over the anvil or somewhere nearer to hand with a special license. Scotland, being one hell of a journey, was the less likely of the two. Marcus would put money, if he'd had any, on Sarre having procured a license; and, if that was the case, there was almost certainly only one place he'd go. The house in that God-forsaken spot on the east Kent coast that he'd always been so bloody fond of.

By the time this much had become clear to him, he was more than half-way down the bottle and starting to feel its effects. He considered spreading the word that Sarre had run off with Caroline Maitland for her money. But though that would ruin the Earl's reputation, it would also make Marcus look rather foolish. And gossip like that would only bear fruit if Sarre married the girl – which Marcus didn't think he would. Why should he? Why would *anyone* marry that plain, annoying chit if they didn't have to? No. Sarre had only run off with her to queer Marcus's pitch and to make her an even less desirable *parti* than she already was. The elopement, should it become known, would achieve that. Sarre didn't even need to take her to bed. And if Caroline was holding out for a wedding ring, Marcus knew he'd never force her. But if they weren't married ... if he was just keeping her for a few days before returning her to her family with her reputation in shreds ... well, if *that* was the case, the game wasn't over, was it?

He could track them down. It wouldn't be hard. If he set off on horseback first thing in the morning, he could be in Sandwich by noon. No, that wouldn't do. If he got lucky, he might find a way of carrying off the girl and he wouldn't get far with a struggling, screaming female tossed across his saddle-bow. He'd have to take the carriage. He could take a room at the coaching-inn in Deal and hire a horse there. That would work. It would enable him to reconnoitre unnoticed.

Of course, if he *wasn't* lucky and Sarre got in his way ... well, the idea of putting a bullet through the Earl's brain was by no means unattractive.

* * *

Later that same evening, Lord Nicholas Wynstanton walked into Sinclair's in order to ask Aristide if *he* knew where Sarre had got to. Unfortunately, before he had the opportunity to do this, his brother arrived hard on his heels and said, 'Ah. Nicholas. How fortuitous.'

'Is it?' Nicholas eyed the Duke with his usual caution. 'Why?'

Rockliffe smiled slightly.

'Two things – neither of which need cause you undue concern. Firstly, I shall be taking Adeline down to the Priors tomorrow and will most probably remain there until after Christmas.'

'She's still not well?'

'She is … less well than I would like.' The truth was that, roughly three months into her pregnancy the Duchess was still suffering severe bouts of nausea which her husband was beginning to find extremely alarming. 'In truth, I would prefer her to remain here within easy reach of her doctor … but she is convinced that country air will suit her better.'

Nicholas nodded and added awkwardly, 'She'll be fine, I'm sure.'

'Of course.' As ever, Rockliffe hid his feelings behind an apparently lazy façade. 'All being well, Nell and Harry will be staying with us for the festive season; and, if you don't consider a family party too dull, you are more than welcome to join us.'

'Thank you. Yes. I might well do that.' Expecting the Duke to stroll off in search of his own friends, Nicholas added, 'You'll give my love to Adeline, won't you?'

'With pleasure.' Toying idly with his snuff-box, Rockliffe said, 'On another issue entirely … do you know where your friend, Lord Sarre, is just at present?'

Nicholas stared. It shouldn't surprise him, this peculiar omniscience of his brother's – but somehow it always did. He said, 'Actually, no. I was hoping someone here might know.'

'Aristide Delacroix, for example?'

'How did --?' he began unwarily and then stopped. 'Why should Delacroix know anything?'

'One would imagine because he and Sarre have been acquainted for some time. Most probably, since one would guess them to have met in Paris, well before the advent of this club.' He paused and appeared to take an infinitesimal pinch of snuff. 'I've a suspicion, you see, that they may own Sinclair's jointly. But perhaps I'm allowing my imagination to run away with me?'

'How would I know whether you are or not?'

The Duke's smile was distinctly disquieting but he said merely, 'It was just an idea I had. As to my enquiry regarding Sarre's current whereabouts, that was in response to a … whisper … that has reached my ears.'

As was normal when his brother became involved, Nicholas knew the feeling of being thoroughly out of his depth. He said, 'What sort of whisper?'

'That his lordship has eloped with the Maitland heiress.'

'*What?*'

'Precisely.'

'But he … no. That can't be right. Where did you hear this?'

'I looked in on Serena Delahaye's party earlier this evening. It appears that Cassie – having conceived an affection for Mistress Maitland – asked Lily Brassington if the girl was ill. And Lily, in somewhat veiled and convoluted terms, gave Cassie to understand that Mistress Maitland had left London for a time and would return a Countess. Able to think of only one unmarried Earl, Cassie took the question to her father … and Charles mentioned it to me.'

Following this without difficulty but no little disbelief, Nicholas frowned.

'I know Dev's out of town – but an elopement? Why would he do that? If he wanted the girl – which I doubt – there's nothing to stop him marrying her properly.'

'That is my own opinion. For what it's worth, I also don't see Sarre running off with a girl and *not* marrying her.' Rockliffe ran a thumb over the enamelled Aphrodite on the lid of his snuff-box. 'What I *do* see is a possibility of him … er … putting a spoke in Lord Sheringham's wheel, so to speak.' The dark eyes rose to encompass his brother. 'It may surprise you to learn that I am disposed to be helpful.'

'Oh.' Amidst the thoughts whirling through Nicholas's head was the knowledge that no one could be more helpful than Rockliffe if he chose to exert himself. Deciding that, since his Grace seemed to know most of it anyway, he might as well know the rest, he said, 'Right, then. We'd better go and find Aristide.'

'Thank you,' sighed the Duke. 'I suppose it would have been too much to expect you to say that in the first place?'

They found Monsieur Delacroix chatting with sundry guests near the Hazard table but, when he caught sight of Lord Nicholas's expression, he excused himself gracefully and walked over to join him.

'Your Grace ... my Lord?' He bowed. 'Is there something I may help you with?'

'Yes,' said Nicholas. 'But in private.'

Aristide's brows rose but he said nothing, merely leading the two gentlemen up to his office and offering them brandy. Then, looking at Nicholas, he said, 'Well?'

'Where's Dev?' asked his lordship bluntly. And, with a gesture of impatience, 'Sarre – Adrian – whatever you call him. Where *is* he?'

Mindful of Rockliffe's silent presence, Aristide said calmly, 'What makes you suppose that I might be privy to aspects of the Earl's personal life?'

'You can cut line, Aristide. As far as the club goes, Rock's guessed most of it ... and he's just heard something damned peculiar. So if you know anything, you might as well say.'

'Ah.' There was a moment of hesitation and then, 'Adrian is in Kent where, so he said when last I saw him, he was planning to marry Caroline Maitland. The two of them left Town on Monday and I believe the appropriate notice will appear in the *Morning Chronicle* tomorrow.'

There was a long silence. Then Nicholas said, 'He's mad. He's completely and utterly insane.'

'Both Bertrand and I have said as much,' shrugged Aristide. 'It didn't make any difference. And I should think the deed would be done by now. Wouldn't you?'

'He had a marriage licence?' asked Rockliffe.

'I presume so – otherwise he'd need banns or the Great North Road.' The Frenchman looked at the Duke and said, 'Pardon me for asking, your Grace ... but what is your interest in this?'

'Two things – the principle one of which relates to Marcus Sheringham.' Rockliffe took a sip of brandy and then appeared to contemplate his glass. 'Sheringham has been hurling accusations of murder against Sarre for ten years. I, for one, have never believed them. I do, however, suspect that there was more to Evangeline Mortimer's death than was ever made public ... and that, for reasons of his own, Sheringham doesn't want the whole truth to come out.'

'You think *he* pushed her?' asked Nicholas.

'I don't think anyone pushed her. I think it was an accident ... though that is of no particular consequence just now. What we ought to be considering is how, with ruin staring him the face, Lord Sheringham will react when he learns that the lady he doubtless regards as *his* heiress has succumbed to the man he's spent the last decade slandering.' He paused and then added thoughtfully, 'Angry, desperate men tend to take ... extreme measures.'

Aristide said, 'Adrian knows there's a possible risk. After the fire here --'

'Did you ever find proof that was Sheringham?' interrupted Nicholas.

'A hint from a delivery-boy,' came the terse reply. 'Nothing that would stand up in court, unfortunately – and no further trouble since. But Adrian thought it was possible Sheringham might go after him, instead.' He paused. 'To stick a knife in his back, he said. I hoped he was joking.'

'One would also hope that Lord Sheringham isn't rash enough to do anything quite so stupid,' murmured Rockliffe.

'Well, if he is,' returned Nicholas grimly, 'Dev's put himself in the perfect place for it. He won't have gone to Sarre Park. He'll have taken the girl to Devereux House – which is as remote a spot as any would-be assassin could possibly wish for.'

'Indeed.' The Duke rose unhurriedly from his chair. 'Then I have a suggestion you may wish to consider. At some point tomorrow, Sheringham will see the notice of Sarre's marriage and know he has lost the game. As I said earlier, I am taking Adeline to Wynstanton Priors. You could travel down with us and, from there, ride over to check on Lord Sarre's well-being.'

'Yes,' said Nicholas. 'I think I might.'

'Excellent. You might also – if his lordship is not averse to the notion – bring both him and his bride back to the Priors so that we can pretend that his wedding took place with all due decorum in a positive welter of strawberry-leaves.' The Duke smiled faintly. 'And upon that beautifully altruistic note, gentlemen – I will bid you goodnight.'

When the door had closed behind him, Aristide said blankly, 'Strawberry leaves?'

'Ducal crest,' replied Nicholas unexpansively. And then, 'Do you know … there are times when I think I don't know my brother at all?'

'As well, probably, as I know my sister.' Aristide paused and then, with a sideways glance, added, 'Is there something going on between you and Madeleine I should know of?'

'What? No.' Despite his best efforts, Nicholas had failed to meet Mademoiselle Delacroix again which naturally increased his desire to do so. 'Aside from the night of the fire, I've never clapped eyes on her.'

'Ah. Then you wouldn't realise, I suppose.'

'Realise what?'

'That she ducks for cover every time she sees you coming.'

'Does she?' Nicholas blinked in surprise. Then, his dark eyes growing thoughtful, 'Does she now?'

111

NINETEEN

Adrian didn't know what to make of Caroline's sudden change of heart. He knew what she'd *said* but he couldn't help feeling there was something more … something he was missing.

But she'd put back some warmth into a day which – despite having begun so promisingly – had disintegrated into misery and shock. That brief, butterfly kiss had made him yearn to put his arms about her and just hold on. He'd wanted to bury his face in her hair and pretend that her presence was nothing to do with Marcus Sheringham; that she was here with him because she wanted to be rather than because he'd tricked her; that a future containing something honest and real might be possible. Just for a moment, he'd let himself hope.

Of course, he'd been unable to let any of that show. He'd merely inclined his head, brushed her hand with his lips and, inwardly cursing himself, said, 'Thank you. I'll try to be worthy of your good opinion.'

Then he went into the house and gave Bertrand the gist of his meeting with Bailes and its likely results. Bertrand nodded grimly and agreed to make the necessary arrangements, then added, 'There's a word for men like your father …but I daresay you'd rather I didn't use it.'

'I'd rather not talk about him at all,' replied Adrian. 'You can stop doctoring the horse, by the way. It seems that Mistress Maitland no longer wishes to leave.'

'She doesn't?' Bertrand stared at him. 'She's going to marry you?'

'So she says.'

'I'm impressed. After the Claude Duvall business, I didn't think you'd talk her round at *all* – never mind managing it in forty-eight hours. What did the trick?'

'I suspect it had something to do with my offering Mr Bailes a job.' Adrian managed a sardonic shrug. 'She thinks I'm honourable and kind.

Whether she'll still be of the same mind by the end of the evening … I don't know.'

'Ah.' Bertrand nodded thoughtfully. 'Yes. Best to get that out of the way, I suppose. But if you want a word of advice, you'll give her that gown you bought. Now she's said she'll marry you, she can't jump to the wrong conclusions. And, aside from women always liking a gift, it'll show that you thought about her and went to a bit of trouble.'

'That's not why I did it.'

'No – but it's how it will *look*.'

Adrian gave a brief, unamused laugh and rubbed his hands over his face.

'Do you know … I'm getting really tired of doing things just for how they look.'

'Good – because that brings me to the other thing. Stop being the Earl and start being yourself. Not all at once, maybe – but gradually, so it looks natural; as though you're just becoming more relaxed in her company. You're a good enough actor to do that, aren't you?'

'Normally, yes,' agreed Adrian. 'But tonight's a different matter. Tonight the best I can hope for is to get the words right.'

* * *

Caroline stood in her chamber, staring out of the window. She realised that, at this point, a sensible woman would be questioning whether or not she'd done the right thing. Plainly, she wasn't sensible. Instinct had triumphed over both caution and logic … and, so far, she didn't regret it in the least.

She might have been disappointed in the stilted formality of his response had she not caught the expression that had flared briefly in his eyes. Incredulity merging into embarrassed pleasure. An expression that she didn't think had anything to do with Marcus Sheringham because, if Sarre had been applying his usual steely control, it wouldn't have been there at all.

She smiled a little and then swallowed a lump in her throat when she remembered how he'd been with that poor old man who plainly loved him. That had been honest, too … and it had revealed more about his lordship than any amount of questioning. He didn't just see those

221

dismissed servants as his responsibility – though, under the circumstances, that would have been remarkable enough. He actually *cared* about them. And that, thought Caroline optimistically, proved that an affectionate nature lay buried beneath the ice. Perhaps, in time, he might be less wary of letting it show.

The red gown she'd been wearing for the past two days had collected dirt and bits of weed during their walk across the fields, which was no bad thing because she was sick of the sight of it anyway. As for the pink silk she'd been wearing on the journey from London, she had no idea what had happened to it and didn't much care. But her only remaining gown was an old blue one made of light wool which was extremely plain and not in the least fashionable. She sighed faintly. She'd have liked his lordship to see her in something vaguely flattering; but since she had little choice in the matter, she shrugged the thought aside and set about readying herself for dinner.

His nerves at full stretch, Adrian waited in the parlour. The brandy bottle was tempting him with its mere presence but he refused the invitation and sat down with a book pulled off the shelf at random. It turned out to be *The Prince of Abyssinia* by Samuel Johnson which sounded a good deal more interesting than it probably was. Adrian opened it and forced himself to read the first page. He was still scowling at that same page some twenty minutes later when Caroline walked in.

He immediately shut the book and stood up, taking in her appearance. The dark blue gown suited her … as did the way she'd tied her hair high on her head, leaving just a few loose curls to drift around her neck. He wanted to tell her she looked lovely but couldn't seem to frame the right words because everything inside him wanted to walk across the room and take her in his arms. So he took a calming breath, cleared his throat and said, 'I haven't seen that gown before. It looks well on you.'

'This?' Her smile was shy and rather surprised. 'It's quite old. Not, as you can no doubt tell, one of the Harrogate ones.'

He shook his head. 'I like it. And I like your hair that way.' *It makes me want to tug that ribbon free and let it all tumble loose so I can bury my face in it.* 'I have to ask if you meant what you said earlier. About marrying me, I mean.'

She sensed rather than saw his uncertainty and again felt an inclination to put her arms around him and hold him very tightly. Instead, she sat down and said tranquilly, 'Yes. I meant it.'

He was surprised by how far those four words went towards easing the tension inside him. But still he couldn't help asking, 'Does that mean you think that, in time, you might be able to trust me?'

'I'm beginning to suppose that quite likely.' The deep brown eyes rose to look directly into his. 'Of course, it will need to work both ways. I'm hoping you'll feel able to stop hiding what you *are* behind what you think you *ought* to be.'

A half-smile touched his mouth. 'Have you been talking to Bertrand, by any chance?'

'Not recently – and not about that. I presume he's told you the same thing?'

'More or less.'

'And so?'

'So I'll try.'

'That's all I ask. I believe we've come to a better understanding of each other rather more quickly than I'd thought possible.' She smiled up at him. 'Perhaps we can build on that.'

'Yes. Perhaps we can.'

* * *

At some point half-way through dinner, dread once more started gnawing at the edges of his mind, making it difficult to maintain easy conversation and turning the food to ashes in his mouth. He stopped eating but kept up a pretence of continuing to do so by rearranging what was on his plate and sought refuge, instead, in his wine-glass.

For a while, Caroline let him get away with it and then, setting aside her own knife and fork, she stood up and held out her hand to him, saying, 'This is silly. You won't be comfortable until you've said what you have to say. So let's go back to the parlour, away from all this food and you can get it over with.'

Adrian rose reluctantly and took her outstretched fingers in his.

'I ought to be able to deal with this better.'

'I won't know if that's true until you've told me.' She gave his hand a brief squeeze. 'And as for dealing with it … I don't suppose it's occurred to you that I might be able to help?'

'No. But that's no reflection on you. I've been living with this for ten years and am still sickened by it.' He walked with her to the parlour and, shutting the door behind them, added, 'I wouldn't burden you with it at all if I didn't have to.'

Caroline sat down and arranged her skirts about her.

'Why do you think you have to?'

'So that when, as my wife, you hear the whispers and see people turning their backs on me, you'll at least know the truth … and for another reason which I'll come back to later.' He took the chair on the far side of the hearth and, keeping his gaze fixed on his hands, said, 'You asked me once if I had ever been in love and I told you that I had. Once. Her name was Evangeline. She was eighteen, stunningly beautiful and had a fortune of twenty thousand a year. I mention the money, not because it mattered to me, but because, had it not existed, none of the rest of this would have happened.' He paused and then, continuing to keep his tone level and completely impersonal, said, 'I was twenty-one and entering the *beau monde* for the first time since making the Grand Tour. The moment Evie smiled at me, I was lost. I didn't care that we had nothing in common or that the neck-or-nothing way she rode scared the hell out of me. I didn't even care that she was rumoured to have been a little free with her favours or that my parents didn't like her. I just wanted her. I wanted her so badly it hurt.'

He stopped and, crossing to the sideboard, poured wine into two glasses. Then, having handed one of them to Caroline, he resumed his seat and took a drink.

'I asked her to marry me and, for some reason I never understood, she accepted. My father considered her entirely unsuitable to bear the hallowed Devereux name and my mother actually despised her … but there was that twenty thousand a year, you see.' He glanced up briefly. 'I should explain that the Earldom was virtually bankrupt. My grandfather liked the gaming-table and my father liked investment schemes. Neither of them was lucky. As a consequence, my parents decided that Evie's money might just about outweigh her many faults and agreed to let me marry her.' Another pause and this time he drained his glass. 'The wedding was to take place two days after my twenty-second birthday. In the early hours of that birthday, Evie woke me up and led me through a part of the house that had been unusable for decades, then out on to the roof. I can still remember the smell of mice and mildew and rotting wood, followed by the clean crispness of the dawn air. The sun was just coming up and the sky promised a beautiful day.'

He stopped again and showed no sign of continuing. The blood had drained from his skin and a pulse was beating insistently in his jaw. Realising that he was approaching the most painful part of the story and to give him time, Caroline fetched the wine from the sideboard and re-filled his glass, saying gently, 'It's all right. You don't have to finish it if you don't want to. The rest will wait until another day.'

'No. It won't. If I don't do this now, I never will. It's just difficult because I can't talk about it without remembering. And I don't *want* to remember.'

'No. I can see that.' And she could. He was starting to look quite ill.

Adrian hauled some air into his lungs and said rapidly, 'By the time I caught up with her, she was standing on the parapet. She was wearing some trailing white thing. She said ... she said she wasn't going to marry me; that she had a lover and was pregnant by him. She asked me to guess who it was but I couldn't. Not at first. None of it made any sense. Then she told me she'd been sleeping with a man I'd known since I was eight years old and who, until that moment, I'd have trusted with my life. And I wanted to vomit.'

So did Caroline. He'd told her the tale wasn't pretty but nothing had prepared her for just how ugly it really was.

Glancing up again, Adrian read her expression and said desperately, 'I'm sorry but it gets worse. She was still dancing about on the parapet when she got annoyed with me for not responding the way she wanted. And that ... that's when she fell.' He drained his glass in one swallow and snapped it down on the table in order to grip his hands together. 'I tried to catch her but it all happened too fast. I couldn't. So she fell. Sixty feet down on to the terrace.' He swallowed. 'I remember exactly how she looked, lying there, broken. I even recall seeing Mr Bailes and Old Matthew staring up at me from the garden. Then I was sick.'

Unable to stand it any longer, Caroline crossed to sit on the arm of his chair and laid her hand over his. She knew better than to say anything. His fingers were tight and cold under hers.

'I ran down to the terrace – to Evie. There was so much blood. I knew there was nothing to be done but her eyes were still open and I wanted … I wanted …' He stopped again and took a breath. 'Servants appeared and then my parents. My father asked question after question until I'd told the whole sordid story. At some point during that, I realised I had Evie's blood all over me and – and I threw up again. Father was disgusted. Then he and my mother asked if I'd lost my temper and pushed her.'

'*What?*' Even after everything that had gone before, Caroline couldn't believe her ears. 'How *could* they? How could they even *think* it?'

'It's just … it's who they were. Who my mother still is, for that matter. All that signified was preserving the family name.' He paused. 'And then *he* came. He'd supposedly come for Evie. Then, when he heard that she was dead, he started shouting that I'd murdered her and that he'd see me hang for it.' Adrian managed a slight shrug. 'If I'd been in any fit state to think coherently, I'd have known that what happened after that was a foregone conclusion. My father didn't care that no one could prove I killed Evie; he only cared that *I* couldn't prove I didn't. And he wasn't about to let his heir stand trial for murder. So he reminded me that I wasn't his only son, pushed some money into my hand and ordered me out of the country.' Another shrug. 'I went.'

'And didn't come back? Or contact your family at all?'

'No. I thought, given time, my father would take steps to have me declared dead.'

There were no words for what Caroline thought of that, so she pressed her lips together and said nothing.

'If Benedict – my brother – hadn't died in a riding accident, I wouldn't be here now. But it seemed I owed something to my name, so ... I came back.' He stopped and drew a long breath. 'That's all of it, I think. But if you've any questions, ask them now. I won't sleep tonight as it is so I'd as soon not have to dig it all up again if it can be avoided.'

'You dream about it?'

'Frequently.' He turned his head to look at her and said, 'You should think very carefully about whether or not you believe what I've told you.'

She shook her head slightly.

'Having just seen what it cost you to speak of it? Of course I believe you.'

'Even though you know I'm an actor and that I've deceived you before?'

'Yes. Even knowing that.'

'You,' he said simply, 'are a truly remarkable woman.' And then expelling a long, uneven breath, 'You haven't asked.'

She didn't pretend not to know what he meant.

'I don't need to. It was Marcus Sheringham, wasn't it?'

'Yes. Nothing can change the way he betrayed me with Evie or what happened to her as a result. But after ten years, I hoped he'd stop calling me a murderer. Since he hasn't ... and since, by the time I returned to England he was already a hairsbreadth from ruin, I decided to give him that final push. He can rant against me all he likes from the debtor's ward in the Fleet prison – or from the other side of the Channel, if he decides to flee the country.' He managed the travesty of a smile. 'And now you know I'm neither good nor kind. I'm just very tired of being smeared by something I didn't do. Also, I'm not averse to giving Sheringham a taste of the kind of hell he gave me.'

Leaving her hand in his, Caroline said, 'No one could blame you for that.'

'*You* could if you really thought about it. Do I need to point out the symmetry ?'

'No. It's clear enough. He took Evie from you and you're taking me from him. But thank you for pointing it out.'

'Yes. I'm very clever.'

'I know.' She looked at him. 'Do you *want* me to change my mind?'

'No – though I'd understand if you did.' He looked down and began toying with her fingers. 'What I want is for none of this to lie between us. Ever.'

'Then we won't let it.' She thought for a moment. 'I suppose I'm not allowed to tell people the truth?'

'I'd rather you didn't. It wouldn't do any good. I can't prove any of it and people believe what they want to. Also, badly as Evie behaved, it doesn't seem fair to speak ill of her when she can no longer defend herself.'

Which is a damned sight more consideration than she ever showed you, isn't it?

Swallowing her momentary flash of anger and, having no further excuse to stay where she was, she rose from her perch beside him and returned to her own chair, saying, 'Very well. It's done now so we can put it away and talk of happier things. When shall we be married?'

'As soon as it can be arranged. I'll ride into Sandwich tomorrow and see the rector at St Peter's.' Adrian wished she hadn't moved away. His relief that the truth was out and the skies hadn't fallen was producing a wave of inevitable euphoria and he'd been wondering what she'd do if he put his arm around her and just held her for a moment. 'Taking, as it turned out, a bit too much for granted, I took some preparatory measures before leaving London. One of them was speaking to my lawyer. If you want a formal contract which includes provision for your family drawn up immediately and can tell me what you want done, I'll write to him. Otherwise, that and other matters will have to wait until we go back.'

Taken by surprise, Caroline said, 'You'd do that?'

His brows rose. 'Yes. I promised, didn't I? Do you want me to?'

'No. It's not urgent. But I thank you for offering.'

'You are entitled to have some say about what's done with your own money,' he shrugged. 'Speaking of which ... you may wish to write to your grandfather. On the whole, since it doesn't cast me in the best possible light, it might be best not to mention that I ran off with you. But I'll leave that decision to you.'

The brown eyes filled with laughter and she said, 'You don't think he'll applaud me for running off with an Earl?'

'No. I think he'll probably want to kick me down the steps. And since I'm looking forward to meeting him, I'd prefer not to start with a disadvantage.'

'He's a plain, self-made man with no airs or graces. Do you *really* want to meet him?'

'Yes. I really do.' He smiled suddenly. 'You love him, don't you?'

That all-too-rare smile made her breath catch. She said, 'Yes. Very much.'

'Well, then. Having heard from Mr Bailes what kind of stock I come from and knowing how I've made my way these last years, it should come as no surprise that a plain, self-made man sounds just the kind of fellow I'd like. Also ... I can ask him how much you *really* know about sheep.'

'You were listening?'

'Hardly at all – though I did catch phrases like *first clip* and *parasites* and *foot rot* which naturally did something to dampen my romantic notions of fluffy little lambs.'

'And you have so many romantic notions, don't you?' she teased.

'One or two.' He paused and then added, 'The one I have in mind at the moment involves kissing you. But I'm reluctant to risk another slap.'

This time the air simply evaporated in her lungs, making speech impossible.

'No. Of course not.' Adrian kept his tone light and entirely free of regret. 'Our wedding, then. Unless Mr Bailes turns up before it and you've no objection to inviting him, it will just be the two of us and Bertrand. Not, I imagine, quite the occasion you'd have hoped for.'

Caroline tried to control her whirling thoughts. *He was joking. He didn't mean it. Did he? If he did ... if he did, how do I say "Yes, please" without* actually *saying it?*

'It doesn't matter – and neither is it your fault. If I'd chosen differently, we could have married openly in London. But I didn't.'

'True.' He leaned back in his chair, apparently relaxed. 'Since we've had an evening of confession, I should probably admit something else. When Claude Duvall first mentioned marriage to you that night at the Pantheon, he didn't know where the words came from. He certainly never planned them. And when he proposed again in the Sunken Garden, it had a great deal to do with the possibility that you were the one woman in a million who might choose the highwayman over the Earl.' He spread his hands in a manner unconsciously French. 'I knew you didn't like me very much. I also knew what a thicket of thorns I'd be plunged into if you chose Duvall. But I couldn't resist the chance to find out if you were truly as rare as I suspected you might be. And you are. Even more so than I originally thought.' He smiled again. 'Now you're trying to decide whether to say something suitably self-deprecating or throw something at my head.'

'No. Actually, I'm not.' Caroline decided that, after what he'd put himself through in the last hour, he deserved to have something made easy. And so, tossing caution to the winds, she said, 'I was wondering why, unlike Claude Duvall, Lord Sarre feels he needs prior permission to kiss his future bride.'

Something flared in the silver-grey eyes.

'It's because, unlike Duvall, the Earl was reared to be a gentleman. Also, of course, Duvall had reason to suppose his advances might not be unwelcome ... whereas his lordship has received no such encouragement.'

'Oh. And how – in a ladylike manner – might that lack be remedied?'

He uncoiled smoothly from his chair and held out a hand to her.

'You could start,' he murmured, pulling her to her feet and into his arms, 'by calling me Adrian.'

TWENTY

On the following morning, Adrian rode into the town with a smile on his face. There were two reasons for this. One was that, against all expectation, he'd had a perfectly peaceful night's sleep. The other was the memory of how practical, down-to-earth Caroline had looked after he'd kissed her.

He'd been careful. A lot more careful, as it turned out, than he'd have liked to be. But still she'd melted into him exactly as she'd done when he'd been Claude Duvall; her mouth just as sweet, her response just as honest. And afterwards ... afterwards her face had been filled with such shy confusion, her eyes so wide and dark and unwittingly inviting, that letting her go had been unexpectedly difficult.

At some point before he fell asleep, something even more unexpected occurred to him. The idea that his feelings for Caroline were becoming more complex than mere liking.

* * *

The rector at the church of St Peter was a youngish man and a stranger. Lord Sarre introduced himself, produced the marriage licence and explained that he required the ceremony to be performed as soon as possible.

The Reverend Conant looked openly disapproving.

'Am I to understand that the young lady is already residing under your roof?' he asked frigidly. 'If so, I will feel impelled to speak to her privately before I can agree to do as your lordship asks. I must be assured that she is not being constrained in any way.'

'She isn't. But you are welcome to call at Devereux House at your convenience.'

'Also, there is the matter of parental consent.'

'No,' said Sarre with pleasant finality, 'there is not. You have in your hand a special licence, signed by the Bishop of London. If he was satisfied, there's no reason why you shouldn't be.'

The Reverend pursed his lips.

'I am not personally acquainted with His Grace.'

'I wasn't aware there was any requirement that you should be.' The Earl assumed an expression of chilly hauteur and restored the licence to his pocket. 'Yours is not the only church in the town. If you feel yourself unable to oblige me, say so.'

* * *

Back at Devereux House, Caroline caught herself smiling inanely at the coffee pot and was forced to conclude that she was well on the way to being completely bewitched.

Having recently been more than a little bewitched by Claude Duvall, this would have been cause for concern had not the two men been one and the same. As it was, however, she told herself that it was perfectly acceptable to fall in love with one gentleman twice.

Unnoticed, Bertrand stood in the doorway watching her for quite a long time before he made his presence known by saying, 'You find Adrian is not so bad, then. Yes?'

'Yes,' she agreed vaguely. And then, 'No. Not so bad at all.'

Nodding, Bertrand sat down and poured a cup of coffee.

'I 'ope you will be 'appy. Better still, I 'ope you will make Adrian 'appy.'

'So do I. I'll certainly do my best.'

'No more charming 'ighwaymen?'

'That,' retorted Caroline with a demure smile, 'would be telling.'

Bertrand laughed.

'Bravo, Mademoiselle. You will do well together, I think.'

* * *

An hour later, when she was half-way through a letter to Grandpa Maitland, Sarre strode in and threw his riding gloves on the table.

'The vicar of St Peter's is an irritating ass who insists he can't marry us until Saturday and refuses to marry us at *all* until he's assured himself that I'm not planning on dragging you to the altar in chains. Unfortunately, the incumbent at St Clement's is prostrate with some ailment or other which leaves us with little choice but to wait on the other fellow's convenience.'

'It's only one more day,' said Caroline placidly.

'Two, actually.'

'From today? Yes. I suppose so. But that doesn't make much difference, does it?'

At some point on the ride home, he'd realised that he couldn't hide what he'd done forever. Sooner or later, she was going to find out and it would be best if she found out from him.

He delayed his answer just long enough for it to be his undoing.

During the short time they'd been together, Caroline had become aware that, while Sarre never hesitated for a second, Adrian frequently did so when he was uneasy.

Without giving him chance to speak, she said, 'What have you done?'

He lifted his chin and looked back, coolly defiant and every inch the Earl.

'What makes you think I've done anything?'

'Haven't you?'

There was a long pause during which Adrian decided that aristocratic superiority wasn't going to get him out of this one – but that confession and contrition might.

'I may have done a couple of things that, with hindsight, could be considered … premature. But they were done with the best of intentions.'

Caroline managed not to laugh but didn't entirely hide the fact that she wanted to.

'Save your excuses and tell me what you've done.'

Adrian saw the dimple peeping out beside her mouth and was tempted to simply sweep her into his arms. Resisting it, he said, 'I instructed my lawyer to put a notice of our marriage in the *Morning Chronicle*. Today, as it happens.'

The dimple disappeared and she stared at him.

'You put an announcement in the newspaper?'

'Yes.'

'While I still thought I was eloping with Claude Duvall and didn't know he was you?'

He nodded. Put like that, it sounded particularly arrogant. Certainly, she wasn't laughing any more.

'You *were* sure of yourself, weren't you?'

'I was fairly sure of myself before we left London,' he agreed uncomfortably. 'It didn't last five minutes once we arrived here.'

'I should think not.' Not inclined to make this easy for him, she kept her tone deliberately cool – even though it was quite enjoyable watching him come as close to squirming as made no difference. 'I presume you had a contingency plan for if your charm failed?'

'Not exactly ... but I'd have thought of something.'

'I can imagine.' She folded her arms and kept him trapped with her eyes. 'What else?'

'I beg your pardon?'

'You said a couple of things. What else?'

He very nearly groaned. He should have got this out of the way last night when she was still sympathetic. She didn't sound very sympathetic now and, by the time he'd finished, she'd probably want to murder him.

All right. Confess, by all means but remember why you did it. And stop behaving like a schoolboy who's been hauled in front of the headmaster for scribbling on the walls.

Dropping negligently into a chair, he said, 'I thought your mother would worry less about your safety if she knew you hadn't run off with some nameless man. So I left her a note.'

Just for a second, Caroline didn't know whether to give way to hysterical laughter or throw something at him.

'A note. I see. How ... considerate. But Mama wouldn't have been worrying about my safety so much as having spasms at the thought I was marrying a Nobody. *You* have made it possible for her to boast to the butcher, the baker, the candlestick-maker – and, for all I know, the fellow who sweeps the street – about her daughter, the Countess. Well done, my lord.'

'Adrian,' he corrected.

'I'll call you Adrian when you stop playing the Earl,' she shot back. And then, 'Is that everything?'

'Not ... quite.'

'Ah. Adrian again, I see.'

He frowned at her, startled. 'How do you know?'

'It's obvious when you know what to look for. Equally obviously, I'm not telling you what that is. In fact, I may never speak to you again unless you finish what you've started.'

Quite suddenly and without any warning whatsoever, he grinned at her.

'Yes, you will. You're having too much fun hauling me over the coals.'

'What brings you to that conclusion?'

He shrugged and then, unable to resist, said, 'It's obvious when you know what to look for.'

Caroline wished he'd stop smiling. It made it impossible to hold on to her perfectly reasonable annoyance and almost as hard not to dissolve into a mindless puddle. She cleared her throat and said, 'Very clever. Well? And I'd sooner we left Lord Sarre out of it, if you don't mind.'

'Sit down, then. This may take a little longer.' And, when she had done so, said, 'I paid a call on Lady Brassington. And I told her everything.'

It was the last thing she had expected.

'*Everything?* No. You can't have done!'

'I did. My masquerade as Claude Duvall; Sheringham and what happened at the Pantheon; which proposal you accepted and which you didn't; the intention to elope. Everything.'

'Oh good God.' Caroline dropped her head in her hands. 'What on earth possessed you?'

'I wanted to be sure that, in the event of any rumours about an elopement, your good name wouldn't suffer too badly but knew I couldn't do it alone. So I trusted her ladyship with my own deception in the hope that she'd be sufficiently fond of you to help. Fortunately, she is.'

'What did she say?'

'Quite a lot after she decided to have her butler bring brandy instead of tossing me into the street. She asked a good many questions, of course ... but, at the end of our talk, she promised the help I asked for.

When we return to London, you'll have Lily Brassington firmly on your side.'

'Oh.' She looked at him helplessly. 'I suppose I'm going to have to forgive you, aren't I?'

'Eventually. I wouldn't want to curtail your enjoyment.'

She shook her head, laughing.

'You're impossible.'

'I *was* impossible.' He rose and crossed to drop a light kiss on her hair. 'From now on, I intend to work at becoming utterly, tediously *possible*.'

Caroline looked up into his face and murmured, 'Don't try too hard. I quite like you as you are.'

The silvery eyes widened slightly and he reached down as if to draw her to her feet.

The door opened and Bertrand walked in, saying, 'You have visitors.'

Adrian immediately stepped back and said, 'Not the damned vicar?'

'No.' He moved aside. 'Two old friends of yours.'

For perhaps three seconds, Adrian simply froze. Then he was off across the room, his hands outstretched. 'Mr Bailes. And – and *Betsy*.'

The short, slightly plump woman in the doorway stood rooted to the spot, her face crumpling. 'Oh. My little lord. I've prayed and prayed but I never thought ... I never ...'

And then she was in his lordship's arms and sobbing into his shoulder.

Just for a second or two, Caroline watched Adrian apparently not minding that Betsy was soaking his immaculate coat and then walked smilingly towards the gardener.

'Mr Bailes – please come in and sit down. Bertrand ... perhaps you could ask Sally to bring tea? And you'll be joining us yourself, of course.'

Bertrand grinned, made a tiny gesture which clearly said, '*Not a chance*' and left the room.

Betsy, meanwhile, was still hiccupping incoherent words into the lace at Adrian's throat in between trying to brush the tears from her cheeks. Pulling a handkerchief from his pocket, he tried to do the job for her and, when she wouldn't raise her head, closed her fingers around it, saying, 'Take this, my dear.'

She eyed it blearily and sniffed.

'N-no, indeed, my lord. It's far t-too good.'

'Nothing's too good for you, Betsy. When I think of all the times you've mopped my face, cleaned the mud from my knees and salved my cuts and bruises ...' He stopped, his voice becoming a little ragged. 'You were a better mother to Ben and me than the woman who bore us – so just take the damned handkerchief, will you?'

This did the trick.

Betsy stepped back and said severely, 'My lord! Such language – and in front of the young lady, too. Shame on you! A body would think you'd never been taught proper manners – which I know for a fact you were!'

Caroline managed not to laugh. Mr Bailes didn't.

Looking duly chastened, Adrian said gravely, 'I beg your pardon, Betsy. But the young lady and I are to be married on Saturday – so it's probably best that she knows all my faults, don't you think?'

'Married?' Betsy's reddened eyes immediately impaled Caroline. 'Is that so, Miss?'

'It is.' She smiled. 'I daresay his lordship will presently remember the rest of his manners and introduce us properly – but, in the meantime, I'd be delighted if you and Mr Bailes would agree to attend our wedding.'

This produced a ripple of shock in both Betsy and Mr Bailes and caused Adrian to bathe Caroline in a sudden, dazzling smile.

It was perhaps fortunate that Sally chose that moment to enter with the tray. By the time everyone was settled with a cup of tea, Adrian had steered the conversation beyond the inevitable exclamations of the great honour of being invited to his lordship's wedding but that acceptance wouldn't be fitting and into more practical channels. Once Mr Bailes had formally agreed to take up the post of head-gardener and Betsy – or Mrs Holt, as she was to be known to the servants under her command – had been appointed as house-keeper, he moved smoothly on to the question of accommodation and other practicalities.

Caroline watched him and thought, *You must have been a very nice little boy and a charming, open-hearted young man if the affection these two old people have for you is any indication. And all that warmth is still there … buried beneath the damage done by Marcus Sheringham, that wretched girl and your blasted parents. If two of them weren't already dead, I could murder them all.*

But she kept smiling and, deciding that Betsy and his lordship would probably appreciate a few moments of privacy, waited until Mr Bailes had finished his tea before asking if he would care to take a tour of the garden and see the mammoth task that awaited him there.

Adrian watched them go and, when the door closed behind them, turned back to Betsy, saying, 'You will have to humour me, Betsy. I've a lot to make up for.'

'You've *nothing* to make up for, my lord. None of it was your fault and the way the old Earl treated you was downright disgraceful,' she replied heatedly. 'And if he thought any of us would have said a bad word about you, he was a nodcock.'

'Among other things. But stupidity doesn't excuse what he did.' He smiled persuasively. 'Come to my wedding, Betsy. Aside from yourself and Mr Bailes, the only other witness will be my old friend, Bertrand.'

She looked at him sideways. 'Not your lady mother?'

'My lady mother has no idea of either my present whereabouts or my immediate intentions. She'll be informed after the event by letter – and politely requested to remove to the dower house forthwith. Even if I could stomach the thought of living with her – which I can't – I won't have her looking down her nose at Caroline.'

There was a pause and then Betsy said cautiously, 'She seems a very pleasant young lady.'

The chill vanished and he laughed.

'She's a very *straight-forward* young lady who doesn't do things just because they're correct. If she asked you to the wedding, it's because she'd like you to be there and because she's guessed that I would, too.' He rose and drawing his new house-keeper to her feet, said, 'If you want to know more about her, come to the other window and see how she and Mr Bailes are getting on.'

Out in the hopelessly overgrown garden, Mr Bailes was pointing to something and Caroline appeared to be listening with interest to what he was saying. The two of them studied the ground for a moment and Caroline sank down to pull at a small plant, then rose again to show it to the gardener.

'You see?' said Adrian quietly. 'You need have no fears.'

'She's not much like that other one, is she?'

'Nothing at all.'

'It doesn't do to speak ill of the dead, of course ... and what happened to the poor girl was terrible. But she wasn't good enough for you, my lord. Not *nearly* good enough.' She shook her head. 'Mr Bailes told us how him and Old Matthew saw her up there, prancing about on the ledge until she got all tangled up in her robe. They didn't know you were up there as well until she started to fall and you shot forward to try and catch her. It's hard to know how horrible that was for you.'

Suddenly very still, it was a long time before Adrian spoke. Then, in an odd tone, he said, 'Mr Bailes saw it?'

'Yes, my lord. He says he saw it all. Ask him yourself and he'll tell you – just like he tried to tell the late Earl.' She scowled and added bitterly, 'It's the greatest pity in the world that he wasn't listened to.'

* * *

Adrian insisted on Bertrand taking Mr Bailes and Betsy home in the carriage and arranged for him to collect them and their belongings the following morning. As soon as the carriage rolled away, Caroline turned to him with a smile only to recognise something in his face that she hadn't seen in two days; an impervious remoteness that told her something was wrong.

Unfortunately, before she could ask what it was, a horseman appeared round a bend in the lane and Sarre said expressionlessly, 'It's the vicar. Since I'm likely to tell him to go to the devil and it's you he wants to see anyway, I'll leave you to deal with him.' And he turned on his heel and strode into the house.

Polite but firm, Caroline disposed swiftly of the Reverend Conant. Having thanked him for calling and apologised for the fact that Lord Sarre was much occupied at present and therefore unable to receive him, she explained that the understanding between herself and the Earl was of a long-standing nature but, due to private circumstances, they

239

wished to marry quietly. She was quite sure, she said cheerfully, that the Reverend would understand.

Then, as soon as she'd sent the affronted cleric on his way, she went in search of Adrian. He was in the back parlour, staring out of the window.

Caroline said, 'What is it?'

'What is what?' He didn't turn round and his voice was faintly dismissive.

'What's wrong?' And, when he still didn't turn, she walked over to grasp his arm and pull him to face her. His eyes were no longer expressionless. They were full of something stark and painful and angry. 'Adrian? What did Betsy say? *Tell* me.'

For a moment, she thought he was going to refuse and simply walk away. Then he said carefully, 'She told me that both Mr Bailes and Old Matthew saw Evie on the parapet that day and they saw her fall. The first they saw of me was when – when I flung myself over to catch her.'

This didn't sound like a bad thing. In fact, it sounded the opposite. It meant that, if he chose, he could prove he didn't commit murder. But because his expression was still bleak enough to make hell freeze, Caroline said cautiously, 'That's good, isn't it?'

'Yes.' He paused, a pulse beating in his throat. 'It would have been even better if my father had felt inclined to listen when Mr Bailes tried to tell him what he'd seen.'

She looked at him, absorbing the final, damning blow contained in that one sentence. If there were words that might make this any better, she didn't know what they were. She only knew that he looked as if his guts had been wrenched out … and that she wanted to cry for him.

She whispered, 'Oh my dear …' And, using the only comfort she knew how to give, wrapped her arms about him and held him tight.

Little by little, she felt his muscles relax and eventually his own arms crept about her. He leaned his cheek against her hair and she heard a long, sighing breath. Finally, he said, 'I don't know why I'm shocked. I shouldn't be. And I ought to be immune to it by now.'

'Of *course* you're not immune to it,' she said fiercely. 'Only a man as cold-hearted as your father could *possibly* be immune to something like this. And, though you sometimes give a fairly accurate appearance of it, *you* are not cold-hearted at all.' She paused and then muttered, 'It's a pity he's dead. There are a few things I'd like to make clear to him.'

She felt rather than heard the tremor of his laughter and also felt him gathering her a little closer. He said, 'I appreciate the sentiment ... but granite doesn't scratch easily.'

'Grandfather always says one should never back away from a challenge.' The warm skin of his throat was very near her mouth. She wanted to lick it but didn't quite dare. 'The Reverend hoped I'd explain why we're marrying in secret, by the way.'

'That's no surprise. What did you say?'

'I more or less told him to mind his own business.'

'Excellent.' Adrian was beginning to enjoy the feel of her body against his more than he should but wasn't quite ready to let her go. 'Am I forgiven for my earlier transgressions?'

Caroline smiled into his neck.

'Grandfather also says that bearing grudges is bad for business.'

'I'm becoming quite fond of your grandfather.'

'I expect that comes of knowing which side your bread is buttered, my lord.'

'That is undoubtedly true.' Realising that good intentions weren't sufficient, he let his arms slip away from her. 'I was Adrian a little while ago. What happened to him?'

Far too much and none of it good.

'Nothing. I just think that he and Lord Sarre ought to be better acquainted.'

* * *

Having left Town without troubling to open the newspaper, Lord Sheringham arrived in Deal very much later than he'd anticipated owing to one of his horses casting a shoe in an inconvenient spot a few miles short of Canterbury. The resulting delay along with the knowledge that he would be completing his journey in the dark resulted in a mood of profound irritation. This was not improved by the discovery that the only available bedchamber at The King's Head was at the front of the house and of miserable proportions. Marcus scowled at the landlord, barked orders at the ostler regarding his own horses and the one he wished to hire the following morning and then stamped into the coffee room, demanding a decent supper.

The food was better than expected and the brandy that followed it, exceptionally fine. This, reflected Marcus, was no particular surprise since the Trade flourished all along this part of the coast and presumably kept the inn well-supplied. The evening was further improved by the company of two garrulous locals who, without realising it, gave him a good deal of useful information.

They recommended that, if his lordship was wishful to ride to Sandwich, he'd do best to take the old road along the coast. Then, when he reached a big old house with twisty chimneys, he'd need to turn inland and head across country.

The old house?

Well, aside from a caretaking couple, the place has been empty for years now ... though somebody had told somebody else that the lord who owned it was back from foreign parts.

The owner?

Why that'd be the new Earl of Sarre, your lordship ... and everyone hoping he'd be less of a bastard than the old one.

Marcus bought them both another drink and then retired to his inadequate bedchamber to plot his strategy. There could be no doubt that Sarre had Caroline at Devereux House. So far, so good. But before anything further could be accomplished, he would need to discover two things. First, whether the Earl had done the unthinkable and married the girl; and second, how many servants he had who might get in the way. Hopefully, not too many.

Opening his valise, Marcus took out the flat box containing a pair of faultlessly maintained pistols. In one sense, it would be best if he didn't have to use them. In another, if he couldn't get his hands on Caroline Maitland's money, he was going to have to flee the country anyway ... so leaving Sarre's corpse in his wake wouldn't make his problems any worse than they already were. Indeed, it would add a much-needed bright spot. Fortunately, he'd always been a good shot.

TWENTY-ONE

The Duke of Rockliffe's party – which included the Duchess, Lord Nicholas, his Grace's valet and her Grace's maid – had arrived at Wynstanton Priors near Sittingbourne at around the time Lord Sheringham was having his horse re-shod at Upper Harbledown. The Duchess had retired to take a very light supper in her rooms; the Duke and his brother had dinner and then settled down to a few hands of cards.

After a while, Nicholas said, 'I've been meaning to ask. How did you know that Dev was in partnership with Aristide Delacroix?'

'I didn't. I merely made an educated guess.' Rockliffe laid down the king of clubs and said gently, 'My point, I think.'

Nicholas grunted, reached for the deck and shuffled it with casual expertise.

'Based on what? The fact that one of them is French and other might as well be?'

'A little more than that. Some time ago I mentioned to Monsieur Delacroix that one of his regular patrons seemed possessed of uncanny good fortune. Delacroix said he would investigate the matter ... and, on my next visit, seemed oddly determined to keep me from the upper salon. Naturally, I was curious.'

'So you went up there and found what?'

'I found the gentleman whose play I had questioned losing heavily to an elderly Austrian Count,' replied the Duke, picking up his cards. 'Only, of course, he was none of those things. Even tinted spectacles can't quite disguise Lord Sarre's extremely distinctive eyes and, of course, I'd seen him playing an old man before.' He looked up, smiling a little. 'If Delacroix called his lordship in, it follows that they know each other rather well. It also follows that the Earl possesses some unique ability of his own at the card table.'

'He didn't the last time I played piquet with him,' objected Nicholas, choosing to ignore all mention of tinted lenses. 'He lost every game but one.'

'Did he indeed?' Rockliffe reached for his wine-glass, his expression unreadable. 'That is extremely comforting.'

* * *

The following morning dawned wet and windy. Nicholas entered the breakfast room in time to hear his brother saying, 'Adeline ... you have to eat something more than dry toast and tea. Couldn't you at least *try* an egg?'

The Duchess shuddered. 'No. I couldn't. And if you love me, you won't suggest it.'

'If I didn't love you I wouldn't be holding your head over a basin at six o'clock in the morning,' began Rockliffe in something very unlike his normal lazy tones. And then, noticing his brother in the doorway, 'Good morning, Nicholas. Not that it is, particularly – as you'll have noticed if you have looked out of the window.'

'The roads won't be good,' agreed his lordship, investigating the covered dishes on the sideboard. 'I'll probably leave riding to Sandwich until tomorrow.' He turned around, looking confused. 'There aren't any kippers.'

'No. And there will continue to be no kippers until Adeline stops finding the smell insupportable.'

'Oh. The same being true of bacon and sausages, no doubt?'

Despite the ever-constant feeling of incipient nausea, Adeline laughed.

'If you want kippers, Nick, you can have them – just not in here. And tomorrow you shall have whatever you like because I'll breakfast in my rooms.'

'You will not,' said her husband promptly.

'Yes, Tracy. I will. And though you're welcome to join me, I think you'll be much more comfortable eating in here with Nicholas.'

'Not if he's having kippers.'

'Stop being difficult.' Making it clear that she considered this part of the conversation at an end, Adeline looked across at her brother-in-law and said, 'Since, according to the *Morning Chronicle*, Lord Sarre can only have been married for two or three days at the most, perhaps you might delay your visit a little longer?'

'No.' His lordship took his seat, staring disconsolately at a plate of scrambled egg. 'I've no intention of staying more than a night. But I want to make sure all's well with him and his new lady and warn him to keep an eye out for Sheringham.'

'It all sounds very melodramatic. Are you seriously worried?'

'No. But now Rock's put the idea in my head, I can't get rid of it.'

The aquamarine eyes encompassed his Grace.

'*Your* idea?'

'I may have mentioned something of the sort in passing.'

'That's different, then. Perhaps you'd better visit this Actor-Earl along with Nick. Aside from anything else, it will give you something to do other than hovering about me.'

'I do not hover,' said Rockliffe, with deliberate hauteur. 'Furthermore, I never have.'

'No. You're right, of course.' Adeline rose and walked around the table to place a kiss on her husband's cheek. 'With you, it's better described as *looming*.'

* * *

Unaware of the forces gathering about them, Adrian and Caroline spent the latter part of the morning introducing Mr Bailes and Betsy – now transformed into Mrs Holt – to the household and seeing them comfortably settled in their quarters.

Mrs Holt immediately demanded a notebook, a pencil and Caroline's company on a tour of the house. When Caroline ventured to suggest that her presence might not be strictly necessary, she was given a stern look and told that, if she was to be mistress of the house, it was her duty to know every nook and cranny of it.

Mr Bailes was about to conduct a similar inspection outside when Adrian caught him and said, 'Oh no. You are not going out there in this downpour. And there's nothing to be done at this time of year, anyway.'

'I could mark out where the flower-beds is supposed to be,' said Mr Bailes hopefully.

'No. If you *must* look at the garden, do it through the window.'

His lordship found his betrothed in the linen-cupboard, meekly listening to a lecture on the correct way of whitening linen. Grinning at her over Betsy's shoulder, he said, 'Pardon the interruption – but I'm riding into town and will take your letters to the carrier along with my own if you wish.'

'Oh – yes, please.' Then, 'But must you? In this rain?'

'I've won't dissolve,' he shrugged. 'And actually, yes – I must.'

By the time he reached the town, Sarre's greatcoat was heavy with moisture and he rather feared that his hat would never be the same again. But, having taken the letters for delivery, he spent time getting even wetter as he searched – and eventually found – a fellow who was both willing and able to do what he wanted.

He rode home, face lowered against the driving rain but happy with the success of his mission.

He didn't notice the lone figure far away to his right, charting his progress through a small telescope and would probably have thought little of it even if he had.

Meeting Bertrand in the hall, he asked for a bath to be brought up and took the stairs two at a time to get out of his wet clothes. Whilst luxuriating in a tub of hot water, he wondered with some amusement how Caroline was getting on with Betsy's version of *A Lady's Guide to Practical Housekeeping*. Then he turned his mind to the question of when to give her the green gown so she'd be able to wear it to their wedding.

It was nearly time for dinner when he finally tracked her to the back parlour where she sat in dazed contemplation of numerous lists. She looked up when he entered the room, opened her mouth as if to say something and then seemed to forget what it was.

It was one of those moments that came upon her every now and then. A sense of incredulity that she'd once thought his face too severe to be handsome. The high slash of his cheekbones, the hard, clean lines of his jaw and the firm, faintly sensual mouth could have been the work of a master-sculptor. And, as if those tailored bones were not beauty enough … pale, clear eyes fringed with thick lashes and set beneath level dark brows; thick, richly-brown hair in which sun or candlelight found every shade from antique gold to bronze; and a lean, perfectly proportioned body which moved with seemingly effortless grace.

Oh God, thought Caroline weakly. *He's quite appallingly good-looking. How am I ever going to hold a man like him? And no matter what he says, we both know why he's really marrying me.*

'You look,' remarked Adrian, 'as if some dire thought has just struck you. Has it?'

'No.' She turned away and gestured to the litter of paper. 'I've lost the ability to think at all. Betsy is a martinet.'

One of his not always popular talents as an actor had been the ability to immediately spot an off-note in any performance. This one was easy. He didn't think she'd ever lied to him before.

He looked down on the nape of her neck, tempted to discover if the skin there was as silky as it looked. Then, putting his hands safely behind his back, he said softly, 'Second thoughts, Caroline?'

'No. No – of course not.'

Another lie. And this time a small cold quiver of something like panic stirred in his chest.

'You should tell me, you know. If it's to do with my less than spotless and far from respectable past --'

'It isn't. It's just ...' She tossed down her pencil and took a breath. 'If you must know, I suddenly realised that I'll never be able to live up to you.'

'*What?*'

He sounded so stunned that she risked turning her head to look at him. He was frowning, plainly confused. Not wanting to have to put the whole thing into words, she said, 'It's not that complicated. Go and look in the mirror.'

Just for a second, Adrian continued to stare at her. Then the unpleasant feeling inside him relaxed its grip and he gave a shaken laugh.

Caroline scowled at him. 'It's not funny.'

'Yes. Forgive me – but it is.' Seeing the trouble still lurking in her eyes, he said deliberately, 'You know that looks aren't everything and

247

can frequently be deceptive. If you didn't, you'd have taken Marcus Sheringham.'

'That's different.'

'I don't think so. Ten years ago, I lost my head over a lovely face. You know how that turned out. And as to your own looks ... my dear, it's time you started seeing yourself clearly. You are *not* plain. No woman with eyes and hair like yours could ever be called that. And best of all ... you glow with warmth and kindness and honesty.' He hesitated and then, because convincing her mattered so supremely, forced himself to say, 'I find that I need those things rather badly.'

Caroline looked back at him, torn between hope and doubt. It almost sounded as though the words meant something more; something she'd never thought to hear from him. But, if that was so, he was clearly not ready to say it yet. So she smiled at him, just a little shyly, and said, 'All things considered, it's very gallant of you to say that.'

The grey eyes narrowed.

'Gallantry has nothing to do with it. You *are* all the things I said. But at times, you are also damned infuriating.'

She eyed him thoughtfully. He looked very cross and also slightly sulky. Quite suddenly, her pleasure in the knowledge that he'd stopped hiding his feelings made her want to laugh. However, realising that this might not be a good idea just at the moment, she rose from her chair, patted his arm and said understandingly, 'I know what it is. You're hungry. Grandfather always becomes tetchy when he wants his dinner.'

'I am *not* tetchy,' he snapped before he could stop himself. And then, catching the gleam in her eyes, 'Mistress Maitland ... are you trying to provoke me?'

'Not particularly – though I imagine it might be informative. And I was Caroline a little while ago. What happened to her?'

'She got too clever for her own good,' he retorted. And smiled.

Inevitably, that smile was Caroline's undoing. Her blood heated and she knew in a more definite and fundamental way than she'd known before that she wanted this man; that he was beautiful to her, both inside and out – that she wanted his hands on her body and hers on his and, more important than either of those, for him to be hers alone.

She'd noticed that he still never touched her unless she invited it. This, as he'd said, could be a matter of gentlemanly scruples. Or it could be that he didn't particularly want to. It occurred to her that, in the years he'd spent abroad, he'd probably had a good many beautiful, sophisticated mistresses. The practical side of her nature decided that this was a thought best not pursued. The part of her that, where Adrian was concerned, wasn't practical at all felt unaccountably depressed. She could only pray that, not having his skills of concealment, neither this nor any of her other feelings for him showed on her face.

Over dinner they talked about Mr Bailes and Betsy and about their wedding the next day – though there seemed little to say about that. And so, after a small, empty pause, Caroline said curiously, 'What was it like, being an actor?'

'Exhilarating … terrifying … extraordinary.'

'Do you miss it?'

'Every day.'

She toyed with an apple, so that she didn't have to look at him.

'It's hard now to understand how I never connected you with Claude Duvall. I must have been either blind or very stupid.'

'No. One uses a whole arsenal of tricks to create the illusion. Some are obvious – such as the highwayman's mask or my hair being powdered and Duvall's not. Also, I made sure you never saw Duvall in full light. For the rest, it's all smoke and mirrors. A different accent; an alteration in the pitch of one's voice; and adjustments to one's posture, gait and mannerisms. Distractions.' He gave an almost imperceptible shrug. 'The only time I sailed seriously close to the wind was that night at the Pantheon. Shifting between myself and Duvall, then back again was risky enough. But when I hit Marcus, I got close enough for him to recognise me.'

'But he didn't.'

'Apparently not.'

Caroline tilted her head and looked across at him.

'Will you show me?'

He grinned. 'Show you what? My acting skills – or how they're created?'

'Both, I suppose. Will you?'

'If that's what you want. But not in here, I think.' He rose and offered his hand. 'You realise, of course, that some of the tricks will be missing ... and that, on-stage, one's audience is somewhat further away?'

'Are you asking me to make allowances?'

'Perish the thought,' he returned blandly, twitching a cane from the hall stand as he went by. 'I'm better than that.'

And he was. He really, really was.

He gave her Count Rainmeyr first because it was one of his favourites and because he wanted her to join in. When, without ever actually asking her to do so, the crusty old fellow had made her pick up his cane three times and even wrung a respectful curtsy out of her, Adrian decided to switch roles. He became a lisping Macaroni, all pursed lips and sucked in cheeks, mincing along on seemingly high heels and plying an imaginary fan. Caroline stared, momentarily stunned by the contrast, then dissolved into giggles.

Finally, he freed his hair from its ribbon, tossed down a handful of coins and sat hunched over the table to begin fussing with the papers she'd left there earlier. He was suddenly old, untidy, short-sighted and profoundly irritable. He pulled at strands of his hair while he grumbled incomprehensibly and squinted at one particular sheet. Then he started totting up lists of medical treatments of the kind not usually mentioned in polite company and studied apothecaries bills which he claimed were scandalously over-priced. He counted out coins, then complained and produced a logic of his own that enabled him to reduce the amount by half. Caroline didn't know who he was playing – only that what he was doing now was way beyond anything she'd ever seen on any stage. She was entranced and more than a little dazzled.

When he stopped, sat up and smiled at her and became Adrian again, she felt disorientated.

'Well?' he said. 'Did I prove my point?'

'Yes. That was ... remarkable.' She paused, not sure what to say next. 'Who was the last one?'

'That, my child, was Molière's *Hypochondriac*. My favourite and generally most popular role – though, as I hope you appreciate, I'm not accustomed to playing it in English.' He rose and went to pour wine for them both. 'The previous two were inventions of my own, formerly used at the card table to disguise my other dubious talent. I also do a Scottish Major, a timid French clerk and an extremely annoying Russian – but I think we'll save them for another day.'

She accepted the glass from him, watching how his loosened hair fell about his cheeks and throat. She'd touched that hair when he'd been Claude Duvall. She knew how it felt, thick and rich, sliding through her fingers. She told herself to stop thinking about it ... and when Adrian rifled through the litter on the table to find his ribbon and set about re-tying his hair she had to prevent herself asking him not to.

Swallowing hard and trying to recover her wandering wits, she said the first thing that came into her head. 'I asked Sally to press my blue gown for tomorrow since it's the one you find least objectionable. I wish I had something better – but my pink silk has mysteriously disappeared. Not that one could call that a misfortune.'

'True.' He was facing away from her, his fingers busy making a loose bow. 'A blessing in disguise, perhaps.'

'Not when one has only two gowns,' Caroline pointed out. 'Luckily, you will be magnificent enough for both of us and thus draw attention from my deficiencies.'

Adrian sat down and picked up his wine, his expression unreadable.

'I enjoy being well-dressed.'

'I've noticed.'

'However, I am not – as Bertrand would have it – a peacock.'

She gave a little choke of laughter and shook her head.

'You'll have to forgive me – but there's definitely a bit of the peacock about that vest you're wearing.'

He glanced down. Scarlet peonies, edged in silver rioted across a background of violet so dark one might almost think it black.

'You don't like it?'

'On the contrary. It's so exactly you. A touch of drama under a cloak of icy reserve.'

He grinned. 'Well, at least you see it. It's more than Bertrand ever has.'

There was a long pause while the grin faded and he seemed to contemplate his wine-glass. Then he said slowly, 'This seems the time to confess that I bought something for you. Like all my other mistakes, it was well-meant so I'm hoping you won't feel either insulted or offended.'

'You bought something? For me?' A hint of colour washed her cheeks. 'When?'

'In Canterbury. The day after we got here.' He sounded suddenly diffident. 'It seemed a good idea at the time ... only then I realised you might not think so which is why I've delayed giving it to you.'

'I don't understand.' She looked about her as if hoping to see some mysterious parcel. 'Since you don't need to give me anything but were kind enough to think of it, how could I be offended?'

'It is not strictly ... appropriate. But as we are to be married tomorrow, I hoped you might overlook that fact.'

'I'll do my best.'

Her eyes were bright with anticipation and she had somehow shifted to the edge of her seat. She looked as eager as a child and he was reminded of his little brother on the day he'd been given his first pony. He said, 'In that case, I think you'll find Sally has put it in your bedchamber.'

'Already? I mean – it is there now?'

'I would imagine so.' The fact that she could barely wait to run upstairs was written all over her. He found it surprising but curiously endearing. He also couldn't resist teasing her just a little so he reached for his glass and took a lazy sip of wine. 'It will still be there when you're ready to retire, however.'

'Oh. Yes. Of course.'

Caroline tried to damp down the burst of happiness that was fizzing inside her at the idea of him tramping around Canterbury in the rain to buy her a gift. She didn't care what he'd bought – only that he'd taken the trouble to do it. She reached out to her own wine, changed her mind and folded her hands in her lap.

Adrian watched her sitting there like a good girl, politely waiting to be dismissed. It made him want to laugh but he merely said casually, 'Would you like to try beating me at piquet?'

'No. That is ... I can't, can I? You always win.'

'I could try not to.' He saw her shoulders slump in frustration and decided that enough was enough. 'Or you could go upstairs now, if you felt so inclined. Just to look.'

'Really?' She was on her feet without knowing how it happened. 'You wouldn't mind?'

No, darling. I wouldn't mind at all.

He rose and offered her a slight bow. 'I believe I can manage to entertain myself for a little while.'

She beamed at him and virtually ran from the room.

Adrian sat down, reached for the pack of cards and idly practised a few slick moves. Ten minutes passed. *She might hate the gown; she might be sitting in her room, grossly insulted; or perhaps, just perhaps, she might ...* He cut the last possibility short in case it was tempting Fate.

He dealt a few hands and toyed with his skill. Ten minutes passed and then twenty. He realised that, unusually, he was making mistakes. He found that interesting. Perhaps letting his mind wander worked better than intense concentration. Then the door opened.

Caroline stood on the threshold as if unsure whether to enter or not. Adrian rose and waited for her to step into the light. Slowly, she did so. His breath caught.

She looked far from annoyed. She looked awed, confused and adorably shy. And something much better than beautiful. She looked utterly desirable.

The dark green silk moulded her figure and made her skin look almost translucent. The elbow-length sleeves ended in falls of soft, creamy lace and a narrow band of it emphasised a *décolletage* just low enough to engage a man's interest. Her waist was reduced to a handspan below which the green silk drifted over a cream underskirt, embroidered like a magic forest. Her hair fell in a torrent of dull gold from a green ribbon, her cheeks were flushed, her eyes wide and dark. Adrian's brain promptly ceased functioning. His body didn't.

She said hesitantly, 'You chose this yourself?'

'Yes.' He cleared his throat. 'Do you like it?'

'I – yes. Very much. Do you?'

More than I expected. And much more than decency permits me to say.

'It ... was certainly worth getting wet.'

He heard the words come out of his mouth and immediately despaired of himself.

Worth getting wet? Christ. What kind of ass says something like that?

But she didn't seem disappointed. She seemed lit from inside with a degree of delight far greater than that deserved by the simple gift of one gown. She positively *glowed*. Then, before he had time to recognise her intention, she literally flew across the room and threw her arms about his neck. Absorbing the shock of impact, Adrian's arms automatically closed about her and then she was saying shakily, 'Thank you. It's beautiful. I love it. I don't know how ... it's such a kind thought. Thank you.'

He tried to think of something to say and then gave up when she pressed warm kisses against his throat and jaw. Instinct took over. Sliding one hand to her nape, he tilted her face up and brushed her lips with his. She sighed and closed her eyes. He kissed one corner of her mouth, then slid his tongue slowly across her lower lip to the other. Her breath hitched and her lips parted. Adrian arms tightened about her and he covered her mouth with his own. He wanted to be careful, to take it slowly. And had it not been for the tiny sound in her throat and the way she instantly responded to his kiss, he might have managed it. As it was, desire flared hot and insistent and the most he could manage was to stop his hands going anywhere they shouldn't.

Caroline didn't even try to think. She tangled her fingers in his hair and gave herself up to physical sensation and the intoxicating joy of being in his arms. He trailed little kisses along her jaw and his teeth grazed her ear-lobe; then his mouth returned to ravish hers, sending little tremors rippling through her and causing her to press herself more tightly against him.

Much though he was enjoying it, it was this last that succeeded in bringing back some semblance of self-control before she became aware of his physical state. He wanted her so badly it alarmed him ... but they weren't married yet. Tomorrow, he'd have the right to ask. Tonight, he didn't. Slowly, gently, he released her mouth and set a little distance between them, breathing rather fast. Equally slowly, her eyes opened and she looked up at him, her expression not unlike what he imagined his own to be.

Holding her gaze, he said, 'Should I apologise for that?'

And Caroline said huskily, 'Not unless you're sorry.'

'I'm not.' He drew an unsteady breath. 'If you want the truth, I'm only sorry we're not married yet.'

'Oh,' she said, vaguely. 'Good.' And, after a moment, 'So am I.'

TWENTY-TWO

The previous day's rain had dried up over-night and the morning of the wedding dawned bright and cold.

At Wynstanton Priors, the Duchess of Rockliffe shooed her husband and his brother out of the house with instructions to call on the newly-weds but not to outstay their welcome. Ignoring Nicholas's knowing smile, Rockliffe pulled his wife into his arms for a lingering kiss and informed her that he'd be back to resume looming no later than the following afternoon – sooner, if possible.

At The King's Head in Deal, Marcus Sheringham ate an early breakfast and prepared to resume his vigil on Devereux House. He now knew exactly how many people resided there. Aside from Sarre and the girl, the household consisted of two elderly couples, a pretty young maid and a sandy-haired French fellow. He'd also surreptitiously scanned the parish registers of all three Sandwich churches and found no record of any marriage. Since it hadn't taken place so far, it was unlikely – as he'd always suspected – that it ever would. He'd tracked Sarre into town and back again through yesterday's rain, taking care to remain out of sight. He hadn't seen the Earl go near a church – but it would do no harm to check. If there was no activity around the house during the morning, he decided he might ride over to have a chat with the various vicars.

* * *

At Devereux House, Caroline spent the morning bathing, washing her hair, counting the hours until it was time to dress and day-dreaming about Adrian. Downstairs, Betsy pursued a relentless campaign of preparations for after the ceremony which had Sally, Mr Clayton and Mr Bailes running hither and thither carrying things and turned every room upside down.

Evicted in due course even from his own bedchamber while the bed-linens were changed and the hangings thoroughly beaten, Adrian stole a bottle of wine and sought refuge with Bertrand saying, 'Thank God one only has to do this once. Mrs Clayton is apparently too busy to brew a pot of coffee and everywhere looks like a battle-zone.'

Bertrand poured two glasses and handed one to his lordship.

'Mrs Holt is a force of nature.'

'That's one way of putting it. Caroline's got the right idea. I gather she's barred her door against invaders. I wish I'd thought of it.'

'Bride's prerogative. And either your room or hers has to be made ready for the wedding-night.'

'Ah.' Adrian took a sip of wine. 'Yes. I suppose so.'

Bertrand's brows rose. 'You sound unconvinced. Didn't you give her the gown?'

'Yes.'

'Did she like it?'

'Yes.'

'How much?'

Adrian stared down into his glass, a small smile curling his mouth.

'Quite a lot.' He looked up. 'And that is very definitely all I have to say on the subject.'

For a long moment, Bertrand said nothing. Then, 'You once admitted to liking her. But it's more than that, isn't it?'

'Perhaps. But if you think I'm going to make a declaration to you that I haven't made to Caroline, I suggest you think again.'

'Fair enough.' Bertrand grinned. 'In that case – as the fellow who'll be standing up for you this afternoon – it's part of my duty to give you some good advice.'

'Oh God.' Adrian laughed. 'You think I need it?'

'Not in the general way, maybe – but you've never been married before.'

'Neither have you. And we are not – we are absolutely *not* having this conversation.'

'Nobody said you'd got to join in,' observed Bertrand. And launched into a ribald and cripplingly funny dissertation on what he called *Practical Guidance for the Newly-Wed Gentleman ...* or *How to Avoid Having Things Thrown at Your Head.*

Three doors down and engaged in drying her hair, Caroline listened to gales of masculine laughter and grinned with delight that Adrian sounded so relaxed and happy. It was going to be a beautiful day.

* * *

From the top of a dune some way along the beach, Lord Sheringham saw one of the old men bring the carriage into the yard and set about washing the mud from it. This might mean something or nothing. With the roads still drying out, they'd hardly be wasting their time cleaning up the carriage for a journey. Still, it was worth keeping an eye on … and there was precious little else to see. There was no other traffic in or out of the house and so far he hadn't managed to clap eyes on the girl at all. One would think, after being trapped inside all the previous day, she'd want to walk outside and get a breath of fresh air. Or perhaps Sarre wouldn't let her. Perhaps he'd got her locked up somewhere. Marcus hoped not. Even if the Earl went off again on some errand or other, breaking into a house of no more than five or six bedrooms, getting passed half-a-dozen servants unnoticed and liberating the girl would be a damned sight more difficult than winnowing his way through a crowded gaming club. Impossible, in fact.

He pulled his cloak around him and tried to make himself comfortable on the grassy hummock. If nothing transpired in the next hour or so, he'd take himself into town for a hot meal and a chance to get warm before he consulted the vicars.

When the need arose, he was capable of endless patience.

* * *

Betsy freed Sally from her duties below stairs to help dress the bride. By the time this happened, Caroline – who had been perfectly calm all morning – could feel her nerves tying themselves into knots. She stared at her reflection while Sally put the finishing touches to her hair and said, 'Has someone told Mr Bailes that I want him to walk down the aisle with me?'

'Yes, Miss. His lordship spoke to him about it himself. And we all thought Mr Bailes was going to burst, he was that proud.' The girl stepped back. 'There, now. That looks very nice, even if I do say so myself. Now let's get you into your gown.' She stroked the figured silk lovingly. 'It's ever so pretty, isn't it? His lordship's got lovely taste.' She lifted the gown, flung it deftly over Caroline's head and settled it on her shoulders in order to begin lacing it up. 'It's a pity he saw you in it last night. But I expect he was glad to know it fitted and everything.'

'Yes.' Caroline could feel herself blushing. 'He seemed quite ... pleased.'

Downstairs in the hall, Adrian had also started to feel tense and, seeing it, Bertrand suggested a fortifying slug of brandy.

'No. I had a glass of wine with you earlier – and I'm not getting drunk before my wedding.'

'You never get drunk at all,' remarked Bertrand. 'If you ask me, that's half your trouble.' He glanced upwards to the sound of footsteps. 'Ah. Reckon she's on her way.'

Adrian stood at the foot of the stairs, his hand resting on the carved newel. Then, as Caroline appeared around the turn on the half-landing, the tightness in his chest simply disappeared. She looked as she had last night. The gown, her hair, that soft uncertain smile ... all of them exactly the same. And if he'd had even a shred of doubt about the rightness of what he was about to do, it evaporated like mist at the mere sight of her. He smiled.

Caroline descended the stairs, drowning in that smile. As always, he was the epitome of elegance. From his beautifully-cut black brocade coat and bronze-green embroidered vest, to the buckles on his polished shoes he was every inch the Earl of Sarre. But the smile ... that was pure Adrian. And when she reached his side and he took her hand, her heart simply flipped over.

'You look ... beautiful,' he said softly for her ears alone. Then, with a slight, formal bow, 'And now, if you're ready, we should go.'

Not unnaturally, it was a bit of a squeeze with four of them in the carriage but Bertrand waited until everyone was settled before slamming the door and climbing nimbly on to the box. Inside and facing the prospective bride and groom, Mr Bailes and Betsy were dressed in their Sunday best and seemingly unable to stop smiling. Caroline smiled back at them and, as unobtrusively as possible, tucked her hand into

Adrian's. Although he neither spoke nor looked at her, he wrapped his fingers around it and held it firmly.

Arriving at St Peter's and leaving Bertrand to escort Betsy into the church, his lordship produced a small posy of pale pink roses from inside the porch and handed them to Caroline, saying simply, 'I think I found the only fellow in town who grows flowers under glass. These were all he would spare.' And seeing the sudden brightness in her eyes, added, 'You are *not* going to cry. The Reverend Conant already thinks I'm some sort of villain. If he sees a single tear, he'll stop the wedding.' Then, when she managed a shaky smile, he placed her hand on Mr Bailes's arm and said, 'That's better. I'll see you inside.'

With no music, no flowers aside from the ones Caroline was holding and an openly disapproving vicar, the ceremony was both simple and no longer than necessary. Mr Bailes performed his part with dignity, Betsy sobbed quietly into her handkerchief and Bertrand grinned as if he'd orchestrated the entire thing himself.

Caroline was aware of nothing except Adrian, holding her eyes with his own and speaking his vows in clear, level tones. Her own voice was a little less steady but she managed not to stammer or get his lordship's string of names wrong.

I take thee, Francis Adrian Sinclair Devereux, to my wedded husband ... to have and to hold from this day forward ... to love, cherish and obey till death us do part ... and thereto I give thee my troth.

The ring slid on to her finger, warm from Adrian's hand. She stared at it for a second, transfixed, before looking into his face to discover that he was doing the same thing, his expression oddly intent. Then the silver-grey eyes flicked back to her face and the shadows vanished in a dazzling smile.

At the moment they were pronounced man and wife, the words *Now she won't leave!* exploded exultantly through Adrian's head ... immediately followed by the startling realisation that, up until this moment, he'd feared she still might. He tried to convince himself that his sudden euphoria was merely perfectly natural relief that the ceremony was behind them ... but the growing bubble of joy inside him gave the lie to that. And so, giving way to impulse, he pulled Caroline into his arms, kissed her and murmured, 'Well done, my lady. Now you shall go home and eat as many lemon cakes as you like.'

And that was how it came about that Caroline walked to the vestry for the conclusion of the formalities, clinging to her new husband's arm and laughing up at him.

The appropriate entry was made in the register, the marriage lines written out and witnessed then solemnly handed to Caroline.

'You are now,' whispered Adrian, 'officially responsible for keeping all my secrets. And if that doesn't scare you to death, nothing will.'

Once out in the church-yard, there was much kissing, curtsying and well-wishing. Then everyone squeezed back into the carriage and they set off on the drive home. This time, Adrian drew Caroline's hand through his arm and covered her fingers with his own. She allowed herself to lean against his shoulder and dream.

* * *

Some fifteen minutes before Caroline joined Lord Sarre at the altar, Lord Sheringham was sitting in a tavern on Knightrider Street. He'd eaten a bowl of largely indifferent stew, washed down with a tankard of equally indifferent ale and was just considering going in search of the rector of nearby St Clement's when three fellows at a neighbouring table invited him to join them in a game of *vingt-et-un*. Though rough and ready, they seemed amicable enough and were playing for low stakes. Furthermore, his lordship hadn't touched a deck of cards for the best part of a week. Deciding that another half-hour couldn't hurt, he ordered a second pot of ale and settled down to play.

At first, it seemed that his luck was in so he was happy to agree when one of his new friends suggested raising the stakes. But then the tide turned and the couple of guineas he'd won soon became a loss of ten. Suspecting that he'd been gulled but not daring, in this company, to say so, he tossed the money on the table and strode out, cursing under his breath. It was almost half past two.

Having only recently risen from his sickbed, the Reverend Marten at St Clement's proved entirely unaware of the Earl of Sarre's presence in the district. He did, however, appear to think that Lord Sheringham

STELLA RILEY

would be interested in his various ailments. Lord Sheringham stalked off, leaving the fellow still talking.

Next was the church of St Peter in the centre of town. Half-way there, he was forced to leap back into a doorway to avoid being drenched in muddy water when a passing cart rumbled through a puddle. Unfortunately, his manoeuvre wasn't completely successful and he was so busy swearing and trying to brush off the worst of the damage, that he didn't notice the plain black carriage that drove past in the wake of the offending cart.

Reverend Conant listened to the mouthful of lies Marcus used to camouflage his enquiry and didn't bother to hide his disbelief. He said coldly, 'How unfortunate. Had your lordship arrived a little over half an hour ago, you would have been in time to witness the ceremony.'

'What?'

'Am I not making myself clear?'

'They're *married?*' There was a roaring in his ears and he shook his head to clear it. 'No. It's not possible.'

'If you doubt my word,' said Mr Conant even more frigidly, 'you may see the Register.'

Marcus opened his mouth, then closed it again as the vicar's first words hit home.

'*You* married them? In this last hour?'

'I did.'

Marcus spun on his heel, swearing violently. Leaving the indignant cleric behind him, he raced back to the inn to reclaim his horse and then swore some more when he had to wait for it to be saddled. There was a red haze in his head. Sarre had ruined him ... and he'd done it deliberately. He'd taken the girl and her money and left Marcus with no option other than flight. In his saner moments, he'd always known it might come to this. But now that it had ... now that it had, there was no way in hell that he was going to quit the country leaving Sarre alive to enjoy his victory.

Turning his horse's head towards the coast, he set off to do murder.

* * *

262

Bertrand swung the carriage into the yard in time to see Mr Clayton rubbing down a pair of horses that hadn't been there when they left. Jumping down from the box and opening the carriage door, he looked at the Earl and said, 'Visitors.'

'So I see.' Adrian stepped down and extended a hand to Caroline. Then, leaving Mr Bailes to assist Betsy, he asked his caretaker who he was going to find in the house.

'His Grace of Rockliffe, my lord. And his brother. Been here near half-an-hour, I reckon.' He grinned at Caroline and said, 'Mrs Clayton and me wish you very happy, your ladyship. Very happy indeed. And you, too, my lord.'

Aware that Adrian and Bertrand were exchanging brief and hurried sentences in French, Caroline decided that, since she was now a Countess, she'd better start behaving like one.

'Thank you. You're very kind. I hope that later, when his lordship and I have greeted our unexpected guests, you and Mrs Clayton will join us in the parlour for a small celebration.'

'Very good of you, milady. Very good indeed.'

She smiled and then looked around. Betsy was disappearing into the kitchen almost at a gallop with Mr Bailes in hot pursuit and Bertrand was pulling off his driving gloves ready to help Clayton with both the visiting horses and their own.

Adrian offered her his arm, his expression enigmatic.

'Don't ask me why they're here. Nicholas, I might understand. He'll have prised everything out of Aristide. But Rockliffe? True – his estate lies only about thirty miles away but that's not enough to put us on visiting terms.'

Having been hoping for a few precious minutes alone with her new husband, Caroline repressed a sigh and said, 'They'll know we're here so we'd better go in. Is there anything – aside from the obvious – that I shouldn't say?'

'I should think what you call *the obvious* gives us enough topics to avoid, wouldn't you? Especially as they're going to have to stay the night.'

They were walking now, towards the front of the house but she stopped and said, 'Oh. I should go and make sure rooms are being prepared and --'

'I imagine Mrs Clayton already has that in hand.' He glanced down at her, his eyes still unreadable in that disconcerting way he had. 'Or were you hoping to escape?'

Yes - but with you.

'Should I be? Or are you calling me a coward, my lord?'

'I know you're not – so let's go and face them together.'

They found the Duke and Lord Nicholas comfortably ensconced in the back parlour beside a cheerful blaze and nursing glasses of wine. As soon as they appeared, Nicholas surged to his feet and crossed the room, one hand outstretched, saying, 'Dev! What's this they're telling us? You were only married this afternoon when the notice was in the *Chronicle* two days ago?'

Sarre grinned and gripped his friend's hand.

'There was a slight delay.' He drew Caroline forward and added, 'But now you may be one of the first to congratulate us.'

Nicholas shot him an odd look but immediately took Caroline's hand and, with both warmth and sincerity, said all the proper things before immediately turning back to Sarre.

'What do you mean – there was a delay? You eloped, for God's sake!'

'Nicholas.' The Duke of Rockliffe's smooth, almost indolent tones saved Adrian from having to answer. 'I'm sure you have a great deal to say on this and many other subjects ... but perhaps it might wait until Lord Sarre has presented me to his lady?'

Caroline looked at the Duke, seeing not only the resemblances to his brother but also the differences. They were both tall, black-haired and dark-eyed. But where Nicholas had a relaxed, loose-limbed posture and an easy, open smile, there was something about Rockliffe that was very different. Something that seemed to command the space about him and which, despite his exceptional good-looks, made Caroline understand why it wouldn't be a good idea to under-estimate him.

264

He smiled, bowed gracefully over her hand and said, 'My warmest felicitations, Lady Sarre ... and my apologies for our lamentable timing in descending upon you on your wedding day.'

Caroline shook her head and said, 'I'm only sorry you didn't arrive in time for the ceremony, your Grace. We would have been delighted for you to have been there.'

'And, if we'd had the least idea of what was going on, we could have been,' grumbled Lord Nicholas. 'If it gets out that her ladyship has been here with you for the best part of a week before you got round to tying the knot --'

'Since I assume only we two know of it,' interposed the Duke smoothly, 'there is no reason why it should. As for her ladyship's recent whereabouts, I imagine the only other person who knows of them is Monsieur Delacroix ... whose lips are doubtless sealed. Lord Sarre?'

'Aristide won't talk. I also confided in Lily Brassington and am hoping she won't either.' He paused, then added, 'If your Grace will keep our secret, I'll be in your debt.'

'Your lordship has a great many secrets, do you not?' Laughter gleamed in the night-dark eyes. 'Fortunately, I am the soul of discretion. Nicholas, of course, is not.'

'I can keep my mouth shut as well as you can,' said his brother, affrontedly. 'And I don't gossip about my friends.'

Adrian said, 'You don't need to tell me that, Nick. But, though your visit is most welcome, I'm not at all sure what prompted it.'

'I'm staying at the Priors with Rock and Adeline – so I thought I'd just ride over to make sure that everything was all right with you.'

Adrian's brows rose.

'Did you have any reason to think it might not be?'

Lord Nicholas cast a fleeting glance in Caroline's direction and then said, 'Nothing definite. Just ... you know.'

'Ah. You're talking about Marcus Sheringham.' He smiled faintly. 'It's all right. You can speak freely before Caroline. She isn't prone to the vapours.'

'That is no doubt fortunate,' murmured Rockliffe, still with that glint of amusement. Then, to Caroline, 'I'm sure you'd like a few minutes alone with your husband … so if there is somewhere Nicholas and I might remove the dust of the road, perhaps we could absent ourselves for a time?'

'Of course, your Grace. I'll have Mrs Holt show you to your rooms and bring up hot water if she hasn't done so already.' She smiled. 'And then – since the kitchen has been hard at work since yesterday – I hope you and Lord Nicholas will join us for our wedding-breakfast.'

When the Duke and his brother had gone upstairs, Adrian looked at Caroline and sighed.

'Not quite the celebration we'd planned with Bertrand and Betsy and the rest of them. Do you mind?'

'Of course not. It's rather touching that Lord Nicholas was sufficiently concerned about you to come here – though he's fairly annoyed you didn't tell him everything before you left London. As for the Duke … you once described him as a very good friend or an undesirable enemy. It seems that he's decided to be your friend.'

'For which I'm duly grateful, believe me.'

'I imagine he could be quite … intimidating.' She grinned suddenly. 'But then, so can you when you choose to be.'

'Acting,' he shrugged. 'Something, as I hope you've noticed, that I've been doing a lot less of recently. In a way, it's --'

The door burst open and Mr Bailes appeared on the threshold with his hair standing on end. He said breathlessly, 'Beg pardon, m'lord – but it's Betsy. I think somebody's took her.'

'*What?*'

'She went across the yard to ask Mr Clayton to bring in some more logs for the fires and when she didn't come back I wondered what was keeping her.' He stopped, then ringing agitated hands, 'Mr Clayton's out cold on the stable floor and Betsy isn't *anywhere*.'

Before he'd finished speaking, Adrian was striding across the hall, through the kitchen and out into the yard. Caroline picked up her skirts and charged after him with Mr Bailes bringing up the rear. Clayton was sitting on the ground, clutching his head but when he saw the Earl, he struggled to rise, saying weakly, 'I'm sorry, my lord. Somebody gave me a clout on the head and --'

'Stay where you are.' Adrian pressed the man back down. 'Where's Betsy?'

'Don't know, my lord. She was here when --'

Vaulting on to the top of the log-store, Adrian scanned the beach. Dusk was falling and wisps of mist drifted over the marshy ground behind the dunes. Some distance way to the right, he could just make out the silhouette of a horse ... and close by it, the shape of a man grappling with a struggling woman. Then he saw the breeze catch a swirl of red skirt; the same red of the gown Betsy had worn for the wedding.

Dropping back to the ground, he snapped, 'Mr Bailes – saddle my horse in case I need him. Caroline – send Bertrand after me but keep everyone else inside the house. And that includes you.'

Then he left the yard at a run and took off along the track.

Caroline wasted no more than a second staring after him. Useless to call him back. This was Betsy so nothing was going to stop him. Whirling round, she spared a glance for Mr Bailes already grabbing his lordship's saddle and Mr Claypole staggering to his feet. Then she flew back towards the kitchen door.

She was just pushing it wide and opening her mouth to shout for Bertrand when she heard the shot.

TWENTY-THREE

Without stopping to think, Caroline spun back the way she had come, yelling, 'Mr Bailes – get Bertrand. *Now!*' Then, snatching her skirts up in both hands, she was racing out of the yard in Adrian's wake.

She'd hardly got through the gate when a second shot set her heart ricocheting against her ribs. 'Adrian? *Adrian!*'

Oh God, oh God. Don't let him be hit. Please, please don't let him be hit.

In just the last fateful few minutes, the sky seemed to have grown darker, as if promising a deluge. She ran, half-tripping, along the narrow, rutted track and then, seeing no sign of Adrian ahead of her, turned to cross the line of the dunes, her breath coming in ragged gasps. A clump of something or other caused her to stumble and fall to her knees. She pulled herself up and ran on, screaming his name.

Where is he? Where? Why don't I see him?

Then, just when panic and despair were beginning to merge into absolute terror, two things happened more or less simultaneously. She saw Betsy running towards her … and she found Adrian by tripping over him.

He was on his back and seemingly unconscious, an ominous stain spreading over the brightly embroidered vest. Sobbing a little and, unable in the poor light, to see if he was breathing, Caroline laid one hand on his chest and the other against his neck, hoping one or the other would tell her if he was still alive. Her fingers came away sticky with blood

Betsy arrived to crouch on the ground beside her, struggling to breathe. She said, 'He's … gone. That man. Went after … second shot … brought his lordship down. Is … is he dead?'

'I don't know. I don't think so.' *He can't be dead – he can't be. How shall I bear it?* Hands shaking and her vision hopelessly blurred, Caroline was fighting with the buttons of the vest. 'Go back, Betsy. Bertrand's coming but we need more help. Get Lord Nicholas.'

Betsy stood up and then, with relief, said, 'Look – they're coming. I'll go … water and bandages.'

Bertrand dropped on his knees beside her. The Duke of Rockliffe and Lord Nicholas were two steps behind him.

'He's not dead,' said Caroline, raggedly. 'Tell me he's not dead.'

Before Bertrand could speak, Rockliffe said crisply, 'Sheringham, no doubt. Nicholas – get a horse saddled and go after him. He'll be headed for Deal but if you miss him there, ride on to Walmer and call out the Lord Warden. Use my name. Go – and try not to do anything stupid.'

Without a word, Nicholas took off, running back to the house.

Bertrand, meanwhile, had shed his coat in order to strip off his shirt. Folding it into a rough pad, he placed it over the bullet-wound in Adrian's shoulder and, seizing Caroline's hands, said, 'No. 'E is not dead. Now, press 'ard, Madame.'

She did as he said for the few seconds it took for him to drag his coat back on and take over from her, swearing under his breath.

Through chattering teeth, Caroline said fiercely, 'Adrian? Don't die. Do you hear me? You can't die. Not on our wedding day.'

The thick sepia lashes fluttered a little and Adrian's eyes opened, dazed and frowning.

'Don't move,' said Rockliffe quickly. 'You've been shot.'

'Gathered that,' managed Adrian, his voice a mere thread but tension in every muscle. 'Betsy?'

'Safe,' said Caroline, finding his hand and holding it tight. 'She's safe.'

'Good.' He seemed to relax. Then, peering down at his chest, 'Damn. This vest was new.'

And Caroline, her face wet with tears, gave way to sobbing laughter.

Rockliffe said firmly, 'He's not going to die. Not from a bullet in the shoulder. He won't die. Do you hear me?'

She nodded, wiping a hand across her face. It occurred to her, somewhat belatedly, that his Grace was in his shirt-sleeves and had a smear of soap below one ear – all of which told her how fast he'd reacted on hearing that first shot.

'Good. Now this gentleman and I are going to get his lordship back to the house. It will be helpful if you precede us so that everything is ready when we arrive.'

'I don't want to leave him.'

Bertrand looked up from what he was doing and said, *'C'est bien, Madame. Monsieur le Duc* is right. And I am 'ere.'

'There goes Nicholas,' remarked Rockliffe, watching his brother ride away. 'And someone is coming with a lantern. Excellent.' He held out his hand and pulled Caroline to her feet. 'Go, my dear. We'll bring him to you.'

Reluctantly and with one last, lingering look at her husband, she went.

Dropping back on to one knee, Rockliffe slid his arm under Adrian's shoulders saying, 'You're going to sit up slowly. You may feel a little light-headed. Blood loss and having a bullet in you has that effect.'

'I'm fine,' protested Adrian, struggling to his knees. 'I can manage.'

'Be still. You're bleeding like a damned pig,' grumbled Bertrand in French. And added a vulgar epithet describing both Lord Sheringham and Lord Sheringham's antecedents.

A tremor that stopped just short of laughter ran through Adrian and he said, 'Bertrand … you should know that his Grace's French is as good as my own.'

'Not quite,' murmured Rockliffe, levering Adrian upright. 'That particular expression isn't one I'm familiar with. Ah … the gentleman with the lantern. Perhaps we can now accomplish this without tripping over our own feet.' He paused and then added, 'Since you're likely to bleed all over me, you'd better start calling me Rock. There are times when formality becomes more than a trifle ludicrous.'

* * *

They got back to the house without mishap and without Adrian passing out on the way. Once in his bedchamber, Bertrand and Rockliffe eased him out of his coat and vest, leaving Caroline to cut away his ruined shirt.

When it was done, Adrian found he was quite glad to lie down. Though his shoulder was on fire, the rest of him was a block of ice. But what troubled him most was the expression in Caroline's eyes and the tear-stains on her cheeks. He said, 'Don't worry. Once the bullet's out, I'll be as good as new.'

'He could have killed you!' she said explosively. 'He nearly did, for God's sake. And it was deliberate. He took Betsy just to draw you outside so he could ... so he could murder you.' She stopped, drew a steadying breath and removed the pad she'd been holding against his shoulder in order to take a look. Then, turning to Bertrand, 'It's not bleeding as much but he needs a doctor. Will you go?'

'*Bien sûr.*'

'One moment,' said Rockliffe quietly. 'If I might take a look?'

'Be my guest.' Adrian started to shrug and immediately regretted it. 'I gather you've some experience of bullets?'

'As much as one would wish to have.' The Duke pushed Adrian back against the pillows and began gently pressing the area around the wound. 'I served in the Hussars for a couple of years before inheriting the title. I've seen bullets being removed ... one of which was from myself.' He stopped what he was doing and sat back. 'From what I can tell, the ball has made a nice straight entry and is lying not far below the surface. Removing it ought not to be too difficult ... though the doctor should still be summoned.'

Caroline stared at him.

'Are you saying *you* can do it?'

'I believe so.' Smiling a little, he rose and went to wash his hands. 'Unless his patients include the odd poacher or smuggler, the local doctor may have had little or no practice with bullet-wounds. But the choice must be Lord Sarre's, of course.'

'Adrian,' said his lordship, with a strained grin. 'If you're going to dig holes in me, formality is *definitely* ludicrous.'

Rockliffe nodded and started issuing instructions; more hot water and linen; knives – razor-sharp and perfectly clean; a bottle of brandy. Then, when things began arriving and he'd placed a large glass of brandy in Adrian's hands with instructions to down it quickly, he said, 'I'd suggest you leave the room for a while, Lady Sarre ... but I suspect I would be wasting my breath.'

'Yes.'

'You should go,' said Adrian, draining the glass. 'This isn't something you want to watch.'

'I'm not leaving you,' she said flatly. 'And I've no intention of watching. I'm going to help.'

'Good.' The Duke rolled his sleeves up, washed his hands a second time and perused the array of gleaming knives Bertrand had laid out on a towel. Then, glancing back at the open doorway where Betsy hovered beside Mr Bailes, 'I suspect Adrian might prefer a little more privacy.'

Managing a smile and hoping she looked calmer than she felt, Caroline crossed the room saying, 'Go downstairs and make some tea for yourself and Mr Bailes, Betsy. You've both had a shock – and I'll need you to sit with his lordship later.'

Then she closed the door, leaving herself, Bertrand, the Duke … and Adrian, now starting to look marginally less tense.

'What should I do?' she asked Rockliffe.

'Stand nearby and have some pads of linen ready when I ask for them. Bertrand …' He switched smoothly to French, 'Sit on his other side and get a firm hold. I need you to keep him as steady as you can.' Then, once more in English, 'The brandy will help, Adrian, but there's no point in pretending it won't hurt. Quite a lot, as I recall.' He turned away to pick up the blade he'd decided was most suitable. 'In the meantime – and to give your thoughts a different direction – you may wish to know that Nicholas is in hot pursuit of Lord Sheringham with instructions to get help from the Lord Warden. Try to be still now … and I'll do this as quickly as I can.'

The knife slid in following the passage of the bullet and Adrian's breath hissed through his teeth. *'Merde.'*

'Quite.' Without removing either his eyes or his concentration from what he was doing, Rockliffe said, 'If Sheringham is caught, you'll need to decide whether or not you want to bring charges against him. Be *still*. Either way, he's finished in England since it would be quite useless to expect me to put attempted murder in the vault along with all your other secrets.'

Adrian said nothing. Sweat was breaking out all over his skin and blood was blossoming about the knife.

Caroline found that watching someone sliding sharp, pointy metal into her husband's flesh didn't agree with her.

'Ah. There it is,' said Rockliffe calmly. 'Very, very still now. I've been meaning to tell you how much I appreciated your performance in *The Hypochondriac*. At some point, I'd enjoy hearing how you got into that line of work.' He made a slight adjustment that had Adrian clamping his teeth together and digging his fingernails into Bertrand's restraining arm. Then, reaching for the slender pincers beside him, he drew the bullet out, saying in a tone of profound satisfaction, 'And we have it. Do you know ... there are times when I amaze myself.'

Adrian gave a low, involuntary groan and let his muscles slump.

'Bertrand, you can let go now. Caroline, press down hard directly over the wound.' He poured a second glass of brandy and approached the bed, the bottle still in his hand. 'Adrian ... brace yourself. Caroline ... remove the pad, if you will.' And he poured neat brandy over the wound.

The shock of it nearly caused Adrian to hit the ceiling and he swore, long and hard in French.

'Really,' remarked the Duke, handing over the glass, 'you and your friend are a linguistic education – though perhaps not of the best sort.' He smiled at Caroline and said, 'He's all yours, my dear. Wrap him up, let him finish the brandy and leave him to sleep. As for myself ...' he gestured distastefully to the state of his apparel, 'I shall go and attempt to restore myself to some semblance of respectability.'

When Adrian's shoulder had been dressed and he'd been tucked underneath the blankets, Bertrand also left the room. Caroline stood for a moment, looking at her husband. His eyes were shut, his brow furrowed and his jaw was tight. She realised that she had no words for what she felt. The sheer, grinding terror of the last hour had paralysed her brain. So she crept on to the bed at his uninjured side and, not wanting to jar him in any way, slid as near as she could without actually touching. Then she slowly released a breath she didn't know she'd been holding.

Adrian's eyes opened and he turned his head. He said, 'You're shaking.'

'Yes. A little.'

'I suppose this has been nearly as unpleasant for you as it was for me.'

'When I found you, I didn't know … I was afraid you were dead,' she said unevenly. 'Then, watching the Duke putting that knife into you …' She shook her head. 'He did it so delicately … but it was still horrible.'

'I won't argue with that. Come closer.'

'I don't want to hurt you.'

'You won't.' Transferring the glass to his other hand, he managed to slide an arm round her. 'Come closer.' And when she was nestled against his good shoulder and he could inhale the scent of her hair, 'Not quite the wedding day either of us imagined.'

'No.'

'Not that it would have been much of a wedding anyway.' He looked into the still half-full glass and then drained it, grimacing slightly. 'But I didn't bargain for getting shot.'

'No.' Caroline took the empty glass and set it aside. 'One can't predict these things.'

'True. That's very true.' His eyes felt heavy and his tongue was having trouble forming words correctly. With some surprise, he said, 'I'm drunk.'

'A little, perhaps.'

'I don't drink, you know. Not much, anyway. It worries Bertrand, that. But you can't drink when you're going on-stage. And playing cards to win, pretending to be somebody else is pretty much the same. So I don't. Drink, I mean.' He frowned, trying to concentrate. 'Shouldn't be drunk in front of you. Sorry.'

Caroline's nerves settled and she turned, smiling, to brush his hair back from his face. 'I don't mind. Just sleep for a while. You'll feel better. And, when you wake, I'll bring you something to eat.'

'Don't go yet.'

'I won't.' *Not until you're sleeping.* 'Betsy will want to see you later.' He nodded, allowing his eyes to drift shut.

'I was going to ask you something, you know. I'd been thinking about it all day. Not a lot of point, now.'

'Isn't there?' She lowered her voice to merest murmur and continued stroking his hair.

He said hazily, 'That's nice. I was going to ask ... going to ask if you'd consider sharing my bed. But not like this. This wasn't at all what I had in mind.' A pause and then he added vaguely, 'You could have said no. I knew you might. But still ... I was going to ask.'

With a flood of pure joy racing through her veins, Caroline had trouble controlling her voice. She said, 'I wouldn't have.'

'No? No. I suppose not.' He sounded regretful. 'Too soon.'

'No. I meant that I wouldn't have said no.'

Adrian forced his eyelids open. 'You wouldn't?'

'Absolutely not.'

'Oh.' His eyes flickered shut again and a smile curled his mouth. 'Ask you tomorrow, then. Or the next day. Ask you when I've stopped bleeding.'

'Yes, darling,' she said softly, watching him drift into sleep. 'Ask me then.'

* * *

Outside his door, she found Betsy patiently waiting. Caroline said, 'Sit with him now, if you wish. Hopefully, he'll sleep for a while. But I must go and play hostess to his Grace. I don't suppose Lord Nicholas is back?'

'No, my lady.' Betsy's face crumpled a little. 'I'm so sorry, my lady. If his lordship hadn't come after me, this wouldn't have happened.'

Caroline put her arms around the older woman and said, 'We can't know that. Lord Sheringham has wanted to destroy his lordship for a very long time. And you must know that the little boy you mothered would walk through fire for you.'

Before going downstairs, Caroline took a few minutes to wash her face and tidy her hair. The beautiful green gown was crumpled and no longer clean but it was Adrian's gift and she couldn't bring herself to remove it just yet.

Rockliffe rose when she entered the parlour, poured a glass of wine and handed it to her. He said, 'I hope you will forgive me for making myself rather more at home than is generally considered polite – but I've asked Bertrand to order a light supper. I doubt you've eaten properly today and I'd rather you didn't faint.'

'I've never fainted in my life.'

'There is, as they say, a first time for everything.' He pressed her into a chair and then said, 'He's sleeping?'

'Yes. Betsy is with him.' Caroline looked up at him, aware that his Grace was once more restored to a frankly alarming degree of elegance. She said baldly, 'Thank you. I don't know … if you hadn't been here, I don't know how we'd have managed. So thank you – for everything.'

An almost imperceptible shake of his head indicated that Rockliffe didn't consider that he'd done anything very much at all. Taking the chair on the other side of the hearth, he said, 'It's been an interesting day. Your husband lives a very eventful life.'

'You seem to know a lot about him.'

'Let us say that I know certain things and have deduced others.' He paused, toying thoughtfully with his snuff-box. 'Since, as you so rightly said, Lord Sheringham came here to kill Adrian, he presumably had every intention of fleeing the country afterwards. He may try getting passage with the smugglers at Deal … although, if that was his plan, he'd have done better riding to Pegwell where I believe the gentlemen of the Trade are extremely active. His other alternative is to take the packet from Dover.' He appeared to take snuff and dropped the box in his pocket. 'It might be in everyone's best interests if he were allowed to escape – but that decision rests with Adrian. And until my brother returns, we won't know if there's any choice to be made.'

'I hope Lord Nicholas is all right,' she said, randomly. Then, 'You told him to go to the Lord Warden for help. I don't understand who that is exactly.'

'The Lord Warden of the Cinque Ports wields a great deal of authority hereabouts. He can call out the Militia, he can prevent a ship from sailing if he has reason to search it and he has powers of arrest. If Nicholas can't catch up with Sheringham, the Lord Warden almost certainly can.' He smiled faintly. 'And if Adrian elects to simply let his lordship slip the net, that can still be arranged.'

'*Adrian* might do that,' said Caroline tightly. 'I wouldn't. After everything his lordship's done – and you wouldn't believe just how wicked some of that is – I'd like to string him up by his thumbs.'

'Most understandable.' Rockliffe took a sip of wine and watched her without appearing to do so. 'It began, one would imagine, with Evangeline Mortimer.'

The brown gaze sharpened but she said nothing.

'You see,' he continued imperturbably, 'I always wondered why Sheringham was so eager to make the world believe that Adrian had killed her. Of course, with any other woman ... yourself, for example ... one would inevitably suspect either foul play or suicide. In the case of Mistress Mortimer, however, anyone who knew her would merely suppose her a victim of her own rash stupidity.' He paused, in apparently idle contemplation of his glass. 'But Sheringham wanted people to think otherwise ... for which, presumably, he had a reason.'

Caroline waited and, when he didn't appear disposed to add anything further, said, 'What do you expect me to say? It's not my story to tell. But if you were to ask Adrian, I think he might share it with you. After all, you know virtually everything else.'

'A thought he has doubtless found disconcerting.'

A tap at the door heralded Sally, announcing that supper was laid out in the dining-parlour.

His Grace rose and offered Caroline his arm.

'As it happens, I didn't expect you to say anything,' he remarked, leading her from the room. 'You are neither stupid nor disloyal. And Adrian is fortunate.'

Over a supper largely composed of the dishes Mrs Clayton had intended for the wedding-breakfast they'd never had, Rockliffe conversed smoothly on a number of topics. Most of these were impersonal but, when Caroline asked after the Duchess, a touch of worry appeared in the dark eyes and he said, 'Adeline is expecting our first child and not finding these early months as easy as I would like.'

'Oh.' Caroline hesitated and then said bluntly, 'I'm probably not supposed to ask – but I gather she's feeling nauseous?'

'Constantly.'

'Peppermint?'

'We've tried it.'

'Ginger?'

'That, too. Nothing helps. I am assured it will stop in due course.' His smile was slightly crooked. 'Needless to say, at present that is not a comfort … which will explain why I will be leaving for home first thing in the morning.'

'Of course.'

Caroline found herself envying the unknown Duchess. Having the love of a man like this would be a rare and precious gift.

They were about to leave the table when there were sounds betokening an arrival.

'Nicholas,' said Rockliffe, rising from his seat. 'Good.'

His lordship entered the room, splashed with mud and grinning.

'Done,' he said succinctly. Then, 'Food. Thank God. I'm ravenous.'

Caroline fetched a clean plate from the sideboard, saying, 'Then please sit down and eat. Your doings can wait for a little while.'

'No they can't,' said his brother. 'What, precisely, does 'done' mean?'

'What it sounds like.' Nicholas piled his plate with slices of ham and chicken. 'I tracked him to the King's Head in Deal. The silly fool had gone back for his luggage and his carriage.' A dish of creamed leeks caught his eye so he helped himself to those as well. 'If *I'd* just tried to kill somebody, I think I'd do without a clean shirt or two in favour of getting the hell out of the country – but not Sheringham. He was even using his own name, the idiot.'

'Clearly. So, having found him, what did you do next?'

'I paid a couple of fellows to stop him leaving and then rode to Walmer.' Nicholas swallowed a mouthful of ham and groaned appreciatively. 'I may have given the Warden the impression Dev was at death's door – just to speed things up a touch.' He looked up. 'How is he, by the way?'

'On the mend, thanks to his Grace's skill in removing the bullet,' supplied Caroline.

'Did you?' Nicholas stared at the Duke. 'I didn't know you could do that.'

'One of numerous things you don't know,' said Rockliffe patiently. 'And Lord Sheringham?'

'Safely under lock and key in Walmer Castle – where he'll stay until charges are laid. Or not, as the case may be. Lord Holderness sends his regards, by the way.' He picked up his knife. 'And now – do you think I might be allowed to eat?'

'By all means.' The Duke smiled at Caroline. 'I can see you are itching to run back to your husband ... but, before you do, there's one other thing I'd like the two of you to consider.'

'Oh?'

'The announcement of your marriage in the *Morning Chronicle* was bereft of all but the basic details and any whisper of an elopement would be damaging. I would therefore suggest that, as soon as Adrian is fit to travel, you come to Wynstanton Priors and remain with the Duchess and myself for a few days. That way, we can make it appear that your wedding was conducted in a fog of ducal respectability which no one will dare question.'

Caroline felt her colour rising. She said, 'That is uncommonly kind, of you. I am at a loss to know why you should do so much for us.'

'If it helps, I will admit to having an ulterior motive.'

'And what is that, your Grace?'

'I think my Adeline would like you. I also think she would enjoy seeing Adrian play Molière, if he could be persuaded to do so,' came the bland reply. Then, with a particularly charming smile, 'And most people call me Rock.'

TWENTY-FOUR

She found Betsy in chair by hearth with her knitting and Adrian asleep in a tangle of sheets.

'Has he woken at all?' she asked.

'Oh yes – and as sulky as a bear, he was too,' came the soft-voiced but perfectly cheerful reply. 'He thought I was going to bring him a couple of chops and a mug of ale, then threatened to fetch them himself when I told him all he was getting was a cup of beef tea and a bit of egg custard.'

Caroline stifled a laugh.

'You obviously won that battle.'

'I said if he wanted to be up and about again sooner rather than later, he'd do as he was bid. So he ate what I gave him and settled down again – though he didn't seem very well-pleased when I said you were supping with the Duke.' Betsy folded up her knitting and stood up. 'I daresay you'll want to stay with him yourself now, my lady. He'll probably sleep for a good long while because I slipped one of my powders into his hot milk. Are we to send for the doctor in the morning?'

'I think so, yes.' Caroline glanced down at her gown and said, 'If I take this off, do you think Sally might be able to do something with it?'

'I'll see to it myself, my lady. You just get yourself changed so as you can settle down in comfort. It might be a long night.'

* * *

The hours passed slowly and, throughout most of them, Adrian barely stirred. Wrapped in a chamber-robe, Caroline sat by the fire, yawning over *Clarissa*. Though it didn't help that she'd picked up Volume Two by mistake, the main problem was the man sleeping a few feet away. The man who, just a little while ago, had said, *I was going to ask if you'd consider sharing my bed.*

She tried reminding herself that he'd been mildly drunk when he said it; then she pointed out that a man would naturally expect to sleep with his bride on their wedding-night. Neither of these sobering reflections helped. He wanted her. And if the day had turned out differently, she'd be lying with him right now.

She looked at the bed. It was large and Adrian was only occupying half of it. Surely it wouldn't hurt to lie down at the far edge and sleep for a little while?

Don't lie to yourself and stop making excuses, said a sardonic voice in her head. *You just want to be near him. You want to reach out and touch his hand. You want to watch him wake up, fuddled with sleep and utterly beautiful. So do it. It's not as though you haven't been invited.*

She uncoiled from the chair and crossed slowly towards the bed. Very, very carefully so as not to disturb the covers, she lay down, one arm underneath her head, facing him. She looked at the tousled brown hair, the long dark eyelashes and the softness of his mouth in repose. She thought, *I could look at you forever and never be tired of it. Why did it take me so long to realise?*

She was still wondering that when she slid into sleep.

* * *

Adrian awoke slowly and became gradually aware of three things. His head hurt, his shoulder felt as though a red-hot poker had been rammed through it and someone was holding his hand. Very cautiously, he opened his eyes.

Caroline was fast asleep amidst a cascade of rippling, honey-blond hair. It spilled over the pillow, coiled around her neck and one long strand had drifted across her nose, making it twitch. Despite his physical ills, Adrian found himself grinning. Gently slipping his fingers from hers, he reached out and brushed the annoying lock aside. She made a tiny snuffling sound and burrowed a little deeper into the pillow. He became aware that the ribbons of her robe had loosened during the night and were providing him with a very interesting view that the parts of his body which didn't hurt appreciated more than was appropriate, given the circumstances.

Damn.

The most sensible thing, he decided, would be for him to get up and leave Caroline to sleep. Unfortunately, that presented him with certain difficulties. He had vague recollections of Bertrand spoiling his brandy-induced haze in order to remove what was left of his clothing. A brief exploration beneath the sheet told him that, in certain respects, Bertrand had been very thorough ... a glance about the room showed him that, in others, he'd been less so because there was no sign of the dressing-robe that usually lay on a nearby chair. It was probably hanging tidily in the closet. And Caroline was lying on top of the bed-covers.

Double damn.

There was no way he was going to risk her opening her eyes to see him tripping across the room in the buff and randy as a schoolboy – which meant staying precisely where he was until she woke up.

Well, there were ways to speed that process.

Not like that, you idiot. Focus on something else, can't you?

Reaching out, he took one silky tress and drew it lightly across her lips. Her brows contracted briefly and she blew it away. Adrian smiled and did it again. This time, her hand came up to bat his away and her wrist connected with his. With a small, annoyed sound, she opened her eyes to squint at him ... and was suddenly wide awake.

'*Oh!*' She shot upright and immediately realised how much of her was showing. Pulling helplessly at her robe, most of which she was sitting on, she said, 'I'm sorry. I didn't mean to fall asleep. Did I wake you? How is your shoulder?' And, swinging her feet to the floor, 'I'll go and call Bertrand, shall I?'

'Stop,' said Adrian calmly. 'Just stop for a moment. You didn't wake me; my shoulder hurts like hell, thank you; and, if you'll be so good as to get my robe from the closet, I don't need Bertrand for the moment.'

'Yes. Of course.' Scarlet-cheeked with what part of her brain told her was perfectly needless embarrassment, Caroline all but flew across the room. 'I've no idea what the time is but I'm sure I ought to be dressed by now.' She produced a luxuriously patterned gold and black robe. 'Is this it?'

'Yes.' He waited until she came to lay the garment across his lap and then, catching hold of her wrist, drew her down to sit beside him. 'Take a breath, will you? Everything will wait for another ten minutes. And it's rather nice finding you beside me when I wake.'

'Is it? Oh. Good.'

Had it not been for the feeling inside him that had been growing for some days now … a feeling that, for years, he'd told himself wouldn't – couldn't – happen again, he might have laughed. As it was, he toyed with her fingers and said, 'This hasn't been the best start, has it? I hope you'll trust me to make it better.'

'None of what happened yesterday was your fault.'

'Even so.'

She sensed something in him that she didn't understand and couldn't concentrate on while his thumb was making lazy circles on her palm and his hair was falling loose around his neck. She looked at the bandages lying white and stark against his skin and, for want of something better, said, 'His Grace is impatient to get home to his wife and will probably wish to take his leave of you first. But Bertrand will fetch the doctor, so you should remain in bed until he's been.'

Seeing the confusion in her, Adrian tugged slightly at her hand and pulled her a little closer. His voice low and soft, he said, 'Anything else?'

'No. Yes. The Duke has invited us to spend a few days at his home so no one will be able to guess we eloped. That's thoughtful of him, isn't it?'

'Very.' His eyes dropped from hers to linger on her mouth. 'And Nicholas?'

'Nicholas?' Caroline's breath started to shorten and a number of unfamiliar sensations were taking place inside her. 'Nicholas. Yes. He found Lord Sheringham in Deal and the Lord Warden's locked him up in Walmer Castle. He'll probably want to see you, as well.' It was becoming very difficult to think. 'The Lord Warden, that is.'

'I think I understood that.' Another little tug brought her within reach of his good arm so he used it to draw her all the way against him. 'Is that everything?'

'Yes.'

'Good.'

He nuzzled her ear, heard her breath catch and was just about to kiss her when the door opened. Caroline sprang to her feet, straightening her robe.

Stopping dead on the threshold with a breakfast tray in his hands, Bertrand grinned and said, 'Looks like you're feeling livelier this morning. Wonderful what a night's rest will do, isn't it?'

Smiling pleasantly, Adrian told his friend, in the vernacular, what he could do with himself.

'I'll bear it in mind,' came the unabashed reply. 'In the meantime, the Duke wants a word before he leaves and Lord Nicholas is asking whether it'll inconvenience you if he stays on for a while.'

'It won't – and we should stop doing this.'

'Doing what?'

'Rattling on in French when we're not alone.' Switching to English, he said, 'My apologies, Caroline. That was rude and won't happen again. Nick wants to stay after his brother leaves. Will that be all right with you?'

Caroline said briskly, 'Lord Nicholas can stay as long as he likes. And now – before any other visitors arrive – I'm going to dress.'

Adrian stretched and lay down, every muscle a deliberate invitation. 'You'll be back later, though. Won't you?'

'When the doctor comes,' she nodded. And was gone.

Adrian met his friend's knowing gaze and said irritably, 'Your timing is bloody awful, you know. In fact, I'm tempted to wonder if it isn't deliberate.'

* * *

His Grace of Rockliffe spent roughly fifteen minutes with Lord Sarre prior to taking his leave of her ladyship and departing for home. He repeated his invitation to Wynstanton Priors, along with his reasons for offering it. Then he spoke with what, for him, was unusual bluntness about Marcus Sheringham. At the end of it and whilst waiting for the doctor, Adrian drank a second cup of coffee, ate a piece of toast and sat frowning into space while he tried to decide what he wanted to do.

The doctor was pleased to approve the Duke's handiwork and seemed relieved not to have been asked to do the job himself. He pronounced the wound clean, said he saw no sign of infection and condemned the Earl to spending at least one more day in bed. Then he left.

As soon as the door closed behind him, his lordship informed Bertrand that he wanted a bath and a shave. After some argument, he was finally allowed to have his way and soak some of his aches away in a tub of hot water. There was another argument when he insisted on putting on a pair of breeches under his dressing-robe. Again, Bertrand gave way but said, 'And that's it. If you think you can pull a shirt over your head without damaging your shoulder, think again. Now lie down before you fall down. You lost a lot of blood yesterday and you're as white as a damned sheet.'

By the time Caroline re-appeared, it was mid-morning and he'd made a number of decisions. As soon as she entered the room, he said, 'As Rock no doubt told you, I accepted his invitation. We'll leave the day after tomorrow, if that suits you.'

She thought of the state of her wardrobe and a Duchess who'd been described as the most elegant woman in London. If she hadn't more important things to think of, she might have despaired.

'Yes. But only if you're well enough.'

'I'll be well enough before that – but there are other matters requiring my attention before we go.' He smiled at her to disguise what kind of matters these might be and added, 'Also, when I bought the gown you wore yesterday, I ordered three others which are supposed to be delivered tomorrow. In case you were wondering what on earth you're going to wear whilst staying in a ducal household.'

Caroline's face lit up. She said, 'Three others? Really?'

'Yes. There are better modistes in London, of course – but this will do for the time being. Now I need to speak to --'

The rest of what he had been going to say was lost as Caroline dropped on the bed at his side, slid her arms round his neck and pressed her cheek to his.

'Thank you.'

He enclosed her in his good arm and breathed her in. He murmured, 'If you're going to do this every time I buy you something, I suspect I may be doing it quite a lot.'

Laughing a little, she shook her head and kissed his jaw.

'It's not the gift. It's the fact that you thought of it.' *I love you, I love you, I love you. How long must I wait before I tell you?* She drew away a little and said, 'Now. Who is it you want to speak to? Nicholas?'

'Yes.' He pulled her back against him. 'But there's no hurry. And it seems a pity to waste such an unexpected advantage.'

Lightly, he brushed her mouth with his … once, twice; and then settled in to kiss her properly. She tasted of honey and cinnamon and Caroline. He wanted her and could feel her wanting him in return. The sweetness of it sent everything inside him reeling.

How long before his damned shoulder stopped being an impediment? And how much longer after that before he could admit that his feelings for her had become much more than either liking or lust? Something he had thought he would never feel again and which made her frighteningly indispensable to him.

I didn't expect this. I want to trust it but, after so long, I'm not sure I know how.

Slowly, he let her go and trailed the back of his curved fingers down her cheek. He said huskily, 'An object-lesson about not starting things one can't finish. I should let you go, shouldn't I?'

'Probably.' Her fingers were still tangled in his hair. With reluctance, she withdrew them and said, 'I'll get Nicholas, then.'

'Yes.' He sighed. 'I suppose that would be best.'

* * *

Lord Nicholas regarded him doubtfully.

'I can understand why you might want to do this … but are you sure it's a good idea?'

'No. I just know that I have to do it. As for understanding – I doubt very much if you do. But you might if you knew the whole story.'

'Does that mean you're going to tell me?'

'No. It just means that the parts you don't know are worse than the parts you do.' Adrian took a sip of the wine his lordship had smuggled

286

upstairs past Betsy. 'Your brother thinks I should just let him flee the country. He's financially ruined and Rock has no intention of keeping yesterday's events to himself, thus giving me poetic justice. Also, if Sheringham shows his face in England again, he could be tried for attempted murder. He'd have done the same to me in a heart-beat, after all.'

'But somehow all of that isn't enough?'

'It would be enough if all I wanted was an eye for an eye.' Adrian paused, then added simply, 'It isn't. And that's one of the reasons why I need to look him in the face and watch him recognise that he's the author of his own downfall … and why I want you there as my witness.' He smiled wryly. 'Look on the bright side, Nick. If you want to know all the grisly details of my past, tomorrow is your best chance.'

* * *

Caroline wasn't especially happy on the following morning when Adrian announced that he and Nicholas had some undisclosed business to attend to. But when she also found out that he intended to ride, she turned pink with annoyance.

'No. You will *not* ride. I won't permit it. You've got a hole in your shoulder, you stupid man. And if you think Betsy and I have nothing better to do than to patch you up when it starts bleeding again, you have another think coming. You shouldn't be going out at all, in my opinion. But if you *must* do so then you'll take the carriage. And that, my lord, is an end of it!'

'Whew!' grinned Nicholas, as she whirled off to instruct Bertrand to ready the carriage 'That's certainly told you, hasn't it?'

'Shut up,' muttered Adrian. And thought, *If she can get that fired up over me taking a ride, God knows what she'd say if she knew where I'm going.*

For the first ten minutes, a heavy silence filled the carriage and, seeing the expression on the Earl's face, Nicholas made no attempt to break it. But finally, still staring out of the window, Adrian said, 'I should probably have asked your brother this question rather than you but somehow it got missed. Will the Duchess object to having someone with my unsavoury reputation as a house-guest?'

'No. Adeline's not what you might expect. And she's got a whole set of dirty dishes in her own family, you know. A mad cousin and a slimy, card-sharp of an uncle, to name but two. So I'd imagine an alleged murderer won't make her turn a hair.' He paused and, with a short laugh, added, 'The only thing you need to be prepared for is that she and Rock are completely besotted with each other. At times, being around them is like living in the pages of a damned romance.'

Lucky Rockliffe. That sounds incredibly nice.

Walmer Castle had originally been built as one of Henry VIII's coastal defences. More recently, of course – this being the official residence of the Lord Warden – the interior had been substantially changed. Shown into a large parlour whose inner walls resembled a fashionable house but whose outer ones were still those of a fortress, Adrian found it somewhat disorientating. Nicholas, however, merely introduced him to Lord Holderness and withdrew from the ensuing conversation.

Having listened to Sarre's request, the Lord Warden said dryly, 'I am relieved to see you alive and kicking, sir. I had the impression you were on your death-bed. However ... I've no objection to you interviewing Lord Sheringham, if that's your wish. But I *will* want to know what I'm supposed to do with him afterwards. I don't generally keep would-be murderers in the house. My wife doesn't like it.'

'That's most understandable, my lord – and I'll discuss the matter with you before I leave.'

'See that you do.' The Warden pulled the bell for a servant. 'He's in a secure room downstairs and I'll put one of my own men outside the door. Not, from what I've seen of him, that he's likely to give you any trouble. Cowardly fellow, in my opinion. Just the sort to go round taking pot-shots at a man rather than look him in the eye.'

As soon as the door opened, Lord Sheringham spun round looking wild-eyed and dishevelled. Then, when he saw who his visitors were, the blood drained from his face. He made an odd sound and backed away to lean against the wall.

'Did you think you'd killed me, Marcus?' asked Sarre sympathetically. 'You really don't have any luck at all, do you?'

Marcus swallowed. 'You were hit. I saw you go down.'

288

'Yes.' A slight gesture of one hand indicated his shoulder. 'A small inconvenience.'

'So I see. Come to gloat, have you?'

No. I've come to rub your nose in the mess you've made of your own life and done your damnedest to make of mine. And to find out why.

'Not exactly.' He sat down, crossed one leg over the other and removed an imaginary speck from his sleeve. 'Perhaps certain things about your current situation have eluded you. You set out to murder me and can be proved to have done so. Basically, your life is now in my hands. All I have to do is walk back upstairs to the Lord Warden and press charges.'

'Go and do it, then. You will anyway.'

'It is what *you* would do, certainly.'

It occurred to Nicholas, watching from his place by the door, that Sarre looked perfectly relaxed and even amicable ... unless you saw the ice in his eyes and caught the note of contempt underlying that smooth voice.

'You want me to beg?' said Marcus. 'I won't.'

'You would if you thought it would get you out of here. Principles have always been an alien concept to you, haven't they?'

'Go to hell.'

'And join you there? I'd sooner not.'

'Always so clever, aren't you? If you hadn't set out to ruin me --'

'I can't claim the credit for that. You did it all on your own. You inherited a substantial fortune and threw it away at the gaming table. Your choice – no one else's.'

'And you did nothing? What about the Halifax chit? You knew her dowry could save me – so you made sure I'd never have it. You only married the bloody girl so I couldn't.'

'Untrue – and you'd be wise to take care what you say about my wife.' The Earl uncrossed his legs as if about to rise. 'In fact, I'm beginning to wonder if we have anything useful to say to one another. Unless, of course, you wish to engage my attention by telling me how we came to this.'

'What?' Marcus's hands were sweating and he wiped them down his breeches. 'How we came to what?'

'How we got from friendship to the point where you want me dead. There must have been a moment when – for you, at least – something changed.'

'Do you care?'

'Not especially. Things have gone too far for that now and much of it happened a long time ago. But I suppose you could tell me why you seduced Evie ... aside from the glaringly obvious fact that she let you.'

Christ, thought Nicholas, shocked. *Is* that *where all this started?*

'I did it because I could,' said Marcus spitefully. 'Because she made it so easy ... and because I was sick of seeing the way things just fell into your lap.'

'I have no idea what you're talking about.'

'No. You wouldn't have. We'd been friends for years but as soon as we went to Oxford you barely had time for me and the set you moved with only tolerated me for my money. Then, of course, you had to go and get a damned Honours degree!'

'For which I worked extremely hard,' remarked Sarre, frowning a little. 'It was your choice not to bother and to walk away with a bare pass. Is that *really* all it took to make you hate me?'

'Does it sound like nothing to you? Trust me – it wasn't. The older we got, the more charmed your life became.'

'If you thought that, you can't have been looking very closely. Don't you remember my parents at *all?*'

Marcus made a gesture of impatience.

'Parents don't matter. They die. My father had and so would yours, eventually. Meanwhile, every time I set foot anywhere there was always somebody or other asking me where *you* were. I got bloody tired of it. First, the fellows at university and then all the prettiest girls in Town. Everybody seemed to think you were something special when I knew you weren't. You stood to inherit an earldom but precious little else – yet there wasn't a female you ever met who didn't want you to cast your eyes in her direction. And then along came Evie Mortimer. All that beauty and a fortune as well. The biggest catch of the season. And who did she choose? Viscount bloody Eastry ... with his empty pockets and a house falling down about his ears. And you were so sodding lovesick and pleased with yourself, it made me want to vomit.'

There was a long silence when he stopped speaking.

Although Nicholas could think of a few things he wouldn't have minded saying, he kept his mouth shut and waited.

Finally, the Earl said slowly and in a tone of pure disgust, 'Correct me if I'm wrong – but you seduced my affianced wife and got her pregnant because you were *jealous?*' And then, when Marcus said nothing, 'Not because you loved her and wanted her ... but because you couldn't bear seeing me happy? Do you have the least idea how *pathetic* that makes you?' He stood up and watched the other man tense as if expecting a blow. 'And then there's the rest of it. You knew I didn't push Evie off the roof – that I'd never have hurt her, no matter what she did. You also knew – or should have done – that she wouldn't be able to tell me about the two of you without turning it into a five-act drama. That's why she was on the roof and it's how she came to fall. Two seconds' thought must have told you that. But that didn't stop you accusing me of murder, did it? Not then ... and not now, ten years on. If there is any logic to this malicious obsession of yours, I can't see it. Christ, Marcus. What the hell is the *matter* with you?'

'If you ask me,' remarked Nicholas, unable to stay silent any longer, 'he belongs in a straight-jacket. Give it up, Dev. There's not a thing in him worth saving. Just go on upstairs and tell Lord Holderness to send him for trial.'

'That is clearly the obvious course.' Sarre paused, appearing to think about it. 'Shall I do it, Marcus? Shall I supply the last act to this farce you've created?'

He shrugged, his face pale and glistening with sweat. 'Why ask me?'

This time the silence was a long one. But finally Sarre said, 'Do you regret *anything* you've done? Any single part of it?'

'Yes. I regret letting you win. Is that what you wanted to hear? Why you came?'

'No. I wanted you to understand that, in setting out to destroy my life, you've only succeeded in ruining your own ... and that you have no one but yourself to blame for your current predicament. You've thrown your good name down the drain in the wake of your money – and if you'd married Caroline you'd have done the same thing all over again. There isn't a shred of honour in you.'

'And you'd know, I suppose?'

'After your final piece of lunacy two days ago, I think I'm as fair a judge as anyone. If you wanted to kill me that badly, I've offered to fight you more than once – but you hadn't the nerve for it. As to your bungled attempt at murder ... it's your misfortunate that, along with Lord Nicholas, his brother was also a guest in my house at the time.' He watched the import of this strike home and a hard smile curled his mouth. 'Rockliffe isn't about to keep what he knows to himself and he will be believed. So even if you walked out of here a free man and found the pot of gold at the end of the rainbow, you would still be finished in England.'

Suddenly Marcus's nerve broke. He said, 'You can't prove it was me. You can't.'

'Don't be a bigger fool than you can help. You used my – my housekeeper as bait. Do you think she'd have any difficulty identifying you? It's over and you've lost. Face it,' snapped Sarre. 'And there's one other thing you should know. I didn't marry Caroline either for her money or to hurt you. Odd as you may find it, you are not that important to me. I did it because she makes me happier than I've been in a very long time. And that, though you won't appreciate it, is the only thing that's stopping me putting a noose around your neck.'

Silence stretched out on invisible threads while Marcus worked it out.

'What are you saying?' he asked weakly.

'I'm saying I'm going to ask the Lord Warden to put you on a boat at Dover – from where you can go to hell in your own way. But if I ever see you again ... if you ever come near Caroline, I shall very probably kill you myself. Aside from that, you're welcome to spend the rest of your miserable life knowing that you owe every day of it to me.'

TWENTY-FIVE

Bertrand had a great deal to say on the subject of Adrian's idiocy in deciding to let Lord Sheringham go.

Adrian listened patiently enough but, in the end, said flatly, 'Yes. I know. He's a bastard in every sense but the true one and you think I should cut out his black heart and fry it – something I'll consider if he ever surfaces again. But if he'd been brought to trial for trying to kill me, the ramifications don't bear thinking about. It would come out that Evie was carrying his child when she died, thus causing speculation as to whether she jumped because neither of us would marry her – meaning that Mr Bailes would have to testify. I don't want that. Meanwhile, mud would be flying in all directions and some of it would stick. Even if Rockliffe stood at my back throughout it all – which isn't something I'd ask him to do – Caroline would still find herself embroiled in a scandal that was none of her making and I won't have that either.' He paused and drew a short breath. 'Finally, I'm damned if I'm going to sink to Sheringham's level. And it's done now – so can we please stop talking about it?'

He found Caroline sitting on her bed in rapt contemplation of three large dress boxes. He said, 'Ah. They arrived, then.'

'Yes.'

'But you thought looking at the boxes would be more fun than opening them?'

'No. I thought opening them would be more fun if you were here. So I waited.' She turned, her eyes brimming with mock-accusation. 'You were *ages!*'

Adrian doubted there was another woman in the length and breadth of Europe who could leave a dressmaker's box unopened for more than five minutes. Really, his Caroline was an unfailing source of delight. Looking back at the boxes, he said thoughtfully, 'Given that they're all identical, how is it that the middle one manages to appear superior?'

'I don't know. It's a mystery.'

'It is.' He grinned and decided to stop teasing. 'Caroline ... if you don't open them, *I* will.'

'You're so impatient,' she scolded, dropping to her knees on the floor to investigate the one he'd called superior. 'Don't you know that anticipation is half the pleasure?'

A wicked gleam lit the silver eyes and he said, 'Some of the pleasure, I grant you. But not half – nor even a quarter.'

Her head remained bent over the ties of the box but he saw a hint of colour rise to her cheek. 'I'll have to take your word for that.'

'Yes.' The truth was that his shoulder was aching like the devil. 'Unfortunately, you will.'

Caroline had got inside the box and was peeling back layers of paper with excruciating care. Then, when the gown was finally revealed, 'Oh. It – it's beautiful.'

'You're allowed to take it out of the box, you know,' remarked Adrian, hoping her attention would remain riveted on the new gown long enough for him to conduct a discreet examination beneath his brocaded vest and find out whether the wound was bleeding again. 'In fact, I wish you would. Ordering something from patterns and scraps of material is a chancy business. I'd like to know I got it right.'

She stopped stroking the heavily embroidered pale gold silk and stood up in order to lift the gown from the box. 'You got it *absolutely* right.' She held the gown against her and gazed at her reflection in the mirror. Then, turning, 'Tell me you think so.'

He whipped his hand away from his shoulder. Tilting his head, he conducted a leisurely appraisal of the golden gown against Caroline's skin and hair. He said, 'Yes. I always suspected that shade might look well on you – but it's even better than I thought.' He grinned. 'Clearly, I'm a genius.'

'Or you've had a lot of practice buying ladies' clothes,' she retorted. And then, looking stricken, added quickly, 'I'm sorry. That sounded like a – a criticism or a question. It wasn't meant to be either.'

The grin faded.

'There have been women, yes. I'm not a monk – but neither am I a rake. And it's all in the past now. You needn't worry that I'll insult you by straying. In truth, I haven't the least desire to do so. And I take my promises seriously.'

Caroline opened her mouth, then closed it again. Finally, she mumbled, 'I wouldn't be insulted. It ... it would just hurt.'

Something squeezed at his heart and, for a second, he let himself wonder how she felt about him; whether it might be more than liking and physical attraction. Then, shutting the thought away for future consideration, he said gently, 'It won't happen. I know our relationship began with a deception but you can trust me not to lie to you – and certainly not about this. Now ... smile for me and open the other boxes.'

She didn't smile. She laid the golden gown down and took a step towards him, frowning.

'You look tired. And pale. Are you all right?'

'I'm fine. My shoulder aches a little but I'll get Bertrand to look at it presently. I may have over-done it this morning.' He paused and then said, 'You haven't asked where I went.'

Not satisfied but knowing better than to fuss, Caroline sat down by the next box.

'I don't need to ask.' She kept her eyes on her hands. 'You went to see *him*, didn't you?'

'Yes.'

'Do you want to tell me about it?' She had the ties undone and was lifting the lid. 'It doesn't matter if you'd rather not.'

He was silent for so long that she thought he wasn't going to answer. But finally, he said, 'I didn't expect it to be pleasant ... and it wasn't. But in the end, certain things made my decision easier. One of them was that he's a sad excuse for a man; another is that he'll never trouble us further. So he'll be on his way to France with the next tide.'

'Ah.' She sat back on her heels and looked at him. 'He's lucky his fate rested in your hands rather than mine, then. *I'd* be doing something creative involving red-hot pincers.'

He smiled at this. 'You're very blood-thirsty.'

'What do you expect? He could have *killed* you.' Caroline turned back to the second box. 'However ... after everything he's done, letting him go was something very few men would have managed and I respect you for it.'

He looked down on her bent head, resisting the impulse to drop on to the floor beside her and take her in his arms. He said, 'Bertrand doesn't. He thinks I'm an idiot. But I'm glad that you don't. Thank you.'

* * *

Mercifully, Adrian's shoulder had not started bleeding again and by the following morning, it felt a good deal better – enabling him to face the journey to Wynstanton Priors with both equanimity and optimism. His mood was further improved by the sight of his wife, elegantly-clad in a misty-blue velvet travelling gown, sparsely trimmed with black braid. Her obvious pleasure in it and the proud tilt of her head made him smile.

'What?' asked Caroline, catching his expression and feeling suddenly suspicious.

He shook his head. 'I was just enjoying looking at you.' And laughed when she blushed.

For a time, they passed the journey in desultory conversation that mostly revolved around the Duke of Rockliffe and his Duchess. Eventually, however, the talk inevitably returned to Adrian's decision to waive his options on Marcus Sheringham's future; and that was when he said hesitantly, 'There's something I ought to tell you about the consequences of that.'

Caroline frowned a little, suddenly anxious.

'Consequences? To you?'

'To both of us.' He paused and then said, 'It's possible you won't feel quite so tolerant towards me when I tell you what setting him free is going to cost.'

'What do you mean?'

'He owes money all over the place. It's not just Sinclair's. It's his tailor, his bootmaker, his servants and God knows who else. If he remained in the country, these people stood some chance of recouping at least part of what they're owed. With him gone, they don't. And that doesn't seem very fair.'

Oh Adrian. Caroline's heart melted all over again. *You of all people know that life isn't always fair and can't be made so. But I love you for trying.* She said carefully, 'He would have fled the country anyway.'

'I know.'

'And the mess he's left behind isn't your responsibility.'

'The debt to Sinclair's is. Aristide continued allowing Marcus credit far longer than he'd normally have done because I asked him to – so I have to make that good. But it's the servants and smaller tradesmen who stand to suffer most. They are the ones who can't afford the loss. You'll think it unreasonable, I daresay – but I can't just ignore them.'

'No,' she sighed. 'You can't. Anyone else – but not you. Do you honestly think that, after Lady B's pearls and Mr Bailes and Betsy, I don't know that?'

He shrugged slightly, looking a little embarrassed.

'Don't you want to argue about it?'

'No. I want to know what you're going to do.'

'Thank you.'

He reached across to take her hands and lift each in turn to his lips. Smiling a little, Caroline wondered if he had any idea how very Claude Duvall the gesture was.

'I'll do as much as I can. I own the mortgages on two of his properties. The interest on both is significantly in arrears so I'll foreclose, sell them and use the proceeds to pay off as many of the smaller creditors as I can. The debt to Sinclair's will come out of my own pocket.' He stopped, his fingers tightening on hers and, looking her in the eye, said, '*My* pocket, Caroline. I'm only telling you all this because, as my wife, you have a right to know. I have no intention of touching your grandfather's money. That wouldn't be appropriate. Besides ... I want the gentleman to like me.'

'I don't think you need worry about that,' she said. 'I, on the other hand, am beginning to realise that I've married a very stubborn fellow. What *am* I going to do with you?'

He sent her a slanting smile of pure invitation.

'I don't know. But I could suggest a few things, if you like.'

* * *

They arrived at Wynstanton Priors in the early afternoon to be greeted on the front steps by Lord Nicholas who had ridden on ahead.

'How is the Duchess?' asked Caroline immediately.

'She's fine,' he replied with a laugh. 'Apparently Rock arrived home to find her drinking coffee and working her way through a plate of macaroons. She swears she started feeling better the instant he stopped looming over her.'

'Oh, that's splendid news! His Grace must be so relieved.'

'He's back to being his usual annoying self, if that's what you mean,' said Nicholas, ushering them inside. 'How's the shoulder, Dev?'

'Still a little stiff – but otherwise, nearly as good as new.'

'In that case, you can come riding with me in the morning. There's a filly for sale in Sittingbourne that I've a mind to buy.'

The Duke and Duchess rose from the fireside to greet them and his Grace made the necessary introductions. Caroline was surprised that, though every bit as elegant as Cassie had said, the Duchess was not a stunning beauty. But then Adeline smiled and took her hands ... and she realised that perhaps her first impression had been overly-simplistic.

When they were all seated and tea had been brought, Rockliffe said, 'Well, Adrian ... Nicholas says you sent Sheringham packing. I imagine that cannot have been easy.'

'In the end, it wasn't as difficult as I expected,' came the faintly guarded reply. 'And I'm hoping that we have seen the last of him.'

'No question of that,' remarked Nicholas, reaching for another slice of cake. 'There's nothing left for him here other than disgrace and possibly prison. I sent a note to Aristide, by the way. I thought he'd like to know that the club is no longer under threat and that you're still in one piece. Oh – I also passed on Rock's suggestion that, if asked, he might give the impression that your wedding took place here at the Priors.'

'Thank you. That would seem to cover everything.' He looked at the Duchess and said, 'It's extremely good of you to involve yourself in our deception.'

Adeline laughed. 'It might surprise you to know how much practice we've had. You are not the only couple whose wedding became fodder for the gossips.' Rising, she said, 'Lady Sarre ... let me show you to your rooms. I'm sure you'd like to refresh yourself after your journey and I'd like the opportunity to indulge in a little feminine conversation. Unless I miss my guess, Nicholas is about to use your husband's presence to renew his attempts to persuade Tracy to let him ride The Trojan – which is an argument he will never win and which I'm quite tired of hearing.'

As they climbed the stairs, Caroline said shyly, 'I'm so glad you're feeling better. His Grace was very worried.'

'His Grace,' replied Adeline serenely, 'was beginning to drive me demented. And you should call him Rock, you know. Aside from myself, everyone does. Also, I understand you spent part of your wedding day helping him dig a bullet out of your husband. I imagine that must have been spectacularly awful.'

'It was. But I should admit that his Grace – Rock – did all the digging. He was splendid.'

'Yes. He always is.' She opened a door. 'Here we are. I hope you will find everything you need but, if not, don't hesitate to ring. I gather you haven't yet acquired a maid so I'll send mine to help you dress for dinner, if you wish.'

'That would be kind. Normally, I can manage by myself but Adrian has bought some new gowns that defeat me.'

The aquamarine gaze dwelled on her thoughtfully.

'Tracy says his lordship is a very talented actor – which is a thing I'm having trouble believing. Is it true?'

'Perfectly true.' Caroline beamed and turned pink with pride. 'He's wonderful.'

'Ah.' Smiling a little at having learned what she wanted to know, Adeline turned to go. 'Then I'll hope that he may be coaxed into giving us a brief performance.'

'I don't think you'll find him difficult to persuade, your Grace. To tell the truth, the difficulty is *stopping* him doing it.'

* * *

299

Later, when Rockliffe was alone with his wife, he said, 'Well? What do you make of them?'

Adeline settled more comfortably into the curve of his arm.

'It's as you said. He's very reserved – which makes it difficult to believe in the acting except that Caroline implied he frequently presents a façade. She, of course, is hopelessly in love with him ... but what he feels is impossible to say.'

'Quite – though I have my suspicions. However, being shot on his wedding day has probably ... delayed a few things.' He laced his fingers with hers and added, 'If that's so, he has all my sympathy.'

'Yes. He would do. So I thought I might help with that.'

'Dear me. Should I be alarmed?'

'No. It's very simple. Jeanne will help Caroline dress but be ... unavailable ... later. I'm sure Lord Sarre is capable of dealing with his wife's laces.' She smiled. 'And, if he's not, you can always give expert instruction.'

TWENTY-SIX

Reluctantly deciding that the gold, embroidered gown was probably unsuitable for what the Duchess had described as 'a simple family dinner', Caroline allowed Jeanne to lace her into the third of Adrian's gifts. A deep, Nile-blue watered taffeta with a pearl-trimmed *décolletage*, it clung to her shoulders and waist and made her hair look the colour of honey.

Jeanne gave the skirt a final twitch, stepped back to inspect her handiwork and said, 'That's very nice, my lady. Perfect for you, if you don't me saying.'

'Thank you.' Caroline smiled and couldn't help adding, 'My husband chose it.'

'You're lucky he has such good taste, then. Some gentlemen have no idea. Now … let's see what we can do with your hair.' She picked up a strand and let it slide through her fingers. 'It's very fine and almost straight … but there's a great deal of it. Yes. Something simple but unusual, I think.'

By the time Adrian emerged from the adjoining room, wearing a coat of unadorned black brocade over a riotously-embroidered gold and scarlet vest, Caroline had been ready for ten minutes. But glimpsing an expression she'd never seen before, she said doubtfully, 'You don't like the gown? I think it's beautiful.'

'*Now* it is,' he agreed, walking slowly towards her, his eyes oddly intent. 'Now you're wearing it.'

'Oh.' The dimple quivered into being and she said naively, 'What a lovely thing to say.'

'It's true.' Adrian suddenly realised that, though it was a joy seeing her suitably gowned, he'd arrived at the point where it wouldn't matter if she was dressed in a sack. He said, 'Your hair looks charming, too … but I'm afraid to touch it.'

Her breath caught. 'Do you want to?'

'Oh yes.' He gave her a brief, dazzling smile. 'But I think I'd better not. Not yet, anyway.' And, offering her his arm, 'Shall we go, my lady?'

* * *

Dinner was a pleasant affair and every bit as informal as the Duchess had promised. Then, after it, the gentlemen chose to take their port in the parlour with the ladies and Rockliffe said, 'Far be it from me to expect you to sing for your supper, Adrian ... but there will be no peace until Adeline has seen a sample of your theatrical talent. She believes me prone to exaggeration, you see.'

'And you are,' said his wife firmly. 'But I'll admit I'm curious, Lord Sarre. Tracy insists that your skills are quite unlike those we see at Drury Lane.'

'I never saw you on the stage, either,' remarked Nicholas. 'But then, I don't go to the play at all if I can help it. It's just a lot of fellows waving their arms about and bellowing.'

'That's not what Adrian does,' objected Caroline. And, to her husband, 'Show them.'

Almost before anyone had time to register what was happening, Adrian somehow became a muscular fellow of military bark and bearing who spoke with an almost incomprehensible Scottish accent. For perhaps three minutes, he had Lord Nicholas standing to attention whilst he tore verbal strips off him as a "sorry excuse for a soldier". Then the illusion dissolved and was recreated as a lisping, mincing Macaroni. Adeline laughingly handed him her fan and Nicholas groaned, 'God – it's Viscount Ansford.'

The fan dropped neatly back into the Duchess's lap and the effeminate Viscount briefly became a gloomy Russian before turning into Count von Rainmayr. He leaned heavily on a poker in lieu of a cane and thanked Adeline with old-fashioned courtesy when she retrieved it after it slipped from his grasp. At some point, the Count's eyes met those of the Duke and he gave the merest suggestion of a shrug. A gleam of amusement lit the night-dark eyes but Rockliffe said nothing.

After a few moments, Adrian straightened his back and replaced the poker. Glancing round at his audience, he said, 'Enough?'

'Just one more?' pleaded Caroline, her face glowing with pleasure.

He looked at her, a small half-smile touching his mouth.

'You have a specific request?'

'Yes.' She smiled back at him. 'Please.'

'Ah. I gather I'm to guess?'

'Can't you?'

'*Bien sûr, Madame.*' In the space of a heartbeat, Adrian relaxed his posture, altered the timbre of his voice and dropped seamlessly into Claude Duvall. 'Since it appears I have been so careless as to forget my pistol, I cannot demand your money or your life, *Monsieur le Duc.* This is an embarrassment, you understand. So perhaps,' he continued, swinging round to Adeline, 'I will say instead, "Your money or your wife".' He bowed and held out a hand, 'Come, *Madam la Duchesse. Venez danser avec moi.*'

'I think not, Monsieur,' she laughed. 'You are a stranger – and, I suspect, a rogue.'

'Of the very blackest, *Madame*,' he agreed, cheerfully. 'But if you will not dance, I must claim instead your jewels. As to my name,' he glanced around, 'does no one guess it?'

'Claude Duvall,' drawled Rockliffe. 'The so-called gentleman highwayman, who danced with the wives before robbing the husbands and thus went from the scaffold into legend.'

'Romantic as that sounds,' said Adeline, 'one can't dance without music.'

Claude Duvall's laughing grey eyes flew to Caroline's brown ones.

'And you, *ma petite*? What do you say to that?'

Smiling, she said softly, 'There is always music. One has but to listen.'

'*Tout à fait.* Come ... tread a measure with me.'

Duvall drew her smoothly up into his arms. This time, however, instead of the swaying dance she remembered, he guided her into a slow, graceful turn before catching her close against his chest and whispering, 'Our interval isn't over, *mignonne.* It is only now beginning.'

And dropped a fleeting kiss on her lips before handing her back into her chair.

The Duke and Duchess of Rockliffe exchanged glances.

Baffled, Nicholas said, 'A French highwayman? That's an odd choice.'

'Not at all,' said Caroline, drowning in her husband's eyes. 'He's a particular friend of mine.'

There was a small silence. Then, Rockliffe looked across at Adrian and said, 'That breeds a suspicion I suspect I would prefer not to have verified. But if you plan to adopt mundane respectability at any point, I'd recommend that you do it sooner rather than later. Meanwhile ... more port, anyone?'

* * *

By the time Adrian appeared, Caroline had managed to unpin her hair and was starting to loosen the parts of it that Jeanne had braided. Catching sight of her husband in the mirror, she was immediately aware that he had shed both coat and vest and, for the first time ever, was standing there in his shirtsleeves. She swallowed hard, wondering if he knew how well it suited him ... and why he was lurking, with apparent nonchalance, in the doorway.

She said, 'I thought you'd sit talking with the Duke and Lord Nicholas for hours yet.'

'Nick wanted me to play cards.'

'Oh. Perhaps you should just tell him why you won't?'

'I did. Thanks to Rockliffe, he wasn't as surprised as he should have been.' He shifted his shoulders against the door-frame, hesitated for a moment and then said, 'Would it be all right if I came in?'

Caroline's hands dropped from her hair and she turned to face him.

'Of course it's all right. Why are you asking?'

Because I'm totally out of my depth and likely to do something crass.

'In order not to appear presumptuous.' He crossed the room towards her and, reaching out, took one of the long, plaited strands in his fingers. 'May I?'

Startled but pleased and suddenly a little shy, she nodded.

Adrian began gently unplaiting and smoothing with slow deliberate hands. He said conversationally, 'Have I ever mentioned that your hair is beautiful?'

'Not in so many words.' She strove for something else to say and added, 'It's too long.'

'Only a woman would say that.' He smiled at her in the mirror. 'No man ever would.'

'Really?'

'Really. A man would only think of losing himself in the scent and silk of it.'

A wholly unexpected tremor shot along her nerves and a pulse throbbed, just once, deep in her body. She said, 'A man ... such as yourself, for example?'

'Yes.' Adrian combed his fingers through the loosened plait, enjoying the way it rippled and aware that her breathing had changed. He moved on to the next braid and said in a tone wholly devoid of expression, 'Why did you want me to do Claude Duvall?'

'I just ... I think I just wanted to meet him again.'

'I see.' He gave the merest suggestion of a shrug. 'He's very charming, of course. And light-hearted and ... uncomplicated.'

Unlike myself. The words remained unspoken but Caroline heard them nonetheless.

Meeting his eyes in the mirror, she said, 'Yes, he is. He's exactly the sort of romantic, not-quite-a-hero to make a girl sigh. I should know, after all.' She managed a faintly self-deprecating smile and then added, 'But that's not why I wanted to see him.'

'No?'

'No. I haven't any secret, lingering regrets, if that's what you thought.'

'I ... wondered.'

'You need not. Ever. Claude Duvall was wildly attractive and I'm not sorry I met him. But he pales into insignificance beside Adrian Devereux – who is every bit as attractive but also possesses a myriad of other incredible qualities. No woman fortunate enough to know Adrian would have chosen Claude. In fact, I don't believe that any woman fortunate enough to know Adrian would look twice at any other man at all.'

A hint of colour crept along his cheekbones.

'That's more than I deserve.'

She rose from the stool and turned to lay a hand against his cheek.

'No. It's a good deal *less* than you deserve.' Her heart was beating erratically fast but she knew that if she did not say this now, she never would. 'I love you. I love your honesty, your unfailing kindness and the fact that – though you've had precious little of it yourself or perhaps *because* of that – you have a passion for justice. I think you are the most remarkable man I've ever met and utterly beautiful, both in body and spirit. And your smile doesn't just make me sigh, Adrian. It steals my breath and lights the world.'

'Oh God.' His arms went around her and he hid his face against her hair. For a long time, he remained silent but eventually, in muffled accents, he said, 'I never expected ... that is to say, I hoped, of course ... but, after everything, I didn't think you would ...' He groaned. 'Listen to me – not even able to manage a whole sentence. I sound like an imbecile. It's just that I can't ... that there are things I can't seem to get right without acting. That's how I manage, you see. How I've managed for a long time ... because it's easier.'

'I know. It's all right.'

'No it isn't. I don't want to do that – particularly not with you. I want us to build a life together and for every part of it to be *real*. But I'm not good at simply being myself. I know that sounds ridiculous but --'

'It doesn't. And you're a lot better at it than you think.'

'Thanks to you, I'm learning. And if I make mistakes, it won't be because I don't try.' He lifted his head and looked down at her. 'On our wedding day, after Rock got Marcus's bullet out of me, I recall promising to ask you something.'

She smiled at him. 'Do you still think you need to?'

'Yes. No. Probably not.' He drew an unsteady breath. 'Since I haven't got much right so far you couldn't be blamed for telling me to go away. But I hope you won't. I want you so very much, you see. And I'd like the chance to do better.' He stopped and, as if it was the last straw, added, 'Now I'm making you cry – and, of course, I've no idea why or what to do about it.'

Caroline wound her arms round his neck and blinked the foolish tears away.

'Why don't you just kiss me? Preferably without asking permission first.'

'That's a good idea,' murmured Adrian, the ghost of a smile back in his voice. 'I wish I'd thought of it.'

And with a tiny gurgle of laughter, she said, 'Yes. So do I.'

Using one arm to pull her closer, he slid the other into her hair to cradle her skull and burned a trail of kisses along her cheek and jaw until he arrived at her lips. Caroline sighed, feeling the warmth of his breath; and then his mouth was on hers, suddenly not tentative at all but making it clear what he wanted. He'd kissed her before, both as Claude Duvall and as himself, and every time had been sweeter than the last. But this was different. This was need and hunger and demand … oddly mingled with invitation. *This* sent sparks spiralling through her veins until her bones started to dissolve in the resulting conflagration. And when he released her mouth to nip gently at her earlobe and slide his tongue over the hollow beneath, a wave of answering desire washed over her.

Adrian found the acutely sensitive dip at the base of her throat and savoured it while his hands moulded her back and hips. Her skin was soft and honey-sweet. He wanted to taste every inch of her and take his time doing it. He felt her untie his hair and gather it into her hands while she rained kisses over his throat and jaw. A small purring groan escaped him and he took her mouth again while his fingers sought and found the laces of her gown. Distantly, he wondered how, in little more than a week, he had come to feel this way. It felt as if he had been waiting for this one moment all of his life.

He eased the gown from her shoulders and let it slither to her feet. Feeling it go but continuing to explore the contours of his back through the fine lawn of his shirt, Caroline murmured, 'My lovely dress.'

'Mm,' breathed Adrian, lifting her clear of the pool of silk. 'My even lovelier Caroline.'

He kissed his way across her shoulders and let his hands stray to new, uncharted territory. She gasped and clung, pressing herself as close as she could to the hard length of his body. Molten heat was flooding every part of her and setting up a clamour in her blood; a clamour for more of some mysterious thing she could only identify with one word. *Adrian.*

Her stays followed her gown to the floor and when his hands found new paths to follow, she gave a sobbing moan and tugged at his shirt.

'Please.'

'Yes.'

His breathing as disrupted as hers, he released her for the second it took to pull his shirt over his head and cast it aside. Immediately aware of the dressing on his shoulder, she said helplessly, 'Oh. I forgot. Perhaps we shouldn't …'

'It's fine. *I'm* fine,' he managed. 'And we absolutely should. Unless … unless …'

Then she pulled his head down to hers and his brain stopped functioning.

Time sped up, slowed down … ceased to exist. Clothing melted magically away until they were lying skin to skin on the bed, burning with mutual fires as Adrian's mouth followed the teasing trail of his hands.

His every touch produced shocks of heat and pleasure. Tremors shook her body and incoherent words tumbled from her lips. She hadn't known it was possible to feel like this; her entire body alight with sensation that left her poised on the brink of some momentous discovery; and throughout it all, like a shining, golden thread, the knowledge that this man … this beautiful, incredible man was finally hers.

Adrian waited until he was sure, beyond any shadow of doubt, that her hunger was as great as his own and that his self-control was sufficient to offer the grace and care she deserved. And then, he finally allowed himself to go where he most wanted to be.

He soothed the first, inevitable moment of discomfort away with kisses and murmured endearments in French. Then he watched her eyes open on his, full of wonder and love. For a few seconds, emotion gripped him even more fiercely than physical pleasure, almost stopping his breath and driving out every thought save the one that thundered so loudly through his head than he thought he might actually have said it.

308

I love you.

Later, drifting in a sea of lassitude and bliss, Caroline dozed for a time, her head pillowed on his good shoulder. Then she said dreamily, 'I thought I knew what to expect ... how it would be. But I didn't. Not at all.'

'I hope you weren't disappointed.'

She heard both the smile in his voice and the fact that it wasn't a question.

'You know I wasn't.'

'Good.' He settled her a little closer. 'It will be better next time.'

'Better?' She investigated the muscles of his chest. 'Is that possible?'

The smile became a laugh but he said, 'That and many other things, sweetheart.'

Silence fell between them for a time but, at length, Adrian said, 'Do you remember that arrogant, bloodless fellow who offered you marriage in Kensington Gardens?'

'The one who said we might "deal agreeably together"?'

'Yes. Him.' Propping himself on one elbow, he concentrated on twining a lock of her hair about his fingers. 'I expected my re-entry into society to be fairly unpleasant and thought a cold, forbidding demeanour would deflect the worst of it – so I invented Sarre. He was the last in a long line of similar parts. Until this last week, I'd become a rag-bag of all of them; a collection of miscellaneous bits and pieces – so many that, somewhere along the way, I'd forgotten who I really was. Or, at least, who I might have been had life worked out differently.' He raised his eyes to hers and said simply, 'You made me remember ... and I could love you for that alone. Except, of course, that there's so much more.'

Caroline's breath snared in her throat and she said raggedly, 'Adrian – you don't have to say anything. I know you care for me and it's enough.'

'No. It's not.' He laid a finger lightly against her lips to stop her speaking. 'Let me say it. It's the least – the very least I owe you. And you deserve something better than an emotional coward.' He paused briefly, struggling to find the words he needed. 'You should know that there's been a … a sort of void inside me for years. A dark empty place that I'd become so used to, I no longer noticed it was there. And then you came along and, in some way I can't explain, you made me whole again. So I don't just care for you, my darling. I need you and want you and … love you.' Sliding his hand to cup her cheek, he said softly, 'There. I've finally managed to say it. I love you, Caroline Devereux. And I've known it since the moment that objectionable parson declared us man and wife because that was when – though I tried not to admit it, even to myself – I realised how afraid I'd been that you might change your mind. The possibility that you could still leave … the idea of you no longer being here to fill my life is the very worst thing I can think of.'

'Then don't think it.' She twisted her head to kiss his palm. 'Don't ever think it again.'

'No. Perhaps now I won't.' He kissed her slowly and then folded her against his chest. 'There's one other thing.'

'Yes?'

'There were a lot of good, practical reasons for letting Marcus go … but the truth is that the thing that tipped the balance in his favour wasn't any of them. I let him go because I realised that, albeit unwittingly and unintentionally, he'd finally done me a favour.'

Caroline held him a little tighter. She said, 'He shot you. I don't see anything good in that – or anything else he could do that might outweigh it.'

'Then you haven't thought, darling.' There was a smile in his voice, along with rare, naked emotion. 'But for him, you and I might never have met. So in essence, he's brought me the most precious gift in the world. You.'

'That is so …' She swallowed hard. 'I don't know what to say to you.'

'No? Don't you want to take advantage of my currently weakened state by making me promise something I'll probably regret?'

'You've already promised me everything I want. How could I possibly …?' She stopped, realising that he was teasing because he didn't want her to shed tears now – not even ones of undiluted happiness . 'Oh. Anything?'

'Anything,' he agreed, wondering what she'd choose.

'Then … will you take me to your gaming-club?'

She felt the shock of his laughter.

'God. I expected a surprise – but not that.'

'Will you?'

'If that's what you want – yes.'

'And to visit Grandpa Maitland?'

'Yes. And to the stars, if you like.'

For a moment there was silence as Caroline nestled a little closer. Then she murmured wickedly, 'What – again?'

Author's Note

The Legend of Claude Duvall

Here lies Duvall; Reader, if Male thou art
Look to thy purse – if Female, to thy heart.
Much havoc has he made of both; for all
Men he made to stand and Women he made to fall.
The second Conqueror of the Norman race
Knights to his arms did yield and Ladies to his face.
Old Tyburn's glory; England's illustrious thief
Duvall, the Ladies' joy
Duvall, the Ladies' grief.

Born in France in 1643, Claude Duvall was hanged at Tyburn on January 21st, 1670.

Stella Riley

Printed in Poland
by Amazon Fulfillment
Poland Sp. z o.o., Wrocław